THE MAN IN THE DRAGON MASK

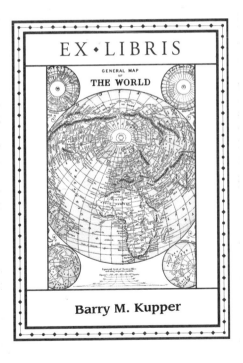

EX · LIBRIS

GENERAL MAP
OF
THE WORLD

Barry M. Kupper

THE MAN IN THE DRAGON MASK

AMANDA ROBERTS

Red Empress Publishing
www.RedEmpressPublishing.com

Copyright © Amanda Roberts
www.AmandaRobertsWrites.com

Cover by Cherith Vaughan
www.shreddedpotato.com

ALSO BY AMANDA ROBERTS

Fiction

Threads of Silk

The Man in the Dragon Mask

The Qing Dynasty Mysteries

Murder in the Forbidden City

Murder in the British Quarter

Murder at the Peking Opera

The Touching Time Series

The Child's Curse

The Emperor's Seal

The Empress's Dagger

The Slave's Necklace

Nonfiction

The Crazy Dumplings Cookbook

Crazy Dumplings II: Even Dumplinger

PROLOGUE

The empress's labor had finally begun, but it had lasted far longer than it should have. Though it should not have been surprising. The pregnancy had been difficult. The empress had not even been able to leave her bed in months for fear that the child would come too early to live.

"Breathe, my lady," the midwife coached the empress as she watched for any sign that the little prince would soon enter the world.

"I cannot!" the empress cried. "He is dead! And I will soon join him!" The empress moaned in pain and terror, for she knew that if she did not deliver of a healthy son, it would be best for her if she died as well.

"You can do it, my lady," Dong Hai, the empress's chief eunuch, said as he grabbed her hand tightly. He turned her face to him, forcing her to open her eyes to meet his. "You did not live through years of war, and famine, and hardship to die at your own moment of greatness! This is why you were chosen. This is why Heaven has always smiled on you.

You will no longer simply be the consort of a beggar king, but the mother of a dynasty!"

The empress nodded and pushed herself to sitting. She grabbed the cords that were tied to each side of the large bed. Her life had been difficult from the beginning. Born to poverty. Married too young. Forced to watch her husband ride off into battle time and time again, always wondering if this would be the day he finally fell and she would be carried off as a war prize. But her husband never fell. And she was never raped or murdered. She was at her husband's side as they were anointed as emperor and empress of a new China. The vanquishers of the invading Mongol hordes. Together, they had torn down the oppressive Yuan Dynasty and ushered in a new one. The Ming Empire. The bright and shining light of the dawn.

But they were not yet a dynasty.

Until the empress fulfilled her sacred duty and delivered a son to her lord and husband, she was not finished.

The empress held tight to the ropes as her ladies crowded around her, holding her up, wiping her brow, kneeling in prayer to Guanyin.

"I...I see him, my lady!" the midwife said. "Push! Do not stop!"

The empress screamed as the little creature tore his way free and slipped into the waiting arms of the midwife.

"I have him!" the midwife said, and the empress fell back, desperate to catch her breath. But the pain did not stop. She could feel the blood pouring from her body and her insides writhing as though she needed to continue pushing. She barely even registered the sound of the pitiful cries that told her the baby was alive.

"A boy!" the midwife announced, and everyone in the room cheered except for the empress and her eunuch.

Dong Hai knew his mistress well, and he could clearly see the distress on her face. As the ladies crowded around the little prince, Dong Hai moved to his lady's side, taking her hand in his.

"I...I think I shall die a happy woman," the empress told him as she moaned, clutching her stomach, begging for death to relieve her of her suffering.

"No," the eunuch said as he wiped her brow. "You will live. You will raise your son to be the greatest emperor China has ever seen."

The empress could only weep as she shook her head.

The door to the bedchamber was open and the midwife stepped out. She held the tiny bundle to the emperor. "A son! A healthy son!"

The emperor took the child in his arms and smiled. "Now the Ming is no longer an empire, but a dynasty," he said. He then turned to his many waiting magistrates, vassals, and servants, holding the child aloft. "My son and heir!"

"May the emperor live ten thousand years!" the people chanted. "May the prince live ten thousand years!"

The emperor laughed as he left the bedchamber, showing his son to the many gathered people and ordering endless cups of wine to be poured. He asked not of the empress as she lay on her bed, sure the end was near.

The midwife closed the door to quiet the sounds of celebration. When she returned to the empress's side and saw the state she was in, she pressed on her still full stomach. Her eyes grew wide and she ordered everyone from the room, the maids and lesser eunuchs.

"I am dying, aren't I?" the empress cried, tears streaming down her cheeks.

"No, my lady," the midwife said, "but you are going to have to push again."

The empress let out a groan from deep inside. "No, no, no. Bring me a knife. I will end the suffering myself!"

"My lady," the midwife said, keeping her voice calm. "You are not going to die. You are not going to give up. You are going to push, and you are going to bring more life into this world."

The empress could hardly understand what the woman was saying. Had she not already delivered a son? But she could not make sense of the midwife's words because she could only feel the need to push. Even though she was certain she had no strength left, her body—and whatever was still inside of it—forced her to continue. The empress squeezed her eunuch's hand and pushed. She felt the hands of the midwife slip inside her body, and then, the pressure finally stopped. This time when the empress collapsed onto her pillow, she felt nothing but blessed relief.

"You did it, Your Majesty!" the midwife said as she rushed across the room to a basin of water.

"What...what happened?" the empress mumbled as she caught her breath.

The midwife approached her with a small bundle in her arms. "You have delivered a second son, my lady."

The empress, the eunuch, and the midwife were silent.

The empress, in her pain and exhaustion, wondered if she had heard the woman correctly. A son? A second son? How was it possible? Did they not have the blessing of Heaven?

The eunuch worried his bottom lip. He still held the empress's hand, and he felt her grip tighten as she tried to comprehend what the midwife had said.

The midwife cared only for the life of her tiny patient.

She knew what fate awaited him, and she hoped that she could show him love in the short amount of time he had left.

"A...son?" the empress said as her senses returned to her. She wiped the tears and snot from her face. She released the hand of her eunuch and reached for the bundle, which the midwife gently placed into her arms.

The baby's skin was red in the golden light of the fires from the braziers, but his skin was smooth. He had a beautiful nose and mouth and thick black hair on his head. He was perfect. The empress held the baby close and breathed in his scent. The baby opened his mouth and let out a little noise. The empress felt tears form in her eyes again, but this time, it was love for the tiny creature that swelled her heart.

"I...I do not know what to do," the empress implored the midwife. As a girl of only sixteen who had been taken by her husband at only twelve, she did not know how to meet the needs of the beautiful baby in her arms.

The midwife sat on the bed and showed the empress how to hold him to her breast so as to give him his first—and last—meal. In her line of work, the woman knew nothing more joyful than helping to bring a child into the world. And she knew nothing more painful than having to snuff the life of a new baby out. Unwanted girls, babies of both sex with hideous deformities, and cursed twins—all these and more often did not even feel the loving arms of their mothers or the warmth of her milk in their bellies before they were plunged into a bucket of cold water and then tossed into a river. Perhaps it was more cruel for the midwife to allow the baby to feel warmth and love before being killed. Maybe it was better to die never knowing just how caring the world could be.

"Someone should call the emperor back," the empress

said, unable to take her eyes from her baby as he gripped her finger and sucked from her breast. "He will be so proud! Two sons! I have done double my duty. The empire is secure!"

The eunuch and the midwife looked at each other. Could the foolish girl not know?

"My lady," the eunuch said gently. "We...we will have to send the child away. The emperor can never know about him."

"What?" the empress asked. "Send him away? Why wouldn't we tell his father? He will be so proud!"

"No, Chun," the eunuch said. He had become so dear to the empress that they often used each other's given names in private. "You know this is bad luck. If the emperor finds out—"

"Just a country superstition," the empress scoffed. "We are above such stupidity. This is my son. A prince. A *dragon* prince."

"All the more reason why no one can ever know about him," the eunuch said. "If the people hear about this, they will surely see it as a curse from above. As proof that the Ming do not have the Mandate of Heaven. That His Majesty acted against the gods in overthrowing the Mongol."

"No...No!" The empress clenched her teeth and held her baby tight. "I will not let you take him. He is a prince! A Ming prince!"

"If the emperor finds out about him," the eunuch tried to continue gently, "he might kill both babies. He might believe they are both cursed. A second baby does not bring stability—it brings chaos and ruin. There will always be questions over which baby is the true heir. The emperor will surely set you aside if he believes your womb is cursed."

"I care not for myself!" the empress spat. "I only care for

my baby. My precious baby! You cannot take him! I will not allow it!"

"My lady, please. I beg of you." Dong Hai folded his hands before him and sank to his knees. "Do not make this more difficult. We have all sacrificed to see your husband on the throne. This is only one more thing that must be done to ensure the success of the Ming Dynasty. Not just for your husband. Not just for yourself. But for your son. Your first-born. The one the emperor is presenting to the people right now. Do you want him to live? Do you want him to rule? Do you want your grandchildren and great-grandchildren to carry the Ming Dynasty on for generations and generations?"

Tears poured from the empress's eyes. She thought she had wanted all those things. She had promised her husband that she would do whatever was necessary to see him on the throne and be a successful emperor. But now, all she wanted was the babe in her arms.

"Please," the empress begged of her eunuch—her friend. "Don't do this."

"I must," the eunuch said as he ripped the baby from the empress's arms.

"No! Dong Hai!" the empress yelled as she grasped for her baby, but the eunuch moved out of reach. She tried to crawl out of the bed after him, but pain ripped through her as she moved and the midwife held her back.

"You must lie back, Your Majesty," the midwife said. "Shh. Please, you must relax. You will hurt yourself."

The empress cried out in pain, not just in her body, but in her heart as well. She heard a door slam as the eunuch secreted the baby away into the dark night. The empress wept as the midwife worked to clean and stitch up her torn body.

Eventually, the empress stopped crying, stopped shaking, and a numb calm fell over her. The baby was gone. There was nothing she could do for him now.

"Is there anything else you need, Your Majesty?" the midwife finally asked when her work was complete.

The empress only shook her head. "Unless you can bring my son back to me, I no longer wish to see your face."

The midwife felt a pain in her heart. She loved children even though she had none of her own. Even though the deaths were often necessary to ensure the success of the families, she felt the pain of the loss of each child accurately. Even the babies that were sick and deformed—what she wouldn't give to take them home and love each one for as long as she could. But the healthy babies, the girls and the twins, those deaths were the worst. They reminded her that the gods were not only kind and merciful, but cruel as well.

"I am sorry, Your Majesty," the midwife said. "May the gods bless you with many more children."

The empress only stared at the wall. "I will never have another..." She heard the door to the room shut and was glad to be alone for a moment. She would never be allowed to grieve her son publically. She could never be able to speak of him. There would be no funeral. How would he navigate the spirit realm if there was no ancestor tablet made for him? She would have to burn clothes for him. Sacrifice her milk. Send him money. And she would have to do it all in secret. No one could ever know. But how would he navigate the spirit realm when he could not even walk? Would the ancestors find him and carry him to Heaven? Would they feed him and clothe him? Would they tell him of her love for him?

The door opened and closed once again, and the empress could hear the soft shuffling footsteps of Dong Hai.

"Did you do it?" the empress asked coldly, never tearing her eyes from the wall.

"The dynasty is safe, my lady," he replied.

There was nothing more for either of them to say. The empress closed her eyes, begging for death. Perhaps if she died, she could care for her son in the spirit realm. She could carry him to the next life and maybe they would be reincarnated together.

"Bring me a white scarf," she ordered Dong Hai, but the eunuch only scoffed.

"Do not be stupid," he said. "You have another son who needs you. You are still the empress. You can have more children. Morn your son in private, but do not think I will let you leave this world before your time. Your work is not finished."

The empress clutched her pillow tightly and cursed the eunuch. She also cursed herself. She should have protected her son. She never should have let him go. Wasn't that the only job of a mother? To protect her children? She had been a mother for only a few minutes and she had already failed.

The door to the room opened and sounds of revelry poured in. The empress forced herself to sit up and bow her head to her lord.

"You have done well, wife!" the emperor announced. "I will pour gold upon your head, the likes of which no wife has ever received from her husband."

"You honor me, Your Majesty," the empress said.

The emperor walked over to the bed and handed the squalling infant to her. "I believe he is hungry."

The empress looked down at the red, scrunched face of

the baby and felt sick. She could not imagine putting her breast into the mouth of something so hideous.

The emperor laughed. "I believe my wife is shy."

"She is only exhausted, my lord," Dong Hai said, kneeling on the floor. "The labor was difficult. But the midwife was certain she would recover."

"Excellent!" the emperor crowed. "After all, more sons will mean more security for the future. And why not daughters? I have many alliances I must shore up, and quickly!"

"Yes, Your Majesty," Dong Hai said, knocking his forehead to the floor.

"Yes, my lord," the empress said as the baby continued to wail in her arms.

"I will leave you to your work and rest, then," the emperor said. He placed a gentle kiss on the empress's head. She tried to hide her grimace from his stink of sweat and wine. When the door was shut, the empress laid back on her pillow once again, leaving the crying baby on the bed out of her reach.

The eunuch ran to the bed and picked up the baby gently. "My lady, you must nurse him. He is hungry. Do you not want him to grow strong?"

The empress scoffed. She could not even look at the hideous little beast.

"Bring a wet nurse," she said.

The eunuch did as he was ordered.

ONE

Twenty-Six Years Later

The Hongwu Emperor, the founder of the Ming Dynasty, the scourge of the Mongol, was dead. In the grand courtyard of the imperial palace in Nanking, a thousand eunuchs, maids, slaves, magistrates, and courtiers garbed themselves in white and smeared ash on their faces as they prostrated themselves in mourning. And leading them all was the emperor's son, Hongdi.

At the front of the mass of mourners, facing the main palace where the body of the emperor lay in repose, Crown Prince Hongdi's heart was heavy. He kowtowed before his father with his mother, the now Dowager-Empress Chun, on one side, and his wife, the soon to be Empress Wen, on the other. Among the crowd were his half-brothers and -sisters by various concubines. They had been scattered throughout the empire to govern their own lands and secure alliances, but all had returned to mourn their father, and many of them had brought their own children with them.

Hongdi's concubines were also present to pay homage to the dead emperor, but none of them had children of their own to guide, for Hongdi was childless. At twenty-six years of age, with a wife and seven concubines, Hongdi should have already had a dozen children of his own, but no one dared suspect why he did not. To speak of the prince's lack of virility would be treason and worthy of death.

"Sit straight," Chun ordered her son as he lifted his head from a kowtow. "Do you want everyone to whisper of your lack of respect?"

Hongdi did not know how he could sit up any more straight, but he thanked his mother for her guidance and kowtowed again. Every part of him ached as he had kowtowed dozens of times already, and would have to kowtow dozens of times more before the public mourning completed. But he would gladly kowtow a thousand times if it put off what would happen next—when he and Princess Wen would sit upon the dragon and phoenix thrones and be appointed as the new emperor and empress of China.

How could you leave me, Father? the prince lamented to himself. *I am not ready. I am not half the man you were. How can I ever uphold your legacy and build my own?*

As he looked up toward his father's body, he felt a warm hand on his own. He looked over at the smiling face of his wife, Wen, and he felt stronger. He squeezed her hand in return and resumed his kowtowing.

He had not chosen Wen to be his wife. Her father had been as instrumental in overthrowing the Mongol as his own. The two men had fought side by side, and very nearly ruled side by side. When Hongwu became emperor, General Kang was the emperor's top advisor and military strategist, and he continued conquering territory and putting down rebellions around the empire in the name of his friend. The day Wen was born, she was betrothed to the emperor's son. On her sixteenth birthday, they were wed. In eight years of marriage, he could find no fault with her, except that she had not given him a child, not even a daughter.

As the sun set, and their bodies were stiff, sore, and exhausted, the prince and his princess were allowed to leave the courtyard and prepare themselves for the crowning ceremony. Empress Chun escorted her daughter-in-law to her quarters to prepare her for what was to come.

Princess Wen was bathed, her skin scrubbed until it was pink, every hair of her head lathered and rinsed. Her body was then rubbed with perfumed oils and she was draped in an exquisitely embroidered gown of red with golden threading. The gown was so heavy, the princess did not know how she would be able to walk up the steps to the throne without toppling over. Her maids worked to style her hair, piling it on top of her head and decorating it with pins of gold and rubies. Another maid worked to prepare her face, outlining her eyes with kohl, adding pink to cheeks, and painting her lips bright red. All the while, her mother-in-law watched from across the room.

"What do you think, Mother?" Wen asked when she was ready. She stood and turned in front of a tall mirror, taking in the beauty of her gown and her own face. The old empress scoffed.

"You may look like an empress, but you do not have what it takes to truly stand at an emperor's side," Empress Chun said.

Wen frowned and felt her heart grow cold. Could the cruel old bat not let her have one day of happiness?

"I was raised for this," Wen said as the maids fussed around her to keep her gown free from wrinkles. "From the day I was born, I was destined to be empress. Educated by the best tutors in books and courtly manners. You were born the daughter of a peasant farmer and taken against your will by a rebel soldier. Which of us truly knows what it means to be an empress?"

The old empress chuckled. "You were raised a spoiled child and nothing more. The fat of cows sits on your hips and the silk from worms caresses your body. You do not know what hardship is. What sacrifice means. When adversity comes, you will abandon my son and your kingdom."

"You will not speak to me so impudently when I am empress!" Wen said quietly, even though she wanted to scream.

"What can you do to me?" Chun asked. "You have taken my son, and now you will take my throne. At least I can say that I am the mother of a dynasty."

"A terrible mother," Wen said, her eyes nearly watering. But she refused to cry. She would not ruin her makeup today. "When I have a child, he will know love and gentleness and be a prince all will envy."

Chun grunted as she turned away. "We will never know, will we?" She stepped out of the room to lead the procession of ladies to the imperial audience hall, where the dragon and phoenix thrones were waiting.

As soon as she was gone from sight, Princess Wen picked up a makeup jar from her dressing table and hurled it at the tall mirror, shattering it into a thousand pieces.

"Princess!" Eunuch Bojing said, rushing to her side. "Do not let the old empress taunt you. In mere moments, you will be the empress of the greatest kingdom on earth. Surely, the gods will bless you with a son then. They will not want to see the Ming Dynasty come to an end or the country plunged into chaos."

"Don't they?" Princess Wen asked. "If the gods loved the Ming, wouldn't they have given me ten sons by now?"

"Shh," the eunuch said. "We cannot presume to know the ways of the gods. But there is no one more pious than you. No one who donates more to the temples. No one who prays to them more fervently. Today is your crowning achievement. As you said, you were raised for this. You will be empress and your family will be honored. Do not despair, Your Highness."

"Hmm," Princess Wen said. "I think you mean, 'Your Majesty.'"

The eunuch laughed. "I will, once you sit on that throne."

Princess Wen nodded and held her head high as she walked out of the room. She climbed up into a sedan chair and was carried across the palace grounds to the main audience hall. Bojing had trotted alongside the chair and opened the silk flaps to the chair as soon as it stopped. He placed a stool on the ground and took her hand, assisting her to the ground. The princess looked up the steps to the building and felt her heart flutter at the knowledge that she was no longer a princess—but an empress.

Prince Hongdi waited just inside the audience hall for the ceremony to begin. His mother had arrived first, carried in her own sedan chair. As she approached, he kneeled before her.

"May the empress live ten thousand years!" he said.

"May the empress live ten thousand years!" everyone else in attendance echoed.

The prince then took his mother's hand and led her across the room to the stairs that led up to a raised dais where the dragon and phoenix thrones sat side by side, though the dragon throne was set a little higher. The empress released her son's hand and climbed the steps to sit on her throne for the final time. Everyone then kowtowed before her and repeated the blessing, "May the empress live ten thousand years!"

The empress gave a small smile and nodded to the gathered crowd. She did her best not to cry. She could not show any hint of weakness or sorrow. And why should she? She had sat upon the phoenix throne as empress for nearly thirty years. Her husband had honored her as the mother of his son. She was the most powerful woman in the country.

But as she sat there and watched Princess Wen approaching, taking each step slowly and surely, to usurp her place, she could not say that it had all been worth it.

For what did she have now to show for it? Her husband was dead. There would be a new empress on the throne. She had no other children or grandchildren to dote on. Is this why she sacrificed her other child? The precious babe who had lied in her arms and suckled at her breast? In her heart was only sorrow and regret.

The prince held his hand out to his princess as she approached the dais. Together, they stood at the bottom of the stairs and waited for the empress to stand and take her place beside the thrones. It seemed to Prince Hongdi that his mother waited far longer than necessary to vacate her seat. But finally, Empress Chun stood, taking her new place as *Dowager*-Empress Chun, and the prince led his princess to the thrones.

Prince Hongdi and Princess Wen turned to face those gathered and sat on the thrones.

"May the emperor live ten thousand years!"

"May the empress live ten thousand years!"

"May the dowager-empress live ten thousand years!"

As the empress's father stepped forward and handed the

new emperor his official seal of State, Hongdi was disappointed that his own father was not present for such a momentous occasion. Though, if his father had still been alive, he would not be emperor. It was a heavy burden to know that no emperor ever saw his son at his height of power. Only when a man was dead, could his son take his rightful place on the throne. He prayed that one day he would have a son of his own to succeed him.

I cannot believe the ceremony is already over," Empress Wen said as she lay in the emperor's arms that night.

"It does seem rather bittersweet," Hongdi said as he rubbed her arm. "After the funeral and the ceremony, then the dinner for all the guests, I am amazed I had any energy left."

"Well, we could not let the day end without our own celebration," Wen said teasingly, rubbing her nose against her husband's cheek.

Hongdi rolled to his side and held Wen's naked body against his. He felt his desire for her rising once again. He kissed her cheek, her neck. He spread her legs and moved to take her again.

But Wen pushed him away. "No," she said.

"What?" Hongdi asked. "No? You cannot refuse your emperor."

Wen laughed. "You have been emperor for only a few hours and already you are throwing your weight around."

"I don't weigh that much," the emperor said, motioning to his body, which the empress had to admit was pleasing. Still, she shook her head.

"I know that you love me," she said, making sure her words were as sweet as honey. "And you have always performed your duty admirably. But now that you are emperor, it is even more imperative that you have an heir."

Hongdi turned away from her and sat up, pulling a thin robe around himself. "Is it not enough that my mother constantly berates me for not yet having a son. Or that my ministers whisper about such things. Or that my advisors urge me to name one of my nephews as heir? Now, you must turn against me as well?"

"I have not turned against you, my love," Wen said, sitting up and hugging him from behind. "I am trying to help you."

"Then why did you turn away from me now?" Hongdi asked. "I will put a son in your belly, I swear it."

"It is your duty as emperor to spread your seed," Wen said. "You have many women who could carry many children for you, not just me. If the gods think me worthy, they will make sure that the seeds you have already planted take root. Please, husband, if you feel vigorous enough, visit the concubines. I feel that tonight is a night that we will be truly blessed."

The emperor sighed. "Fine, I will go." He wrapped his robe around him and tied it tightly. He grabbed a wine bottle and cup and went to the door. "I will obey your every command, *empress*."

"Go!" she said with a laugh, tossing a pillow at him.

"Fine, fine," he mumbled to himself as he walked out of the empress's palace. He had told his attendants that he would be spending the night with his empress, so there was no one waiting for him as he began meandering down the many paths that ran through the palace grounds. His own palace was some distance away, but the palaces for the consorts were quite near. He started to walk toward them, but as he poured himself another cup of wine, he meandered in a different direction. If his own empress didn't want him, why would any of his consorts? Wen at least loved him...or she claimed to. They had been barely more than children when they were wed. They had grown up together. But the consorts, they came later. Every year that passed without Wen conceiving a child, a new consort was added to the harem. He tried to do his duty by them, but he did not enjoy it. He felt like a horse sent to stud instead of an emperor making love to his women.

And he knew the blame was his alone.

Eight women and not one pregnancy. Not even a miscarriage. No, he could not have that many barren women. It had to be his own seeds that were fruitless. What would he do if he never had a son of his own? What would happen to the Ming Dynasty? He began to climb the stairs of the main bell tower in the center of the imperial palace grounds.

His father had been a nobody when he was born. A peasant farmer. Kicked out of his own home as a young boy because his family couldn't afford to feed him. He had joined a monastery just so he would have food to eat. After the monastery was destroyed by rebels, he joined the army for the same reason, to have something to eat. He fought his way through the ranks, switching from one side to the other, until he became so powerful he overthrew a dynasty. He ran the Mongol right out of China.

And what had Hongdi done to follow in his father's footsteps? He couldn't even sire a child.

As he walked around the bell tower, he looked at the stars above him. The brightest star, the purple star, the Heavenly Abode, twinkled brightly.

"Are you there, Father?" the young emperor asked,

pouring himself another cup of wine. But this one he did not drink, but spilled upon the ground. "That one was for you and all you accomplished. I have done nothing. And you're great Ming Dynasty will die with me."

True, the emperor could appoint one of his many nephews as heir, but he did not think the people would accept a break in the line of succession. There were still many people who believed that the Mongol had earned their right to rule China. The Manchu, another northern tribe of barbarians, were also causing problems along the northern borders. Still, other powerful clans in the west thought they should rule China. No, there were too many threats, both outside the empire and inside it, who would be waiting to use such a break in tradition as evidence that the Ming did not have the Mandate of Heaven.

The emperor had to find a way to make the people love him. Believe in him, even if he never had a son of his own. Then, perhaps the gods of Heaven would bless him with a child.

The emperor tried to set his cup on the wall of the walkway around the top of the bell tower, but it slipped from his hand, tumbling to the ground far below. The emperor shook the drowsiness from his head and drank directly from the wine bottle. He then threw that from the bell tower as well. He laughed as the bottle crashed to the ground, the sound echoing off the wall that surrounded the palace.

"Stupid walls," he grumbled. He looked north, south, east, and west, and could see each wall that surrounded the palace clearly. "This place is too small for a growing family. A growing empire!" The emperor let out a fearsome roar.

"I need a palace equal to...no, greater than my own magnificence." He chuckled as he heard the guards and eunuchs gathering below, trying to figure out who was making such a ruckus above them in the bell tower.

"Come and catch me," the emperor taunted the tiny people below him. "I am not just an emperor, I will be the greatest emperor China has ever seen. The richest, most powerful. With the largest, most opulent palace the earth has ever seen."

He heard footsteps on the stairs coming up toward him. He leaned against the wall and sank down to sit and wait.

"Come and stop me if you can," he mumbled as he drifted off to sleep.

TWO

*T*he emperor looked out from his throne over the gathered advisors, ministers, and magistrates while the empress sat at his side.

"My father accomplished more in his short life than any other Chinese since the first Han emperor thousands of years ago," he said, his voice loud enough to carry through the large room. Those in the audience nodded and murmured their agreement. "To oust an invading force and establish a new dynasty was not an easy task, and few men, even myself, will be able to ever come close to being his equal."

"You are still young," one of the magistrates spoke up. "Your father had high hopes for what you would accomplish after he was gone."

The young emperor nodded. "Yes, how I will uphold his legacy has weighed heavily on my mind and heart since his death."

"Many emperors expand their territory," the empress's father, General Kang, offered. "True, your father and I took back what the Mongol stole, but their power was waning.

China is a fraction of the size it was during the reign of Ghengis Khan, the first Mongol emperor. We could take back some of the lands that his worthless offspring let slip from their grasp."

Empress Wen leaned forward just enough that Hongdi could see her from the corner of his eye and noted the satisfied smile on her face. He knew that praising her father would please her, even if the man held enough sway over the court already.

The emperor nodded. "I agree. There are warlords to the west that have been causing troubles. We should assert our authority there soon."

"Many great leaders focus on public works," one of the emperor's advisors, a Buddhist monk who had served at the same temple his father once had, said. "A new temple devoted to the Buddha in dedication to your father would surely please the celestial beings, who would then send down blessings on your new reign. Helping the poor, the sick, the widows and orphans, a new temple could bring much-needed relief to the people of Nanking."

Many people clapped at this. After all, who could oppose the idea of caring for those of great need within the realm?

"There is wisdom in this," the emperor said. "Thank you for your suggestion. But on the topic of building a temple, it is this idea of embarking on a great building project that I am thinking of."

While several people nodded their agreement, far more stayed silent on the matter.

"My father did not just establish a new dynasty," the emperor went on. "But he gave the country back to true Chinese. In many ways, the Ming is not a dynasty he started, but it is a continuation of the Qin Dynasty. When

Qin Shi Huangdi came to power, uniting the warring states, he built palaces, tombs, temples, and started the Great Wall."

"We should build a monument to your father," one of the ministers said. "The founder of the Ming Dynasty should loom large over Nanking and the people in it."

There were many murmurs of approval at this.

"This is a good idea," the emperor said. "But I have something bigger in mind. Something that will show not just the people of Nanking that the Ming are a force to be reckoned with, but the world."

"We could reinforce the Great Wall," General Kang spoke up. "The Mongolian barbarians will forever want to try to return. And the Manchu have been amassing forces as well. If we build up our defenses to the north, we will demonstrate to all the northern tribes that we will not be easily overrun."

"But the wall did not prevent the Mongol from coming the first time," another minister spoke up. "A wall is outdated technology. And it is crumbling in many places. The money and manpower required to build the wall would far outweigh the benefits. We should increase our northern forces, yes, but let the wall rot."

The men grumbled as they argued about the benefits and drawbacks to building up the Great Wall. The emperor sighed and gripped the arms of his throne in frustration. He had to let the men say their piece before he could make a decision, lest the men feel unheard.

"Gentlemen," the emperor finally said, raising his hand. "The threats from the north cannot be ignored. Which is why I believe we do need a plan for reinforcing the wall and the northern armies. But more than this, I believe we should make a show of force in the north that cannot be ignored. Not by the Mongol, nor the Manchu, nor even forces from across the sea should they dare taunt us."

The men looked from one to another, worrying their hands, their eyes glancing about for some hint about what the emperor could be planning to do.

"We shall move the capital city from Nanking to Peking and build a new palace, the likes of which the world has never seen!" the emperor said. He sat back in his seat, satisfied at his words, but the room did not react the way he expected. Everyone was stunned into silence, afraid to speak. "Well? Do you not think this is the best way to emphasize my sovereignty? My power?"

"It is one way," General Kang said, the only man who dared to challenge the young emperor. "But you could build up the palace here. Though, I dare say the cost would be exorbitant either way, at least building one here would not mean relocating thousands—"

"Hundreds of thousands!" one of the ministers piped up.

"Yes," the general went on. "Perhaps hundreds of thousands of people. We who serve the throne have lived in the south for generations. You would not just be moving courtiers, but their families. Servants and their families. And if we leave, what about the farmers and craftsmen who have been supporting the imperial families for hundreds of years? This is..." The general wanted to say madness, but he knew better than to make any insinuations about the emperor's mental state. "This is an undertaking the likes of which the country has not seen in hundreds of years."

"But it has been done," the emperor said. "Chang'an was once the capital city, to the west. And Kublai Khan built his palace in the north. We are only here in the south because many of my father's supporters were here—such as yourself, General."

The general could not deny that Nanking was the logical choice for the late emperor to set up a capital. But it was also the logical choice to stay.

"But what benefit is there to moving?" the general asked. "Other than to set up a uniquely Ming capital, the cost...the manpower...the disruption to the daily order of running the country. The troubles will never end."

"My father was from the north," the emperor said, sitting high on his throne. "I am a northerner. The people here in the south do not appreciate having an emperor in their midst. In the north, among my own people, I will be welcome like the Son of Heaven that I am. It was my father's dream to return to the land of his birth, was it not?"

"He did often speak of returning home," the general begrudgingly admitted. "But he knew that it was impossible. Nanking is the capital, and he had accepted that to be emperor meant staying here."

"Then my father did not dream big enough," the emperor said, standing. "I will finish what my father started. I will move the Ming capital to the north. I will fortify the northern wall against any incoming attack. And I will build a palace that blazes yellow in the light of the sun. All who see it will know the might of the Ming Dynasty and of China!"

The room erupted into cheers and clapping, whether they truly believed the emperor's words or not. The emperor believed them. And it was clear that nothing would stop him from seeing his plan through.

Empress Wen clapped as well, and she smiled as her husband looked at her. But when he looked away again, her eyes landed on those of her father, and then on and her two brothers standing toward the back of the room. They all knew this was foolish. A waste of funds the throne did not have. It would diminish their own power, to be taken far away from their family home where they had amassed vast tracts of land and countless tenant farmers and even their own army.

After the emperor took his leave, the empress retired to her own quarters. Her father and brothers soon joined her there. As soon as the general entered the room, he grabbed Wen roughly by the arm and shook her.

"Why did you not talk him out of such foolishness?" he demanded to know.

"He didn't tell me!" she said, pulling out of her father's grasp and rubbing away the pain. "He never mentioned a desire to build a new imperial city to me."

"Then you are failing in your duties as a wife and empress," her father said. "And not for the first time."

Wen knew that her father was referring to the fact that he had not born a son, but she bit back tears. She would not show weakness in front of the men of her family.

"If your husband does not confide in you and you cannot guide his actions, what good are you?" Wen's eldest brother, Jun, asked her.

"Is there another woman?" her younger brother, Sun, asked. "A concubine who has his eye and ear and tongue?"

"No," Wen said. "Not that I know of. He does lay with the other consorts, but they are not his confidants."

"Then why did he keep this from you?" the general asked.

Wen shook her head. "I do not know. Perhaps he knew that I would not approve. He must know that no one would be supportive of such a decision. We have been married a long time and know each other well. And considering your place here in the south, he must have known that I would try to talk him out of it."

"Well, he would not be wrong," Jun said. "We can't move our lands. And even if we demanded an equal parcel in the north, there would be no men loyal to us there. The farmers would not know or trust us. And no one would join our army."

"Sun," the general said to his youngest child, "you must stay here and govern the estate in my stead."

"Yes, Father," Sun said, placing his hand over his heart.

"Do not disappoint me," the general added. "If this foolish plan comes to fruition and we have no choice but to move north, Jun will come with me. We will set up a new estate there, near the capital city."

"We will not be able to build in even one generation what has taken us hundreds of years to amass here in the south," Jun said.

"No," the general acquiesced. "But we might have no choice but to try. Besides, we will not be starting from nothing. Two generations ago, we were tenant farmers as well. Now, look at us, the most powerful family in China. Even more powerful than the emperor himself if he does not have a son. We will ride north and build power there as well. It never hurts to spread power and influence throughout the land."

The sons nodded at their father's wisdom, imagining just how great their landholdings would be by the time they inherited them.

"And you, my daughter," the general said, turning to Wen. "You must regain your husband's favor. Or find a young woman you can control who will please him."

"Yes, Father," Wen said with a bow. "I will not disappoint you again."

"And for the gods' sakes, get pregnant," the general said. "If you do not, it is only a matter of time before you end up on the street, banging at my door for food. And you know what will happen then."

"Yes, Father," Wen said.

"No daughter of mine will bring home such disrespect and live," the general said anyway, even though from the time she was old enough to know she would be married to the emperor, she knew that any failure on her part would lead to her death. But her father seemed to take some perverse pleasure in reminding her of that fact as often as possible.

"Come," the general said to his sons, and they all exited the empress's palace. As soon as they were gone, the empress began to pace. Her eunuch, Bojing, rushed into the room before the door was even closed.

"My lady," Bojing said. "Is this really happening? We are moving north?"

"I must speak to the emperor," Wen said, untying the sash to the gown she had worn to the formal audience. "Something blue. Hurry! Call the maids."

Bojing opened the palace door and summoned the empress's maids and they got to work dressing the empress in a beautiful dark blue robe with golden phoenixes embroidered on it. They reworked her hair and makeup to make her look less intimidating and more alluring. They sprayed her with a light floral scent that was sure to tempt the senses, and she ate the seeds of a pomegranate, which were said to increase fertility. Once she was ready, she was taken to the emperor's office, where he was speaking with the minister of finance about how to begin planning for the move to Peking.

"...take time. I cannot imagine the move taking place for at least a year—"

"A year?" the emperor yelled, jumping to his feet. "That is outrageous, minister!"

"For the move itself," the minister went on. "But that is only because there currently is no palace suitable for the royal family in Peking."

"But my father started work on the Purple Palace years ago," the emperor said.

"Yes, Your Majesty," the finance minister said. "He was actually remodeling an old Yuan palace, but the project became too costly and was abandoned. I have no idea of the state the buildings are in now."

"Put together a group to travel to Peking at once," the emperor said. "I need to know the state of the palace and what it would take to bring it up to livable standards. We can continue the remodeling to make it into a palace fit for an emperor after we move."

"Yes, Your Majesty," the minister said, backing away with a bow. As he reached the doorway and caught the eye of the empress, he seemed to be pleading with her to change the emperor's mind. He quickly averted his gaze, as it was against the law for any man who was not related to the empress to look upon her face, but the weight from his plea weighed heavy on her shoulders. How many more people would be counting on her to convince the emperor to change course?

Bojing announced the empress's arrival, and she entered the office without waiting to be admitted.

"You could not even wait until this evening to chastise me, my love?" the emperor said, not looking up from the papers on his desk.

"My heart is beating rapidly in shock," she said, moving

to his side. "I could not rest, could not think on anything else until I spoke with you on the matter. How could you make such a decision without discussing it with me?"

He looked up at her, his mouth open as if to yell, but her eyes had watered of their own accord and he bit back his harsh words.

"Have we truly grown so far apart that you would not even speak to me about something that will so drastically change not only our lives, but that of every person in the kingdom?" she asked, her heart truly pained.

"Because I knew it would displease you," the emperor said, looking away from her, fingering the papers before him.

"Then why keep it secret?" she asked. "Why should I find out at the same time as the ministers and eunuchs? Am I not your empress? Your wife? The one you love? Have I fallen so very low in your eyes?"

The emperor stood and took her face in his hands. "I value your words, your counsel, above all others. But I must do this, and I knew you would try to talk me out of it. And perhaps you would have been right to try and do so. But I do not want to hear it. This place...it is stifling me."

"Whatever do you mean?" she asked.

"I cannot be the emperor I need to be with the ghost of my father lingering around every corner," he said. "My father, the great hero. The founder of the Ming Dynasty. The beggar king who banished the Yuan. How can I ever outshine such a legacy?"

The empress said nothing. Indeed, how could anyone hope to ever be greater than the Hongwu Emperor?

"That is why I must leave," the emperor said. "Why *we* must leave. I believe that staying here is why I have been unable to sire a son. I cannot...fulfill my duty to you when I am surrounded by ghosts."

"No!" the empress said. She could not let him think—or at least say out loud—that he was unable to sire children. "You have always performed your duty admirably. It is I who have failed to give you a son. It is I who should be cast aside. I will bring you new consorts. Younger women. Women who will light the fire inside that you need to bring forth a palaceful of children!"

The emperor smirked. "Only admirably?"

The empress licked her lips. "Fantastically." She sat on his desk, pushing his papers aside and tugging at the sash of his robe.

"Get out!" the emperor ordered the servants as he picked the empress up, situating her higher on the desk as he pulled aside the layers of her robes. He pulled her body to him, entering her with ease, causing her to squeal in delight. As she tossed her head back, he nipped at her neck and chest. With each thrust, he begged the gods, the ancestors, anyone who might be listening to give him a son. If he had a son, he might not need to leave this place. The only home he had ever known. His father might have been a northerner, but he had barely left the Nanking palace in his whole life. There were no wars to fight, no lands to conquer. Only the day to day drudgery of running an empire. His only joy, his only release, was taking his empress and his consorts to bed. But even there, the joy was tainted by the need to have a son. Lovemaking was not purely for pleasure, but for duty. If he only had a son, he could relax. He could be happy. He could have a future to look forward to.

As he spilled his seed into Wen, he grabbed a kerchief and held it to her opening.

"Do not lose a drop," he said. "You would not want my son to accidentally slip out.

Wen leaned back, her legs spread enticingly as she held the cloth to her body. She bit her lower lip, and he could tell that she wanted more. She could make love over and over again and never be satiated. But the need to have a son squashed his ability to pleasure her as much as he truly desired. No matter how much he wanted to, he could not rise again to the occasion so quickly.

"Go to your rooms," he said. "I have much work to do. Take your vile herbs that will make your body more hospitable to a child."

The empress left his silk kerchief in place as she stood, straightening her robe. "Come to me tonight," she whispered, her hot breath on his ear sending shivers down his spine. But he knew he would be unable. He kissed her hand and sent her on her way.

He straightened the papers on his desk that had been rumpled in their lovemaking. He ran his hand over the plans for his new palace to smooth out the wrinkles. He grabbed a brush, dipped it in ink, and then drew a new room next to the empress's chambers. He labeled it "the crown prince's quarters."

THREE

*E*ighteen months later, the emperor, the imperial family, countless servants, scores of courtiers and their families, and the entire standing army marched into Peking, the new imperial city. The empress had been unable to sway the emperor from his course. Instead, every month that she—and the rest of the consorts—failed to conceive, the emperor seemed more intent to move the court to Peking. "Everything will be different," the emperor told Wen. "And all for the better."

She had her doubts, but she could not voice them to her husband. If he was determined to move, no force on earth could persuade him otherwise. And now, after weeks of traveling in a carriage never stopped swaying from side to side, the empress and her eunuchs and ladies were pulling into Peking. Ahead of her, the emperor was riding a great black stallion. Usually, it was forbidden for commoners to look upon a royal personage. But the emperor wanted everyone to see him as he rode into his glorious new city.

The cart pitched forward as the wheels jumped from

the dirt-packed road they had been riding on for weeks onto the cobblestoned streets of the city. The empress pulled the red silk curtain of her cart back and peered out at the city that was to be her new home.

"My lady!" the eunuch Bojing cried out as he tried to tie the curtains closed again. The empress slapped his hand away and continued to look out. Ahead of her cart, she could see her husband, sitting tall astride his horse, a broad smile on his face as he waved to the crowd. She could not remember a time when she last saw him so happy. Perhaps this move would be for the best, after all.

But then she looked at the faces of the people along the road and she wondered who the emperor was waving too. There were many people, so many that she could see no end to them, but they were not gathered as though to watch the imperial procession. They seemed to be merely going about their daily lives. Peking had always been a bustling city, and even though the city was about to be changed forever, you would not know that by looking at the people along the street.

In spite of the cobblestones, the city was exceptionally dusty. The empress coughed and black dirt smeared her handkerchief. She had never been in such a dry and dusty place. Placed so far to the north, the empress had expected Peking to be cold and wet, like a perpetual winter. Instead, the air was as hot and dry as the Gobi Desert, which lay several thousand li to the west. Even the faces of the people looked dry as shoe leather, and the empress had to wonder how prone the city was to droughts.

The smell was also abhorrent. Wen had spent most of her life in the city of Nanking, but as the city was surrounded by green trees, every home had a luscious garden, and the rains came regularly, the city rarely smelled anything but sweet and clean. Peking smelled like a pigsty, and the empress was sure that the piles of dry dirt along the road were actually the droppings of animals.

Empress Wen was about to sit back in her seat and close the curtain to the dust and smells when she saw it. The large red wall that surrounded the new palace. The Purple Forbidden City. The palace had been named after the Purple Star, the home of the celestial beings, which resided just above Peking. The empress had seen the plans for the Forbidden City, and the emperor had spent many nights describing his vision to her, but nothing had prepared her for seeing the palace walls for herself.

The wall itself was almost eight meters high, taller than any building she had ever seen in Nanking. It was painted bright red, for luck and protection, and the top of the wall was covered in golden bricks that shone in the sun. Beyond the wall, she could see buildings even taller than the wall, each one painted red and shining with golden roofs. She imagined that even in the Celestial Palace, the gods must be able to see the shining Forbidden City below. She felt pride swell in her chest at what her husband—her emperor—had accomplished.

The empress turned to tell her ladies to look at the magnificent city before them when she heard angry voices. She looked back along the road as a small group of people gathered, yelling and shaking their fists at the emperor as he passed. The empress saw him slow his horse so he could better hear what they were saying. But he did not see the man in the very back of the group who lobbed a ball of rotten cabbage at him until the fetid vegetable hit him in the arm.

The people laughed, and the empress stared in wide-eyed shock. Who would dare insult the Son of Heaven in such a way? The emperor, too, looked down at his arm, now wet from the assault. He shook off the surprise and motioned for some of the guards to arrest the man.

But that seemed to send the entire group—which had somehow doubled, no, tripled in size—to break out into a frenzy of screaming and fighting.

The people rushed the procession, pulling at the riders atop the horses and rocking the carriages. "My lady!" Bojing yelled, pulling the empress back from the window, but he could not tie the silk cords closed. As bags of clothes, furniture, and other household items fell from the carriages, the people in the crowd fought viciously for the goods before dragging them away.

"They are stealing from us!" one of the maids shrieked.

"They mean to kill us!" another cried.

"Go! Go!" Bojing yelled to the cart driver, banging on the roof.

"Hai-ya!" the cart driver yelled as he cracked a whip to get the startled horses to move. The carriage lurched forward and bounced as the wheels ran over something that had fallen in the path. One of the maids stumbled to the floor of the carriage, banging her head on the wooden seat.

"Help her!" the empress ordered as she gripped onto her own seat, doing her best to stay upright. But when Bojing lifted the girl to sit, the other maids shrieked when they saw blood pooling down the poor girl's face and onto her dress.

"Lay—" The empress grunted as the wagon hit another bump. "Lay her down. Press a kerchief to the wound!"

Bojing and maids did their best to attend the girl, but the constant jostling of the wagon made it difficult, the blood smearing not only on the girl's face and clothes, but on those who tried to tend to her as well.

Finally, the carriage came to a stop and a eunuch opened the door from the outside, offering his hand to the empress. "Please hurry, my lady," he said.

The empress took his hand and stepped out. "My maid was injured," she said. "What happened—" But her voice died away as she saw that the other carriages were in much worse condition. The outsides were coated with rotten food, wheels were busted, and some horses had broken loose. Almost all of the precious goods that had been put atop the carriages were gone. Eunuchs, maids, and even consorts being carried out of the carriages also had all manner of injuries. The empress looked beyond the line of carriages and saw that the guards had formed a protective barrier between the imperial procession and the angry mob of people, which had grown in such number she could not see the whole of them.

"Empress!" a eunuch called, and she allowed herself to be led through a small door in the massive red gate and into the Forbidden City.

The inside of the Forbidden City was not nearly as opulent as the empress had imagined after seeing the outer wall. The cobblestone paths were uneven. There were piles of browning trees that had never been planted. Half-naked men were moving to and fro carrying all manner of building materials. And the sounds of construction were deafening.

"What...what is going on?" the empress asked, though she was not sure who she was even speaking to, her own entourage having been thrown into chaos along with the rest of the traveling party. She did not even see the emperor.

"My lady," one of her lesser eunuchs said as he bowed before her. She could not recall his name right now, but he had been sent ahead with some of her other eunuchs and ladies to prepare her palace for her arrival. "Please follow me."

"What is happening?" the empress asked. "Where is Bojing? The emperor? What of my lady? The one who was injured?" She was very near to tears.

"Please, follow me to your quarters," the eunuch said. "Bojing is taking care of everything."

The empress nodded her head. She had every faith that her chief eunuch would have everything well in hand. She saw that two of the ladies who had been with her in the carriage were nearby, so she waved for them to escort her. They squeezed her hands tightly, helping her navigate the uneven path as the small group made their way to the Palace of Earthly Tranquility, which was supposed to be the finest palace in the Forbidden City.

On first glance, the palace was exquisite. The stairs leading up to the palace were newly laid and smooth, and the latticed windows would let in the right amount of light and breeze. In fact, it was precisely how she had imagined it. The emperor had allowed the empress to help design the palace so she would be happy with it.

But once the doors opened, her mouth gaped in shock.

It wasn't finished.

The floor was bare wood, without a rug or carpet to be seen. There was no bed, only silk blankets and pillows on the floor. The braziers had been set in the middle of the room, as though waiting to be moved to the four corners later. And she could still hear the banging of construction going on in another building nearby.

"Wh-wh-what is this?" the empress asked the eunuch.

His head was bowed and his hands folded tightly in front of him. "We did the best we could, Your Majesty," the man said. "But the palace...none of the palaces have been completed."

"But...where am I to sleep?" she asked, stepping through the room and looking into the various side rooms that were to serve as her bedchamber, dressing chamber, dining room, sitting room, library, office, and wardrobe. "Where is my furniture? What am I to do with my clothes? Where have my jewels been placed?"

At this point, she thought the eunuch was crying. "I am sorry, my lady," he said between sniffles. "I have checked with the Ministry of Household Affairs every day. They claim your items are accounted for, but they have yet to be delivered. I told them you were arriving today and demanded they hand the items over, but they still have not arrived."

"This...this is unacceptable!" the empress yelled. "Where are my things? Where are my maids? Where is Bojing? And what is that incessant *banging*?"

"Empress!" Bojing stepped into the room, and the empress ran to him, sobbing into his arms.

"I cannot live like this!" she said. "It's filthy. Horrible!"

"I understand, my lady," Bojing said as he led the empress away from the door. He clapped his hands together sharply, and two eunuchs carried a large chair into the room. They set the chair down and placed a silk cushion on it to make it more comfortable. Bojing then helped lower the empress into the seat. Bojing then continued to bark orders, and at once, a calming cup of tea appeared in the empress's hands. She watched, as if by magic, as the quarters that were unlivable only moments ago slowly turned into the palace she had dreamed of.

Right before her eyes, her *kang*, her bed that would be heated by warmed stones underneath, was built, and her blankets and pillows piled atop it. Chairs, tables, her writing desk, shelves, and all the furniture she remembered, along with some exquisite new pieces, were placed throughout the rooms. Handwoven rugs were brought in and spread out along the floors. Several very strong men were brought in to carry the immense bronze braziers to their proper places. Finally, trusted eunuchs from the Ministry of Household Affairs brought in trunk after trunk of the empress's finest gowns, along with countless boxes of her most precious jewels.

It took several hours to set everything to right, but by evening, the empress felt something akin to normal again. Even the banging had stopped. She let out a satisfied sigh and sat on her *kang*. She reached out to Bojing and took his hand in hers.

"Thank you," she said. "I was of half a mind to mount a horse and ride back to Nanking."

Bojing chuckled. "No, you would not have done that. You could never admit defeat. Especially by a little dirt."

"A little dirt?" the empress scoffed. "You act as though I was hysterical for no reason. Without you, I would be sleeping on the floor tonight. Can you imagine?"

"I am glad to be of service to you," Bojing said.

"What of the maid?" the empress asked. "Was she terribly injured?"

"She will heal in a few days," Bojing said. "Thankfully, the apothecary arrived some days ago and his quarters and office were already arranged."

"That is a blessing," the empress said. "Any idea what

caused the riot in the first place? I thought the people were glad we were moving to the city."

Bojing said nothing, but looked away.

"Bojing?" the empress prodded. "Tell me. What is happening?"

"The people of Peking..." He shook his head. "They are not pleased with the arrival of the imperial family. They have been taxed beyond reason to pay for the building of the Forbidden City."

"What?" the empress asked. "Why?"

"The emperor ordered it," he said. "He said that Nanking had supported the imperial family for long enough. It was now Peking's turn."

The empress shook her head. She knew better than to criticize the emperor out loud, but she could not see the reason behind laying the cost for the move on one city.

"Many people have also lost their homes," Bojing went on. "The palace was quite small before. To be expanded to house the entire imperial court, many, many blocks of homes had to be destroyed."

"Were the families fairly compensated?" the empress asked.

"I do not know," Bojing said. "I am not privy to such information. But judging by the way the people reacted today..." He did not need to continue.

"I will speak with the emperor," Wen said. "We cannot live in a city where the people hate us. We must find a way to endear the emperor to the people before things grow worse."

"I think that is an excellent plan, Your Majesty," Bojing said. "How will you do that?"

"I have no idea," the empress said, rubbing her forehead. The banging outside had stopped, but it seemed the banging inside her head had only begun.

"I will prepare you for sleep, Your Majesty," Bojing said. "Perhaps tomorrow will be a brighter day."

The empress sighed. The sun might shine brightly on Peking, but it seemed that only clouds surrounded the Forbidden City.

FOUR

*I*n his own quarters, the emperor fumed. He paced the length of his dressing quarters like a caged tiger, ready to lash out at the first person to dare come within reach. His chief eunuch kept his head down as he prepared to dress the emperor for the throning ceremony to officially name the Purple Forbidden City as the imperial capital and primary residence of the emperor.

"Why were my rooms not ready?" Huangdi asked his eunuch.

"I do not know, Your Majesty," the eunuch said as he laid the emperor's glorious yellow robe across a chair to smooth it out. "I was not part of the group sent ahead to prepare for your arrival."

"Who was?" the emperor barked. The eunuch hemmed and hawed, not wanting to possibly endanger the lives of his fellow servants.

"There was so much to prepare, and so many people involved. And I was busy with you back home making sure today would go perfectly—"

"What?" the emperor roared, turning on his eunuch. He

stomped toward the eunuch as he cowered, unsure of what he had said that had enraged the emperor so. "What did you say?"

"Just that I was helping you in Nanking—"

"No!" the emperor said. "You called it home. That place is no longer our home. This, the Purple Palace, Peking, this is our home now. Do you understand?"

The eunuch kowtowed, knocking his forehead to the floor. "Yes, of course, Your Majesty. Forgive my stupid words."

"Hurry and help me dress," the emperor said. "We are already late for the ceremony."

"Yes, Your Majesty," the eunuch said. He helped the emperor remove his dusty and sweaty traveling clothes, making no mention of the bits of rotten food that had gotten on them from the angry mob that had formed along the procession route. He then helped the emperor into a warm bath to wash him from the dirt and smell of horse. He washed and combed and oiled the emperor's magnificent long hair and used a special cream to massage the emperor's scalp. The emperor sighed as he seemed to relax into the tub, and the eunuch hoped that the emperor had forgotten the unpleasantness of their arrival in their new city.

"Who was in charge of preparing the procession route through the city?" the emperor suddenly asked. The eunuch's hands froze in place for a moment, caught off guard by the question.

"I couldn't say," he said as he resumed rubbing the emperor's scalp.

The emperor slapped the eunuch's hands away as he stood, the soapy water dripping down his perfectly formed body. He snatched a towel from the side of the tub and dried his face and arms, then wrapped the towel around his waist. He called for the rest of his servants, who would help him dress. They bustled in quietly, each knowing exactly what was required of him.

"You seem to be quite out of your element here, Wangzhu," the emperor said. "Since when have I ever asked a question and you not have an answer for me? If you cannot get me the information I need, what use are you to me?"

The other eunuchs who had been busy fussing around the emperor and the room all slowed in their movements and eyed the chief eunuch. Wangzhu looked at each of them in turn with a warning in his eyes. If they thought there might soon be an opening for his position, they were wrong.

"Forgive me, Your Majesty," Wangzhu said as he stood aside and another eunuch brushed and styled the emperor's hair into a knot on top of his head. "I simply did not want to tax you further after the unpleasant morning you had. Do not worry. I will make sure the appropriate people are punished."

"No," the emperor said. "This is my home. My city. My *country*. I am the emperor, and the way those peasants treated me and my family today was disgusting. It was dangerous! What if the horses had been spooked into a stampede and my mother had been injured? You will find out who was responsible for order in the city today and bring him to me. Do you understand?"

"Yes," Wangzhu said. "I will do so immediately." Wangzhu bowed low and backed out of the emperor's dressing room, sweat dripping from his brow as he tried to decide where to lay the blame.

After the emperor's hair was styled, his body rubbed in

fragrant oils, and his facial hairs trimmed, the eunuchs helped don him in his exquisite robe. After dressing him with his silk underclothes, the heavily embroidered yellow robe was placed around him and secured with a sash that tied in the back. On the front of the robe, a large blue five-toed dragon was embroidered. Only the emperor was ever allowed to display a five-toed dragon, and the emperor wanted to make sure there was no mistaking who the ruler was in this new immaculate palace.

Once the emperor was dressed, the main doors of his palace were opened and he stepped out into a hazy sunshine. He covered his mouth as he let out a small cough.

"Why is the air so dirty?" he asked.

"The air is very dry this time of year, Your Majesty," one of the eunuchs answered.

"And the redecorating has loosened much dust," another added.

"When will the redecorations be completed?" the emperor asked.

Taking note of the conversation the emperor had with Wangzhu earlier, the other eunuchs were more cautious with their answers.

"I will seek out the master designer and find out for you, Your Majesty," one of them said.

"Good," was all the emperor replied as the silk curtains of a palanquin were pulled back for him. The Forbidden City was four times as large as the palace in Nanking, and it would take much time and be incredibly exhausting for the emperor to walk so far. So instead, all members of the royal family would be carried around the Forbidden City in palanquins while their servants would trot along aside.

When the emperor arrived at the main audience hall, his heart filled with pride. The building was immense.

Much larger than any building at the palace in Nanking. Indeed, it was larger than any building he had seen in his entire life. There were more than a dozen stairs leading up to a raised level with a terrace where people who wished to seek an audience with the emperor could wait, and then there were several more stairs that led to the front doors of the audience hall. Usually, for typical audiences, the emperor would enter from a side door to the rear of the building. But today, for such a momentous occasion, he would enter from the front.

Another palanquin soon arrived, and Empress Wen stepped out wearing an equally stunning yellow robe, but her's was embroidered with a phoenix, it's five tail feathers a rainbow of colors.

The empress kneeled before the emperor. "Your Majesty."

The emperor took her hand and kissed the back of it. "My lady. Shall we?"

The empress nodded and allowed the emperor to lead her up the stairs, which she could feel the heat from even through her heavily embroidered slippers. Still, she kept a smile on her face and stood straight. She would not let anything else ruin this day. A new home. A new throne. A new city. A new life. The gods had to be smiling down on them. It had to all be worth it.

As they entered the audience hall, hand in hand, all of the magistrates and ministers, the empress's father, and the emperor's mother were in attendance, lining the long red carpet that led to the raised dais where the emperor's throne sat.

Only the emperor's throne.

Wen did her best to contain her shock. There was only one throne present, situated in the center of the dais. In

Nanking, there had been two thrones. Of course, the empress's throne had been smaller, set slightly behind the emperor's, but still, she had pride of place at the emperor's side.

As they approached the throne, there were several Buddhist monks present, bowing, chanting, and burning incense before the throne. The empress's eyes were drawn upward to a giant golden dragon with a large golden pearl in its mouth situated directly above the throne. She could not begin to calculate what the great beast must have cost. No wonder the people were enraged over taxes. If they found out that their money had been used to cast such an idol, they would probably burn the Forbidden City to the ground.

The emperor and empress kneeled before the throne, and the monks moved toward them, waving their wands of incense around them and chanting blessings for the empire and for fertility. When the monks were done, the emperor stood and then helped the empress stand. He released her hand and climbed the few steps to the throne without her. He then turned and faced the crowd.

"These monks once worshipped beside my father when he had nowhere else to go," the emperor said. "No family. No lord. No one to turn to in times of deep distress, these monks took in a beggar from the streets. And that beggar became not only my father, but the father of the new glorious Ming Dynasty!"

The crowd erupted into cheers.

"Today, I have asked these men to bless this new throne, this seat of power, and the dragon that sits above it. The Dragon Throne. Only the one true emperor shall sit upon it. If anyone who is not the Son of Heaven dares to attempt to usurp the throne, the pearl from the dragon's mouth shall fall and crush the usurper. Never again will China be ruled by barbarians from the north or any other invading force."

The crowd cheered again, and the empress clapped as she kept a smile upon her face and her chin lifted in pride.

The emperor stepped back, and it seemed as though the whole room held its breath. The emperor sat, and the excited cheers let loose once again. The cheering lasted for so long, the emperor had to raise his hand to quiet them so he could continue with what else he had to say.

"Today was to be a day of joyous celebrations, but the day was marred by an angry mob who attacked me and my family on the road as we arrived," the emperor said. Many people hissed and grumbled their dissatisfaction at this.

"They are lawless peasants," someone said. "These northerners have no culture, no grace. They have no idea what it means to be in the presence of the Dragon Emperor."

"Hear, hear!" the crowd cheered.

"That may be true," the emperor said. "But who was responsible for ensuring the people were prepared for my arrival? Who was supposed to make sure the way through the city was safe? My own dear mother or wife could have been severely injured if any of those foolish peasants had thought to lift a weapon and not merely garbage."

Murmurs began to circulate through the room. In spite of his calm facade, the emperor was clearly angry about the mob that morning and was looking for someone to blame. Everyone shuffled nervously, wondering who the finger would be pointed at.

"Wangzhu," the emperor said, calling his chief eunuch forward.

The eunuch shuffled toward the dais and kneeled before the emperor. "Yes, Your Majesty?"

"What have you found out about the riots this morning?"

Wangzhu quickly searched for an answer. He had only left the emperor's presence not even an hour before. He had no idea who had been in charge of any part of the emperor's arrival, and he had been planning for this very ceremony. He thought the emperor would give him at least a day to find a scapegoat.

"Your Majesty," Wangzhu said, sweat dripping from his brow. "I still need more time. I was hoping to confer with General Kang about the arrangements that had been made for the procession—"

"You blame General Kang?" the emperor asked.

"No!" the eunuch said, not wanting to make an enemy of any member of the empress's family. "I only meant that as a military man, he would know better than I the arrangements for making sure you and the imperial ladies were well protected."

"Hmm," the emperor said. "I see. General Kang."

"Yes, Your Majesty?" the general said, stepping forward with seemingly no concern at all about being questioned on the topic.

"What arrangements did you make to ensure the safety of your daughter and my mother?"

"None," the general said plainly.

"None?" the emperor nearly spat, and the room gasped.

"No, Your Majesty," he said. "I have never before set foot in this city. What would I know about its people or how to make it secure?"

"So you just left us to be slaughtered by rioters?" the emperor asked as he sat on the edge of his throne, his knuckles white as he gripped one of the arms.

"Not at all," the general said. "It was my understanding

that the local magistrate of Peking would want to make sure the city was prepared for your arrival."

Everyone among the crowd began to whisper as they tried to figure out who the magistrate of Peking was. The people looked from right to left, shuffling from one side to the other until an aisle cleared and a portly middle-aged man was revealed.

"Lord Hai," the emperor said. He had not met the man, but he had corresponded with him frequently during the preparations to move the capital to Peking.

Lord Hai rushed forward, kowtowing before the dais. "Your Majesty, your safe arrival in Peking has been of utmost importance to me since I first learned of your internet to move here."

"And yet our very lives were threatened this very morning," the emperor said.

Lord Hai raised his head and waved off the emperor's concerns. "They were nothing but greedy beggars. They only threw a bit of rotten food. My men ran them off quickly. I am sure you were never in any danger."

"Are you saying that I am overreacting?" the emperor growled. "That I am easily cowed by a bunch of starving peasants?"

Lord Hai realized he had gravely misspoken and he could not see a way to clear himself without invoking more of the emperor's rage.

"I would never say such a thing," Lord Hai said, knocking his forehead to the floor so hard the banging could be heard throughout the audience hall. "The rioters were scattered and your family arrived safely. Please, I beg of you, have mercy! I failed you, but I swear I will never fail you again."

"That is right," the emperor said. "You will not."

Lord Hai, his face dripping with blood from a gaping wound that had formed on his forehead, looked up pleadingly at the emperor.

"You have severely neglected in your duties," the emperor said, and Lord Hai felt his bowels go weak. "Your people are starving and rioting in the streets. The lives of the imperial family were threatened under your watch."

Lord Hai began to cry. "Please, Your Majesty—"

"For endangering the lives of the imperial family, which is no less serious a crime than treason, I sentence you to death," the emperor said. Lord Hai cried out in anguish, but the emperor went on. "And not just any death, but the Death by a Thousand Cuts."

"No! Please!" Lord Hai pleaded as those in the room gasped and murmured. But his pleas fell on deaf ears.

"Take him away," the emperor ordered. "See that the execution is carried out immediately."

The crowd parted as several guards approached and carried Lord Hai away as he continued to cry and yell for mercy.

The emperor looked around the room, believing he would see nods of support for his heavy hand in dealing with the situation, but everyone avoided his gaze. No one wanted to be the next target of his anger.

Only one person dared to raise her eyes to him.

Empress Wen.

The smile that had been so firmly planted on her face all through the ceremony was now gone. She did not frown, exactly, but she was not pleased. He wondered for a moment if he had gone too far. If the punishment was indeed too cruel. The Death by a Thousand Cuts was rarely used, it was so horrific. The style of execution was explicitly used to prolong the suffering of the victim for as long as possible by removing parts of the person's flesh, little by little, until the person finally died. In the hands of an extremely skilled executioner, death could take days.

The emperor opened his mouth to speak, to amend the sentence to beheading, but he stopped himself. The emperor never made a mistake. And to contradict himself now, in front of all of his most illustrious subjects as he sat upon the dragon throne, would inevitably cause him to lose much face.

No, Lord Hai would face the most terrible of executions. Every resident of Peking would hear his screams. And no one would doubt that Hongdi, ensconced in his new Forbidden City, was the most powerful ruler China had ever seen.

FIVE

*W*hen the emperor signaled the end of the audience, everyone kneeled, even the empress. The emperor did not hold his hand out to her to lead her from the room by his side as he had when they resided in Nanking. After the emperor and his attendants left the room, the empress rose and exited next, followed by her eunuchs and ladies. As soon as they left the audience hall, the empress grabbed Bojing, her chief eunuch, and pulled him aside. She removed one of her pearl earrings and placed it in his hand.

"Give this to the executioner," she whispered. "Make sure Lord Hai is dead on the first cut."

"Yes, my lady," Bojing said. He gave a quick bow before scurrying away, hoping to bribe the executioner before the poor man's suffering had begun.

The empress then continued on to her rooms. It was growing late, and the day had been long. The sun had not yet set, but after traveling and the ceremony and the punishment meted out to Lord Hai, the empress was ready for an evening of rest.

Wen sat down before her dressing table with a long sigh. She removed her other earring and put it in a drawer with other mismatched jewels she often used as gifts or bribes. She wished she would have had time to send a more expensive bribe with Bojing. The executioner would be risking the emperor's wrath if Lord Hai did not suffer. But she could not sit by and let such a barbaric tactic be used on their very first night in their new home. She did not believe the practice should ever be used. It was archaic and cruel. It was only supposed to be used in the most extreme of cases, not tossed around arbitrarily to make a point.

What was the emperor's purpose, anyway, the empress wondered. Was it not enough that he had moved the imperial court to the other side of the country? That he had built —or at least started building—a magnificent palace? That he had installed that cursed dragon over his throne? Did he not already feel secure enough in his role as emperor that he had to resort to such base cruelty to frighten the magistrates into submission?

No, she supposed he did not. After all, without a son and heir, it would only be a matter of time before the magistrates and ministers would begin looking for the next emperor on their own. The emperor could appoint one of his nephews as heir, but history had shown that such a decision often led to divisions within a family, and not a little bloodshed. If the nobles were upset with the emperor's choice of heir, the country could once again fall into civil war, and everything her father and the emperor's father had fought for would be for nothing.

The empress sighed again as she washed her face and slathered her skin, from her scalp to the soles of her feet, in fragrant oils said to preserve her youth and beauty. She was already twenty-five, had been a wife for nearly a decade, an empress for almost two years. Her age and responsibilities were already weighing on her heart and mind. Many sleepless nights were leading to dark circles forming under her eyes. She did not doubt that Hongdi still found her desirable, but if she did not conceive a child soon, no amount of beauty would be able to entice him to her bed. He had already removed her from his side at court. How much longer would she be able to remain by his side in other aspects of his life?

Bojing soon returned and gave her a nod, indicating that he had been successful. That, at least, gave her some measure of comfort.

"What of his family?" the empress asked. "Should we do something to get them out of the city?"

"I do not think it would be wise to get more involved, my lady," Bojing said. "You have done enough for the poor man's soul. He blessed you with his last breath."

Tears rushed to the empress's eyes, but she wasn't sure why. She didn't know the man. And she thought that, surely, she had done what any decent person would. She supposed it was merely exhaustion from the day clouding her rational thoughts.

"Yes," she said, "I suppose you are right. Help me prepare for sleep."

The ladies had already removed her heavy ceremonial robe and silk undergarments. They had dressed her in her favorite light sleeping sheath, but the night had been cooler than she was used to. She had to remember that they were thousands of li north of Nanking. Even in the depths of summer, it would always be cooler than what she had been used to. She shuddered to imagine just how cold the winters would eventually get.

While the empress's ladies were allowed to change her

clothes, she only allowed Bojing to prepare her feet every evening before she was finally able to crawl into bed. She sat in a chair while Bojing brought over a bowl of hot water mixed with goat milk and rose petals. One at a time, Bojing took the empress's feet into his lap, where he removed her splendid slippers, which he handed to one of the maids to store in a special cabinet, and then he unwound the long strips of silk that were used to keep her feet in the tightly bound lotus shape that had been achieved when she was six years old after two years of excruciating training. If her feet did not remain tied with the silk ribbons, the weight from her body would eventually force the feet to straighten back out again, leaving them horribly disfigured. She had heard that unbinding a woman's feet was even more painful than binding them in the first place.

As Bojing removed the red strips of silk, the empress let out a long sigh. It was as if not only her feet, but her whole body was being released from its bindings, if only for a few moments. Bojing then placed her feet in the warm water, washing them with exquisite tenderness, making sure to carefully clean in between each of the countless folds that formed the tiny petals of her lotus feet. If necessary, he trimmed her nails and treated any wounds that had developed over the course of the day. Even the smallest boil or blister could fester and turn gangrenous if it was not immediately and properly tended to. One of Wen's younger sisters had died after having her feet bound when an infection settled in. Wen supposed that would be one blessing of bearing a son for the emperor, she would not have to go through the process of binding a daughter's feet.

Bojing then made sure the feet were completely dry before rubbing fragrant oils on them, taking much more time than was necessary on the relaxing massage. The empress was nearly asleep when Bojing began re-wrapping the empress's feet with new strips of red silk, just as tightly as before. The empress took a deep breath and waited for the new round of pain to subside before she stood and made her way over to her large kang. She looked at it for a moment, realizing that this would be the first time she slept here. This was truly her new home—and she would have to get used to it.

She was about to remove her robe and climb under the warm, inviting blanket when there was a knock at the door. The emperor's chief eunuch, Wangzhu, entered the room and kneeled before the empress.

"The emperor has summoned you, Your Majesty," he said.

The empress looked out the latticed windows and saw that it was now well past sunset. There was only one reason the emperor would be summoning her so late.

"Tell the emperor I am tired and to summon a lower consort instead," the empress said. She heard Wangzhu gasp. "What is it?"

"My lady," Wangzhu said, "you saw how he was at the audience today. He has been in an unhappy mood since our arrival. I would not want to deny him anything he desires."

"You won't be," the empress said. "I am the one saying no."

"But I will have to be the one to tell him, Your Majesty," Wangzhu said. "Please, my lady, have pity."

The empress groaned. Had she not shown enough mercy today? Besides, she was still hurt over the fact that he had not had a throne placed for her beside his own. And she truly was exhausted.

Still, she realized that as empress, lying with the

emperor in the hopes of providing an heir was her primary duty.

"Very well," she said. "Allow me to change."

"Thank you, Your Majesty," Wangzhu said with not a little relief.

The ladies helped the empress change from her comfortable sleeping clothes into something more enticing. They then wrapped her in a heavier robe so she would not catch a chill on her way to the emperor's palace. Finally, she climbed into the waiting palanquin and was carried to the Palace of Heavenly Purity, the emperor's palace.

As she stepped into the palace, she was somewhat relieved to see that his rooms were in as much disarray as her own. At least he had not put his own comfort above her own. The construction was simply taking longer than they had anticipated.

The emperor was in his night robe as well, and he dismissed the servants as soon as she entered. He poured her a cup of wine and offered it to her. She smiled and crossed the room toward him, accepting it happily, but sipping it slowly. She did not want the wine to enhance her exhaustion and send her to sleep before she had done her duty.

"My empress," Hongdi said after he had emptied his glass. "Can you believe we are finally here?"

"I cannot," she said, placing her own goblet near his. "It seems as though we are simply at a winter retreat and will return to Nanking soon."

"Eventually, that feeling will wear off and this will become as much a home to you as Nanking was," he said. The empress gave him an agreeable smile, but she doubted it. There was no replacing the home where she had spent the whole of her life. She and the emperor were betrothed at her birth, and since their fathers were dear friends and her mother was a lady-in-waiting to the empress, Wen was raised in the palace at Nanking instead of her father's home.

"You doubt my words?" the emperor asked her.

"No," she said. "It will only take time."

"We have all the time in the world right now," he said. He gripped her hand and pulled her to him, running his hands over her hair and her cheeks before placing his lips on hers. She leaned into him, hoping to hurry him along so she could return to her own bed soon, but he pulled away with a questioning look on his face.

"What is wrong?" he asked.

"Nothing," she said as she leaned in to kiss him again.

"No," he said. "I've been kissing you since you were thirteen years old. I can tell when your mind is elsewhere."

Even after so many years together, the emperor knew how to make his empress blush. They knew from a young age that they were destined to be married, so as soon as she was old enough to know what love was, she had loved Hongdi. She would often sneak away from her mother, out of the women's quarters, to Hongdi's study, where he was supposed to be reading long texts about how to be a good ruler. And when they were too young to know better, he had kissed her. Many months before they were married, she allowed him to make love to her. Up against a willow tree near the koi pond at the far end of the palace grounds. She did not fear any repercussions. In fact, if she had become pregnant before they were married, it would only have meant that the gods smiled on their union. But, alas, no child ever came from their frequent joinings.

Wen stepped away and shook her head. "I am only tired. We traveled so far. Sleeping in a different nobleman's home every night for weeks. I was looking forward to sleeping in my own bed finally."

"You would rather sleep than make a son with me?" the emperor asked, and for once, the empress could not interpret his tone. Was he truly angry or only teasing her?

"Of course not, my love," she said as she went to the bed and pulled her robe open. "Come to me."

Hongdi did as he was bid, taking her in his arms as he lay atop her, spreading her legs and squeezing her breasts. She did love the feel of his body against hers. He was still strong, his stomach flat and rigid. She wrapped her legs around him, urging him on. But once again, he pulled away.

"No," he said. "You are upset with me. Why? Tell me."

The empress grunted in exasperation. "If you do not want to make love to me, then call a consort. That is their only purpose. I am your *empress,* not just a vessel for children."

"What is that supposed to mean?" Hongdi asked. "Your job as empress is to bare my children."

"But not *only* to bare your children," Wen said. "We were supposed to rule together side by side, as we always have done."

The emperor scoffed. "So, that is what this is about," he said. "You are angry about your throne."

"Yes," Wen admitted crossing her arms. "I have always sat beside you. I have always supported you. Been a source of confidence and advice. When you said that things would be different after we moved, I did not think you would sequester me behind closed doors."

"The decision to sit by myself on the dragon throne had nothing to do with you," Hongdi said. "I am the emperor. China has no other ruler but me. When people see me, that should be abundantly clear. Having a woman at my side could make me look weak."

"Weak?" Wen repeated, disgusted. "You think I make you weak? Your wife? Your empress? The daughter of China's greatest general? You dare to say that I am weak?"

"You twist my words," Hongdi said. "I hold you in the highest regard. You know that. But you know that a woman ruling is like a hen crowing. It is unnatural. For you to sit by my side, it undermines my authority with the ministers."

"I have never undermined you," Wen said. "We have always been partners."

"Haven't you?" Hongdi asked. "So when you paid the executioner to give Lord Hai a quick death, that was not undermining my order that he should suffer?"

The empress felt her stomach sour. "You didn't..." she started to say but could not finish.

"I did," he said as he walked over to a table and reached into a drawer. He tossed something at her that landed beside her on the bed. It was her pearl earring. "My men intercepted Bojing. I am sure you recognize that. I did not punish your eunuch, which you can thank me for, but you can be sure that Lord Hai will suffer even more for your meddling. I am having his wife and daughters taken to the slave market tomorrow."

"You...you lie," she said. "Even you would not be so...so monstrous!"

The emperor stomped over to Wen, grabbing her by the arm. Without any regard for her feet and her need to take smaller, more cautious steps, he pulled her to one of the windows, throwing the lattice open.

"Do you hear that?" he asked her.

"Hear what?" she asked. The emperor was silent. She felt a cool breeze on her face. At first, she could hear nothing but the rustling of leaves and the chirrup of frogs in the lily ponds. But then, far in the distance, she could hear the sound of a man screaming. The sound of torture. Wen swayed on her feet and held her breath, determined not to be sick.

The emperor slammed the lattice shut. "I am sorry to cause you pain. I have never loved a woman the way I love you. But we do not have a son, and that cannot continue. The most unfilial act is to be without a son. I will not fail my father by letting his dynasty die with me."

"So, what are you going to do?" Wen asked. "I have never failed you in my conjugal duties. Nor have I been jealous when you have taken lower consorts. Indeed, should any of your ladies become with child, my heart would rejoice."

"I believe you. But we have failed the gods by not following the teachings of the old masters. You have been given too much freedom. Too much authority. You must be put in your place."

"You mean by removing me from my place at your side?" Wen said. "That is why you did not give me a throne."

"Exactly," Hongdi said. "But I have given you your own throne. Your own audience hall. It simply has not been built yet. But when it has been completed, I am sure that you will be overjoyed."

"How magnanimous," the empress said. "Thank you for finally telling me the truth of the matter. I knew something had changed between us, but I did not know what it was. I only wish you had told me sooner."

The emperor nodded. "Indeed. I did not wish to hurt you. But I see my delay was unable to prevent it. I am sorry."

"An emperor need never apologize," Wen said. "If there is nothing else, may I retire back to my room now? I am quite overcome with emotion. Perhaps you can send for a consort and the gods will bless you now."

"Perhaps I will," the emperor said as he picked up Wen's robe, which had fallen to the floor when he dragged her across the room. "I am sure you are tired. Rest well, my love."

"And you, my lord," she said, forcing a smile to her face and holding her head high despite the burning pain in her feet.

As she exited the emperor's palace, Bojing was waiting for her by the palanquin. His head was facing the ground, but even in the pale light of the moon, she could tell he was crying. He undoubtedly heard everything that had been said.

Wen placed her hand on his shoulder. "I do not blame you."

"I am so sorry, my lady," he said as he sniffed. "I had hoped that you would never learn the truth."

For a moment, she listened to the screams of pain on the night breeze. Then she shook her head.

"Come, let us retire," she said. She climbed into the palanquin and rode back to her own palace in silence.

SIX

*T*he emperor sat on his dragon throne, overlooking his many advisors. He was tired, but did his best not to show it. He had not slept well. The new bed was not as comfortable as his old one, and he assumed it would take some time to get used to. He was also frustrated. He always slept better after spilling his seed into one of his women, but after his row with Wen, he was in no mood to deal with any of his consorts. And now, the incessant banging and yelling and drilling from the workers who were doing their best to complete the designs he had planned for the Forbidden City were grating on his nerves. He knew they were working diligently on his behalf. On his orders. But the constant noise was giving him a headache. But he could not say anything about it. He was the person who had insisted on building this new palace. On moving north before it was ready. If he showed his discomfort, he would be admitting that he had made a mistake, something an emperor could not do. So, instead, he cleared his throat and sat up straight as he addressed his ministers.

"What is being done to help endear me to the people?" the emperor asked.

The men went quiet and looked from one to another. After the way he had dealt with the city magistrate, none wanted to provoke the emperor's displeasure.

"You are the emperor, Your Majesty," one of the men said. "The people love you. The little skirmish on the day of your arrival does not reflect the true feelings of the majority of the people."

"Doesn't it?" the emperor challenged. "The city magistrate has been dealt with, but the people still need a new leader, someone to handle the taxes and other city issues in a way that will not bring reproach upon the throne."

"Yes, Your Majesty," another man said, stepping forward with a stack of papers. "I have already put together a list of possible candidates for the position. All up-and-coming young men."

The emperor motioned for Wangzhu to take the papers from the advisor. "Have those taken to my study. I will examine them later and make my decision."

"Yes, Your Majesty," Wangzhu said, accepting the papers and handing them off to one of his assistant eunuchs for them to be sent to the emperor's study.

The emperor then turned back to his advisors. "Finding a new city magistrate is all well and good. But what about me? What can be done to encourage the people to revere me?"

"Lower taxes," one advisor spoke up.

The emperor scoffed. "Was that in jest?"

The man smiled uneasily. "Of course, Your Majesty."

"We could send rations of rice into the poorer *hutongs*," another advisor spoke up. "A satisfied belly is a satisfied citizen."

"Can we spare any rice from the stores?" the emperor asked. "We will need to make sure there is enough to last the winter, which will be much longer here."

"I will check and report back to Your Majesty post haste," the agricultural minister said.

"Good," the emperor said. "What else?"

The men went quiet for a moment and then shared looks between one another. The emperor could see that they clearly had something to say, but no one wanted to speak up.

"Out with it," the emperor said, his voice raised. The men winced.

"It has been more than three years since you last took a new consort," one of the ministers said quickly. "You were so preoccupied with the designs for the Forbidden City and the move north, we let the topic slip to the wayside."

The emperor sighed and cleared his throat again. He knew that his lack of an heir was an important topic, one that made him angry and ashamed in equal measure.

"Indeed, the move has been difficult for myself, and even more so for my ladies, I believe," he said. "Their lack of...affection toward me has been a side effect of their exhaustion from the move and sadness at no longer being close to their families."

Most of the consorts had come from southern families from all social classes. And while they were not permitted to see their families very often, it was a comfort to know their families were close. The consorts' mothers were allowed to visit, and the girls were allowed to return home if their fathers were ailing. Now, living so far from their homes, it was unlikely that many of them would ever see their families again if they were not wealthy.

"Yes, exactly that, Your Majesty," the minister said. "How

astute you are. I...we...believe it may be time to take a northern consort...or several...to show the northern people that we are, indeed, all one family."

The emperor groaned inwardly. The idea of taking more women into the Inner Court increased his headache tenfold. He already had...he could not remember how many consorts. He had not even slept with all of the ones he had. He preferred his empress, and only took the other women to his bed because it was his responsibility. He knew the women were lonely, especially since none of them had children to raise. The idea of bringing more women into such a lonely life filled him with guilt. But he knew that providing the country with an heir was his primary duty as emperor. So if he had to bring one more woman into the court, and could placate the people at the same time, he supposed he would have to do it.

"Inform the empress to prepare for the consort selection process," the emperor said. "I assume you think I should choose a woman from Peking?"

"Actually, Your Majesty," the minister said, his head bowed, "we believe that we should have a mass consort selection. As many as the new women's quarters can support. Women from all walks of life should be selected. It would please the nobles and the peasants if they knew their daughters were equal in your eyes."

The emperor felt his stomach turn sour at the thought. He had already been through a massive consort selection process when he had been a young man. It was always arranged that Wen should be his empress, but he was also required to take several consorts at the same time. He knew that most men envied his ability to support as many wives as he wanted. Only the wealthiest of men could afford more than one wife. Having many wives was a status symbol, so, of course, the emperor had to have more wives than anyone. He supposed if he'd had many children, he would find the work of visiting a new woman every night more enjoyable. There would be less pressure on him to perform with such regularity, and the women would be happier. As it was, he found the visits to the consorts exhausting, and he knew the women were miserable, often fighting amongst one another for pride of place before his mother and Empress Wen. They had to find some purpose in their lives, some reason for living, if they were not to be empresses or mothers.

"Surely one woman would be enough for now," the emperor said.

"It is not the number of women that is important," the minister said, "but the display of power. The pageantry. The visual spectacle of thousands of women all coming to the Forbidden City dressed in their finest garments, each with the same hope of becoming an imperial consort." The minister rubbed his hands together and chuckled at the mere thought. "What a sight!"

"Not to mention the money the families from further abroad would bring to the city," the finance minister said. "They will need places to stay, food to eat. They will shop in the markets and visit the operas and theaters. Such an event would surely ease the burden of the increased taxes on the city."

The men in the room mumbled their approval at this plan. And at the very mention of money, the emperor knew he had lost any chance of keeping the consort selection small. He sighed and gave a small wave of approval. He would have to see if the apothecary had any suggestions to improve his stamina.

*E*mpress Wen sat in an ornate high-backed chair on a very slightly raised dais in the formal sitting room of her palace so she could see all of the consorts, the dowager-empress, and the other ladies of the court. There were only twelve consorts presently, but three of the emperor's youngest sisters by his father's lesser consorts were still among the court ladies, waiting to be married off. Two of his elder sisters were also present as they had been widowed and had to return home, along with their female children. If they had had sons, they would have been allowed to stay in the home of their husbands until their sons came of age. But with only daughters to their name, they were forced to return to the home of their natal birth.

Behind each of the ladies, a lady's maid stood. Depending on the rank of the lady, she could also have more maids and eunuchs waiting for her outside of the sitting room. As large as the room was, it was already crowded and loud.

The women chatted among one another as they waited for the young empress to call them to attention. It was tradition for the empress to hold court among the ladies every morning, to give them instruction on how each could improve their service to the emperor, deliver announcements, and handle any disputes among the ladies, which seemed to take the vast majority of her time.

Today, the empress was in no hurry to call the ladies to attention. She had been informed of the emperor's plan to hold a massive consort selection to add northern ladies to the Inner Court. She saw the wisdom in the decision. It would endear the imperial family to the northern people. It would increase the emperor's chance of siring a child. Surely his yang would be compatible with some woman's yin eventually. And the families who could afford to travel with their daughters to Peking for the selection process would spend substantial amounts of money in the city.

Despite all that, though, she knew that bringing more women into the Inner Court would bring not a little trouble to the ladies' already pitiful lives. The Ministry of Household Affairs kept meticulous notes on all the goings-on of the imperial ladies. The empress knew for a fact that three of the consorts were still virgins. She also knew that there were several ladies who had spent their wedding night with the emperor and then were never visited by him again. She knew that she was fortunate that Hongdi still found delight in her bed—when they weren't fighting at least. That the emperor was going to be bringing more supposed lovers into an already loveless harem was going to cause more than a little heartache among the consorts, and not a little strife among all the ladies.

Dowager-Empress Chun hmphed and then mumbled loudly enough for Empress Wen to hear, "When I was in charge of the Inner Court, morning court never started later than the hour of the snake."

Empress Wen squared her shoulders and clapped her hands together. "Good morning, ladies."

The ladies all stood from their chairs and then curtseyed to the empress. "Good morning, Empress." Then they turned to the dowager-empress. "Good morning, Lady Mother." Then they returned to their seats.

Empress Wen smiled to the ladies, but she could feel her lips quaver. She spoke quickly, hoping the dowager-empress wouldn't see her nervousness.

"I know that many of you have complained about the noise in the day and the dust in the air at night," the empress began. "The apothecary will be making his rounds, administering draughts to help with pain and sleeplessness, but it might take him a few days to get to all of you."

The ladies began talking again, mostly about the poor state of the rooms and the toll it was taking on their health.

"Ladies," Wen said, clapping again. "There is no need for further discussion on the matter." The ladies quieted. "The emperor also sends his love and affection for each one of you." Wen raised her hand and summoned Bojing forward. As he walked through the room, he handed each of the consorts a box containing a unique hair decoration for each one of them.

"He remembered that pink is my favorite color," Lady Qin said, her eyes tearing up.

"You would have said that no matter what color it was," Lady Zhou sniped as she admired her own blue butterfly jewel.

Lady Qin's lips quivered and she did her best not to cry. She was one of the virgins.

"The emperor has been very busy with taking over after his father's death and moving us north," the empress said. "But he wants you to know that he has not forgotten you and that he will be spending more time in the Inner Court in the future."

The ladies exploded into excited chattering about what this could mean for all of them. All it would take was one night with the emperor to become pregnant and change their lives forever.

"Ladies," Wen said with a clap. "Quiet!" But the ladies chattered on, each one wondering which of them would be blessed with the emperor's attention first.

"Quiet!" Empress-Dowager Chun barked, and the ladies were instantly silent. The old empress glared around the room, saving her most withering stare for Wen last. "The way you ladies behave is shameful. Empress Wen should be training you better."

There was a snicker from somewhere in the room, but by the time Wen tried to find the source of the voice, the room was completely quiet.

"Thank you, Lady Mother," Wen said politely. "There is one more thing I need to speak to all of you about." The room remained quiet as the ladies examined their baubles or stared longingly out the window. Wen cleared her throat. "There are going to be many changes here in the Inner Court in the coming months. The emperor, in his boundless wisdom, has decided to take new consorts among the families of the north to—"

Empress Wen was not able to finish her sentence before the ladies erupted into yelling, crying, and shrieking.

"That's not fair!" one lady cried.

"I have to share a palace with Jinli already!" another said.

"I'll never get to see the emperor!" Lady Qin cried, burying her hands in her face as her tears flowed freely, her lady unable to provide her any comfort.

"Quiet!" Empress Wen said, but she could hardly hear her own voice over the commotion. "Ladies!" She clapped her hands to no avail. Out of the corner of her eye, she could see her mother-in-law smirking. Empress Wen jumped up, ignoring the pain in her feet. "Silence!" she yelled. The ladies all went quiet in surprise. "Do not speak again unless you are directly addressed."

Aside from some sniffling, the ladies did as they were ordered, waiting for the empress to elaborate on the worst news the ladies could have received.

"I know you are worried," the empress said. "More ladies for the emperor means less time with him for each of you. But, please, believe me when I say that I will be working closely with the Ministry of Household Affairs to ensure that the emperor divides his time fairly among each of you. And that includes myself."

The ladies fidgeted, anxious to speak their thoughts on the matter, but the empress stared them down, not calling on a single one of them to speak.

"The emperor makes no mistakes," Wen reminded them. "If the emperor believes that bringing more women into the harem is the best decision, then he is right. Never forget that."

The ladies all nodded in agreement.

"We all must hope that this new batch of consorts will bring blessings from Heaven, and not one, but that many children will soon join our happy household," the empress concluded.

The ladies all nodded, whether they agreed with the empress's assessment or not. Out of twelve consorts and an empress, the likelihood that the emperor would have a child with any woman was a dwindling dream. But the empress was right. The emperor was infallible. They could not speak against his decision.

"That is all," the empress said as she stood. "Return to your rooms and await the visit from the apothecary."

The ladies all stood and kneeled before the empress. "Thank you, Empress. May you live one thousand years." Their maids all helped them to their feet as they tottered out of the sitting room and to their waiting sedan chairs.

The empress followed them, standing in her doorway as she watched them leave. She did not realize the dowager-empress was standing behind her until she spoke.

"More women will not result in a child," the old woman said.

"What are you talking about?" Empress Wen asked.

"It's a punishment," the dowager said as she walked past Wen, shaking her head.

"A punishment for what?" Empress Wen called after her, but the empress did not reply. Wen sighed, wondering what the old woman was talking about, when she noticed that Lady Qin was standing aside, waiting for a chance to speak with her.

"What is it, Lan?" Empress Wen asked, using the girl's given name in private.

Lan dropped to her knees and crawled to the empress in supplication, giving no attention to the way she ruined her exquisitely embroidered robe in the process.

"Please, Your Majesty," Lan said through her tears. "Have mercy on me!"

"Stand up," Wen said, motioning to Lan's attendants, but Lan shook them off, remaining kowtowed before the empress.

"I beg of you, send the emperor to me before the new consorts arrive," Lan said. "Please, give me just one chance to please him! He has already forgotten me. When the new consorts arrive, I will die the way I am now. Please, please send him to me."

The empress kneeled down and pulled Lan to her feet. "This is not becoming for the future mother of the emperor."

"You mean...?" Lan asked.

The empress nodded. "I will make sure he visits you, and soon."

"Oh! My lady!" Lan exclaimed, taking the empress's hands in her own and kissing the back of them. "I will be forever in your debt."

"You owe me nothing," Wen said. "Go. Clean yourself up."

"Yes, my lady," Lan said, and she could not stop smiling as her attendants helped her into her sedan chair.

The empress sighed and called for her own sedan chair to take her to the Ministry of Household Affairs. She had much to do to prepare for the arrival of the new consorts.

SEVEN

*H*undreds of li from the Forbidden City, a young woman named Fei sat beside a rushing river, taking a moment to rest her feet from the long walk from her house to the fresh, clean water that was best for drinking. There was a well closer to the house, but Fei thought it tasted as though it had never seen sunshine. As if the water itself was dark and gloomy. So when it was her turn to retrieve the family's drinking water, she took the time to walk through the woods and down the hill to the river.

Fei leaned back on her elbows and took in the bright sunshine. Her walks to the river were also the only times that she was alone. Her family was of moderate size. Her mother was still alive, as were two of her father's concubines. She had three sisters who had already married out, three brothers who lived at home, only one of whom was married, and two younger sisters. Her married brother had one child only a few months old. The family was comfortable, though not particularly wealthy, so there was never any privacy. Fei even shared her bed with her sisters. And she was never far from the scrutinizing eye of her mother.

Her mother would never allow her to sit in the sunlight as she was now for fear her skin would darken. But Fei did not worry about such little things. She knew that her parents would arrange a marriage for her eventually, and her poor husband would have to accept her, dark skin and all, since he would not see her until after they were wed.

Her only concern was that she was already nearly nineteen years of age. After paying dowries for three daughters, her family had struggled to come up with a dowry for a fourth. She was not overly worried. She knew her family would scape the funds together eventually. Though it might only be enough for her to be a second wife instead of a first wife. She was concerned, though, for her younger sisters. Perhaps if her brothers married well, the dowries from their wives could then be used to pay the dowries for her sisters. She yawned and stretched to keep from falling asleep under the sun's rays. Her mother would never forgive her if she fell asleep and came home with a bright red burn.

She stood and glanced across the river to the old, burned-out house that had been long abandoned but never torn down. She always wondered what happened to the family that used to live there.

When she was younger, she would play with the boy who lived with his parents, an older couple, whose name was Shihong. He had been an only child and seemed rather lonely. He had fashioned himself a bamboo raft and would cross the water when it was calm to play with Fei and her siblings.

One night, the little house caught on fire. The flames had been so bright and the smoke so strong, her whole family was roused from their beds. Fei watched in horror as the house was destroyed in only a matter of moments. She thought initially, though, that the family had survived, as she saw dark shadows of people running away from the house and into the woods. But by the time the flames went out and Fei's father and brothers had taken a boat across the river, the family was gone and never returned. Fei's father told her the family had perished in the fire. She insisted that she had seen people leaving the burning building, but if that had been true, why did the family not return and rebuild?

As she grew older, she knew that it had simply been a childish hope that her friend had escaped. No extended family ever arrived to mourn the dead, tear down the house, or claim the land. Fei often felt that she was the only person in the world who remembered and mourned the little family and Shihong. Every New Year, during the spring festival, she would set out extra food for them so they would not wander as hungry ghosts and burned joss sticks in their memory.

Fei shook her head from the memories and filled the two buckets and looped them over a long pole on her shoulders to carry them back up the hill and through the woods to her family home. The extra weight was excruciating on her tiny bound feet, but she knew it was making them smaller, stronger, and, thus, making her more marriageable. Tiny feet were prized over a pretty face for many families.

"Miss Fei! What are you doing?" a maid called as she ran to help Fei with her buckets of water.

"It was my turn to fetch water, so I went to the stream," Fei explained.

"You are dirty and sweating!" the maid said. "Your mother will be furious if she thought I was making you do my work. You only need to dip the water from the well."

Fei smiled and rolled her eyes. There was no explaining to anyone in her family, even the servants, why she enjoyed her weekly walk to the river. She could only nod, hand over the water, and then retreat back into the sequestered rooms of the women's quarters and have a relaxing bath before her mother saw her face streaked with sweat.

Fei helped the maid fill a tub with heated well water, then she completely submerged herself in the tub, scrubbing her hair and body with the same harsh soap that was used for their clothes. She had some friends who were much wealthier who used sweetly scented soap, but Fei's father saw no reason to waste money on such frivolities.

When she was finished, her maid helped her from the tub, tied her feet in long red ribbons, and then helped her dress in a plain robe for the afternoon. The maid tied Fei's hair up in a simple style and did not bother with any face paint. Fei's afternoon would consist of embroidery, calligraphy, perhaps a bit of reading, and then she would have supper before practicing on her erhu and then dressing for bed. She would see no one other than the women in her family, so there was no reason to have the maid create an elaborate hairstyle or wear a heavily embroidered robe. But Fei had no more than sat down by a window to work on embroidering a handkerchief when she was summoned to appear before her father.

"Why would Father wish to see me?" Fei asked as the maid now worked quickly to make Fei more presentable.

"Fei is getting married!" her younger sisters sang as they danced around her.

"Why else would the master call for you at such an unusual hour?" the maid asked as she pinched Fei's cheeks to make them pink.

"But I have heard nothing of Father accepting inquiries," Fei said. "The harvest this year is not looking promising enough for us to earn a decent dowry."

"Perhaps he has had an offer from a rich man who needs no dowry," the maid said. "Only a young, beautiful wife to provide him with sons."

Fei blushed. "I am hardly a great beauty. If an old man with that much money wants a pretty wife, there are many more out there he could choose from."

"Shush," the maid said. "It doesn't matter. Just go see what your father has to say."

Fei nodded, having to settle for the few jewels attached to her hair and a quick change of clothes before being ushered to her father's study.

When she entered the room, she saw that her mother and her eldest brother were there as well, and they were all smiling. Fei kneeled before them and knew that the maid must have been right to some degree—an offer of marriage had arrived, and it seemed to please her family greatly.

"Baba," Fei said. "You sent for me?"

"Yes, my girl," he said, motioning for her to stand. "I have received a summons from the Forbidden City. The emperor is looking for new consorts, and you have already made it past the first round of inquiries."

"I...I have?" Fei asked. "How?"

"Some weeks ago, all the families of the north were ordered to send in the birth charts of their daughters of marriageable age," her father explained. "I saw no reason to mention it at the time, but, apparently, you have birth numbers that complement those of the emperor. You will be going to Peking for the next rounds of examination."

Fei's hand flew to her mouth. "I...I am to go to Peking?"

"This is a sign from Heaven!" her mother said as she smiled near to bursting. "The last time the emperor took consorts, you were too young. Your other sisters were of the right age, but their birth charts were not auspicious. This must be a sign that you are destined for great things!"

Fei's heart was beating hard in her chest. She was going to Peking, to the newly built Forbidden City for the consort selection. She could become a palace lady! If she did, her family would be showered with gifts and gold. They would never have to worry about money again. Her brothers and sisters would make excellent marriages. Her parents could spend their graying years in the most lavish comfort.

But she would probably never see them again. She shook her head. She would never be chosen as an imperial consort. She was too old, her skin too dark. For the first time, she cursed herself for not listening to her mother and taking better care of her skin.

Not that she wanted to be chosen, anyway. From what she had heard, the emperor already had a dozen consorts— and no children. His father had also died fairly young from years of heavy food and drink. Fei had no interest in becoming a barren widow, cursed to live out the majority of her life in the Hidden Court of retired consorts. She was grateful she had no real chance of being chosen.

"The emperor honors me and our family," Fei said. "But I am old and ugly. Surely I will not be chosen. Would it not be better to find a husband for me here?"

"At this point, you have been forbidden to marry until the emperor has dismissed you," her father explained. "All eligible young ladies north of the Yangtze River are to attend the examination in Peking two weeks from today."

"All of them?" Fei asked, her eyes wide. "Oh, Baba. There must be hundreds...thousands...hundreds of thousands of girls! I'll never be chosen. Is it not a waste of money to send me? Tell the emperor I am horribly deformed or disfigured. Is that not a basis for exclusion from the selection?"

Her parents and brother laughed.

"If you want to be sent home immediately, be sure to let the emperor know how funny you are, little sister," her brother said.

"No!" her mother said, swiping at her son. "Do not say such a thing. Fei has a real chance to change her life. To change all of our lives. She must do her best to catch the emperor's eye."

"Oh, Ma," Fei's brother said. "Be reasonable. She's right. She's too old to be a consort. Sending her to Peking is a waste of money. We are all tightening our belts as it is."

"The last thing I want is to be a burden on the family," Fei said.

"Quiet, all of you," her father said. "Fei, you are going to Peking. And you are going to do your best to pass the examination and become a consort. While I agree your chances of selection are not good, the farther along in the process you go, the more marriageable you will be upon your return. With any luck, the emperor will send you home with enough gifts that you can pay your own dowry."

Fei nodded. She had not considered that. She knew that there would be several rounds to the examination process. If she passed at least two or three rounds before she was rejected, it made sense that men here in her hometown would then be very interested in taking her as a wife.

"Unfortunately, I cannot afford to send anyone with you except your maid, Lina," her father continued. "You will travel with Ruolan's family."

Fei's mood picked up at that. Ruolan was her dearest friend. How exciting it would be to travel together and be able to have a friend by her side as they went through the examinations together.

Fei's mother wiped a tear from her eye. "Oh, that I could go with you. I know that you will bring such honor to us."

"You just want to see the Forbidden City," Fei's brother jibed.

"That is enough from you!" their mother said as she pinched his arm and pushed him from the room, he laughing all the way.

Fei shook her head and smiled. She hoped she would not be chosen. She loved her family and would miss them greatly if she were picked. Of course, no matter who she married, it was unlikely that she would see her family very often. Once a woman married, she was no longer a part of her father's home and family, but her husband's. Still, if she was married to a local man, she could at least see her mother and sisters on days that they went to temple.

"Come, come," her mother said, tottering over to Fei. "We have much to do to prepare you for the examination."

Fei followed her mother from the room. She chanced a glance back at her father and saw him looking at her with pride on his face. She never imagined that of all her siblings, she would be the one to bring honor and prosperity to her family. As a middle child, a girl, she had very little to offer a husband other than her ability to have children, and that hardly made her unique. Still, she would spend the next two weeks obeying her mother's every order and do her best to succeed in the examinations.

At least for the first few rounds.

EIGHT

"*H*urry, Fei!" Ruolan yelled as she waved Fei toward the open door of her carriage.

Fei's heart thumped quickly in her chest as she kissed her mother and sisters goodbye. She then bowed to her father.

"I will do my best, Baba," she said. The old man took Fei's cheeks in his hands and kissed the top of her head.

"If you are chosen, this could be the last time I ever see you," he said. "It is a bittersweet day."

"I hope we will meet again," Fei said.

Her father chuckled and tapped her on the nose. "As much joy as you bring to my heart, I hope we do not."

Fei nodded and tried—and failed—to not cry as she gingerly walked to the waiting carriage. Lina helped her climb up, and then the maid climbed up beside her. They sat across from Ruolan, her mother, and her maid. Fei did her best to bow to Ruolan's mother from her sitting position.

"It is most kind of you to allow me to accompany you on our journey," Fei said.

The woman smiled. "Our families have been good friends since long before either of you girls were born. It is an honor to escort you to meet your future husband."

Fei chuckled in embarrassment. "You are too kind. You know that next to the beauty of Ruolan, I don't stand a chance at being chosen."

"Your humility speaks well of you," the woman said. "But I hope you do not truly think so little of your own chances. The selection process is based on far more than just beauty."

"Ugh," Ruolan groaned. "If I have to read one more scroll from Confucius, I think my eyes will fall out of my head."

"At least Fei will then have a better chance of being chosen next to your eyeless face," Ruolan's maid quipped. Ruolan slapped her maid's leg and the girls all burst into laughter.

"Fine," Ruolan said. "Fei, if I am chosen and you are not, you shall come with me as my maid. If we can't both be consorts, at least we can still live together and be friends."

Ruolan's maid's eyes went big and glassy. "You would cast me out, mistress?"

"No," Ruolan said. "Even the lowest concubine is allowed to have two maids. You *and* Fei can come with me."

"What if I am chosen and you are not?" Fei asked. "Would you be a maid for me? Would you wash my clothes and give me a bath and clean my porcelain bowl?"

The girls all laughed again, knowing that Ruolan would never lower herself to be anyone's maid, not even for her dearest friend.

"I do not believe that will ever happen," Ruolan said. "I am completely confident that I will be chosen."

"There will be thousands of girls there!" Fei exclaimed. "What makes you so sure you will be chosen?"

Ruolan shrugged her shoulders. "It's better than thinking I won't be, isn't it? Why bother going at all if I plan to just turn around and take the long journey back? I'll be chosen. And more than that, I'll be the first woman to give the emperor a son."

Despite Ruolan's preening smile, the other girls and Ruolan's mother all went silent for a moment. It was common knowledge that the emperor had no son—had no child at all—despite his young age and dozen consorts. In the weeks leading up to the selection day, many had speculated that the emperor was looking for new consorts to increase his chances of having a son. But Fei did not see what twenty women, or even a hundred, could do for a husband that thirteen could not. Indeed, if even one wife could not bear him a child, what was the point in having more wives at all?

Ruolan's mother cleared her throat and smiled at the girls. "Yes, a positive attitude can go a long way toward making your dreams come true. But a stable mind and elegant manner will take you much farther when it comes to being selected. Who can recite for me one of the poems of Wen Pu?"

"Fitful and falling, autumn moonlight fills the clumps of chrysanthemums..." the girls—even the maids—all began reciting together.

For the two days of their long journey, they passed the time quizzing each other over the various questions they might be asked if they were lucky enough to move up the ranks in the selection process.

ei had been to Peking twice before with her father, but both times had been before the Forbidden City had been built. The city had always been busy and crowded, but it had always had its own sense of order. The people had moved to their own rhythm.

Now, the city was in chaos. The Forbidden City, with its vermillion walls and golden roofs, loomed large over the squat homes and buildings that spiraled out beyond sight in every direction. Roads and even whole neighborhoods that had once existed were now gone. The city was covered in a layer of grime, and even the air comprised of dust from the construction on the emperor's massive new palace.

The carriages parked outside an inn, and Fei and Ruolan were ushered inside where they would bathe and be made presentable for the first stage of the examination process. The girls had no chance to sleep from the exhausting journey. They arrived at the inn after midnight, but they had to arrive at the Martial Spirit Gate of the Forbidden City at the hour of the rabbit, less than five hours away.

The girls were washed thoroughly, their hair and bodies scrubbed with soap that smelled of sweet flowers that Ruolan had brought and shared with Fei. The soap smelled divine and made her skin softer than she knew was possible. She could not help but dream that if she was chosen to be a consort, that she would always be able to bathe with soap just like this. When the girls were done bathing, the maids cleaned and wrapped their feet before rubbing their whole bodies with scented oils.

The maids then tied up their hair in tall styles, using black puffs of cotton to make their hair look even bigger and fuller than it was naturally. They added fresh flowers and jewels of butterflies and dragonflies. They then painted Ruolan and Fei's faces with rice powder to make their skin as white as possible. Lina grumbled to herself when she could not make Fei's skin appear as white as Ruolan's.

"It doesn't matter," Fei whispered to Lina. "I am not here to be chosen."

"Then why come all this way?" Lina asked, her voice low. "Don't you want a chance to be a consort? You could become the mother to the next emperor!"

Fei shook her head. "I just want to go home and marry well. It is enough for me."

Lina sighed as she watched Ruolan's maid helping her lady into a beautiful new gown, most certainly created just for today.

"I do not think anything will be enough for that one," Lina mumbled.

"Whatever happens to Ruolan, I just hope she is happy," Fei said.

"Do you think she will be?" Lina asked. "A low-ranking concubine out of dozens, if not hundreds of women?"

"Well, she will certainly outrank anyone who ever came from our village," Fei said. "That alone will bring her joy, I am sure."

"And what of you, my lady?" Lina asked as she used her pinky finger to rub red coloring along Fei's lips. "What will bring you joy?"

"I just want to make it far enough along in the process to provide dowries for my sisters," Fei said. "I will go home with my head held high if I can accomplish only that."

"Hurry! Hurry!" Ruolan's mother said with a clap of her hands as she fussed over her daughter first and then Fei. "Oh, you both look so beautiful! The emperor will surely miss out on owning the finest jewels in his kingdom if neither of you is chosen."

Fei could not help but take a glimpse of herself in one of Ruolan's mirrors and she had to agree. She had never felt so beautiful. Maybe she did stand a chance at being chosen.

The girls were taken back to the carriage while it was still dark and the stars were twinkling over the silent city. But they had not traveled far when their carriage came to a stop.

"We are not there already, are we, Ma?" Ruolan asked.

"Certainly not," her mother said, leaning out the window. "Driver! What is happening?"

"Hundreds of carts, mistress!" the driver called back.

The girls gasped and leaned out the windows to get a better look. All they could see were the carriages in front and behind them, where other girls with similarly painted faces were also looking out of their carriages, wondering what was going on.

"Is there another way?" Ruolan's mother asked the driver.

"Afraid not, mistress," he said. "We were given strict orders which way to approach the city and the Martial Spirit Gate."

Ruolan's mother huffed and grunted and sat back in her seat, tugging Fei and Ruolan with her. "Get down, girls," she said to the maids. The girls did as they were ordered, all disappointed at the long wait ahead of them. "This line probably goes all the way to the gate. Carriages must have been lining up since yesterday! We should have come straight here when we arrived."

"And stood before the emperor stinking of travel?" Ruolan asked. "Certainly not. He will just have to wait for us."

"Spoken like a true empress," Fei said.

"Well, at least we have more time for you to practice your recitations," Ruolan's mother said. "Who wants to start?"

🌺

*T*he sun was high in the sky by the time the carriage pulled up to the Martial Spirit Gate and Fei and Ruolan, their maids, and Ruolan's mother all stepped out. Fei gulped as she stared up the side of the red wall that was higher than any building she had ever seen in her life. She couldn't believe she was about to step inside the emperor's palace. Even if she was not chosen to be a consort, simply being invited into his home was a great honor.

At the gate, several eunuchs were waiting, one looking especially important as he sat behind a table, his writing brush in hand. Ruolan's mother led the girls to the gate and handed the eunuch the girls' official summons. The eunuch mumbled to himself as he wrote down their names, the names of their maids, and then some other information.

"Female guardians will wait for their charges in the Garden of Serenity where the empress and dowager-empress are awaiting you," the eunuch said to Ruolan's mother.

"I...I am to see the empress?" the woman stuttered in shock. She then turned to Ruolan, taking her daughter's hands in her own. "Do you know what this means? I will be able to put in a good word for you! You are certain to be chosen!"

"Do you not think every other mother here today has not had the same idea?" the eunuch said with an annoyed sigh as he waved over two younger eunuchs who were standing at the gate. "Let me give you a little advice. Don't say anything. The empress is a shrewd woman. If you try to persuade her to choose your daughter, it will only go badly for you."

Ruolan's mother raised her head and smoothed down the front of her gown. "What would you know of the ways of women, eunuch? It will go better for you if you watch your tongue when speaking to me or my daughter in the future, lest you end up with another vital piece of your anatomy sliced off."

Fei wanted to faint from embarrassment. She did not know who this man was, but she knew that eunuchs were very important servants in the imperial household. He probably would be able to sway the empress much more easily than a stranger like Ruolan's mother. But Ruolan only smiled as she followed her mother through the palace gate, her maid and newly assigned eunuch at her heels.

"I...I apologize for my...guardian," Fei whispered to the eunuch behind the table. "She has not slept in days, nor do I know when she has last eaten. We are eternally grateful for your assistance."

The eunuch looked Fei up and down for a moment, then he looked down at his records. "You are nineteen years of age?"

"Yes, sir," she said.

The eunuch shook his head and used his brush to change something on his paper. "You are seventeen." Then he looked at her pointedly. "Do you understand?"

Fei bobbed her head and kneeled in thanks, doing her best not to cry at the eunuch's show of kindness. She had no idea that her age could disqualify her from being chosen. Indeed, if she was too old, why had she been summoned in the first place? Still, she knew that the eunuch was helping her, in his own small way.

"Yes, sir," she said. "I understand. Thank you."

"This is Yuying," he said, waving a young eunuch over. "He shall be your liaison for the day. He will show you where to go, what to do. If you are chosen, he will be assigned as your eunuch servant. Step aside."

"Thank you. Thank you," Fei said several more times as she bowed her way through the gate and into the Forbidden City to make way for the next set of girls waiting their turn to register.

As Fei entered the palace, her mouth fell agape. It was as if she had stepped into the most beautiful garden in the world. There were paths of pure white stone leading in several directions, and between them were islands of the greenest grass and bluest ponds. There were flowering trees and shrubs of every color. Birds flew overhead and squirrels could be seen in the trees.

And the garden was filled with the most beautiful jewels of all—marriageable ladies from across the empire. While Fei had felt beautiful at the inn, she suddenly felt like sandstone in a box of rubies. She had thought that her finest gown would be appropriate enough for the event, but now she saw that almost all of the other girls wore gowns that were much finer. More expensive. The newness of them shining in the sun. The eunuch might have done her a favor by changing her age, but there was nothing he could do for her plain face or old gown.

"Please, follow me," Yuyang, Fei's new eunuch, said to her with a bow.

Fei did as she was told, wondering all the while why the ladies were all standing around and not going where they needed to go. They were led to another gate in another wall where Ruolan already was.

"What took you so long?" Ruolan asked.

"Sorry," Fei said, not explaining that she had apologized to the eunuch at the desk. Ruolan would be appalled. "What are we doing? Who are all these ladies?"

"They are presenting us in groups," Ruolan said. "Those girls already made it past the first round."

Fei nodded in understanding. No wonder the girls were all so beautiful. Any girl not pleasing to the eye would have already been sent home. She felt her stomach tighten and prepared herself to not even make it through the first round.

"Where is your mother?" Fei asked, thinking it best to know where to find her guardian as soon as she was dismissed.

"In the empress's garden, that way," Ruolan said with a partial wave. "Can you believe how rude that eunuch was earlier? I can tell you now, if I am made a consort, that man —or whatever he is—will be the first to go."

Fei felt her cheeks heat up and she mouthed an apology to Yuying, who was standing silently nearby.

"I am sure it will be some time before you have the authority to fire anyone," Fei said.

Ruolan chuckled. "Oh, just you wait, big sister. I'll have the emperor eating out of my hand in no time."

Fei sighed and shook her head, deciding not to waste her time arguing with Ruolan once she had set her sights on something. And, truly, she hoped Ruolan would be chosen. Ruolan was her friend, and she wanted the best for her.

What Fei was less sure of was what she wanted for herself. Did she want to be chosen or not? Should she try her best or trip over her own feet in an act of self-sabotage?

She had no idea. She only hoped she could decide soon since the doors before her were opening.

Fei and Ruolan were led along with two hundred other girls into a large open area where they were arranged in twenty lines of ten. Their maids and eunuchs were ordered to wait along the wall. Two elderly women then began at each side of the group, saying "go" or "stay" to each girl they passed. Fei realized that this was the first test. A test of visual appeal only. The girls told to go were sent to a door to the right, while the girls who were told to stay did as they were ordered. The women must have had exacting standards, for they were dismissing about half of the gathered girls. Fei's heart began to race as the women got closer to her. She just knew she was about to be dismissed before she even had a chance to recite a poem. She watched the girls who were dismissed cry or stomp their tiny feet as they went to the exit, their dreams dashed. Still, Fei did not know what she wanted. Did she want to stay? Did she want the women to think she was beautiful? Or did she want to be dismissed? If she only knew if the girls would be given some sort of monetary gift as they left, it would lessen her worries. She had only hoped to earn enough money for her sisters. If she had already accomplished that by merely showing up, she would leave happily. But she had a feeling that all the girls being dismissed now would be going home with nothing. No money and no honor. And she just knew that she was about to be one of them.

"Go," the older woman said to her from her right side.

"W-w-what?" Fei asked stupidly.

"Go on," the woman said, nodding her head toward the exit door.

Fei nodded. She had failed, as she knew she would. And yet it still came as a surprise to her. She looked up and saw the hopeful faces of Lina and Yuying as the old woman passed her. Since Fei hadn't moved, they must have thought she had been told to stay. She felt guilty for getting their hopes up. She dropped her head in shame as she headed toward them, leaving the quickly dwindling lines.

"I'm so sorry," Fei said as Lina and Yuying each took one of her hands.

"You did well, my lady," Lina said.

"I wish I could have served you better," Yuying said.

Fei pressed her lips tightly as Yuying started to lead her to the door. "Wait," she said, stopping. "Ruolan."

The three of them looked back and waited anxiously as the women drew closer to Ruolan. Ruolan gave a small wave to her friend, but kept her smile plastered on her face. Few knew that Ruolan could not risk appearing less beautiful by wearing a frown. Fei held Lina and Yuying's hands tightly as they waited for Ruolan's command.

"His Majesty approaches!" a voice rang out.

Everyone gasped as they looked up and saw a man in a yellow robe flanked by several eunuchs, one holding a large umbrella over him to block the sun, walking toward the center of the open space.

"Kneel!" Yuying said as he dropped into a kowtow.

"What?" Fei asked.

"He said kneel," Lina said as she pulled Fei into a kneeling position.

"No, kowtow!" Yuying said.

"How?" Fei asked as she tried to mimic Yuying's prone position but did not think it would be possible in her gown.

"No, you kneel. The maid kowtows," Yuying explained.

"What?" Fei asked again, but as Lina let go of her hand to form the kowtow pose, Fei lost her balance and tumbled on top of Lina.

"My lady!" Yuying exclaimed as he reached over to try and pull her up. But for some reason, he let her go, returning to his kowtow position and letting her fall again, this time banging her elbow on the hard ground.

"Ouch!" she cried.

"Let me help you," a man said with a laugh.

Fei looked up, suddenly remembering the reason they were trying to figure out how to bow in the first place.

She was looking into the face of the emperor.

"Your Majesty!" she said, casting her eyes down. "Forgive me. I was startled and—"

"No need to apologize," the emperor said as he reached for her hand and pulled her to standing. He looked over to the girls who were still standing in line. Fei followed his gaze. "I seem to have startled all of them."

Fei smiled as she saw that the girls in line were all kneeling and kowtowing in different positions, each unsure of how to greet an emperor.

"I only wanted to see how the selection process was proceeding," the emperor said, turning back to Fei. "But if all the ladies are as charming as you, I am sure the selection must be terribly difficult."

"Charming?" Fei asked in shock, then her hand went to cover her mouth as she realized she should not have spoken.

One of the older women who had been performing the elimination process approached them.

"Your Majesty, I am so sorry that this reject has troubled you," she said.

"Reject?" the emperor said. "This delightful rose did not meet your expectations?"

"Of course not," the woman said. "Her skin is too dark. She's too tall. And her nose is too small."

"What?" the emperor said with a chuckle. "Surely you jest."

"I would never jest with Your Majesty," the woman said.

"Look at me," the emperor said to Fei, but she could not. She should not. She knew that it was forbidden to look a member of the imperial family in the face. But she felt his finger on her chin, then he lifted her face to meet his and she gasped.

It was Shihong. The boy who had lived across the river.

NINE

"*W*hat is it?" the emperor asked, a smile tugging at the edges of his lips.

Yuying tugged at the edge of Fei's gown, urging her to kneel—or at least lower her lingering gaze. Fei shook her head and cast her eyes down. Of course this man—no, not a man but the Son of Heaven—was not Shihong. She only saw similarities because she had been thinking of her young friend recently. Fei bent at the knees, but her hand remained in the warm grip of the emperor's palm.

"I...I'm so sorry," she said. "You look like someone I once knew."

The emperor chuckled. "Someone who made you trip over yourself?"

"No," Fei said. "Just a childhood friend."

The emperor nodded and turned his attention to the elderly woman standing nearby, the one who had told Fei to go.

"This woman did not pass your exacting standards?" he asked.

"No, Your Majesty," she said.

"Tell me..." He paused.

"Song," Fei said. "Song Fei."

"Tell me, Song Fei," the emperor said. "Are you a woman of high moral character?"

"I believe so," Fei said. "I have never given my parents a reason to grieve."

"And are you well versed in the classics?" the emperor asked.

"I often sat with my brothers when they were being tutored," Fei said.

"And are you skilled in the womanly arts?" he asked.

"I can play the erhu, and my mother was famed in our village for her embroidery skills, which she passed on to me."

The emperor nodded and turned to the old woman again. "This woman is pleasing to me. Let her advance to the next stage of the examination process."

"But...Your Majesty," the woman protested. "Think of how ugly her children might be."

"Do you really think that I would ever have ugly children, madam, no matter who the mother was?" the emperor asked, and Fei did her best to bite back a laugh.

The woman pursed her lips tightly and then said, "No, of course not, Your Majesty. The children of the Dragon are sure to be the most beautiful in the land."

"Then it is settled," the emperor said. "Song Fei, please move on to the next phase of the examination process...and do not disappoint me."

Fei glanced up at him and nearly lost her balance once more at how handsome he was as he smiled at her with a bit of mischievousness on his lips.

"Th-th-thank you, Your Majesty," Fei said, so excited she wanted to scream. She had passed! And not only had she passed, she had been given approval by the emperor himself! This was surely an auspicious sign! If only her mother were here.

"This way," the older woman said gruffly. Fei stood upright but kept her head down as she walked away from the emperor, her hand finally sliding from his grasp. The woman escorted her across the yard to the line of girls who had been told to stay, but she was sure she could feel the heat from the emperor's gaze on her back as she walked.

"Continue," the emperor called out, and he headed back the way he had come, his attendants shielding him from the sun. As soon as he was out of sight, the girls who still had not been divided rose from their crouched positions and stared at Fei. She felt her cheeks go hot and looked to Ruolan for support. But even Ruolan stared at her with hard eyes. Fei shrugged her shoulders and shook her head. She had no idea what had just happened. Prettier girls than she had been dismissed. How she had earned the right to stay, she had no idea.

The old women clapped their hands to bring the girls back to attention, and they all snapped their heads forward, their chins raised. Once again, the women walked through the rows telling the girls who to stay and who to go. Since Fei was certain to stay, she looked over to her servants, Lina and Yuying. Unlike Ruolan, the excitement was clear on their faces. If Fei were chosen as a concubine, they would be allowed to stay as well. She knew that they would do whatever it took to help her rise in the emperor's favor. She wondered if the emperor would remember her after today.

When the first part of the selection process was over, Fei was overjoyed to see Ruolan standing with her. They were then instructed to return to the courtyard to wait for the next part of the selection process.

Fei grabbed Ruolan's hand. "Isn't it wonderful! We both passed to the next rank!"

Ruolan nodded and gulped as though she had eaten a piece of sour fruit. "So *we* did...barely."

Fei knew that her friend was probably jealous that she had spoken to the emperor, had looked into his face, had touched his hand.

"We both knew that you would pass the beauty examination easily," Fei said. "Look at me. I am so ugly, the emperor himself had to intervene!"

Ruolan smiled at that. "Well, if I am lucky, he will give me a pass on the mathematics exam. That is my weakest point."

"We will help each other," Fei said, giving her friend an encouraging smile. This time, Ruolan gave a strained smiled back, squeezing her friend's hand.

❦

The examination lasted for days. Thousands of girls had passed the first part of the exam, but each new section sent more and more girls home in tears. The girls' bodies were examined in depth. Fei had never been naked in front of so many women in her life. She was peered at from head to toe to make sure she had no moles or rashes. Her hands had to be straight and her nails clean. Her feet were measured to make sure they were no longer than three inches from toe to heel.

The most humiliating part was when she was told to strip naked and lie on her back. An old woman came in and spread Fei's legs. Without warning, the woman stuck her finger into Fei's private areas and scratched her, causing great pain and blood to flow.

"She is whole," the woman said and then walked away. Fei was in tears as she dressed as quickly as possible and fled the room. Of course she was whole. She would never let a man touch her in such an intimate way before marriage! No girl of quality would. Why she had to endure something so degrading in order to be approved as a concubine, she would never understand. If they had told her that such a test was going to be administered, she might have put up a stronger fight to stay home.

But as she exited the examination room, she noticed that there were still more girls who had been dismissed. Apparently, some of them had, indeed, *not* been whole. Fei shook her head in disbelief. How could anyone be so foolish as to risk their future in such a way? They would most likely be unable to find husbands after they were sent home if anyone found out which part of the exam they failed.

Ruolan emerged from her exam looking as though nothing horrifying had happened to her.

"Are you all right?" Fei asked, taking her friend's hand anxiously.

"Why wouldn't I be?" she asked.

"Wasn't it...painful? Humiliating?" Fei asked.

Ruolan scoffed. "That's nothing compared to what our first nights with our husbands will be like," she said as she straightened her robe.

"What?" Fei cried, her face blanching.

Ruolan laughed. "Didn't your mother prepare you for your wedding night in case you were chosen?" Fei shook her head and Ruolan nodded. "I suppose she didn't bother if she thought you wouldn't even pass the first part. She probably thought she had plenty of time to explain it to you when you returned home."

"Will you...explain it to me?" Fei asked with some hesitation.

Ruolan patted Fei's cheek. "If we both make it all the way to the end and you don't go home to your mother, yes, Fei, I'll tell you all about it."

Fei sighed. "Thank you."

Over the next few weeks, all of the girls were given exams meant to test their intelligence and moral character. They were quizzed in literature, math, and even science. They had to recite long poems and passages from the classics. Their calligraphy was examined, as was their ability to embroider and play an instrument.

Finally, Fei and Ruolan were among the final three hundred girls who had survived the examination process. They all stood in line, waiting to hear their names called to see if they would pass to the final level. Fei was shocked when she saw Empress Wen and Empress-Dowager Chun enter the room. They would be making the final decisions as to who would be chosen and who would not.

Empress Wen stared over the collection of the finest maids in all of northern China. The most beautiful. The smartest. The most skilled. Those with the whitest skin and most graceful movements. She had never been judged on such a rigorous scale. Since her father had been the reason the late emperor even sat on the throne, her marriage had been arranged since birth. If she had been ugly or stupid, it would not have mattered. She still would have been empress. She had always prided herself on being naturally above all other women, selected by the Celestial Beings themselves to be empress over the glorious Ming Dynasty.

But now, after so many years of marriage, at least a decade older than all the girls who stood before her, she could not help but wonder how she compared to them. If she had to go through the examination process the way they did, would she have even passed the first level? She would never know, and she could not help but doubt herself for the first time. She feared that among so many great beauties, the emperor would surely find one—or many—who roused him and strengthened his seed. True, he had delighted in none of his other concubines thus far in the way he had with the empress. But it was clear that these girls outshone all others. And they were so young. What man could resist such beauties at his fingertips?

The empress cleared her throat and looked at the papers before her. She and Chun had already spent many days reading about each girl—her exams, her temperament, her family—and they had made some decisions. But there were some girls who needed to be questioned further before they could make their final decisions.

"Song Fei," Wen called out, and one of the women rose from her half-kowtow position that was allowed for ladies of the court. "Come forward."

Fei did as she was ordered, and Wen could not help but admire the graceful way the tall girl seemed to float on her tiny lotus feet. When Fei reached the empress, she returned to her half-kowtow crouch. She did not speak, and Wen noticed Chun nodding her approval. When the girls were not being tested over the past few weeks, their eunuchs were supposed to be teaching them court etiquette and decorum. Fei's eunuch had taught her well.

"So," the empress said, "you are the clumsy girl who caught the eye of the emperor."

"Yes, Your Majesty," Fei said.

"Tell me what happened."

"I did not know how to kneel before the emperor as I do now, my lady," Fei said, never raising her eyes from the ground. "I made a fool of myself. The emperor showed me great kindness in allowing me to stay."

"And here you are, at the very end," Wen said, looking over Fei's papers. "Your education is excellent, your calligraphy beautiful. At least more beautiful than your face." She eyed Fei for a reaction and got none. She was impressed. "However, you never should have come this far. You realize that the emperor should not have second-guessed the decisions of the retired consorts. They know what it takes to please an emperor more than anyone." Wen thought she saw Fei flinch at that. "Well? What do you think?"

"The emperor is never wrong," Fei said without hesitation.

Wen thought she heard a muffled chuckle from her mother-in-law next to her. This girl was clever. Too clever by far. If it were up to her, she would send the girl home immediately. She could not have someone within the harem who she could not trust to uphold her rules, even in the name of the emperor.

But the girl had been right. No one was to question the decisions of the emperor—even the empress. If the emperor believed that Fei possessed the qualities of a concubine, then he was right.

"Return to your place," the empress said.

"Thank you, Your Majesty," Fei said as she stood and backed away, keeping her head down the entire time.

Wen and Chun spoke with some of the other girls they needed to question and then made their final announcements.

Fei and Ruolan were now imperial consorts.

The empress watched as Fei hugged her friend in celebration. If only the girls knew the life they had been selected for. No matter, they would learn soon enough. The empress left the room, leaving the head of the Ministry of Household Affairs to make sure the girls were settled into their rooms and all other arrangements for their life in the Forbidden City made. The mere thought of going from managing a harem of twenty to now nearly seventy was enough to give her a headache. She wanted to go to her room to rest. Tomorrow would be the first time she held a morning audience that would include all the new girls, and she was not looking forward to it...or the rest of her life.

"Your Majesty!"

Wen groaned inwardly at the sound of her name being called. She knew who it was, and she had been avoiding her for weeks, but Lady Qin had finally caught up with her.

Lady Qin tottered toward the empress as quickly as she could and kneeled at her feet. "Please! You promised that I would finally have a night with the emperor. Why has it not happened? Tomorrow is a full moon, the night you are supposed to spend with him. After that, I will then be lost among dozens of new—younger—concubines. I beg you, please send me to him tonight."

Empress Wen's heart went out to Lady Qin. The woman had been beautiful when she first arrived, but years of neglect and sorrow showed in the lines that had developed around her mouth and across her brow.

"I am sorry," Wen said. "I did everything I could to persuade the emperor to take you to bed. But he said he wanted to save his vital energy for the arrival of the new concubines. You must understand—"

"I must?" Lady Qin said, daring to stand and face the empress directly. "Why must I? You know what this means. The life you have condemned me to! I have given my life to the emperor, but he has not fulfilled his duty toward me!"

"Shh!" Wen said, placing her hands on Wen's shoulders in an attempt to calm her. "Do not say such things. You know that the emperor cannot be at fault."

"But how is it my fault?" Lady Qin asked, tears filling her eyes. "What...what am I to do now?"

Wen pulled Lady Qin into her arms and hugged her. "I am sorry, my friend. But it is not over. You will still be among the rotation of concubines. I will still do what I can to see you delivered to his bed."

Lady Qin shook her head as she pulled away, using the long sleeves of her robe to wipe her tears away. "Don't bother. I have lived this long as a nun. Perhaps I will simply join the other retired concubines who have dedicated their lives to the goddess."

The retired concubines were the concubines and consorts of the late emperor. They lived in a secluded part of the palace where they would finish out their days. Wives of emperors could never remarry, but they could dedicate their lives to Guanyin and live as nuns if they wished.

"No," Empress Wen said. "Your life is not over yet. Cultivate patience and you will be rewarded."

"There is no other woman here more patient than I have been," Lady Qin said.

"Then your reward will be greater than all of ours added together," Wen said.

Lady Qin laughed bitterly and shook her head as she allowed her maid to lead her away.

Empress Wen waved Bojing over. "Do your best to make sure Lady Qin ends up in the emperor's rotation."

"I will try my best, my lady," Bojing said. "But the emperor does not delight in her. He will not choose her of his own volition."

"Just do whatever you can," Wen said. Bojing nodded

with a sigh. They had had this conversation many times. Wen had been trying to convince her husband to do right by Qin for years with no success. Still, she would be true to her word and not give up.

Bojing turned to leave, but Wen stopped him.

"And one more thing," she said. "Make sure that Song Fei does *not* end up in the emperor's rotation. I don't need a girl like that catching his eye again."

"Yes, My Lady," Bojing said with a bow.

"Her friend," the empress said. "The girl she was hugging. Who is she?"

"Zhang Ruolan, Your Majesty," he said.

"Send her to the emperor," Wen said, "as soon as you are able."

"I will do what I can," Bojing said.

The empress waved him away with a flick of her wrist. "Good."

TEN

*F*ei marveled at how exquisite her room was. She had thought her room back home was comfortable, but never had she seen so many silk sheets and bed covers, each one embroidered in the brightest thread she had ever seen. Every floor was covered with thick rugs that cushioned her tiny feet with each step.

There were three beds in her room. As there were now so many concubines, they had to share palaces. But each bed was in a separate part of the small palace and were hung with thick drapes that when pulled closed gave ample privacy.

There was a central gathering room where the girls would take their meals together and could meet for talking, playing games, or do other social activities together. Each girl also had a private sitting room where she could read or write alone or entertain her own guests.

There were large closets for each girl that were already full of gowns of the highest quality. Each girl was given three pairs of shoes, furs for winter, and plenty of coal for their braziers. They were given a monthly allowance of cash, from which they would pay their eunuch and maid and could hire more maids if they wished, along with yearly stipends of cloth and thread to make more clothes for themselves. Their families would each be given large gifts of gold, cloth, furs, chickens, goats, and silkworms. The girls could also send money from their allowance home to their families.

"I've never had so much money before of my own," Fei said quietly to Lina and Yuying as she held the heavy silk coin purse in her hand. "I hardly know what to do with it. I don't need another servant. Should I send it home?"

"Not now," Lina said. "The money they receive from the emperor will last them a very long time. Save it for the future should they fall on hard times."

Fei saw the wisdom in Lina's words, but she had no idea what she should do with the money. Should she hide it? Keep it on her person? Did she need to worry about thieves in the Forbidden City? For the moment, she put the money under her pillow.

The only thing that made her unhappy was the fact that Ruolan was not one of her roommates. In fact, Ruolan had been given a room all the way on the other side of the Inner Court. She had no qualms with the girls she was ordered to room with, but she didn't know them, and they were quiet girls who kept mostly to themselves. Even when Fei did try to engage them in conversation or try to get them to join her in a game of cards or to read together, they would demure, offering some excuse of being busy or tired and would then go to their own beds, pull the drapes, and read alone or chat with their maids.

"I don't think they like me very much," Fei grumbled to Ruolan one afternoon after taking the long—and very painful—walk to Ruolan's palace. As such a low-ranking concubine, Fei and the other girls could only depend on the use of a palanquin when they were summoned by the empress—such as for the morning greetings—or the emperor. Otherwise, if they wanted the use of a palanquin, they would have to pay the eunuchs who carried them for the privilege. Fei did not think it wise to waste her limited allowance on being carried from one place to another. Though, it quickly became apparent which girls came from wealthy families and which ones didn't. Those who did not need to save their allowance or send it home took palanquins often, usually with the drapes pulled back so everyone could see them. Girls like Fei, who did not have such comfort with frivolous spending, walked. Girls like Ruolan, who could neither afford a palanquin nor wanted to be thought of as coming from a poor family, stayed in their palaces as much as possible.

Ruolan snorted as she bit into one of the sweet cakes she had ordered to treat Fei with when Fei arrived at her door. The girls were given three meals a day along with one jar of tea per week, but they could also order additional food, treats, and tea whenever they liked...for a price.

"Of course they don't like you," Ruolan said, causing Fei to nearly choke on her cake.

"What?" she sputtered. "Why?"

"Because—"

Ruolan was interrupted by a banging noise from construction being carried out on a building on the other side of the wall that separated the Inner Court from the Outer Court. She grunted and stomped—as much as she could in her bound feet—to the door of her palace.

"Stop that this instant!" Ruolan yelled. "I'm trying to entertain."

The men working on the other side of the wall laughed.

"They enjoy getting a rise out of you," Fei said. "Your screaming is the closest such men as those will ever get to an imperial concubine."

"They make me sick," Ruolan said. "They were working on the roof yesterday and didn't bother to hide that they were trying to sneak a peek at me. Can you believe it? Filthy, sweaty, laborers trying to look at the emperor's concubines? They are lucky he doesn't cut their eyes out."

"How do you know they were filthy?" Fei teased.

Ruolan tossed a pillow at her friend. "What else could they be after spending all day in such dusty air." She coughed and waved her hand in front of her mouth for effect.

Fei sighed and nodded. The construction for the Inner Court seemed to have been given priority, as the decorations were completed before the concubines arrived. Indeed, it would have been impossible for men to work in the Inner Court with concubines present. But they could still hear construction being carried out in other parts of the Forbidden City, and they could not hope to escape the dust that such constant work kicked up.

"So, you were about to tell me why the other concubines don't like me," Fei reminded Ruolan.

"Oh, yes," Ruolan said as she poured them each more cups of tea. "It's because everyone knows who you are. The girl who fainted and caught the eye of the emperor."

"I did not faint!" Fei said. "I fell over like an idiot. And I hardly caught his eye."

"You have talked to him more than any other girl here, except for the few who have already been called to his bed," Ruolan said. "And according to them, the emperor barely said anything. He simply crawled into bed, did the business, and then left."

Fei blushed.

"Oh, right," Ruolan said. "I was supposed to tell you about that, wasn't I?"

"You don't have to—" Fei tried to say.

"There's not much to it," Ruolan interrupted. "You know how the lady stuck her finger inside you and scratched." Fei nodded, almost feeling sick at the memory. "It's like that. You know boys have a penis, right?"

Fei nodded again, remembering when her brothers were young enough to still be in the women's quarters. They often bathed together or ran around naked when it was too hot to wear anything, and she knew that boys and girls looked different in their private areas.

"Well, they stick that into you instead of a finger," Ruolan said. "And it makes you bleed too."

Fei groaned and made a face. "Ugh. Why? That sounds terrible!"

"It's how your husband knows you were whole," Ruolan said matter-of-factly. "If you don't bleed, that means another man was there before him."

"But the woman," Fei said, her face growing hot. "She made me bleed! Am I ruined?"

"No," Ruolan said. "Just a little blood is okay. When the emperor takes you, there will be more. Like when you have your moon phase."

"Do you bleed every time the husband...takes you?" Fei asked.

Ruolan shook her head. "No, you won't bleed again. And Mama said that after a few times, it will actually be enjoyable."

Fei shook her head in disbelief. "I can't imagine ever enjoying such a strange act. Why would it feel good, anyway? The whole purpose is just to make children."

"I don't know," Ruolan said with a shrug as she sipped her tea. "We probably won't be with him enough times in our lives for it to ever become enjoyable."

"What do you mean?" Fei asked. "There are only fifty of us."

"And the twelve from before," Ruolan corrected. "And the empress."

"Sixty-three, then," Fei said. "If he took a different woman every night, we'd still see him...five times a year."

"No wonder you passed the mathematics portion of the exam," Ruolan said with a snort. "But he doesn't take a girl every night. We've been here ten days and he's taken three girls. How many times will we get to see him a year at that rate?"

Fei paused for a moment and tried to do the math in her head. When it started taking too long, she guessed. She knew Ruolan wouldn't know the real answer anyway. "Th... three," she settled on.

"Hmph," Ruolan said, apparently surprised with the high number. "What if he ends up having a favorite and taking her more often than the others? He is known to visit the empress regularly. Believe me, if we see him once a year, we'd be lucky. I've heard that some of the older concubines, the ones that were already here, are *still* whole."

"What?" Fei said. "No! But there were only twelve. Why would they hold the selection process and bring in more concubines if he doesn't even lay with the ones he has?"

"Who knows," Ruolan said as she sucked on a sugar-powdered date.

"What are we supposed to do?" Fei asked. "How can we catch the emperor's attention?"

"You mean you haven't already been trying?" Ruolan asked.

Fei sat back, shocked. "Was I supposed to be?"

"Umm, yeah, dummy," Ruolan said. "Doesn't your eunuch tell you anything?"

Fei shrugged. "He seems nice and helpful. He always fixes my morning tea the way I like it."

"Have you been giving him tips?" Ruolan asked.

"I paid his salary," Fei said. "Why would I give him tips?"

"By the gods," Ruolan said, shaking her head. "We are stuck here in the Inner Court. The eunuchs can go anywhere. They hear everything. They know all the palace gossip."

Fei shook her head. "I don't want to be part of gossip," she said.

"No," Ruolan said, shaking Fei's sleeve. "Don't you see? The eunuchs can go where we can't. Talk to those we can't. Influence those we can't."

"Influence?" Fei asked.

"You can give your eunuch a tip to take the Minister of Household Affairs a bribe to put your name before the emperor," Ruolan explained.

"We can?" Fei asked. "But...I thought that the emperor's calendar was set, and very strict. The schedule is all based on tradition and our moon phases and all that other stuff."

"Only to a certain extent," Ruolan said. "He sleeps with the empress on the full moon. Any other night is up for negotiation."

"How do you know this?" Fei asked.

"My eunuch told me after I paid him a tip the first day."

Fei sighed and leaned back in her chair. "Do you think everyone knows this except me?"

"I'm sure there are some girls here dumber than you," Ruolan said. "But not many."

"But that means there are dozens of girls paying tips and bribes," Fei said. "How much are you paying?"

When Ruolan told her how much her latest bribe was, Fei nearly fell out of her chair. "That's almost our entire allowance! How are you going to pay your servants' salaries?"

"If I spend the night with the emperor, it will be worth it," Ruolan said. "The emperor will give me a gift. If he's exceptionally pleased with me, he'll give me a bigger gift. And if I get pregnant, I'll be elevated to consort and given my own palace and a bigger allowance. If I have a son, I'll be the mother of the next emperor and will be able to have anything I want!"

"But...the emperor has no children," Fei whispered.

"Not yet," Ruolan said with a smile as she sipped her tea. Fei fingered the teacup in front of her. Was Ruolan drinking some sort of concoction to help her conceive? Perhaps. But surely the empress and the other concubines had tried similar methods to try and conceive. Why was Ruolan so sure she would succeed where the empress had failed?

"I hope it works for you," Fei said. There was no way she could spend that much money on a bribe. She could live without Yuying if she had to. But if she had no money to pay Lina, she would be sent all the way back home, and then she would be alone. She would still have Ruolan, but they were already separated by distance. And Fei had a feeling that as Ruolan continued to bribe and scheme her way to the top, they would grow even farther apart.

"Don't worry," Ruolan said. "Once I am a rank one consort, I'll put a good word in for you with His Majesty. I won't leave you behind."

"How magnanimous," Fei said, but she couldn't help

laughing, and Ruolan laughed with her. How could she have doubted her friend, even for a moment?

"I should probably go," Fei said as she stood. "I have a long walk back to my palace."

"When I am court favorite, I'll send a sedan chair for you," Ruolan said, leaning back in her chair and taking another bite of a sweet cake.

"You keep eating cakes like that and you won't find a sedan chair carrier willing to cart you around for any amount of coin," Fei jibed. Ruolan threw a pillow at her, which Fei easily dodged.

She was about to walk through the door when she saw the head of the Ministry of Household Affairs walking up the few steps to Ruolan's palace. Fei stepped back and allowed the eunuch to enter the room.

"Welcome, minister," Ruolan said as she stood, offering the minister some tea.

"I am here to inform you that His Majesty has selected you to be his bedmate tonight," the minister said.

Fei froze, then she turned back to Ruolan. Ruolan put her hand to her heart and plopped back onto her chair. Fei stepped back into the palace.

"Ruolan, did...did you hear what he said?" Fei asked.

Ruolan took a few shallow breaths and then stood again. "Did you say...that I had been chosen?"

"Yes, my lady," the eunuch said. He waved his hand and two maids that Fei hadn't even noticed stepped into the room holding two baskets of bath items.

"Fei..." Ruolan said, and that seemed to be all she could say.

"Ruolan," Fei said, her excitement for her friend growing. "You...you did it!"

"I did!" Ruolan said, coming out of her stupor. "I did it!"

"You did it!" Fei ran over to Ruolan and grabbed her hands as the girls began to scream and cheer and shake.

The eunuch minister rolled his eyes but couldn't completely hide his smile. "A sedan chair will be here to pick you up at the hour of the pig. Be ready."

"Yes, sir," Ruolan said. "Thank you, sir."

Fei had never heard Ruolan speak to anyone except her father with such respect.

"We will prepare your bath, my lady," one of the maids said. "The emperor expects you to be prepared for him in a very precise way."

"Thank you," Ruolan said, her eyes glassy. She squeezed Fei's hands even tighter. "Will you stay with me? Help me prepare? I...I don't think I can even walk to the bath right now."

"Yes, of course," Fei said as she wrapped her arm around her friend's shoulder.

Fei helped as the maids washed and scrubbed and oiled every part of Ruolan's body. Her feet were given extra care to make sure they smelled sweet and were soft to the touch. She was dressed in a long red robe of a silk so delicate it was nearly see-through. She was then given a foul-smelling and bitter soup that was supposed to encourage fertility. Fei only hoped that it did not counteract whatever fertility medicines Ruolan was already taking.

Finally, long after dark, at the hour of the pig, the sedan chair arrived. Fei held Ruolan's hand and helped her climb up.

"Don't wait up for me," Ruolan told Fei once she was settled.

"I'll come to see you first thing in the morning," Fei said as the chair bearers stood and started to pull away, her hand slipping from Ruolan's grasp.

"Wish me luck!" Ruolan called out. "Not that I need it!"

"Good luck!" Fei called with a wave, and she watched until the chair was carried out of sight.

"She'll be lucky if she's gone longer than fifteen minutes," one of the Ruolan's roommates said with a scoff.

The two girls who were sharing a palace with Ruolan had been out visiting their own friends and had returned while Ruolan was bathing. They were obviously jealous of Ruolan's good fortune and had watched the preparations with brooding faces for the entirety of the evening. Ruolan didn't seem to notice their negativity. Indeed, she hardly seemed to notice that the girls were there at all.

The girl who spoke must have thought Fei cared what she had to say because she then continued, "That's how long it took for Meiyang to return to her room after she was summoned by the emperor. If you wait a few minutes, Ruolan can tell you about it when she gets back so you won't have to walk all the way back over here tomorrow since you can't afford a sedan chair."

Fei thought that Ruolan's attitude of pretending the girls didn't exist was a good one and turned to leave.

"Goodnight, ladies," Fei said.

"Finally," Lina said as she ran up to Fei's side. Fei could hear the other girls chatting in low voices as she walked away, but she didn't bother trying to listen to their spiteful words.

When they reached the end of the path of Ruolan's palace, Yuying was waiting with a lighted lantern on a long stick to illuminate their walk home.

"I am sorry you had to wait so long for me," Fei said. "You must both be famished."

"I went back and saved some dinner for you," Yuying said.

"We know it was an important evening," Lina said. "Ruolan is your friend. Her being chosen must make you happy."

"It does," Fei said. "Of course, I would be happier if all of us could be chosen eventually. That would be a perfect world, wouldn't it?"

"Yes, miss," Lina said. "I am sure your time will come."

"Will it?" Fei said. Lina could only shrug. Yuying said nothing. Remembering what Ruolan had said earlier about the eunuchs needing to be bribed, she then addressed Yuying directly. "Will it, Yuying?"

"Oh, of course, my lady," he stammered.

"Yuying," Fei said, stopping. She didn't want her own roommates to hear what she had to say. "Did you overhear what Ruolan said about the eunuch servants needing to be paid tips and bribes in order to get us concubines into the emperor's bed?"

Yuying hesitated before lowering his head and mumbling, "Yes."

"So, it is true, then?" Fei asked. "I haven't been to see the emperor because I cannot afford a bribe? Why didn't you tell me?"

"No, mistress!" Yuying said. "That's...not exactly true."

"What isn't?" Fei asked.

"I mean, yes, it is true that under normal circumstances you would need to send a bribe to the Minister of Household Affairs to be given a favorable position on the schedule," Yuying said.

"What do you mean *normal* circumstances?" Fei asked.

Yuying hesitated and his body shook. Fei wondered if he was about to cry, but Lina reached over and pinched his arm sharply.

"Out with it!" Lina barked.

The boy yelped. "I went there!" he said. "I went to the household affairs department to...make inquiries about how high the bribes were. Believe me, my lady, I would never have needed a tip from you myself. If you rise in the emperor's esteem, I will rise with you. It is in my best interest to help you as much as I can."

Fei nodded. "Go on. You went to find out about the bribe and discovered it was too high for me to pay, so you didn't bother telling me. I understand. I suppose I should thank you for not taking my money knowing I wouldn't get anything out of it—"

"No," Yuying said. "It's not that. I mean, that is partly it. The bribes are very high. Higher than I knew you could pay for at the time. But in a few months, after the initial excitement has worn off, the price will go down and I had thought we could try then. But I found out something much worse."

"Worse?" Fei asked. "Like what?"

"I have a friend in the household affairs office," Yuying said. "He told me...he..." Yuying began to sniff and he wiped his nose with his sleeve.

"What?" Lina asked, reaching to pinch Yuying again.

The boy flinched and spoke quickly. "He told me that the empress herself had given the minister the order to remove your name from the schedule completely."

Fei felt the world around her go black, as though she had been slapped across the face.

Lina gasped. "The empress...? My lady!"

Fei came back to herself but felt nauseous. "Ruolan said it. The other girls hate me because I caught the eye of the emperor. I just didn't realize she also was talking about the empress."

Yuying continued to cry. "I'm so, so sorry, my lady. I...I didn't want you to know. To...to lose hope..."

Fei pulled him to her to comfort him, but as the truth of his words sank in, she found she had no comfort to give. Fei, Yuying, and Lina all cried as they realized their lives would never improve. Fei would be stuck as a lowest rank concubine for the rest of her life and never have a child.

ELEVEN

$\mathcal{A}$ s Fei walked around the garden nearest to her palace, she watched red, white, and yellow koi fish swimming around in a clear pond. She tossed bits of dried noodles to them, which they darted for greedily, ramming each other in the head and splashing clear out of the pool for the measly morsels. After a moment, she stopped. Giving the fish what they wanted seemed to make them more miserable than if she had not given them any food at all. If they won the food, they were then greedy for more. The fish became more aggressive, attacking one another even when there was no food to be had. They swam around quickly, waiting for her to toss them more, driving themselves to exhaustion. What foolish creatures. It was not as though they were starving. The fish had plenty of roots from the pond plants that floated about for them to nibble on. There were also water bugs that floated and skipped along the top of the water they could eat. And every evening, a designated group of eunuchs walked through every garden of the Forbidden City, tossing the day's ration of fish food into the ponds. Fei shook her head and decided she could never hope to understand the ways of pond fish.

Yuying came up behind her, holding an umbrella aloft to shield her from the early sun.

"Thank you," Fei said. "But I never worried overmuch about my skin. And now that I will never see the emperor, I don't see a reason to care for my looks at all."

"Never give up, my lady," Yuying said. "Things can change in the blink of an eye here among the emperor's court."

"What do you know about it?" Fei asked as she turned and walked back down the path back toward her rooms. "How long have you served the emperor?"

"I was recruited only two weeks before you arrived, my lady," Yuying said. "When the emperor decided to bring so many new concubines into the inner court, the Ministry of Household Affairs knew they would need many more maids and eunuchs and cooks and gardeners and guards and seamstresses and so on to take care of them."

"Is that when you were...made a eunuch?" Fei asked with some hesitation. It was a personal question, but she had so few people she could talk to, and she felt that she and Yuying had grown close enough to speak of such things over the last few weeks.

"No, my lady," Yuying said. "That happened when I was but a child. Before I could attend the school for training future palace eunuchs, I had to be castrated. But it was worth it. Here I am, serving at the palace, given a regular salary and my parents paid handsomely for me."

"What if I had not been selected?" Fei asked. "Would you have been sent away without a position?"

"No, my lady," Yuying said, switching the heavy umbrella to his other arm. "I would have been given an assignment elsewhere. Perhaps feeding the fish or working in one of the many kitchens."

Fei nodded. "I am sorry you were saddled with me, then," she said. "If you had been assigned to any other lady, she might still have an opportunity to advance, and you with her."

"But you were nearly dismissed," Yuying said. "And here you are. Your life in the palace nearly ended in that moment, but then everything changed. You never know when your life could change again."

Fei shook her head. "How? I am like those fish in the pond. Nowhere to go, waiting on someone to throw scraps of food at me. Walking, embroidering, and practicing my erhu—the same things I have done day after day since my arrival—are all that will fill my days from now until I die because of the empress."

Yuying shook his head. "You never know, my lady." He stepped close and whispered, "She could die."

Fei gasped. "What? Is she ill?"

"No!" Yuying said. "I am simply saying that anything could happen to any of us at any time. She could die. She could fall ill. She could simply fall out of favor. Any number of things could happen to her that would make her black mark on you vanish in an instant!"

Fei sighed and bit her lower lip. "I suppose."

"Besides, you, of all the ladies, caught the emperor's eye," Yuying went on. "I am not convinced he has forgotten you."

Fei scoffed. "He has dozens of ladies to turn his head. And you think he will remember me?"

"He did not choose any of them, my lady," Yuying said. "They were all chosen for him—except you."

Fei bit her lower lip again, not daring to hope...

"You did not see the way he was looking at you when you walked away from him to return to the selection process," Yuying went on. "The way his eyes lingered. How he touched his lip, as though imagining what it must be like to kiss you."

Fei blushed. "Yuying!"

"I am sorry, my lady," the eunuch said. "I may have been cut, but I am still a man surrounded by beautiful ladies. I know what most men find pleasing in a woman. The other concubines, they are lovely, but they are all the same. I can hardly tell one from another. You are something different."

"Something ugly," Fei said. "Even the emperor did not deny how hideous I was. He only said that his own good looks would be enough to make beautiful babies with me."

"You are a little taller than the others, a little darker of skin," Yuying said. "Your nose a little smaller, your eyes a little wider. I would bet that you were still the most beautiful girl in your village. Of course, anyone would look ugly when compared to the other concubines. But you are far from ugly."

Fei sighed and took her umbrella from Yuying, whose arm must surely be growing tired.

"I am not wholly convinced you are right on that score," Fei said. "But I appreciate your attempts to cheer me up. And you are right, life can change in an instant. I suppose I should not give up on taking care of myself just yet. Thank you."

"Of course, my lady," Yuying said. "I would do anything for you."

"Good," Fei said. "Because there is one thing I would like to ask." Yuying waited expectantly. "When we are alone, in moments like this, please do not call me your lady. It is rather repetitive after a while."

"As you wish," Yuying said with a bow. Even though Fei had asked him to stop calling her his lady, it still came as a shock when he said no more, and they both laughed. They stopped walking when they heard heavy footsteps approaching. They looked and saw two men carrying a red sedan chair pass Fei's palace.

Fei turned to go inside. She did not know of anyone who would bother visiting her. But then she heard someone call her name.

"Fei!"

Fei looked and saw that Ruolan had opened the curtain to her chair. "Stop!" she then ordered the chair-bearers.

"My lady?" one of them asked. "I thought we were going to the temple for prayers."

"Shut up and stop!" Ruolan ordered. "Do as I say. Set me down."

The men stopped and rocked the chair to one side as they lowered it, nearly toppling Ruolan out onto the ground. Ruolan squealed, and Fei and Yuying ran to her side. From around the sedan chair, Ruolan's own maid appeared, but she was a girl Fei had not seen before.

"Are you all right, my lady?" the maid asked as she helped Ruolan out of the chair.

"Yes," she said, taking the maid's hand. Yuying took her other hand and helped pull the girl to her feet. Once Ruolan was standing, she smoothed her gown and hair before reaching back into the sedan chair and producing a birdcage with two marvelous red and green birds.

"A gift," Ruolan said, offering the cage to Fei.

"Oh, Ruolan!" Fei said as she admired the pretty birds as they tweeted and hopped about on their perches. "They are beautiful! But why would you give them to me? Don't you want them?"

"Invite me inside," Ruolan said as she wiped her brow. "I am dying in this heat. I'll tell you everything."

"Oh! Of course," Fei said, taking the heavy birdcage in one hand and Ruolan's hand in her other one. Ruolan's maid also helped escort Ruolan up the few stairs to the palace.

Lina opened the door and stepped outside with a bow. "A pleasure to see you, Lady Zhang. May I prepare tea for you?"

"Please do," Ruolan said. "And bring a fan for me."

"What happened to the maid who came here with you from our village?" Fei asked as she took Ruolan to her sitting room and placed the birdcage on a table.

Ruolan let out a long sigh as she sat on the low stool, as though she had walked the distance across the inner court instead of having been carried. "She left me."

"Left you?" Fei asked in shock. "Why?"

"She missed her home," Ruolan said. "Her family. She said she had a sweetheart back in the village she wished to marry."

"But...why didn't she tell you?" Fei asked. "Why did she come all this way with you just to leave?"

"I suppose she never really thought I would be chosen," Ruolan said as she accepted a cup of tea from Lina, who had quickly appeared with the tea things and prepared Ruolan's cup first. "She thought that we would come, she would have a wild adventure in the capital city, and then she would return home and get married and I would never know she planned to leave me."

Lina dropped a teacup and it clattered to the floor. Thankfully it didn't break.

"Are you all right?" Fei asked.

"Yes, my lady," Lina said, but her voice shook. Fei would have to ask Lina what was wrong later.

Fei then turned back to Ruolan. "I'm so sorry." She watched as Lina handed Ruolan's new maid a wicker fan, which the maid then used to cool her mistress.

"Faster!" Ruolan ordered the maid. "I'm dying."

"Are you feeling all right?" Fei asked, reaching over and putting her hand to her friend's forehead. "It is warm in the sun, but here in the palace, I think it is quite comfortable."

"The whole Forbidden City is stifling," Ruolan said, and Fei could not argue with her on that point. "That is why I had to come see you. Ever since my night with the emperor, my palace has been crawling with visitors."

"I've noticed," Fei said. "I have come by to see you a few times, but each time it seemed as though there was a line of ladies to see you, so I came back home."

"I wish you would have stayed," Ruolan said. "It would have given me an excuse to send them all away while I visited with my one real friend. The vultures."

Ruolan sipped her tea again. Fei examined her own tea and realized it was chamomile. She nodded her approval to Lina but did not drink it herself. Her days were so boring, if she drank the tea she would soon fall asleep. But Ruolan clearly needed something to help her calm down.

"Can you move just a little to the right," Ruolan said to her maid. "A little further, little further. There. Perfect. And move the fan a little faster."

Fei caught the maid rolling her eyes and frowned at her in disapproval. The maid blushed and lowered her eyes, doing as her mistress had commanded.

"So, we have hardly spoken since your night with the emperor," Fei said, lowering her voice and scooting her stool close to Ruolan. "How was it?"

Ruolan looked around the room, over to the other side of the palace where Fei's roommates had their quarters.

"They aren't here," Fei said. "They went...Oh, they went to see you, actually."

"That is why I had to take a sedan chair here," Fei said. "And made a big announcement about going to the temple to pray, so I could finally leave and go somewhere that I could get a moment's peace."

"I'm sorry you had to waste money on a sedan chair for me," Fei said. "Though I suppose if you had sent a note asking me to visit, your room still would have been crowded. What is going on? Why is everyone pestering you?"

"Why else?" she asked with a shrug as she sipped another cup of tea. "They all think I can put a good word in for them with the emperor. They have been coming to me all day, as soon as the sun rises, staying until curfew. Bringing me all sorts of gifts." She motioned to the birdcage.

"Don't you want to keep them?" Fei asked. "They are so lovely."

"I already have two sets," Ruolan said. "And so many embroidered kerchiefs, as if I can't make my own. Here." She reached into one of her bilious sleeves and pulled out a small stack of kerchiefs. "Have these."

Fei chuckled. "Even if I had the worst cold I don't think I could use all these."

"Then send your maid out to the market to sell them," Ruolan said. "That's what I have been doing with most of the gifts I have received. At least I have a nice little purse to help pay my expenses for a while."

"But if you can't help them," Fei said, "shouldn't you return the gifts?"

"I have tried!" Ruolan said. "I have told them that I am nothing special to the emperor, but they don't believe me. They push the gifts into my hands, begging me to just try and then running away before I can refuse! I do feel guilty about accepting the gifts, but what else can I do?"

Fei shrugged her shoulders. "What happened? With the emperor? Was it...as your mother said?"

"I...suppose," she said, smiling behind her teacup.

"Ruolan!" Fei hissed, smacking her friend's shoulder playfully. "Tell me!"

"Well, I was already in the bed when he entered the room," Ruolan said. "And I was far more nervous than I thought I would be. A maid brought in tea and steaming towels. I..." She stopped and looked around. Even though only their own maids were present, she still cupped her hand around Fei's ear to whisper. "I put a sleeping-draught in his tea."

"What?" Fei shrieked. "Wha...what if he fell asleep and couldn't...you know? Or what if he found out and was angry?"

"Mother said that all men grow tired after making love," Ruolan said. "I just wanted to make sure he was tired enough that he slept with me instead of sending me away and going to his own room."

"Oh, Ruolan," Fei said, shaking her head. "That was so risky...Did it work?"

"Yes," Ruolan said. "He didn't drink the tea until after we were finished, so it worked out perfectly."

"Wait, go back, then," Fei said. "Tell me everything."

"When he came into the room, he was wearing a red robe embroidered with a dragon...and nothing else," Ruolan said, and the girls giggled. "He pulled back the drapes from the bed and removed his robe, standing there, *naked*, smiling at me."

Fei gasped, her hand over her mouth. "He had no shame?"

"He didn't need any," Ruolan said. "I can say with certainty that he is a Son of the Dragon. He hasn't an ounce of fat on him. His body is perfect. So muscular. So smooth. So handsome. Did you look at his face that first day, when he took your hand?" Fei nodded. "So, you know. Believe me, every inch of his body is as perfect as his face."

"Wow," Fei said, daring to imagine what a perfect man's body might look like. But she didn't have much to draw from. After her brothers turned seven years old, they left the women's quarters and spent most of their time with other men. She saw them, and other farm and forest workers occasionally, but never naked.

"And he was already excited to see me," Ruolan said. "His penis rearing up like an angry snake."

Fei's face grew hot at the description. "Did it hurt?"

"A bit," Ruolan said. "But not too much. He kissed and caressed me before that. I wanted him to take me. But it didn't take long before he was finished."

Fei felt a little disappointed at how quickly the story ended. "He didn't say anything?"

"Just some pleasantries about how happy he was to see me and he hoped we would have many children together," Ruolan said. "Then he drank his tea and used the warm towels to clean himself off. He stood to dress, but then said he was tired and needed to lie down. The eunuchs who had stayed in the room with us to make sure I was a virgin asked him if I should be sent away or if he wanted to return to his room, but he just grumbled and rolled over against me and fell asleep. The eunuchs took that as a sign that I was to be allowed to stay."

She smiled and cocked her head from side to side, making her earrings shimmer and tinkle.

"But what good did that do?" Fei asked. "If he was sleeping, what did you get out of staying?"

"Because I was still there when he woke up," Ruolan said. Then her voice finally showed an edge of disappointment. "But it did not have the desired effect."

"What do you mean?" Fei asked.

"I thought when he woke up and saw me there, he would be pleased," Ruolan said. "Thankful to have a beautiful, naked woman by his side. That he would talk to me or make love to me again. Give me another chance at a baby. But he just seemed so surprised, he mumbled some excuses and fled the room!"

"He was embarrassed?" Fei asked.

"I think so," Ruolan said, her head drooping sadly. "I fear he will never send for me again after that."

Fei took her friend in her arms. "Well, he has many, many more concubines to visit before he should visit you again anyway. Do not lose heart. At least you saw him, and are no longer a virgin. That sets you above many of the women here."

"I know," Ruolan said. "He did send me this later." She held up her hand, showing Fei a ring with a central pearl surrounded by rubies.

"Oh, Ruolan," Fei said. "It is beautiful! He must have been pleased."

Ruolan shrugged. "I noticed the other concubines he took before me all have the same ring. I am sure it means nothing personal."

"Well, a very wise man once told me that life in the

Forbidden City can change in an instant," Fei said. "Don't lose hope. At least you aren't completely barred from seeing His Majesty like I am."

Fei was surprised when this information didn't seem to be new to Ruolan. "I had hoped to send the emperor a note, thanking him for choosing me and telling him that he should send for you. But my eunuch warned me that any mention of you could diminish my standing with the emperor, so I said nothing. I am sorry."

"Don't be," Fei said. "Don't risk your life here to protect me. I'll be fine. Somehow, I'll muddle through."

Ruolan smiled and nodded. "Well, I suppose I should head back. People will be wondering where I really slipped off to."

Fei stood to see her friend off, but when Ruolan tried to stand, her hand went to her head and she stumbled back down, missing the stool and falling to the floor.

"Ruolan!" Fei cried, crouching down and helping her friend sit up. "What's wrong."

"I...I don't know," Ruolan said, her hand going to her head. "I just got so dizzy all of a sudden. And it's so hot in here." She then leaned over and vomited up the several cups of tea she had drank.

"Lina!" Fei called. "Find the doctor!"

TWELVE

"Pregnant?" the empress nearly shrieked.

"Yes, Your Majesties," the old doctor said, nearly giddy with the news. "I just confirmed it myself. I checked several times to be sure. I did not want to give you false hope. But yes, I am certain that Lady Zhang Ruolan is with child."

Empress Wen was standing to the side of the dragon throne. She knew something either terrible or wonderful had happened when she had been called into a formal audience with the emperor and Dowager-Empress Chun. But she didn't expect this. She did not think the emperor would be able to sire a child no matter how many concubines the man took.

As the shock of the news wore off, the empress began to feel sick. Her eyes watered and she thought she might faint. The emperor had sired a child—and it wasn't with her. She looked over to the emperor, who seemed to have not heard what the doctor had said, his chin propped up in the palm of his hand as he stared at the doctor.

"Ruolan...is with child?" the emperor said dumbly.

"Yes, Your Majesty," the doctor repeated, the smile still on his face.

"How...how far along?" the emperor asked.

"According to court records," the head of the Ministry of Household Affairs spoke up," Ruolan was your bedmate twenty-two days ago."

"And you can tell this soon?" the emperor asked.

"She has all the early symptoms," the doctor said. "It is possible that her body is displaying signs of...some form of distress. Women have very delicate constitutions. Pregnancies are also very volatile in the first few weeks. It would not be uncommon for her to...lose the baby."

"Don't say such a thing," the emperor said, coming out of his stupor. "But you would not have come to me, called us all together, if you thought she was suffering from distress, would you have?"

The doctor laughed. "No, Your Majesty. I have every reason to believe that Lady Zhang is successfully with child. And as long as she is given the utmost tender care, you, Emperor Hongdi, are going to be a father."

The emperor let out a cough like a choke and put his fist to his mouth. Empress Wen could see that his eyes were glassy. She hoped he did not show weakness by crying in front of all of his ministers and advisors. After a moment, Hongdi cleared his throat and stood.

"I'm going to be a father!" he announced, holding his arms up. The whole room erupted into cheers. The empress clapped and did her best to smile, but she was near to tears herself.

The emperor turned to Wen and took her hands in his. "We have been truly blessed. Finally! We are going to have a child. A son!"

"Indeed, we are," she said, squeezing his hands back and gritting her teeth.

"This proves that the Celestial Beings are smiling down on us and that the Ming Dynasty truly has the Mandate of Heaven! Moving to Peking was always the right choice."

"I can see that," Empress Wen said. "I was a fool to ever doubt your vision."

"I forgive you, my love," the emperor said, taking Wen's jaw in his hand and then kissing her tenderly on the mouth. "You are going to be the most wonderful mother."

She shook her head, a single tear escaping and sliding down her cheek. "I...I had given up. I never...never thought...That is why the gods blessed this girl instead of me."

"No!" Hongdi said. "This is your child too! As soon as it is born, you can adopt it and I will appoint him as my heir. Everything will work out perfectly. You will see."

Wen doubted his words, but in her emotional state, she was afraid to say too much. She nodded. "Yes, of course."

The emperor turned back to the ministers. "Ruolan will immediately be elevated to rank three consort," the emperor said.

"Rank three?" the Minister for Household Affairs repeated. "Are you sure?"

"Yes," the emperor said. "But only as a precaution. If the child is indeed a boy, she will then be elevated to rank two."

The empress clenched her fists and bit her tongue. There currently were no rank two or three consorts as none of the ladies had ever fallen pregnant before. This would make Ruolan, this nobody, this girl from the countryside who had been in the palace for a mere month, the second most powerful woman in the Forbidden City. Wen looked to

Chun, who currently held no official status other than one of high respect since her son was of ruling age and had a capable empress of his own. Chun was not smiling, but neither was her face impassive. She seemed to be frowning. Angry, almost. But why? This child would secure her and her late husband's legacy. Isn't that what every empress wanted?

"Ruolan will immediately be given her own palace." The emperor was still going on about his gifts for Ruolan, and Wen forced herself to pay attention.

"Ruolan fainted earlier today," the doctor said. "Which is why I was summoned. She should be allowed to rest for a few days before moving her."

The emperor flew down the steps toward the doctor and gripped his arms. "Is she ill? Is she in danger? What are you doing here talking instead of there caring for her?"

"Your Majesty," the empress said, stepping down from the dais and placing her hand on his shoulder. "I am sure the girl is fine."

"She only got a little over warm," the doctor said. "She will be fine with some rest and ginseng soup, which her kitchen is preparing for her now."

"No!" the emperor snapped. "No, not her kitchens. My own kitchens will prepare all her food from now on. Lady Zhang is to have only the best from here on out, do you understand?"

"Yes, Your Majesty," the ministers all said in unison.

"Her food rations, her furs, her tea," the emperor went on. "Everything is to be increased. Send her three—no, four times her allowance right now as a cash gift, and raise her monthly allowance to that of a rank three consort. Also, send gifts of cash, silk, pigs, donkeys, and chickens to her family. Her father will be given the hereditary title of duke, and it will go back three generations!"

"Your Majesty," the dowager-empress finally said. She motioned for her eunuch to help her down the dais stairs. "You are acting a fool. Stop this."

Wen's hand flew to her mouth, and there were several audible gasps from through the room.

"M-M-Mother," the emperor said. "You dare speak to me in such a way?"

"When the situation calls for it, I do," she said. "You have only just learned of the girl's condition. As the doctor said, it is very possible she could lose it. There is not a family in existence that does not have a history of tragic miscarriages. Your own father's concubines and consorts lost more children than they ever gave birth to."

"Mother," the emperor said, "where are these dark words coming from? Are you not pleased?"

"I will be," she said, "as soon as the doctor places a living grandson in my arms."

"And I am sure I will, Lady Mother," the doctor said.

"Until then," the dowager-empress went on, undeterred, "I would recommend caution. Since no other girl has been with child by you before, I understand your excitement. Elevating her from concubine to consort is acceptable. But only level six. No woman has ever been made a rank three consort without at least one successful birth."

"Fine," the emperor said. "Rank six it is. Rank three upon the delivery of a girl and rank two upon the delivery of a boy."

"This is acceptable," the dowager-empress said. "And you may send her father a modest gift. But bequeath no title until the child is successfully delivered."

"Yes, Lady Mother," the emperor said. "Anything else?"

"No," the dowager-empress said, as though she had not

just given the emperor a severe dressing down in front of the entire court.

"Very well," the emperor said. "I would like to pay a visit to the girl myself now. Let her know that I am coming so she can make herself ready."

"Yes, Your Majesty," several ministers said, then the emperor and ministers left the room, leaving the empress and dowager-empress alone.

Wen considered leaving the room, leaving the old crone to her cruel thoughts, but she decided to find out just what exactly the old woman was thinking.

"It is almost as if you don't want this baby to be born," Wen said. "As though you could put some sort of dark curse upon it simply by wishing it were so."

Chun snorted. "If that girl really is pregnant, then I'll be surprised."

"The doctor seemed awfully sure," Wen said.

"There are medicines that can...alter a woman's state," Chun said. "You know this. Haven't you missed your courses on more than one occasion?"

Wen cleared her throat and ran her hands down her long sleeves. "Yes. I have tried numerous herbs and teas and concoctions to supposedly enhance my fertility over the years. I think some of them did the opposite, though. I would miss my courses for two, even three months before they returned with debilitating pain. The doctor never declared me pregnant, though, no matter how much I wanted it to be so."

"That is true," Chun mumbled. "He is an excellent doctor. He's never given a false diagnosis that I know of. Still...something isn't right about this."

"What do you mean?" Wen asked. "What are you talking about?"

"You don't look stupid," Chun said. "Do you really believe after twelve years of marriage and a dozen concubines and an empress that a girl is suddenly pregnant now?"

"What else am I supposed to think?" Wen asked. "According to the records, they did lay together, and she has all the symptoms. All we can do is...be joyful." She clenched her teeth together, pulling tightly at her heavily embroidered sleeves. It was as though she could not get every wrinkle out of them. "We must prepare for this new child and welcome it as if it were my very own."

"That may be all you can do," Chun said. "But you always did lack a backbone."

"What are you saying?" Wen asked. "What are you going to do? What do you think I should be doing instead?"

"Never you mind, *empress*," Chun said, and she motioned her eunuch to her side to help her totter out of the room.

Wen watched the older woman as she left the audience hall. She wished she had some idea what the woman was up to. She surely would not sabotage the girl. Give her a concoction to intentionally cause a miscarriage. No, that would be insane. Suicide! But why wasn't she happy about the baby? Why did she think the girl was lying, or possibly faking?

Of course, being pregnant would be in the girl's best interest. But faking a pregnancy would be stupid. Dangerous. Ruolan would be risking her life if she dared to try and mislead the emperor. She had been watching Ruolan since she joined the harem. The girl was bold. High-strung. And if anyone was to get pregnant, she was not surprised it was Ruolan. She had perfect confidence that everything would work out in her favor. But, like all the girls, surely she knew that her chances of becoming pregnant were almost nonexistent.

The more Wen thought about it, the more she wondered if Chun was right about...something. Ruolan seemed to know from the day she walked into the Forbidden City that she would fall pregnant. That she would be the one to give the emperor what he most desired. And she had been right.

But how did she do it? If there were some secret to falling pregnant, Wen would have found it by now. She had done far more than taken herbs to try and become pregnant over the years. She had given money to every temple in the kingdom. She had spent days on her knees in prayer. She had visited a witch. She had spent years and a fortune trying to do what Ruolan had done in one night.

How?

She had no idea. And she didn't know how to find out. But Chun seemed determined to discover the girl's trick. Fine, let her. Wen would stay out of Chun's way, and she would be there to comfort the emperor when his mother broke his heart.

THIREEN

a child!

The emperor was beside himself with joy. Finally, after so many years, a child—no, not just any child. A son was to be born. Heaven itself was surely smiling down on him and the Ming Dynasty.

I have done it, Father, Hongdi thought to himself as he walked quickly to the women's portion of the Inner Court. *The dynasty is safe.* He did not even wait for a sedan chair to carry him the distance. He didn't need it. He would have run to see Ruolan if he could. But such exuberance would not be dignified. Still, he walked as quickly as he could, which was still faster than a sedan chair would have traveled.

The gate between the eastern and western palaces of the Inner Court was always open, but the ladies rarely left the eastern palaces unless they were invited by the emperor himself—with the exception of the empress and the dowager-empress, who were free to go where they wanted whenever they wanted. When the emperor went to the eastern palaces, it was usually in a sedan chair, and with the intention of seeing someone specific. Therefore, the emperor was rarely seen wandering the eastern section of the Inner Court.

The emperor's sudden appearance in the women's quarters was immediately met by gasps of surprise and pleasure, and he heard the ladies calling after him as soon as he entered.

"Your Majesty!"

He turned and saw two young ladies giving him a half-kowtow, but it was clear from their quivering forms that they were anxious to approach him.

"Where is the palace for Ruolan?" he asked.

The ladies stood and disappointment was clear on their faces. But he had no time—or inclination—to comfort them.

"She is in the Palace of Falling Leaves," one of the ladies said. "Shall I show you?"

Glancing down at her feet as she began to sway toward him, he knew that she would greatly slow his progress.

"Just...point me in the right direction, please," he said.

She waved her hand down one of the paths, a kerchief she was holding swirling like a snake. "That way. Follow the path to the pond, then turn right. Someone else can guide you the rest of the way."

"Thank you, my lady," he said as he turned to leave, not even taking a moment to consider if he had seen the girl before or had ever heard her name. As he left, he could hear their disappointed grumbles. He would need to move Ruolan to her new palace and place guards around her as soon as possible. If he were a man of many children, he would not need to take such precautions. But with only one child and dozens of jealous concubines, he would need to make sure Ruolan and his son were safe.

But perhaps this was only the beginning. If Ruolan was able to fall pregnant, maybe the other girls could as well. He would have to talk to the Minister of Household Affairs about his current schedule of bedroom activities. The sooner he slept with all of his new concubines, the better. Perhaps by the end of the year, he could have a dozen children. Boys and girls! He chuckled to himself at the idea of his own pretty little princesses running around the Inner Court, each one learning painting and poetry. They would be the most eligible young ladies in the empire—and possibly the east. He would finally have girls of high enough status to form alliances with some of the neighboring kingdoms that were causing problems along the borders.

He knew he was getting ahead of himself. And as he wandered the long white pathways between the green grassy areas and pink and purple flowering trees and shrubs, he knew he was also quite lost. He had never tried to find his way to one of the women's palaces before. He went around a bend and stumbled into a small group of people, knocking one of them to the ground.

"How dare you injure my lady!" a eunuch cried out.

"Let me help you!" a maid said.

"Forgive me," the emperor said. "I did not see you, I was in such a hurry."

"Why would you—" The eunuch stood up and the color drained from his face when he saw he was addressing the emperor. He dropped his lady's hand and dropped to his knees. "Forgive me, Your Majesty. I did not realize it was you."

"What?" the maid asked, looking up. She, too, ceased from helping her lady and kneeled as well. "Your Majesty!"

"Don't be stupid," the emperor said, stepping past them

and offering the concubine his hand. His breath left him when it saw it was Fei, the girl he had met during the selection process. "It's you!"

Fei righted herself and bowed before the emperor, this time quite properly. "Forgive my clumsiness, Your Majesty. I did not see you."

"No, it was I who was rushing and not paying attention," the emperor said as he pulled Fei up to her feet. "You may stand as well," he directed to her servants. He then noticed that in the scuffle, Fei had dropped a basket of goji berries, which the maid and eunuch now rushed to collect. "Again, I am sorry. I was on my way to see Ruolan. I just heard the joyous news."

"Oh, of course!" Fei said, her face beaming. "I was on my way there as well. I was there when the doctor confirmed her condition, then she was swept away back to her own rooms. I wanted to take these to her."

"Very thoughtful," the emperor said, looking at the basket. He noticed that, unlike the other girls he had seen, Fei did not seem at all jealous of Ruolan. Perhaps they were friends. "Would you show me the way to her palace? I seem to have gotten turned around on my way to see her."

"Of course," Fei said. "If you'll just follow me." She stepped ahead of him and walked more quickly than he expected her to be able to with her bound feet.

"Do you know Ruolan well?" the emperor asked.

Fei nodded. "We grew up together in the same village. We rode to Peking together in her family's carriage for the selection process."

"I almost cannot believe she is with child," Hongdi said as he took a deep breath, enjoying the sweet-smelling air of the women's gardens.

"You are very fortunate," Fei said. "I do not think you could have wished for a better mother for your child."

"What makes you say that?" the emperor asked.

"Ruolan is very beautiful," Fei said. "And she is terribly clever. Your son will be smart and handsome."

The emperor nearly shook his head as he listened to her words. She had nothing but kind things to say of her friend who had been given such blessings where she had not. He had asked—several times—for Fei to be brought to his bed. But each time, the minister had some excuse for why she could not be chosen. He could not help but wonder if it should have been Fei in Ruolan's position right now.

"I...I have asked for you...in the past," the emperor said, suddenly shy with his words.

Fei slowed her steps and looked over her shoulder at him. "You have?"

"I was told you were ill," he said.

Fei looked away and continued walking. "Yes, I was. Quite ill. I think that my lungs were not used to the city air after being raised in the countryside."

"I can understand that," the emperor said. "It has been an adjustment for all of us."

"But I am feeling better now," Fei said as they stopped at the edge of the garden path, a palace before them. There were a dozen girls crowded around outside, none of whom seemed to even sense that the emperor was behind them.

"Then perhaps I will send for you again soon," the emperor said.

Fei blushed and looked down. She licked her lips as though unsure of what to say. She then thrust the basket toward Hongdi.

"This is Ruolan's palace," she said.

"Why are you giving me this?" he asked.

"You cannot arrive without a gift!" she said, a smile on her lips that said he should know better.

Hongdi chuckled. "Oh, of course. I was so excited, in such a hurry, I forgot."

"Go," Fei said. "She will be excited to see you too."

"Thank you," Hongdi said, and then he held up the basket. "For the gift."

She nodded. "My pleasure."

The emperor stepped out of the garden toward the palace, and he noticed that Fei did not follow. "Aren't you coming?"

"It is so crowded," she said. "I'll never get past them all."

"You will if you are with me," Hongdi said, offering her his hand. Again, her cheeks went pink as she accepted his assistance to step from the path to the main walkway to the palace. She then nodded and removed her hand from his, turning to her lady for help. Hongdi nodded, knowing how it would look to all his other concubines if he seemed to be showing affection to only one of his ladies.

He cleared his throat and stood straight as he walked to Ruolan's palace. The concubines who had come for a visit, though, were standing so tightly together, he could not hope to get through. Usually, his chief eunuch was with him to announce his presence, but in his desire to get to Ruolan quickly, he had left Wangzhu behind.

"Excuse me," the emperor said, but the ladies ignored him. If anything, they crowded more tightly together against the interloper.

He pressed his lips into a tight line and patted one of the girls on her shoulder. She shrugged him off. He patted her again. This time she let out an irritated grunt and wiped at her shoulder as if there was a speck of dirt on it. He tried again, this time patting her shoulder and clearing his throat.

The girl turned around, a scowl on her face. "Who do you—" She dropped to her knees as soon as she saw his face. "Forgive me, Your Majesty!" She then reached up and tugged at the sleeve of the girl who had been standing next to her. That girl looked down at her friend and then up at the emperor. She, too, was instantly on her knees. That started a cascade, as each girl looked over to see what was causing the girl next to her to kneel. In only a moment, all of the concubines, maids, and eunuchs who had gathered to try and visit Ruolan were on their knees around her palace.

"Thank you," the emperor said as he started to step his way around the throng of people. He turned back to Fei. "Come." Fei's maid helped her navigate the path the emperor had forged and climbed the few small stairs to the front door.

The emperor realized it would not be proper for him to enter into a lady's palace unannounced, so he turned to Fei's eunuch.

"Will you do the honors?" he asked.

The eunuch smiled and nodded with excitement, as if he had just been given an incredible promotion.

"His Imperial Majesty, Emperor Huangdi!" Yuying announced. All of the ladies in the room gasped and turned in shock and then dropped to their knees. At the far end of the room, Ruolan stood up slowly, made eye contact with the emperor ever so briefly, with a faint smile on her lips, and then she too kneeled. The emperor could not help but chuckle at the girl's temerity. She was bold. She knew that she had what Hongdi valued as most precious in the world within her, and she would use it to her advantage. He was not sure if it was endearing or a warning sign about her character. For the moment, he would let her enjoy her elevated position. She was right to celebrate and feel proud. She had done what no other woman—even the empress— had been able to do.

"Leave us," Hongdi said, and the ladies quickly stood and scurried away. Ruolan's maid and eunuch moved to the door so they would be out of listening range, but near enough to go to their lady if she called for them.

"Hmph," one of the girls scoffed as she left. "First, our room is crowded with visitors, and now we can't be here at all."

"Let's hope she moves soon," her friend replied. Hongdi assumed the girls were Ruolan's roommates. Well, he would make sure they were moved to the end of his schedule, if he bothered to sleep with them at all.

"You may stay," the emperor said to Fei, and she gave an appreciative nod. Her servants moved to stand with Ruolan's.

Once the crowd of visitors and well-wishers had left the room—though he assumed they were all waiting outside for him to leave—he crossed the room and took Ruolan's hand, pulling her up to standing.

"As soon as I heard the news, I had to come see you immediately," he said, then he leaned in and kissed her on the cheek. "Please, sit, you should rest."

Ruolan giggled. "You don't need to coddle me just yet. I don't even feel it! I had no idea I was with child until the doctor told me."

"What happened, then?" the emperor asked as he sat in a chair next to hers.

"She fainted," Fei said. "In my quarters."

"Ah," the emperor said, and he motioned for Fei to take a chair opposite him.

"Tea," Ruolan ordered her maid. "Yes, that is true. I suppose I cannot say I feel nothing. I had been feeling warm and a little tired. I thought I was coming down with a flu or something and decided to get out of my quarters and take in the fresh air. Since the trees bloomed, the air has been much cleaner lately."

The emperor nodded. "I have instructed the construction and decoration crews to work in another part of the Forbidden City, well away from the ladies' quarters. I am sorry they have been so disturbing to you."

Ruolan shook her head. "It is nothing. You needn't worry. I haven't had time to think of anything except how to take care of myself for the next few months."

"You will never have to worry about that again," the emperor said, squeezing her hand. "Oh, and...I brought this for you." He handed her the basket that Fei had given him.

"Goji berries!" Ruolan exclaimed. "How wonderful!" She motioned her eunuch over. "Wash these and put them in a bowl and place them on the table here."

"Yes, my lady," he said as he rushed off to do her bidding.

"As soon as you are feeling rested," the emperor said, "you will be moved to your own palace. It is much too crowded here."

Ruolan looked at Fei and the girls smiled at each other. "How kind of you," Ruolan said.

"Unless..." the emperor said, looking from Ruolan to Fei, "you would like your friend, Fei, to share the new palace with you. I would hate for you to be lonely."

"Oh!" Ruolan said, taking Fei's hand in hers. "That would be wonderful, don't you agree, Fei?"

"It would be an honor to room with the mother of the emperor's first child," Fei said. The emperor thought she was trying to hide just how excited she was. He supposed the two friends had missed each other living on opposite sides of the Inner Court.

"Excellent," the emperor said. "I will have the preparations for the new palace completed immediately. When your quarters are ready, a sedan chair will be sent for you... for you both."

"Thank you," Fei said.

The emperor stood. "I should be going. There is much to do and much to prepare."

Fei stood and bowed, but Ruolan remained sitting.

"I will visit you again soon, Ruolan," he said. Then he turned to Fei. "And I do hope to see you again soon as well."

"As do I," Fei said softly. The emperor nodded to them both and then left the palace.

"Shut the doors!" Ruolan barked to her maid, who had just appeared with a tea tray. "I don't want any of those fake well-wishers in here."

The maid nearly dropped the tray as she tried to close the front door, but Lina swooped in to help with the tray and the heavy doors.

"So, what was that?" Ruolan asked, her eyes sparkling.

"What?" Fei asked, her cheeks hot.

"I do hope to see you again," Ruolan said mockingly. "I'm carrying his baby, but he clearly has amorous thoughts of you. What happened?"

"I ran into him on my way to see you," Fei said. "Quite literally! I came around a corner and he was moving so quickly he knocked me down."

"How can someone so clumsy also be so lucky?" Ruolan asked.

Fei shrugged and poured tea for Ruolan and herself. "Anyway, he was apparently quite lost, as he was wanting to visit you but did not come with his eunuch or in a sedan chair."

Ruolan laughed. "He is so excited he has lost his senses!"

"Quite!" Fei said. "So I showed him where your palace was, and while we talked, he said that he would like to call me to his bedchamber soon."

"No!" Ruolan said.

"Yes!" Fei replied. The girls fell into a fit of laughter.

"Can you imagine if you fell pregnant too?" Ruolan asked. "Wouldn't that be wonderful?"

"One baby is a miracle," Fei said. "Two would be too much to even dream of. We should just focus on keeping you safe and happy."

Ruolan sighed and put her feet up on a stool as she took a deep breath and sipped her tea. "Everything went perfectly."

"What do you mean?" Fei asked.

"I did what I came here to do," Ruolan replied. "I was made a concubine and I fell pregnant my first night with the emperor. It couldn't have worked out any better."

Fei nodded, but she worried that there was something more to Ruolan's words. "If you did something to increase your fertility, would you mind sharing it with me?"

"Of course," Ruolan said, and she stood and crossed her room, opening her trunk and pulling out a bag of herbs. "I won't be needing any more for quite a while anyway. It's *danggui*, dried angelica flower. Brew a few petals every morning and drink it all day. It will nourish your blood, making your body more hospitable for a baby."

"That's it?" Fei asked.

Ruolan nodded. "What did you think?"

"I don't know," Fei said as she fingered the little silk

pouch. "You just seemed so confident that you would get pregnant right away. I thought...I don't know. That you had something more than herbs up your sleeve."

"What else is there?" Ruolan asked. "I prayed, as we all do. But, I guess I just believed it. My mother always told me to speak it into existence, whatever it was I wanted. So, if I want to be rich, I just say I am rich. If I want to be beautiful, I just say I am beautiful. If I say the emperor will make me pregnant, then he will!"

Fei shook her head. "If only I had your confidence."

"Don't worry," Ruolan said as she accepted the bowl of goji berries her eunuch brought her and began eating them. "I will help you. We can't have you thinking less of yourself when the emperor sends for you to go to his bed."

Fei blushed and shook her head. "I should go and begin preparing for our move."

The girls said goodbye and Fei headed to her own palace with thoughts of the emperor on her mind. Would he really send for her? Would the empress try to stop him as she already had for so many months? Would it be possible for her to fall pregnant too? Logically, she knew it was too much to hope for, but at the same time, as soon as she arrived in her room, she had her maid prepare the angelica tea for her.

FOURTEEN

*L*ate at night, when most of the Forbidden City was dark and asleep, Dowager-Empress Chun sat in her sitting room, smoking her water pipe and waiting for her eunuch, Donghai, to return.

Somehow, that girl Roulan had managed to get herself with child. It wasn't possible. Chun had cursed herself. Her husband. Her son. Well, not her other son. The one who was taken from her. The precious child who had nursed from her breast. The one who had been killed when he was too little to defend himself.

Chun shook her head from the dark thoughts as the door to her sitting room squeaked open and closed.

"Well?" she hissed to Donghai.

"I have discovered what you wanted to know," Donghai said. "It is as you suspected, at least according to the girls who shared Ruolan's room."

"I knew it," Chun said as she put the stem from her waterpipe aside and beckoned Donghai to come closer. "Tell me all about it!" Donghai hesitated. "What is wrong?" Chun demanded.

"I think that we should stop this," Donghai said.

"What?" Chun screeched.

"I think we should leave the girl alone," Donghai insisted. "The emperor needs an heir. If he doesn't have one, there will be war again. Don't you remember what that was like?"

Chun scoffed. "Of course I remember. You think I would ever be allowed to forget?"

"There is hope again, for the first time since your son—" Chun shot the eunuch a withering glare. "Since the emperor married," he corrected. "People have feared what would happen to the dynasty, to the empire, if Hongdi did not have a child. That fear is gone. At least for the moment. I know the child might be a girl, but everyone seems convinced that it will be a boy. That Heaven is smiling on China once again. Hongdi...I've never known the man to be so joyous."

"The boy is a fool," Chun said. "A blind fool. You are certain that the other concubines will tell the truth when interrogated by the ministers?"

"That's just it," Donghai said. "I don't know that the girls are telling the truth now. I think that they would say anything to ruin Ruolan."

"Why?" Chun asked. "Is the girl not popular among the concubines?"

"Ruolan is a rose in a garden of them," Donghai said. "She is nothing special. Most of the other girls wouldn't even know who she was had she not gotten pregnant. But that's exactly it. They are all so fiercely jealous of Ruolan's good fortune, they would say anything to ruin her, to ruin whoever fell pregnant."

"Or maybe Ruolan is going to get what is coming to her,"

Chun said. "How stupid could the girl be if the other girls in her palace saw everything?"

"I don't think she is," Donghai said. "Overconfident. Demanding. Spoiled. Oh yes, she is all these things. But stupid? No. Not this stupid."

"Does it matter?" Chun asked. "The other girls will testify against her."

"It might not be enough," Donghai said. "The emperor knows that women in the Inner Court scheme against each other. He might punish the girls as liars just to keep Ruolan —and the child—safe. You could be underestimating just how much he wants this child."

"Hmm." Chun considered this for a moment. It was possible that the emperor could overlook any number of sins in order to ensure the child's safety. She would have to find absolute proof of Ruolan's deception before telling Hongdi that he had been deceived.

"Fine," Chun said. "Then find the boy, the one the girls believe is the real father of Ruolan's baby. Make him talk."

"My lady," Donghai went to Chun and kneeled before her, his eyes cast down, his voice gentle. "Do not make me do this. Leave Ruolan alone. I know you are angry and hurt. I am sorry for my part in that. I was protecting you then as I am protecting you now. Stop this."

"How dare you!" Chun yelled, pushing her water pipe over, sending it crashing to the floor. "After all you have already done for me, you would deny me this?"

"I would deny you nothing," Donghai said as he fought back tears. "I can never atone for the pain I have caused you."

"Yes, you can," Chun said. "By doing as I have ordered! Find the boy! Make him confess! By any means necessary."

Donghai took a moment to compose himself and then

nodded. "As you command, my lady." He then stood and backed away to the door of the room.

Chun rubbed her forehead and her hands shook. If she could not trust Donghai, then she could not trust anyone. The only other person who knew the truth was the midwife, and she had long since disappeared.

Chun stood and looked through a latticed window into the night and saw the shadowy form of Donghai slipping away. She sighed in relief. He would not fail her.

He never had.

"*W*hich one?" Fei asked as she stood up and held two swatches of silk in front of her. "The blue or the red?"

Ruolan eyed each one carefully. "They are both beautiful."

"Of course they are!" Fei said. "They are gifts from the empress! She wouldn't send you something of low quality. But which one do you want to be wearing when you are made a rank two consort?"

Ruolan sat back and sighed, running her hand over her stomach, which was only just beginning to show the growing life within her. "I feel like I should wear red for luck. But I know I would look stunning in the blue."

"Then blue it is," Fei said, tossing the silk onto a pile with several others and jotting down some notes. "This will not be an occasion for you to hold back and feign modesty. You'll never go any higher than rank two. You should dress your absolute best."

"I don't know," Ruolan said. "If anything ever happens to the empress, the emperor could—"

"Shh!" Fei said. "Don't even joke about such a thing. I know your ambition is limitless, but the empress has been good to you. Look at all the gifts she has sent." Fei motioned to the pile of silk that was sitting in front of a pile of furs that was sitting next to a box of jewels.

"I know," Ruolan said. "But she has yet to visit me in person except once to congratulate me. That was weeks ago."

"Well, have some sympathy," Fei said. "You know she wishes it was her."

"They all do," Ruolan said as she gazed out of the window. "I'm glad you are here, Fei. I...I admit that I was jealous at first that the emperor himself had chosen you to make it past the first round of the selection process."

"I had wondered," Fei said, remembering how cold Ruolan had been to her during the rest of the selection process and the days after.

Ruolan nodded. "I couldn't help it. I thought you were ruining my plan. My chance to have a child. But I know that was foolishness. I'm glad you are here. Without you, I'd be so alone now."

Fei went to Ruolan and took her hand. "We have each other." Ruolan nodded and wiped away a tear that was pricking the edge of her eye.

Fei pulled away and went to the pile of silk. "Now, I better see these to the seamstress. She's going to have lots of work to do to keep you in clothes that fit over the next several months." She went to the door of the room to call for the maids when the door flung open and two eunuch guards stomped into the room.

"I'm sorry, my lady," Lina said. "I tried to stop them."

"What is the meaning of this?" Fei asked, but the guards pushed her aside.

"Lady Zhang," one of the guards said. "You are to come with us."

Ruolan pushed herself up from her chair and hugged her stomach. "What is going on?"

"Come with us," the guard repeated. "You need to answer some questions for the Ministry of Household Affairs."

Ruolan scoffed. "Then he can come ask me himself. How dare you barge in here, scaring us half to death. Get out of here before I send for the emperor!"

"Our orders come from the emperor," the guard said. "You are to come with us know or we are instructed to use force."

"Force?" Fei asked, the shock of the situation wearing off. She stepped in front of Ruolan. "Don't you know she is pregnant? She could be carrying the next emperor!"

"Don't make us drag you out of here, Lady Zhang," the guard said, looking past Fei to Ruolan.

Fei looked at Ruolan. "What is happening?"

Ruolan's face was panicked. "I have no idea."

"Enough," the guard said, stepping forward and elbowing Fei out of the way as he grabbed Ruolan by the arm and pulled her out of the room, moving too quickly for her on her bound feet. Ruolan stumbled to her knees.

"Stop!" Fei yelled as she tried to help pull Ruolan up. But the guard pushed her aside again, and then each guard took one of Ruolan's arms and carried her out the door of the room, and then out the main door of the palace, Lina and both of the girl's eunuch servants watching in horror. Ruolan screamed and struggled, but there was nothing she could do to free herself from the men.

"Don't worry, Ruolan!" Fei called, chasing after her. "I will go to the emperor! I will go to the emperor!"

The guards deposited Ruolan into a sedan chair and then pulled the curtains shut. One of them then stomped back to Fei.

"You'll do no such thing," he said, grabbing her by the arm and pushing her back inside the palace. "You are under house arrest. If you try to leave, you will be put under actual arrest and taken to the Ministry of Justice, do you understand?"

"This is madness!" Fei said, but it was then that she noticed there were already two guards stationed on each side of the main door.

"Fei!" Ruolan called from the sedan chair.

"I'll find out what is happening!" Fei called as the chair was lifted and carried away. "Don't worry! I'll help you!"

But once Ruolan was out of sight, the fight fled Fei and she slapped her hand to her mouth to stifle her crying. Lina came and took her into her arms.

"What is happening?" Fei asked.

"I don't know," Lina said as she led Fei to a couch and tried to pour some tea, but her hands were shaking. "Those guards just showed up, pushing their way in. I'm sorry."

"And house arrest? What does that mean?" Fei asked Yuying and Ruolan's eunuch. "What have I done?"

"I suspect they don't want you talking to anyone," Yuying said.

"Talking about what?" she asked. "I have no idea what is going on."

"I'll go out," Yuying said. "See if I can learn anything."

"Wait," Fei said, looking around the room. "Where is Ruolan's maid?"

*T*he emperor slammed his fist on the table. "No! I don't believe it!"

"You must believe it," Dowager-Empress Chun said as she sat across from her son in his private sitting room, Empress Wen sitting nearby but stunned into silence, her hand over her mouth.

"No," the emperor repeated. "It's not possible. It is my son. The Minister of Household Affairs said that her pregnancy was in perfect timing with the night I spent with her."

"She could have slept with any number of men before and after that night," Chun said. "The minister wouldn't know the difference."

"Not before," Wen said. "The girl was a virgin. The eunuch's checked the sheets."

Chen shrugged. "After, then."

"I still don't see how," Hongdi said. "The girls are watched at all times. How could she have had a lover?"

"Young girls are tricky," Chun said. "They can get away with anything. The concubines she shared her palace with said the boy slipped into her room at night. They could hear them rutting like pigs when they should have all been asleep."

"The girls must be lying," the emperor said. "They are jealous of Ruolan because she is pregnant and they are not and they want her gone."

"That is what I thought at first too," Chun said pityingly. "Which is why I had Donghai find the boy himself."

"He...he found the lover?" Hongdi asked. "How? Who is he?"

"One of the young men working on the construction of the new sections of the Forbidden City," Chun said.

Hongdi stumbled back to his chair. "What? How? No! They are nowhere near the women's quarters. And they are always out of the palace by nightfall."

"He must have found a place to hide among the chaos and then waited until dark to slip into Ruolan's rooms," Chun said.

"But how would they have met in the first place?" Wen asked finally. "They can't have spoken to each other during the day. Someone would have seen them."

"Someone did see them," Chun said. "Her maid. She said that Ruolan caught sight of the man when he was working on a rooftop and they exchanged words."

"Her own maid spoke against her?" Wen asked in shock. That was damning, indeed. Most maids and eunuchs would do anything to protect their ladies. As the lady grew in rank and esteem, she would take her servants with her, so it was in their best interest to safeguard her reputation.

"Exactly," Chun said, and Wen thought the woman seemed rather triumphant at sharing the information. She should have been devastated to learn such news. Ruolan's life—and the life of the child—was in danger. Wen could not but think that Chun was somehow involved in discovering this information. But why, she had no idea. She pushed the old woman from her thoughts for now and turned to her husband.

The emperor was gripping his face, rocking back and forth. Wen went to him and placed her hand on his back.

"Are you all right?" Wen asked.

"How could I be?" the emperor asked her, looking up with tears in his eyes. "Everything is ruined. Do you know what people will say when they hear I have been cuckolded?"

"We don't know that it is true," Wen said. "We must

conduct our own investigation. Bring the Minister of Household Affairs here, now."

"Yes," Chun said. "But we must act quickly! We cannot let the girl get away with this for a moment. She must be questioned immediately before she can come up with some excuses and find friends and allies to lie for her."

"No!" Wen said. "We do not want to arouse suspicion. Everything must remain as it is until we know the truth."

"Why are you protecting her?" Chun asked. "What do you know? You are the head of the Inner Court. How could this happen on your watch?"

Wen narrowed her eyes at her mother-in-law. "What game are you playing at?" she asked through gritted teeth. "All of the girls are closely watched. The palace is secure. There are guards everywhere, constantly. I...I simply don't believe that Ruolan would do something so stupid and risk her life. Why should she?"

"To conceive an heir," Chun said. "You and Hongdi were so desperate for a child, you would have believed anything that girl told you. You would have raised a bastard as your own and looked the other way if it meant keeping you in gold and silk!"

"How dare you?" Wen said. "I would do whatever it takes to protect the emperor and the empire. If I thought for a moment that Roulan's child was not Hongdi's, I would have said something."

"Would you have?" Chun asked. "Well, I guess we will never know. All we know for certain is that as painful as it is, I am the only person willing to unearth the ugly truth. The only question left is what is, Hongdi going to do about it?"

Oh, the old woman was cunning, Wen had to give her

that. As Wen looked at the emperor and saw him glaring at her, she knew that Chun had planted seeds of distrust.

"Did you know?" Hongdi asked Wen.

"Of course not," Wen said. "I still don't think I believe it. Ruolan is loyal to you."

"That is yet to be seen," Hongdi said as he marched across the room and threw the doors open. "Guards!"

"Yes, your majesty," the men said.

"Go collect Ruolan, Lady Zhang," he said. "Take her to the Hall of Purity for questioning. Do not let her out of your sight and do not let her escape. If she won't go with you, drag her there if you must."

"Your Majesty!" Wen exclaimed. "She is pregnant!"

"Silence!" the emperor said. "You are to stay out of this. My mother is right, you should have kept a better watch on Ruolan, on all of them!"

Wen closed her mouth but kept a careful eye on Chun. She had to find out what the old woman was up to.

"And put Fei, her roommate, under house arrest," the emperor said. "I don't want her talking to anyone."

"Yes, Your Majesty," the guards said.

"Actually," the emperor continued. "Put all the concubines under house arrest."

"This—" Wen started to say, but one glance from the emperor and she closed her mouth again.

"I don't want any of them to leave their rooms until I figure out what is going on around here," the emperor said.

"Yes, Your Majesty," the guards said as they bowed and then left the room.

The emperor then turned to Wen. "You wanted to object?"

"If I am allowed to," she said. "There will be no way to contain the allegations if you arrest all of them."

"I can't trust them," the emperor said. "If Ruolan has a lover, maybe they all do."

"That is preposterous," Wen said, and she nearly broke out in laughter, but the emperor stomped toward her so quickly, she barely had time to flinch before he backhanded her across the face, sending her reeling into a chair behind her. She reached up to her cheek, her head spinning, her hands shaking.

The emperor pointed a finger at her. "Never call me preposterous again," he said. "I am the emperor, and what I say is truth. If I believe that the concubines cannot be trusted, then it is so. Do you understand me?"

"Y-y-yes," Wen stammered in a whisper. "Of course."

"Now," the emperor said as he straightened his robe and sleeves. "I am going to get to the bottom of this. You, too, will stay in your rooms until I deem otherwise."

Wen wanted to protest, but she only nodded. Her face was throbbing and her lower lip quaking. Even if she tried to speak, she would burst into tears, and she would not give him the satisfaction.

"Good," the emperor said, and then he left the room. Wen's maids rushed into the room to their lady's side and helped her to stand.

"I don't know why you did it," Wen said to Empress-Dowager Chun, "but you have just damned the entire dynasty."

"I wouldn't expect you to understand," Chun said as she sat back in her chair. "You never were that clever."

Wen turned away and went to her waiting sedan chair to return to her own palace. She knew she had to do something, but what? There was no way for Ruolan to survive this.

FIFTEEN

*F*ei kowtowed in front of the emperor, tears streaming from her face, her body trembling.

"How could you not know?" the emperor demanded. "She is your closest friend. Don't you share everything?"

"I didn't know anything!" Fei cried. "It's not possible!"

"The Minister of Justice found the boy," the emperor said. "He confessed to everything!"

"He's lying!" Fei said, daring to raise her head to look at the emperor. His face was hard, but there was also pain in his eyes. He had wanted this child more than anything, and now he was about to lose it. Fei seized on that fear to plead for her friend's life. "Ruolan would never be unfaithful to you. She loves you, as we all do. She wanted nothing more in life than to give you a child. If you kill her, you will be killing your own son!"

The emperor grabbed Fei by the arm, dragging her to her feet. She winced from the pain, but that did not stop the emperor from shaking her.

"That is not my son!" the emperor screamed in her face. "That whore Ruolan slept with the construction worker to ensure she would fall pregnant. She tricked me! She wanted me to believe the boy was mine, to raise her bastard as my own. To make him emperor. To heap praise upon her head. Well, thankfully, my mother and others saw through her trick. She will be punished. And you along with her if I find out that you knew anything about it!"

"I knew nothing," Fei insisted. "I know nothing. I was not living with her then. You know that."

The emperor released her with a final shake, sending her stumbling back onto a chair. "But she had to have said something to you," the emperor said. "Did she brag about her plan? Or did you see her flirting with the workers on the other side of the wall?"

"No," Fei said with a surety she did not completely feel. While she did not want to believe that Ruolan would do something so stupid, she had always sensed that Ruolan had some plan up her sleeve. She was always so sure that she would fall pregnant. Could it be possible that she did sleep with another man after sleeping with the emperor in the hopes of becoming pregnant and no one would be the wiser? It was a clever plan, but so fraught with danger, she could not imagine anyone going through with it.

Except, perhaps, someone like Ruolan. Someone with the utmost confidence in herself and her abilities.

Fei shook her head. No. She couldn't believe it. She refused. She would not let the emperor kill her friend—and her unborn child—on the word of two girls who were clearly jealous of Ruolan's good fortune.

"After you took Ruolan to bed," Fei said, "her room-mates were jealous. Why do you believe them over Ruolan herself?"

"Because it is not just them," the emperor said as he

collapsed on a couch and rubbed his head. "Her own maid spoke against her."

"But that is not her maid," Fei said.

"What?" the emperor asked, looking up.

"Her maid went home to marry her sweetheart," Fei said. "That maid is a girl who was only just assigned to serve Ruolan. She has no loyalty to her. What of her eunuch?"

"The eunuch has said nothing except to deny knowing anything, just like you," the emperor said with a sigh. "I also thought that the girls might be lying. Trying to ruin Ruolan for their own gain. But the interrogators, they found the boy. He confessed under torture."

Fei shook her head. "No, I still don't believe it. He could still be lying."

"To what end?" the emperor asked. "He will be put to death."

"What of his family?" Fei asked. "Maybe someone offered to pay the family a large sum if he sacrificed himself."

"There would be no way to prove that," the emperor said. "His word is more damning evidence than your conspiracy theories."

Fei sank back to her keels and clasped her hands before her, pleadingly. "We are talking about the life of my best friend. And your son. I think every possible explanation should be thoroughly explored before any sentence is handed down."

"It...it's too late," the emperor said. "She will be executed tomorrow at dawn."

"What?" Fei shrieked, jumping to her feet. "No! Why?"

"I have no choice!" the emperor said. "I have three

witnesses and her lover confessed. She must be put to death. She is a traitor to the throne. To me!"

"No!" Fei cried as she fell to the emperor's feet, grabbing the ends of his robe. "Please! Please, I beg of you! Show mercy! Banish her! Imprison her! Take her child away and send him to a monastery. But, please, please don't kill her!"

"I must," the emperor grumbled as he stood and stepped over Fei, but she did not release her grip on his robes.

"Please!" she screamed as he attempted to drag her across the floor, but he stopped as he heard his garment start to rip. "What if she confesses? Will you show her mercy then? Lock her in a room forever. Let her serve as a reminder for what happens when someone betrays you."

"If she confessed, how could I show her mercy?" the emperor asked. "If she admitted to what she had done, I would have to execute her. I could not show mercy to a guilty person."

"But that is the very definition of mercy," Fei said. "To forgive those who do not deserve to be forgiven. At least if she confesses you will know the truth. If you execute her while she denies betraying you, you will never know what really happened. If you kill her tomorrow, will that give you peace?"

The emperor pulled his robe from Fei's grip and walked toward the door, but then he stopped and turned back, pacing the room. Fei kept her head down, hoping that her own humility might speak on behalf of her friend.

"She had been interrogated many times and has not confessed yet," the emperor said. "She has staunchly denied any wrongdoing."

"Let me go to her," Fei said. "I am her friend. She will

talk to me. She will trust me. If I have your word that she will not be executed if she confesses, I will get her to talk."

The emperor paced some more. He was sweating even though the room was cool. Fall was coming early to Peking.

"It...it must be in writing," the emperor said. "She must sign a confession. Then I will find a way to show her mercy."

"Oh!" Fei cried as she kowtowed. "Thank you, Your Majesty! You are truly as good as you are wise. Thank you! Thank you!"

"Do not thank me just yet," the emperor said. "You still have work to do."

"I will go to her immediately," Fei said. "Thank you."

"I will let the Minister of Justice know that you have my leave to speak to the prisoner." And with that, the emperor stormed out of the room, slamming the door behind him.

Fei jumped to her feet and collected paper, a writing brush, and a stick of ink. Lina and Yuying followed her, Yuying going to fetch a sedan chair. Fei would pay any amount to get to the Hall of Justice as soon as possible. She could not waste a moment.

❧

*T*he Hall of Justice was an old Yuan Dynasty era dungeon located in the southeast corner of the Forbidden City. There was only one iron gate that led to the maze of cells below where the worst of China's criminals were held. Murderers, political prisoners, traitors, mostly people who were to be executed or held in prison for life.

There were two guards at the gate, and they stopped Fei from entering.

"Turn away, little lady," the first guard said.

"I am here on the emperor's business," Fei said. "I have permission to see Lady Zhang."

The guards burst out in laughter.

"No one sees the prisoners except the Minister of Justice, and you aren't him," the guard said. "So, just be on your way." But he licked his lips and rubbed his fingers together, and Fei realized that she probably could have seen Ruolan before now if she had thought to bribe the guards.

"I'm telling you," Fei insisted. "I am here to see the prisoner. You will not want to anger the emperor by denying me."

The guard sighed. "You were cute at first, but now you are just getting on my nerves. Get out of here before I have you dragged back to the women's quarters."

"You wouldn't dare touch one of the emperor's women," Fei said, standing her ground and holding her head high. Out of the corner of her eye, she could see the other guard watching them, and he seemed less sure of himself than the one she had been talking to.

"I'm going to need you—" the guard started again.

"Stand down," a voice called. Fei looked over and saw one of the eunuchs from the Ministry of Justice, but not the minister himself. "Our office has just been informed that Lady Song does have permission to visit Lady Zhang. She seems to believe she can wrangle a confession out of the prisoner."

"Which is why I brought paper and ink," Fei said, holding up her writing items.

The eunuch nodded. "Your servants must stay here. I will escort you to the prisoner's cell."

Fei nodded, and she couldn't help but take some satisfaction from the guard's stunned face as she passed him after the other guard opened the heavy iron gate.

"Let me help you," the eunuch said, offering Fei his hand. "The stairs are slippery."

Slippery with what, Fei was not sure. The stairway descended underground, the only light coming from torches along the wall. The air grew more moist and fetid the deeper they went. The eunuch sneezed.

"Oh, the mold down here is terrible for my constitution," he lamented. Indeed, Fei was not sure how anyone could survive more than a few minutes down here, let alone days...or years.

When they reached the bottom of the stairs, there was a large room where several more guards were stationed. Some were eating, some were playing a dice game. One sat in a corner and snored away.

The eunuch mostly ignored them as they turned left down a dank hallway. Fei stood close to him as the sounds of the prisoners began to waft around her. Crying, yelling, a scream. The sound of chains being dragged around. As they passed a hall that went off to the right, she heard a banging sound like metal on metal and a groaning like that of a wild animal. She had heard that the emperor had a menagerie of wild beasts. Lions and tigers and something called a giraffe. But she had never seen them. She thought they must have been housed at another palace, or perhaps on a strongly fortified farm. But now, she wondered if they were so dangerous they were kept down here. How terrible for a wild creature like a tiger to be kept in a cage, never to see the sun.

She quickened her pace when she saw that the eunuch had gotten ahead of her. She had to focus. She was here for Ruolan. She had to do whatever it took to save her friend.

They came to another hallway that went to the right, and this time the eunuch took it. They passed several cells with creatures in them that looked so pathetic, so thin and filthy, they could hardly be called human.

Finally, the eunuch stopped and Fei saw Ruolan hunched in a corner of a cell, her bright pink gown the only reminder of the life she had been living before she had been brought down here.

"Ruolan!" Fei called.

"Fei!" Ruolan crawled to the bars of the cell and reached for Fei's hands. Fei squeezed them. "Am I to be freed? Are you here to help me?"

Fei looked up at the eunuch. "Can you open the door?"

He shook his head. "I am afraid I cannot," he said, then he sneezed again. "I must get out of here. Can you find your way back?" Fei nodded. "Good. Five minutes, no more." He then brushed past her and headed back down the hallway as quickly as he could.

"Fei!" Ruolan whined. "What is happening? Wh-wh-why did he leave?"

"I am here to help," Fei said as she passed the paper and writing brush through the bars. "If you confess to having an affair with the construction worker, the emperor will show you mercy. You will be imprisoned, but not put to death."

"What?" Ruolan asked. "Confess? But I haven't done anything!"

"Ruolan," Fei hissed. "Tell me the truth. Did you do it? Is that how you—out of all the girls—managed to fall pregnant? It wasn't just the angelica flowers, was it?"

"By the gods," Ruolan said, her eyes watering. "You don't believe me either."

"It's not—" Fei sighed. "I don't care if you did or not. I am just trying to save your life. If you confess, the emperor will spare you. Will spare your son!"

"I'll be a prisoner?" Ruolan asked, her voice cracking. "Here?"

"I...I don't know," Fei said. "I didn't ask."

"I'd rather die than spend another moment down here," Ruolan said as tears slipped down her cheeks. "I'm filthy. Covered in my own urine. I'm starving. When the guards toss me steamed buns..." She burst into heavy sobbing. "I...I have to fight the rats for them. Look." She held out her hand and Fei saw small puncture wounds. "They bite my hands and feet when I try to sleep. I think they are checking to see if I am already dead."

"I am sure the emperor will not leave you here," Fei said. She had no way of knowing, but if she could just make sure that Ruolan wasn't put to death, she could work on securing a better living arrangement for her later. "Just write out a confession and sign it. I will take it to him and you will be released from this place."

"Why?" Ruolan asked. "If I confess, why would he spare me?"

"It was his promise," Fei said. "He will grant you mercy if you confess."

"Confess...to treason?" Ruolan asked, incredulous. "Do you realize what you are asking me to do? I am innocent! I am carrying the seed of the Dragon in my belly! And you want me to lie and say...what? That I slept with some dirty construction worker? Does that sound like me? Like something I would do?"

Fei shook her head. "Of course not. But...but they found a boy who claimed to have slept with you. And your wretched roommates, they confirmed it as well. All the evidence is against you. If you don't confess...Ruolan, you will die tomorrow."

Ruolan continued to cry, but she nodded her head.

"Good. Get it over with. I can't stay down here another moment. If the emperor sent me a white kerchief, I would hang myself."

"Don't say that," Fei said. "You need to live. For yourself. For your family. For your son!"

Ruolan shook her head and willed herself to calm down. "No. For their sake, for my own sake, I cannot do that. My honor, the honor of my family would be ruined. And what would become of my son? The bastard of a whore? What kind of life would he have?"

"The emperor has no other children," Fei said. "Maybe in time, he will claim the boy as his own—as he should!"

"No," Ruolan said. "It will be a matter of pride. The allegations against me must be common knowledge by now. The emperor will never acknowledge our son. Ever."

Fei took Ruolan's hand. "Please. You know better than anyone how life can change in an instant. You have no idea what the future will hold if you live. But if you die…" Fei sucked in a breath to hold herself steady. "If you die, there will be no future."

Ruolan nodded sadly. "I know. But at least I will die with honor. The gods and the ancestors know the truth. They will protect me in the next life."

Fei burst into tears of her own. "I can't let you die, sister!"

Ruolan reached through the bars and stroked Fei's cheek. "It's not your choice. My fate was sealed the moment I became pregnant."

Fei kissed Ruolan's hand and held it tightly in both of hers.

"There is something I want you to do for me," Ruolan said. Fei nodded, for she could not speak. "Go to our room and collect every jewel you can find. If you move my trunk, under a loose brick in the floor is a box of jewels and money. Send it all to my parents. I fear that the emperor will take his wrath out on them and demand the money back that he sent to them as a gift. He would ruin them. Send them the money along with a message from me telling them that I retained my honor to the end."

"You...you can write to them," Fei said as she handed Ruolan the ink stick.

"Brilliant!" Ruolan said. She went to a corner of the room where there was moisture on the floor and rubbed the ink stick in it. Fei hesitated to imagine what the liquid actually was. Once the ink was thin enough, Ruolan used the brush to write a short letter to her family. She blew on the ink to dry it as best she could in the humid room and then rolled the letter into a scroll and handed it to Fei through the bars of the cell.

"Send this to them, along with the money," Ruolan said. "Promise me."

"I promise," Fei said as she held the scroll to her heart.

Ruolan smiled and nodded. "You should go. The eunuch will be looking for you."

Fei burst into tears again and both girls reached through the bars of the cell door to hug as best they could.

"Goodbye, sister," Ruolan said. "I pray we meet again in the next life."

Fei nodded and gripped the bars to help her stand. Her legs were weak and her feet ached as she tottered along down the cobblestone hallway. When she turned the corner, she put her hand to her mouth to stifle her sobs. She did not want Ruolan to worry about her. After a minute, she was able to control herself, and she wiped the tears and snot from her face with her long sleeve. She walked down the hallway, leaning on the wall, her eyes hazy from the dank air and crying.

When she came to the next corridor, she heard the low moaning sound again. She looked ahead and saw that the guards seemed to be paying her no mind. She slipped down the corridor, wanting to just chance a glimpse of the creature. She might never have another chance to find out what a giraffe was.

She passed several more cells as the sounds grew louder, but they were all empty. Finally, she reached the end of the hall. There was only one cell left. The creature had to be in there. She licked her lips and calmed her quaking breath. She peeked into the cell and saw...

A man.

A man in ragged clothes was bent over so she could not see his head, which he seemed to be banging against a wall. But the sound was...metallic, somehow. As if he had a bucket on his head. But it was he who was letting out the terrible moaning. The sound of a man suffering. She wondered if this man, like Ruolan, was also innocent, and that was what caused the great pain to call out from the depths of his soul.

"H-h-hello?" Fei called out. "Are you—"

The man turned around and she screamed. She turned and tried to run down the hallway, but she slipped on the floor, falling and banging her chin. She scrambled up and ran down the hall, ignoring the throbbing pain in her feet.

That was no man, but a monster. His head...his face... was not human. He looked like a terrifying beast. Like a lion or...or a dragon.

At the end of the hall, Fei ran into something solid and screamed.

"Dear, dear!" the eunuch said as he gripped her arms. "What is going on? What is taking you so long?"

"I...I saw..." Fei looked back down the hallway, but the banging and moaning had stopped. She realized that it must have just been a figment of her imagination. Her terror of being in this place and the low lighting. "I was lost," she finally said.

"Easy to do down here," the eunuch said. "Come." He gently led her, his arm around her shoulders, to the stairs and then helped her up to the gate.

"My lady!" Lina said as she and Yuying took her from the eunuch. "What happened? You are covered in muck."

"I slipped," Fei said as she was led to the waiting sedan chair.

"Did you get it?" Yuying asked her as he reached for the folded parchment she was still holding tightly to her chest. "Did you get the confession?"

Fei sat in the chair and shook her head. "No. She is innocent."

"But...but she will die," Lina said, disbelief on her face.

"Her honor was more important to her than her life," Fei said.

Yuying and Lina nodded, then they stepped back and let the curtains of the sedan chair fall. Fei let the swaying motion of the chair calm her as she was carried back to her palace with images of the man in the terrible mask seared into her mind.

SIXTEEN

*I*n the dim light of morning twilight, while the stars were still winking their last goodbyes, Fei and Yuying snuck to the Gate of Northern Flower, a gate typically only used by the palace servants for food deliveries and rubbish removal. Both were wearing heavy cloaks to hide their appearance, even though once they were outside the palace, no one would know who they were. But if anyone knew what they were about to do, Fei would not be excused easily—if at all. She was risking her life for her friend. But it would be her last time.

As they approached the gate, Fei slipped a small ruby gemstone to Yuying, who then approached a guard. The two spoke for a moment before the guard nodded to Fei and opened the gate for them.

"No trouble?" Fei asked once they were outside. "Are you sure he will let us back in?"

"For another jewel, he will," Yuying said as he took Fei's arm and led her away from the palace wall and into a crowd of people heading south to watch the execution.

Fei shook her head. Luckily, she had brought several

jewels with her, along with an obscene amount of cash, just in case they needed it. When she discovered Ruolan's cache under her trunk, she was shocked at just how much money and jewels there were. She had no idea where Ruolan could have gotten them. Her family was better off than Fei's was, but not by that much. She wondered if Ruolan had somehow been stealing them. Or maybe they had been gifts from the emperor since he found out she was pregnant. Fei didn't know, and she didn't want to know. But she knew she could use them to sneak out of the palace just once. All the money and cash she had leftover, she would then send to Ruolan's family along with the letter, just as she had promised.

But she couldn't let Ruolan die alone. She didn't want the last thing for Ruolan to see to be the executioner's face. She didn't want to see her friend killed, but she would sacrifice her own comfort for Ruolan. She would stand in the crowd and make sure that Ruolan saw her. Know that in her final moment, she had not been abandoned.

When they reached the south side of the Forbidden City, the square where the executions were to be held was already packed with people. People were laughing and eating, sellers were hawking their wares, children were pickpocketing. It was as though everyone had arrived for a great party. Fei had to be careful as she walked so as not to topple over as she balanced on her bound feet among the crush of people. She gripped Yuying's hands tightly as they made their way through the crowd. She could barely even see the platform where the execution was to take place, she was so far away and there were so many people in front of her.

Finally, she heard someone shout, "Make way for the prisoners!" The people all erupted into cheers.

"Move!" Fei said, unsure if she was talking to Yuying or the throng of people around them, but she used her small form to shoulder her way through the crowd, dragging Yuying along with her.

A small side door opened near the massive main southern gate of the Forbidden City, and Ruolan and another man that Fei had never seen before were both led out with ropes around their necks toward the platform. Ruolan had to bounce on her tiny bound feet to keep up with the man who was leading her, which must have hurt her immensely, but she did not stumble or fall, and Ruolan's heart ached for her. She knew that Ruolan would do her best to hold on to her dignity until the end, no matter how much pain it caused her.

Fei tore her eyes away from Ruolan to resume her trek toward the front and center of the platform. As she did, she heard the crowd begin to jeer at Ruolan and the man with her.

"Whore!"

"Traitor!"

"Murderer!"

Fei then realized that some of the gathered people might have heard the rumors about a concubine being unfaithful to the emperor, but most of the people probably had no idea why there was to be an execution today. She finally reached a spot where she would be able to see the platform clearly. She only hoped that Ruolan would be able to see her. She would have no idea to even look for her friend in the mass of people there to enjoy the spectacle of her death.

As Ruolan and the man reached the stairs for the platform, the jeers grew louder, and some people threw rotten food at them at all. Noodles and dumplings and rancid vegetables all hit their mark, splattering on Ruolan's clothes, her face, and in her hair, which was hanging in long matted tangles around her. Fei felt herself choke up at the memory of helping Fei comb out her long beautiful hair before bed just a few nights before.

Ruolan and the man were led to the center of the platform and told to stand as their guards stepped away. Ruolan placed her hands around her small stomach, revealing to everyone that she was pregnant. There were audible gasps through the crowd, and Fei nodded in approval. This was Ruolan's one act of defiance against the emperor. It would spread through the city like wildfire that the emperor had a pregnant concubine executed. The emperor would lose much face among the people for such an act of cruelty.

The Minister of Justice then stepped forward and unfurled a scroll. In a surprisingly loud and deep voice for a eunuch, the man said, "By order of His Majesty, Emperor Hongdi, you, Lady Zhang Ruolan, and you, Yang Chao, for the crimes of adultery against His Majesty, treason against His Majesty, and deception against His Majesty, are hereby sentenced to death by beheading." The minister stepped aside and motioned for Ruolan and the man to kneel. As they did so, Ruolan kept her head high. The man—who was little more than a boy—next to her, dropped his head and sobbed.

There were fewer cheers now as people began to murmur to each other, wondering if they were all seeing the same thing—a pregnant woman and her lover about to be put to death. It was shocking in its barbarity.

"Mercy!" a woman in the crowd yelled.

The minister shot a look out into the crowd and Fei pulled the hood of her cloak down. She wanted Ruolan to see her, but she had not planned on the minister being there. If she were caught outside the palace, her virtue would be called into question and she could find herself executed as well.

"Mercy!" another person yelled, and then another, until the whole crowd was calling for mercy for the pregnant concubine.

But Fei could see that Ruolan did not expect mercy. She sat on her knees, her back straight, her chin high. Waiting.

The minister motioned for the executioner to get on with it. The executioner nodded and stepped forward, unsheathing his long curved sword. The crowd groaned and some began to cry. Many looked away. What was to be a free morning of entertainment had turned into a show of horror. The blade sang as it was swung through the air, and the boy's head left his body in an instant. The body toppled forward, blood spurting across the platform, as the head rolled in front of Ruolan.

Ruolan's will broke as she stared down at the head in front of her. "No!" she screamed. "I'm innocent!" She tried to stand, but a guard stepped forward and pushed her back down. "Please, please, please!"

"Mercy!" the crowd started up again. The Minister of Justice motioned for the executioner to continue his assignment. He seemed to hesitate before stepping behind Ruolan.

Tears rolled down Ruolan's cheeks as she shook her head. "I don't want to die! I don't want to die!"

Fei could no longer bear it. "Help me!" she told Yuying as she grabbed his shoulders. Young as he was, he was surprisingly strong. He lifted her up above the crowd and she pulled her hood back. She lifted her arm and waved to Ruolan. "I'm here!" she yelled.

Somehow, over the yelling of the crowd and Ruolan's

begging, she seemed to have heard her friend. Ruolan looked out over the crowd and her eyes met Fei's.

"I'm here for you!" Fei said. "Look at me!"

Ruolan stared at Fei and nodded. *Thank you*, she mouthed.

The executioner's sword sang for a second time.

The crowd erupted into boos and hisses, this time for the Ministry of Justice and the executioner.

And for the emperor.

"Cruel monsters!"

"Death to the emperor!"

"Kick the Ming out of Peking!"

As Fei watched the body of her friend crumple to the ground, she felt sick. She lost her balance, and Yuying struggled to keep from dropping her.

"We need to get out of here before there is a riot!" Yuying said as he did his best to keep Fei on her feet. "Please, my lady! We must flee!"

Fei nodded and huddled close to Yuying as he led her from the crowd. The people were crushing forward, toward the platform. Fei began to fear what the people might do to the minister if they caught him. But he had the executioner and several guards with him, so she did not doubt he would make it back to the palace alive. She pulled the hood down over her head, thankful the minister did not see her, and concentrated on going in the opposite direction of the crowd, away from the platform and back toward the Forbidden City.

"*T*he people what?" the emperor screamed from the Dragon Throne.

"They...k-k-killed the Minister of Justice," Wangzhu told the emperor, his head down as he shook before the emperor.

Empress Wen covered her mouth in shock.

"Why?" the emperor demanded.

"Because he oversaw the death of Ruolan," Wangzhu said. "The people wanted her to be shown mercy."

"Mercy?" the emperor sneered. "She was a cheating, lying whore!"

"Of course, Your Majesty," Wangzhu said. "And the minister read the charges before she and the boy were executed, but..."

"But what?"

"But...she was visibly with child," Wangzhu said. "The people thought her death was...cruel."

"Cruel?" the emperor asked. "They haven't seen cruel. The rioters, the men who killed the minister, where are they? Have they been caught?"

"Some of them have, Your Majesty, Wangzhu said. "The guards managed to round a few of the men up and take them to the Ministry of Justice. The executioner, however, was also killed."

"Give them the Death by a Thousand Cuts," the emperor said. "In public, but in a way that the people cannot stop it. They want to see cruel? I will show it to them."

"Perhaps now is not the time for such a bloody act of force," Empress Wen said, her voice gentle. "The city is in a state of agitation. Let the people calm down and forget. Execute the rioters in private if you must."

The emperor turned his rage to the empress. "*If* I must?" he asked. He crooked a finger at her, beckoning her forward. She did as he commanded, keeping her eyes downcast. "What did I tell you about questioning me?" he asked, but before she could apologize, she once again took a slap across the face. It was not as painful as before, but in front of the entire court, such an act was meant to send a message.

"Forgive me," the empress said as she slinked away.

The emperor stood and addressed the crowd. "I am done being humiliated by the women of the Inner Court. If one woman of the court was able to have a lover—thanks to the severe lack of oversight by the empress—then how many others have taken lovers? As of this moment, any concubine I have had relations with shall be retired. Never again will they be allowed to come to my bed."

The people of the crowd began to murmur at the implications of this. The empress's heart raced. Surely he did not mean her as well. She was the empress. She could not so easily be set aside. But she thought it best to hold her tongue for the moment.

"Any woman I have not yet had relations with shall be examined again," the emperor went on. "Any concubine found to no longer be virginal will be put to death for treason."

The crowd gasped. The empress stepped forward. She had to speak. She could not allow such madness to continue, but her ladies grabbed her sleeves and held her back.

"Your Majesty," one of the other ministers spoke up, "if you put more ladies to death now...the people will not be pleased. They are already horrified at the death of Lady Zhang."

"Their deaths will not be public," the emperor said. "It will be the responsibility of the empress, as the head of the Inner Court, to order their deaths by hanging from a white kerchief."

"No!" the empress cried.

The emperor turned back to her. "Are you unable to carry out your duty, empress? Or should you be retired as well? I have a palace full of women eager to take your place."

The empress shook with rage and fear. She did not believe he would depose her. Her father was far too powerful. The leader of the military. Why, even now he was defending the northern border against Manchu raiders.

Yet, she did not want to provoke the emperor's wrath. He had already done unspeakable acts. He didn't have to kill her to make her life unlivable.

"I will do as you command," she said humbly, bending her knees.

"Good," the emperor said. He looked out over the crowd. "Any other issues?" The room fell silent. The emperor left the dais, confusion and panic in his wake. Several councilors and ministers approached the dais, asking for the empress's attention.

"You must do something," one of them said to her.

"Taking the concubines into the Inner Court was meant to instill love for the emperor among the people," another said. "If word gets out that he is killing them, the citizens will surely turn against him."

"I know," the empress said. "But what am I to do?"

"You are his wife," the ministers said. "Talk some sense into the man!"

The empress used the sleeve of her gown to remove the

makeup from her cheek, revealing the bruise the emperor had left there only days before.

"Do you think the emperor is listening to my common sense recommendations right now?" she asked as the men gasped at the sight. Of course, many of them probably beat their own wives. It was a common way for men to keep order in their homes. But Wen was the empress. She was supposed to be above such things. And if her father knew, surely he would be furious. No one—not even the emperor —would want the leader of the army to turn against the empire.

"Then what are we to do?" the men asked helplessly.

The empress rolled her eyes. "First, the girls will consent to the exams. Maybe they will all still be intact and he will have no cause for anger against any of them."

"And then?" another man asked.

"I don't know," the empress said. "I don't know.

SEVENTEEN

*E*mpress Wen sat at a low table across from Lady Qin and poured them each a cup of tea, trying her best to keep her hands steady. The midwife had completed her reexaminations of the ladies' virginity. Three had failed the test—including Lady Qin.

The empress's orders from the emperor were clear. She was to sentence Lady Qin to death. But she had to talk to the woman first. The other two girls who had failed were new concubines, young and, presumably, foolish. The empress did not even remember their faces, much less their names. She had sent them their white scarves and expected them to know what to do.

But Lady Qin...She and the empress had been together for many years, nearly eight. The empress had worked tirelessly on her behalf to have her bedded by the emperor, but he simply could not be forced. He had ignored her, finally preferring the younger batch of concubines to a woman who had waited devotedly for him for years. Wen knew that Lady Qin had been devastated by the arrival of the new concubines. But had she been devastated and stupid enough to take matters into her own hands and somehow take a lover? The empress did not think so. But she could not deny that Lady Qin had failed the midwife's evaluation and was no longer a virgin.

"You know the results of the midwife's exam?" Wen asked as she placed a teacup before Lady Qin. "She told you at the time."

"She didn't have to," Lady Qin said as she took her teacup, swirling it in her fingers as she watched the tea leaves. "I could see it on her face as soon as she was done."

"Did you know that you were going to fail the examination beforehand?" Wen asked.

Lady Qin sipped from her teacup to calm her nerves, but teardrops still managed to slink down her cheeks. "I suspected I would," she said in a near whisper.

Empress Wen's face dropped into her hands. "So you admit it? How could you? After waiting so long, how could you do something so stupid as to take a lover?"

Lady Qin looked directly at the empress. "But I didn't! I would never!"

"Lady Qin," Wen scoffed. "How can you sit there and lie to my face? You admit you failed; you admit you knew that you would. How can then deny that you have a lover?"

"Because it is the truth," Lady Qin said. "I never took a man to my bed in the whole of my life! I swear it!"

"Then why did you fail the exam?" Wen asked, not believing a word of Lady Qin's protestations.

"It...it must have been a mistake," Lady Qin said, her face blushing bright red. "I...I am old. My monthly bleeds are not as heavy or as long as they once were. Perhaps I am just...dried up, a husk of a once young and fertile woman."

"You are younger than I am," Wen said. "You are twenty-five?"

"Twenty-six," Lady Qin corrected.

"That is still young enough to have children," Wen said.

"Why are you torturing me with such false hopes?" Lady Qin asked, leaning forward on the table. "No man would have me now at my age, least of all the emperor. And now that he believes me to not be a virgin, he will send me into retirement with the other old and used concubines. My life is over!"

Wen shut her mouth, pressing her lips into a thin line. The emperor's order that any concubine found to be not chaste would be put to death had not spread among the concubines. Wen did not want to scare them unnecessarily. She had truly believed that all the ladies would pass the test and there would be no need to tell them of the emperor's threats against them. But after Lady Qin and the other two were dead, there would be no way to hide their fates from the rest of the Inner Court. The ladies would learn the truth. And even if they had passed the exam, they would be terrified. What arbitrary test would he put them to next and find them lacking? They would live each day in fear.

"What?" Lady Qin asked. "What are you not telling me?"

"You will not be retired," Wen said. "You...will be given a...a white scarf..." She could not finish her words. There was no need to. Everyone knew the significance of such a "gift." Lady Qin's maid, an older woman, gasped, her hands flying to her mouth.

Lady Qin's mouth opened and closed several times before she uttered a simple, "No."

"I'm sorry," Wen said, reaching for Lady Qin's hand, but Lady Qin pulled away.

"No!" she said again, this time with more force. "No, you can't! It...it's not my fault!"

"What do you mean?" Wen asked.

"It was her!" Lady Qin said, pointing to her maid. "She is the reason I failed! She...she tricked me!"

The maid rushed over and kowtowed before her lady and the empress. "I'm sorry! I had no idea! I was only trying to help you!"

"What is going on?" Wen asked. "What happened?"

The maid raised her head slightly, meeting Lady Qin's eyes. Then Lady Qin turned to the empress.

"I...I am so ashamed..." she said.

"Ashamed for what?" Wen asked, growing more frustrated. "Did the maid sneak you a lover? What did she do?"

"No," Lady Qin said. "No, nothing like that."

"Then what?" Wen asked through gritted teeth.

Lady Qin looked at her maid and nodded. The woman stood up and went to Lady Qin's bedchamber. She came back with something concealed in a silk drawstring pouch. When she returned, she set the item on the table in front of the empress with a *thunk*. Whatever it was, it was quite heavy for its small size.

"I have served many ladies in the palace over the years," the maid said. "The emperor's father had many more concubines than your husband has ever had. And while he did have more children, he also neglected most of his women."

"As emperors do," Wen said. "Having many concubines is more about status than anyone's needs or happiness."

The maid nodded. "So, over the years, I learned that many of the women who were no longer called to the emperor's bed found...other ways to satiate their own desires."

The empress raised an eyebrow and looked at Lady Qin, her face red with embarrassment. Wen reached over the opened the silk pouch. She pulled out a long piece of jade. After she examined it for a moment, she realized it was in the shape of a man's penis.

"Oh!" she exclaimed, dropping it on the table with a clatter. "You...you used this yourself to...simulate relations with the emperor?"

Lady Qin nodded and burst into tears, unable to speak.

Empress Wen shook her head and placed the item back into its pouch.

"I...I knew that the older, discarded concubines had used them," the maid said. "So I thought it would help Lady Qin's life be a bit more...bearable. Enjoyable. Give her some happiness if she was to spend her life alone and childless. But I never thought...I didn't consider that since she was a virgin..."

"When I used it," Lady Qin tried to explain through her hiccups and tears. "It was enjoyable at first. I didn't realize that...relations between men and women could bring pleasure to women. But then...I don't know what happened. I started to bleed. I was so scared! I immediately stopped and cleaned myself and the...item and never used it again! I swear!"

Empress Wen had been married for many years. She had brothers and sisters and lived in a world where men could have sex with as many women as they wanted. She grew up knowing all about eunuchs and how they couldn't have relations with women. She lost her own virginity to the emperor before they were officially married. She did not like to think she was a woman who was easily shocked. But as she stared at the silk pouch and realized that a piece of jade was going to lead to the death of Lady Qin, she could hardly speak.

"I am so sorry, Lady Qin," the empress finally said,

reaching across the table and squeezing the young woman's hand. "I believe you when you say that you have never had relations with a man. I believe this is all just a...terrible tragedy."

"Is it?" Lady Qin asked.

The empress nodded and reached into a pocket in her voluminous sleeve, pulling out a white scarf. "You failed your examination," she said. "The emperor will never believe that you are still a virgin."

"But...but I am!" Lady Qin said. "You have to do something!"

"I cannot," the empress said, standing. "The emperor will only say that this...item is a...a disguise. Something that you are using to hide the fact that you have a lover."

"No! No!" Lady Qin screamed as she stood and ran around the table, dropping to the floor in front of the empress and grabbing her hand. "Please! Please save me! It was an accident! I would never betray His Majesty! Never!"

"Please, stop," the empress said, her eyes so glassy she could hardly see through them. "I have my orders, and I must obey them. I am sorry. You know what you must do." She pulled her hand from Lady Qin's grip and walked toward the door.

"No! Please!" Lady Qin screamed, crawling after her, but her maid wrapped her arms around her and held her.

"I'm sorry!" the maid said. "I'm so sorry!"

Empress Wen forced herself to keep walking and not look back as she heard the women crying together. Once she was outside, she turned to the guards, who were aware of the orders Lady Qin was to be given.

"Let me know when it is done," she told them.

"Yes, Your Majesty," the men said. The empress then climbed into her sedan chair to be carried back to her own palace. Once the curtains were closed, she let loose the tears that never seemed to stop lately. Lady Qin had been her friend. She was certain that Ruolan had been pregnant with the emperor's child. She began to doubt that her title or even her father would be able to keep her safe should the emperor turn on her. He was becoming dangerous. Wild with jealousy and suspicion. She dreaded to find out what he would do next.

❦

The emperor watched as Lady Qin's body, covered in a white sheet, was carried from the Forbidden City and loaded onto a donkey cart. The body would not be given an imperial burial, but would be sent home to her parents. It would send the message that the woman had died shamefully.

After the body was gone, the emperor shut the doors to his audience hall and paced before his dragon throne. How could things have gone so badly so quickly? The move to Peking had seemed to be a success. The Forbidden City was growing before his eyes, looking even more beautiful than he had imagined. The selection of the new concubines had calmed tension in the city. The people were still grumbling about taxes, and there had been unrest in the north, but the people were a long way from outright rebellion, and the empress's father knew best how to squash any barbarians at the wall.

But for Ruolan to fall pregnant...That had been a dream come true. Finally. But she had lied. Had betrayed him. The emperor's fists clenched at the mere thought of the treacherous girl and her bastard seed. But she was now gone, as were any of the women who had betrayed him. The women he had slept with were retired while the women who had lost their virginity elsewhere were dead.

Except for the empress.

He growled at the thought of her. There was a time when he had loved her well. Too well. He had spilled more of his seed in her than anyone. And what did he have to show for it? Nothing! His mother had been right. She had not been the empress he needed. He had to put four women to death under her watch. How many concubines had his father executed? None!

But he could not depose her. The people loved her. She was as well known among the populous as he was. The great general's beautiful daughter. The emperor's childhood sweetheart. His equal.

The emperor spit as he stormed from the audience hall toward the empress's palace. He thought that by not giving her a throne next to his, she would have learned her place by now. But she clearly had not. She had argued with him at every turn. Tried to spare the lives of every whorish concubine. She could be unfaithful herself for all he knew. In protecting the girls, maybe she felt she was protecting herself. But he could never prove it unless he caught her in the act with a lover. And she was too clever to ever let that happen. Especially now, when he was being hypervigilant.

No, he would have to show her another way that *he* was the emperor—and that she was nothing but a woman.

He arrived at the empress's palace unannounced, pushing the doors open and startling the servants who were working there.

"Where is she?" the emperor demanded of the trembling maids and eunuchs.

One of the maids raised a trembling finger and pointed to the next room. "Her study, Your Majesty."

By the time the emperor arrived, Empress Wen was already kneeling before her desk, as was her chief eunuch, Bojing.

"Get out," he told the servant. The empress glanced up in annoyance. No one was supposed to order her eunuch around but her. But she kept her mouth shut and lowered her eyes again as Bojing left the room, closing the doors behind him.

"If it were up to me," the emperor said, "I would cast you out with the rest of the retired women right now."

Wen remained bowing, saying nothing. Even her eyes were downcast, so he could not read her expression.

"Those concubines, those whores who betrayed me," the emperor said as he paced, "that is all on you. You should have kept them chaste. They were mine! My precious jewels. And you let them ruin themselves. I should punish *you* for their crimes."

He thought he saw her tremble, but only slightly. Good. He wanted her to be afraid of him. He was tired of her questioning his authority. She had to know that no matter who she was, no matter who her father was, her fate was still in her hands.

He stepped to her and grabbed her arm, dragging her to stand. "You will never defy me again, do you understand?"

"Of course, my—" She screamed as he pushed her back on her desk, shoving her papers and writing brushes aside. He untied her sash, pulling her robe open. "No! Stop!" she screamed.

Hongdi slapped her. "You do not tell me what to do!" He tore at her silken undergarments as she began to cry.

"My lady!" Bojing yelled, opening the door.

"Get out!" the emperor roared. "Do not interrupt me with my wife!"

The empress tried to push him away, pounded his chest with her fists, but still, Hongdi pressed forward. He pulled her hair, exposing her neck to him. As he smelled her skin, his arousal grew. He knew she would never speak against him after this, and seeing her so helpless had never made him want her so fervently.

He lifted her hips higher onto the desk and tore at her clothes to expose her body to him. As he reached down to release himself from his own robes to take her, he suddenly felt something cold as ice against his neck. He looked up and saw that the empress was holding a letter opener to his throat.

"No," she said, her eyes boring into his.

"You wouldn't dare," he said. "I could have you put to death for even threatening such a thing."

"But you won't," she said as she shoved him away from her. "After the way you have been acting lately, after what my own servants just saw, I could kill *you* and no one would blame me. You are acting insane."

The emperor glared at her. "You are making threats you can't possibly follow through on."

"Can't I?" she said. "If you dare ever touch me again, one word to my father and he will ride his army straight through your precious Forbidden City and impale you to your dragon throne. You know he would."

Hongdi kept his eyes on her, but, dammit, he knew she was right. He might be able to put little nobody concubines to death—but not the empress. Not even for threatening his life. Her father would never forgive him, even if her death were justified.

"Very well, *empress*," the emperor said as he backed away, straightening his robe. "But you, along with all the other concubines, are confined to your quarters from now on. You may not leave, even to go to temple, without my permission. Do you understand?"

"Yes, Your Majesty," she said, the letter opener still gripped tightly in her hand.

The emperor then threw the door open, revealing Bojing waiting anxiously just on the other side. The eunuch sighed in relief when he saw the empress brandishing her weapon. He stepped aside and let the emperor leave.

Empress Wen stood still as a statue and did not even breathe until she heard the front door of her palace open and shut. Then, the letter opener fell from her hand and she crumbled to the ground in a heap of tears. Bojing ran to her side and held her in his arms.

"My lady!" he cried, checking her for injuries. "My lady! He didn't...did he?"

She shook her head. "No...no, I stopped him."

"What happened?" Bojing asked. "Why was he in such a rage?"

Wen forced herself to stand. "I don't know. He said that I have defied him too many times. But I have done all he has asked. I...I sent Lady Qin to her death! What more does he want from me?"

"I don't know, my lady," Bojing said. "Maybe he—"

A scream rent the air. Despite the order to stay in her palace, the empress threw open the front door and stepped out into the cold dark night.

"Where?" she asked her many servants who had followed her out. "Where is it coming from?"

There were more screams and pleas to stop.

"There!" one of the servants said. "Concubine Song Fei's palace."

The empress felt sick to her stomach. She saw that the door to Fei's palace was open, and she could hear the girl screaming and crying. She wished that there was something she could do, but she knew she could not. She had only able to stop the emperor from forcing himself on her because of her own power. Her own authority. Even Bojing, who saw what was happening, could not stop the emperor from taking what was his. And now, as much as the empress wished it were not true, she could not stop her husband from claiming his right over his concubine.

"Inside," she ordered her servants, and they all knew that there was nothing that could be done for the girl.

The empress closed the door behind her and then went back to her study to think. She could not stop the emperor from taking Fei, or any of the girls, but she was not totally helpless. She picked up her papers and writing utensils and began composing a letter to her father.

EIGHTEEN

When Fei woke up, the emperor was gone. She was shocked she had slept at all. After he had finished with her, he lay next to her on the bed for a long time. She had pulled a blanket over herself to cover her exposed body and did her best to control her trembles. Her back had been to him, and she counted the tiny embroidered phoenixes on her bed's satin canopy wall, waiting for him to leave, praying he would not take her again. She did not think her body could handle it, she had been in so much pain. But at some point, she must have fallen asleep, and then he had slipped out of the room. She hoped he did not go to the palace of some other poor, unsuspecting girl, but she had no way of knowing.

She turned over and winced, her back aching from where the emperor had banged it into the edge of her bed in his fervor.

"My lady! You are awake," Lina said, jumping up from her place on the floor. "How are you feeling?"

"Like I was pushed from a great height," Fei said. "Everything aches."

"I will draw you a hot bath and prepare some tea," Lina said. "Would you like anything to eat?"

Fei's stomach rumbled and acid bubbled up into her throat. She shook her head. The mere thought of food made her nauseous.

"Very well," Lina said, and she quickly darted from the room.

Fei sat up, swinging her legs off the edge of the bed. As she looked around the room, she was surprised to see that it looked...normal. Tidy. She remembered the emperor pushing over a table and smashing a vase. He was...in such a rage. She realized that Lina and Yuying must have quietly worked on straightening the room while she slept. But as she looked down, she saw that the robe she had been wearing was ripped. She frowned and winced again, feeling pain in her face where the emperor had struck her. She stood and stripped the ruined clothes from her body. She attempted to pull one of the sheets around her, but she saw blood stains...and she could smell him. She tossed the sheet, the blanket, the pillow, all the bedclothes onto the pile with her ruined clothes.

Yuying entered the room and averted his eyes when he saw that his lady was naked.

"Burn them," she said, pointing to the pile of ruined silk and satin. "All of it."

"Yes, my lady," Yuying said as he gathered the items and put them outside the front door of the palace for now. When he returned, Fei had managed to find a clean robe in her trunk and was attempting to pull it around herself. Yuying rushed to her side and helped her cover herself.

"Thank you," she said. She then walked over to her dressing table and sat down slowly. She sucked in a breath when she saw her face. "My father would hit his women sometimes, my mother and his concubines, but he never left a mark. My mother said that bruises diminished a woman's value and a man's honor."

"The emperor showed no honor last night, my lady," Yuying said, and Fei's eyes watered.

"There was nothing you could do," she said. "He was... within his right."

"It was still...terrible to witness," Yuying said, his own voice weak.

"You...watched?" Fei asked him.

"Lina and I," Yuying said. "We...we couldn't leave you alone. We were afraid...We thought he might kill you. And we wanted him to know that he wouldn't get away with it if he did."

A tear escaped and ran down Fei's cheek. She wiped it away. "That was very stupid of you," she said. "He could have killed you too."

"We will never abandon you, my lady," the eunuch said. "No matter the cost."

Fei nodded her appreciation, too overcome to speak.

"Your bath is ready," Lina said in the doorway.

Fei tried to stand under her own steam, but her legs wanted to collapse under her. Yuying put her arm around his shoulder, and he carried her to the bathing room. Together, Yuying and Lina lowered Fei into the hot bathwater, scented with roses and geraniums. Fei leaned back, and Lina lifted her lady's feet up, one after the other, to remove her footbindings before lowering them back into the water.

As the warmth of the water seeped into Fei's bones, the tension melted away, and soon, Fei was crying uncontrollably. It was as though as long as she was being attacked, she had to hold her body, her mind, her emotions stiff. She could not protest for fear of angering the emperor further.

But if she had relaxed any part of herself for even a moment, she would crumble. But here in the water, with both of her servants at her side, she knew she was safe, and she began to fall apart.

"Why?" she cried. "Why?"

Lina sniffed and shook her head. "The man could have any of you at any moment! He only needed to inform you of his intentions. He didn't have to use such force. It was disgusting."

"Brutish," Yuying added. "Not the actions of a gentleman. Of an emperor."

"Ruolan had said that he was kind, gentle." Fei lifted a washcloth out of the water, the sound of water droplets strangely soothing. "That it had been...pleasurable. Why? Why did he hurt me?"

Lina and Yuying shook their heads. They had no answer for her.

"I went out this morning," Yuying said, "under the guise of completing my morning chores. I spoke to several other maids and eunuchs. Apparently, the emperor left the empress's palace in a rage before he came here."

"The empress was the cause?" Lina asked.

"No," Yuying said. "Bojing's assistant said that the emperor arrived at her palace already full of anger. They don't know why he was so angry in the first place. Apparently—" He dropped his voice to a whisper. "—he tried to force himself on the empress in much the same way as he did you, but she fought him off."

"No!" Fei said, her hand flying to her mouth. "How?"

"She threatened to tell her father," Yuying said, raising an eyebrow.

"Does the general have enough power to be a threat to the emperor?" Fei asked.

Yuying shrugged. "Enough to get the emperor to leave the empress unharmed."

"But not enough to protect me," Fei said, her eyes filling with tears again.

"It wasn't just you," Yuying went on. "After he left you, he went to Lady Sui's palace, and then to Lady Kun."

"How many were there?" Fei asked, her eyes wide with horror.

"Including you..." Yuying said. "Five."

"Five!" Fei said, sitting up. "He...attacked five of his own concubines?"

"He said something to Lady Sui about fulfilling his duty now that the...whores had been done away with," Yuying said.

"He can't mean the women he retired," Lina said. "He had relations with those women himself."

Yuying shook his head. "No. He meant Lady Qin, Lady Zhu, and Lady Hui. They...they all hung themselves with white scarves at the order of the empress after they failed their virginity examinations."

Fei leaned over the side of the tub and vomited green bile onto the floor, for she had no food in her stomach to come out.

"He killed them," she muttered. "He killed them!"

"Shhhh!" Lina said, kneeling down and rubbing the warm washcloth and hot water over Fei's hair and face. "It's over. You are safe! You passed the exam. He won't kill you."

"Won't he?" Fei asked. "What if he says that since I am no longer a virgin, I should be put to death as well?"

"He won't," Lina said. "He retired the women he deflowered himself."

"But he didn't beat them," Fei said. "He didn't...force himself into them." She clenched her whole body together, wishing she could magically heal the damage the man had done to her. That she could somehow be a virgin again.

"And what is to keep him from coming back? From... taking me...hurting me again?"

Lina and Yuying looked at each other, and Fei knew the answer. Nothing. There was nothing stopping him. Nothing to protect her.

Fei tried to stand up in the tub, but without her foot wrappings, it was impossible to stand, much less walk.

"My lady!" Lina exclaimed as she tried to settle Fei back into the bath. "What are you doing? You are going to fall!"

"And break my neck?" Fei asked. "Good."

"What are you talking about?"

"Bring me something sharp," Fei said. "I have heard that if I slit my wrists while I am in water, it won't hurt. I'll just fall asleep."

"No!" Lina said. "We aren't going to help you kill yourself."

"Fine," Fei said, and she slipped completely under the water and exhaled all the breath from her lungs.

"My lady!" Lina screamed. "Stop!" She grabbed onto Fei's arms and tried to pull her up, but Fei had a strong grip on the side of the tub and could not be budged. Yuying reached into the water and tried to grab her waist, but the salts and oils Lina had put into the water made her too slippery for him to grab a hold of.

"Oh gods!" Lina cried. "Oh gods! What can we do?"

Yuying reached into the tub again and slipped his hand under Fei's body, pulling the stopper. The water from the tub began to gush out onto the floor. In only a moment, the water level was low enough that Fei's face was exposed and she instinctively gasped for air.

"Why did you stop me?" Fei asked. "I can't live this way. He will come back. I am sure of it."

"He very well might," Lina said, rubbing Fei's back. "But...do you believe that Ruolan really fell pregnant by the emperor?"

"Of course," Fei said. "What does that have to do with anything?"

"Then you could fall pregnant too," Lina said. "You could be pregnant right now."

Fei sat up and looked at Lina for a moment, digesting her words. She was right. Ruolan fell pregnant after only one night with the emperor. The same thing could happen to Fei. She ran her hands over her stomach.

"But...I don't want to have a baby with that man," Fei said.

"It's not about him," Lina said. "If you become pregnant, your child could be the next emperor. You would be safe then. Protected."

"Protected by a baby?" Fei scoffed. "What a terrible burden for one not yet even born."

"I know," Lina said, "but...even though you are suffering now, it could all be worth it in the end. You have no idea what the gods have planned for you."

Fei laid her head back against the side of the tub. Did she not say something similar to Ruolan the night before she died? *You never know how life can change in an instant*, or something like that. Fei sighed and nodded. She would live...for now. She let Lina wrap her feet and get her dressed. Then she let Yuying read to her until she fell asleep. Yes, she would continue living for now. But if the emperor came for her again, she did not know how she would survive.

NINETEEN

The emperor stood up from the tub, steaming water falling from his body. He stepped onto a rug, and Wangzhu rushed forward, wrapping a towel around his waist. The eunuch then came forward with a jar of scented oil to rub over the emperor's body, but the emperor slapped Wangzhu's hand away, sending the jar smashing to the floor.

"Leave me," the emperor barked. Wangzhu did as he was ordered, bowing his way out of the washing room and closing the door behind him. The emperor rubbed the towel over his long, sleek hair that hung nearly to his waist and then tossed the towel to the floor. He stepped in front of a tall mirror, one that showed his full length, and liked what he saw.

The emperor was still a young man, he drank little and was careful with his food. He would not soon run to fat as his father did after only a few years on the throne.

But then he noticed a red mark running across his shoulder that he had not seen before. He stepped closer to the mirror to get a better look. It was a scratch, as though from a woman's fingernail. He then noticed another across his stomach. As he turned, he found one deep enough in his back that it was bleeding. He slammed his fist into the mirror, causing it to crack. Now, instead of one scratch across his shoulder, he saw dozens. He grabbed the mirror and shoved it to the floor, sending the glass pieces scattering.

"Ungrateful whores," the emperor snarled. "I bless them with my body, and they thank me by marring my perfect form?"

Wangzhu opened the door and surveyed the mess. He clapped his hands and a lesser eunuch appeared. "Clean this up before His Majesty cuts himself," he ordered. The eunuch nodded and shuffled away to collect the cleaning materials.

"Who did this?" the emperor asked Wangzhu, pointing to the scratch on his shoulder.

"I wouldn't know, Your Majesty," Wangzhu said. "I averted my eyes during your...husbandly duties with the concubines."

"Then retire all of them," the emperor said as he stepped from the room and held his arms out for Wangzhu to place a robe around him. The emperor pulled the sash tightly around himself and walked to his dressing room, where several more eunuchs were preparing his clothes and accouterments for the day.

"Retire them?" Wangzhu asked, doing his best to hide his disgust. "Any one of them could be with child. It would be best if we waited for a full moon cycle before making any changes to their station."

"You know they are not!" the emperor screamed at

Wangzhu. The other eunuchs all moved as far away from the emperor as they could and fell to the floor in a kowtow. But Wangzhu stood his ground. He lowered his eyes, but not his body.

"I am a worthless, impotent man," Hongdi said as he stomped toward Wangzhu. "Worse than a eunuch! At least cutting your manhood was a requirement for your position. What good is a complete body if I cannot beget my own heir?"

Hongdi's nostrils were flaring as he stared his servant down, but Wangzhu did not flinch. He did not move. He did not speak until he gave the emperor a moment to calm himself.

"You are far from impotent," Wangzhu finally said. The emperor scoffed and turned away from him, burying his face in his hands.

"Then what am I?" Hongdi asked. "If I cannot continue the Ming Dynasty, what am I?"

"You are the emperor," Wangzhu said. "And, eventually, the gods will bless you."

"Even after what I did last night?" Hongdi asked. He shook his head and held it in shame. He was horrified by his own actions. When he closed his eyes, all he could see was Fei as she cried and shook beneath him, her body wracked with terror. Of all the concubines and consorts he had taken, no woman had caught his eye like she did, except for Empress Wen. He had prayed to the ancestors that Fei would pass the rest of her examination process and become one of his concubines. He had hoped that she would be the one to carry his first son.

But last night...He knew that after last night, she would never smile at him again. She would never trust him.

He wasn't sure why he had done it. He knew it was wrong. That he would ruin everything with Fei if he took her. But he couldn't stop himself. Day after day, Empress Wen, his mother, Ruolan, they had taken every opportunity to undermine him as an emperor and a man. He had to remind them just who he was and that their place was beneath him.

"After a moon cycle," the emperor said, "retire the women from last night."

Wangzhu pressed his lips together in a tight frown, but he still forced himself to say, "Yes, Your Majesty."

"Except...except for Song Fan," the emperor said.

Wangzhu said nothing to this except to bow as he went to his office to make a note of the emperor's orders.

Hongdi then cleared his throat and stood upright. He saw that his dressing room eunuchs were still kowtowing on the floor.

"What are you waiting for?" he said to them. "Get back to work."

They all quickly jumped up and prepared the emperor for the day.

❀

"As you can see, Your Majesty," the chief builder of the Forbidden City said as he walked beside the emperor along the outside balcony of the Hall of Imperial Peace at the expansive garden below, "the building work on at least half of the Forbidden City is complete, including the household palaces of the imperial family."

"A little too late," the emperor grumbled as he thought about Ruolan betraying him with one of the workers.

The chief builder began to sweat, and not from being in

the direct sunlight. "The remainder of the city is completely mapped out, and groundbreaking has begun on each section," he rattled on, hoping to avoid any unpleasant conversations. He knew he was lucky that the emperor only punished the boy and not him as the boy's supervisor. Though, how Yang Chow would have found an opportunity to seduce the concubine, he couldn't begin to imagine.

The builder pointed to the various buildings they could see from their vantage point that were under construction.

"The Palace of Cherishing Essence. The Palace of Consecrated Beauties. And in the distance, The Chamber of Joyful Longevity. And those are only the ones we can see. There are dozens more in the works. A palace of shimmering gold stretching as far as the eye can see. Your Majesty, it will be the most splendid palace the world has ever seen."

The emperor placed his hands on the low wall that ran along the balcony and felt a smile tug at his lips. It was certainly glorious. Would that he could build a tower tall enough that he could see all of China.

"It is truly excellent," the emperor said, and the builder let out an exhale of relief.

"Thank you, Your Majesty," the builder said. "And wait until you see everything up close. The best craftsmen from around the country have been brought in to carve and paint elaborate reliefs on every beam. There—" He pointed into the distance. "—will be a stone wall of such opulence. Taller than three men and ten times as long, nine imperial dragons will be carved both to protect the Forbidden City from evil spirits and to sing of your magnificence. Everyone who sees it will be rendered mute in awe."

The emperor chuckled. "Well, if they are rendered mute, how will they be able to sing my praises?"

The chief builder laughed heartily, wanting nothing more than to remain in the emperor's good graces.

"How long?" the emperor asked.

"I have approved the plans for the dragon wall, but it is not a priority, as more palaces and temples and housing for the servants are needed—"

"No," the emperor said. "I mean for all of it. Everything. How long until the building work will be completed?"

The builder cleared his throat to buy himself a moment before answering. "My men are working as quickly as possible, Your Majesty, you have my assurance on that."

"I am sure I do," the emperor said, turning toward the builder, crossing his arms across his chest. "How long?"

"Perhaps another...ten—"

The emperor frowned.

"*Seven* years...Maybe...maybe five..."

"Five more years of this dust and noise?" the emperor asked. "You have already been working on it for three years. I cannot wait another five years before inviting foreign dignitaries to quake before my magnificent palace."

The builder wiped the sweat from his brow. "I understand, Your Majesty," he said. "I, too, am anxious to see the final result of the work of so many dedicated servants."

The emperor narrowed his gaze at the builder. "This is unacceptable. Your men should work faster."

"They are already working from dawn to dusk," the builder said. "And with winter coming, we will have far fewer daylight hours in which to work. I do not see how I can make my men more productive than they have been. Each one is greatly honored to be building this palace for you. I assure you, they are working as quickly as they can."

"Then you need more men," the emperor said.

"I have spent every cent of the hiring budget, Your

Majesty," the builder explained. "I could not hire more men without more money."

"How many more men would you need in order to complete the building in only two years?" the emperor asked.

The builder sputtered. He was already stretching the truth by saying that the building work would be completed in five years. He could not imagine completing the work in only two! It would be impossible. It was not simply a matter of hiring more men, but he himself was only one person. He would not be able to oversee that the work was being done correctly if too many men were working on too many projects at the same time.

"I-I-I do not know, Your Majesty," he said. "I would have to calculate how fast the men could work and how many projects we could complete at the same time. And not just unskilled laborers. I would need more foremen, more craftsmen, people who would require a higher salary—"

"How many?" the emperor asked, doing his best not to lose his temper with the man who he knew had been slaving away on the palace tirelessly for years already.

"Perhaps...a thousand men," the builder said, his voice so soft the emperor could hardly hear him. "A thousand men?" the emperor asked as he looked around at the group of ministers and servants who were following him and laughed. "Is that all?" Everyone laughed, though no one knew why.

"Are there not more than fifty million people in China?" the emperor asked of no one in particular.

"More than sixty," one of the ministers familiar with a census held a few years before clarified.

"Surely, it cannot be difficult to find a thousand more workers in a country such as mine," the emperor said.

"It is not a matter of finding men," the builder said, "but of money to pay them."

"I see," the emperor said. "Where is the minister of finance?"

"Here, Your Majesty," a thin and studious looking man said, stepping forward from the group.

"See to it that the chief builder here is given the funds he needs to hire the workers he requires," the emperor said, then he turned to continue his walk.

"It would be impossible," the finance minister said.

"What?" the emperor asked, turning back to the minister.

"We simply don't have the funds for more workers," the minister said. "The costs for the Forbidden City have been astronomical already. We have had to divert funds from the military, from agriculture, from nearly every other aspect of government to pay for what has already been built."

"Then raise taxes," the emperor said simply.

"The people have already been taxed in the extreme," the finance minister said, looking to the new governor of Peking. But the governor said nothing, lest he follow in the path of his predecessor.

The emperor nodded. He remembered how he and his family had been accosted by rioters when he first arrived in the city, their chief complaint being that of taxes.

"I had hoped to keep the tax increases limited to Peking," the emperor said. "But I now see how foolhardy that was. One city cannot support an entire government. Raise taxes on the top ten wealthiest cities in the country."

"Your Majesty," the finance minister said cautiously, stepping closer so he could lower his voice. "While taxing other cities might help ease the burden here, we would hate to see outbreaks of unrest as we have seen here spread to other cities."

"You think that the other cities will not find it a great privilege and honor to provide for a new palace that will be the envy of the world?" the emperor asked.

"No," the finance minister said. "I don't, Your Majesty. They will resent it heartily."

The emperor pressed his lips as he turned away from the ministers and looked out over the partially built palace again. Once again, he could find no support from the very people who were supposed to obey his every order. And these were not foolish women, but his own men, his ministers and advisors.

"Then what would you advise?" the emperor finally asked, hoping someone had a workable suggestion to this problem.

"Slow the building process," the finance minister said. "Instead of building it in five years, plan for the construction to complete in ten years, or even twenty—"

"Twenty!" the emperor yelled, facing the finance minister. The minister hesitated, but then he continued.

"If we slow the building work, the money will last much longer," he said. "We will be able to not only avoid raising taxes, but we could lower them, which would go a long way toward placating the people."

"The people are stupid," the emperor said. "What can peasants know of what it takes to rule the largest kingdom in the world?"

The finance minister cleared his throat but did not continue. He knew there was no way to convince the emperor of the wisdom in slowing the work.

"The people will be placated when the work is

complete," the emperor went on. "When they see what their money has built."

"I am not sure they will see the Forbidden City as you do, Your Majesty," the finance minister said.

The emperor had had enough of the minister's impertinence. He grabbed the minister by the collar and dragged him to the low wall around the balcony.

"How would you like to see the Forbidden City from a new vantage point?" the emperor asked. He lifted the small man upon the wall and dangled him over the side. The other ministers, guards, and servants who were present all yelled in shock for the emperor to stop.

"Please!" the finance minister begged. "Forgive my impertinence!"

"Do you appreciate the palace I have built now?" the emperor yelled, shaking the minister, letting him slip down the side of the wall a little further.

"Yes! Yes, of course! It is magnificent!" the minister cried. The others gathered around held their breath, certain the emperor was going to drop the minister.

"And you will make sure to find the money, and ensure that those taxed will be grateful for the privilege?" the emperor asked.

"Yes! Yes!" the minister said as he sobbed. "Whatever you want! I am only your faithful servant!"

The emperor chuckled and then pulled the finance minister back up the wall, tossing him to the floor of the balcony. The finance minister was shaking as he got to his knees and kowtowed to the emperor.

"Was that so hard?" the emperor asked. The finance minister only shook his head. The emperor smirked and then walked away. Some of the other ministers and servants rushed to the finance minister's side.

But then the emperor heard the minister groaning.

"He is clutching his heart!" one person said.

"Someone fetch the palace doctor!" another cried out.

The emperor did not turn back, but instead quickened his pace. He had more work to do.

TWENTY

*T*he empress sat in her chair on the raised dais in her personal audience hall, looking out over the throng of consorts, concubines, maids, and other ladies of the court. They were unnaturally quiet, each one holding tightly to the hand of her maid or the lady sitting next to her. They were all still under orders to remain in their palaces, the morning audience with the empress being the only exception. But even though this was the only time the ladies could freely associate with one another, few seemed to feel like talking.

All of the women were on edge. Terrified of doing or saying anything that might lead them to lose favor with the emperor—even though none of them seemed to be in his favor at present. The emperor had not continued his rampage against the girls, but neither had he returned to the bed of the empress.

Today, the empress held in her hand the order to send the women the emperor had taken in his fit of rage into retirement—all except Song Fei. It seemed that the empress's plan to keep the emperor from the girl, and to use her friendship with Ruolan to drive a wedge between them, had failed. In spite of everything that had happened, it appeared that Fei still held a special place in the emperor's heart.

Though, it would be impossible to know that by looking at Fei now. Even weeks after she was attacked by the emperor, the fear was clear on her face, even though the bruise he had left behind was mostly faded. She sat alone, her attendants protectively standing to either side, her head down as to avoid eye contact with anyone.

The empress finally cleared her throat and called the ladies to attention for the audience to begin.

"I have sorrowful news," the empress said, not knowing how to soften the blow that was coming. "The following ladies are to be sent into retirement." She then read the names of four of the women who had been attacked by the emperor. Each in their turn burst into tears at the cruelty of it, but they all stopped when they realized that Fei's name had not been called.

Everyone knew what had happened that night. Which ladies had been the victims of the emperor's wrath. It was impossible not to know. The women all went quiet as they looked from the empress to Fei and back to the empress. Even Fei raised her eyes and looked at the empress expectantly, waiting for her name to be called. But the empress only folded the missive back up, handing it to Bojing.

"You will be taken to your new quarters as soon as the audience has ended," the empress said.

"But...what about Song Fei?" Lady Sui, one of the now-retired concubines, said as she stood. "She is no longer a virgin either. Why has she not been retired?"

"It is not our place to question the wisdom of the emperor," Empress Wen said.

Lady Sui spat on the floor. "Wisdom! Don't speak to me of the nobility of the emperor. He left marks on my back that have yet to heal."

"Lady Sui," the empress said, doing her best to remain calm. In truth, she did not blame Lady Sui, or any of them, for their hurt and anger. But she could not allow the women to speak ill of the emperor. It would not help any of them. "You are walking on perilous ground. Sit down and be silent."

"No," Lady Sui said, holding her chin up. "I'll remain silent no longer. What the emperor did was wrong. Sending me into retirement at sixteen years of age is wrong."

"Take her away," the empress said, motioning to Bojing. Bojing nodded and waved to some of his assistants to lead Lady Sui away.

"Then take me away as well," Lady Kun, one of the other retired concubines, said, also getting to her feet. "I'll not sit here and listen to you blather on for another moment while our lives are forfeited."

"Very well," the empress said, nodding to the eunuchs. They took Lady Sui and Lady Kun by their arms and removed them from the audience hall, their servants following behind.

"Anyone else?" the empress asked, looking over the crowd. The other two ladies who had been ordered into retirement looked at each other, then stood and left of their own volition. The empress clasped her hands together tightly until they were gone. Once the doors closed behind them, everyone turned to Fei to see what she would do.

Fei's cheeks burned, feeling every eye in the room upon her. But she kept her head down, her eyes trained on the embroidered kerchief that she twisted in her hands. She knew she should be among the women who had been retired. She had no idea why the emperor had spared her. She wished he hadn't. If he kept her in the Inner Court, he must have plans to return to her eventually. The mere thought of seeing him again, of looking into his face, of feeling his hands on her body made her ill.

"Let us continue," the empress said when she was satisfied that Fei was not going to leave. Not that she had much more to say. There were no upcoming activities for the ladies. No trips to the country palace. No afternoons on the lake. No festivities planned for the Spirit Festival. The ladies were to all stay in their rooms unless the emperor summoned them—and everyone doubted that he had any plans to summon them, except possibly for Fei.

The empress finally stood and dismissed the girls to return to their palaces. The women all gave the empress a half-kowtow and blessing and then quietly left the audience hall.

"You should have the girls who were taken away or walked out punished," Empress-Dowager Chun said to Empress Wen when all the girls were gone.

"Haven't they been punished enough by being retired?" Wen said.

"The retirement is punishment for failing to provide an heir," Chun said. "Their disrespect for you is another matter entirely. Speaking back? Denying your authority? Leaving without being dismissed? How can you allow such disrespect? No wonder the emperor is displeased with you and the whole Inner Court. You are a shameful excuse for an empress."

"I have done everything in my power to support the emperor and maintain harmony here," Wen said through clenched teeth. "The concubines are barely holding onto their sanity as it is. Do you know how many letters home to their families I had to intercept of them begging to return home?"

"You should have chosen girls with stronger constitutions," Chun said. "You should have submitted your body to your husband. Everything that has gone wrong within the palace is of *your* making."

Wen shook her head. "You know that is not true. I could not have stopped what happened—"

"You were the cause of what happened!" Chun said, pointing a long, boney finger at Wen. "You made the mistake of loving him. Of letting him love you. This is what comes when people fall out of love. Nothing but chaos and ruin. He should have been given a girl who would have done her duty as a wife and no more."

"Someone had to love him if you weren't going to," Wen said, choking back tears.

"It's never your fault, is it?" Chun asked. "There is always someone else to blame for your shortcomings. One day, Wen, one day, all your failures will be laid bare, and then not even your father will be able to save you."

With that, the dowager turned and left the audience hall, not waiting to be dismissed either.

Wen slapped her hand to her mouth to stifle her sobs. How she hated the dowager-empress. The woman had always been cold to everyone, not just Hongdi. She had been a strict empress when she ruled over the Inner Court, never bending the rules for anyone or anything. Wen had always feared the woman growing up, and when she was old enough to understand that she would be married to Hongdi, the only worry she had was having to submit to Chun as her mother-in-law. She thought that things would get better after she became empress, but the woman's stinging barbs only seemed to hurt even more.

When she was finally done crying, she wiped her eyes with a kerchief and then rode in her sedan chair back to her own palace. When she entered, and excited maid ran up to her, brandishing a letter.

"My lady!" the maid said. "This was given to me by one of the eunuchs when I went to collect your tea allowance this morning."

Wen took the letter from the girl eagerly, ripping it open as soon as she saw that it was from her father.

Daughter,

your letter caused me great distress. It disconcerting to hear how brutal the emperor has become. His change of heart toward his ladies had not gone unnoticed. It would appear that some of the other women have reached out to their families as well, all sharing similar stories. The public opinion of the emperor has dropped like a stone into an already turbulent sea. It has caused ripples, but none bigger than the dissatisfaction many already feel over his rule. I wish there were something I could do about his mistreatment of you and the other women. But you are merely that—women. A man has the right to handle his wife and concubines how he sees fit. While there are some who would be interested in talking about a possible coup, it will not be for the sake of a few spoiled girls.

Do not write to me of this matter again until you have information I can use.

General Kang.

Wen scoffed and tossed the letter into a brazier, watching it go up in smoke.

"Mere women," she mumbled to herself. "I will show you what mere women can do."

"My lady?" Bojing said.

"My father says that the people are turning against the emperor," Wen said.

Bojing nodded slowly. "Is this a good thing?"

"Before we moved to Peking?" Wen said. "I would have cut your tongue out for even suggesting such a thing."

"And now?"

"Did you hear that the emperor caused the death of the finance minister?" she said.

"He had a heart attack," Bojing said. "A sudden tragedy."

"Fortunate for Hongdi the man didn't actually fall," Wen said. "He seems to always have a convenient explanation or excuse for his...mad actions."

"You think the emperor is losing his grip on reality?" Bojing asked.

"Isn't he?" Wen asked. "He is hiring thousands more workers than we can afford. According to the new finance minister, the empire will run out of money by winter's end. If we cannot buy grain from the south, those of us in the north will surely starve to death. The emperor will not even live to see the completion of his great palace."

"But what can be done?" Bojing asked.

"I don't know," Wen said. "Not yet. Father seemed to intimate that with the right piece of information, the nobles could be turned against the emperor."

"War?" Bojing asked.

"Perhaps not," Wen said. "Perhaps my father could take the emperor's place."

"There are reasons why he did not take the throne in the first place," Bojing said. "He has never been popular among the people."

"Then he could prop someone else up," Wen said.

"Who?" Bojing asked.

"I don't know!" the empress grunted, pushing her way past him so she could pace the room and think. "It doesn't matter. If we can't turn the nobles against him, we won't have enough support to overthrow him anyway."

Wen nearly chocked on her words. She never imagined she would be plotting to ruin her husband. The man she had loved since girlhood. But she could not sit idly by and allow him to destroy the empire her father and his had built together.

"Then what information do you have that your father could use?" Bojing asked. "You have known the emperor your whole life. Have been closer to him than anyone. If he has any secrets, you are the only person who would know them."

Wen shook her head. "There is nothing. Until now, he was a filial son, an excellent student, a kind husband. Other than what he has done recently, I could never speak a bad word against him."

"Then we must look elsewhere," Bojing said.

"Where?" Wen asked. "His father is dead. His brothers are far away. Who else would have enough knowledge or power to undo the emperor?"

"What about his mother?" Bojing asked.

"The dowager-empress?" Wen said. "Well, if anyone knows more about Hongdi than I do, it would be her. But I can't imagine what. She was a terrible mother. From what I have heard, she neglected Hongdi nearly from the moment he was born. I have only ever seen her be hard on him."

"All families have dark secrets," Bojing said. "It might not be something about the emperor that could ruin him, but something his parents did."

The empress sighed and shook her head as she continued to pace. What could Hongdi's father have done that could ruin his son?

"There is something the old bat said," the empress mused. "What was it? Something about a curse."

"A curse, my lady?"

"Yes," Wen said, doing her best to recall what the dowager had said. "She was certain that Ruolan could not be pregnant because there was a curse of some sort on the family. One that would prevent a child from being born."

"A curse on Hongdi?" Bojing asked.

"I don't know," Wen said. "She wouldn't elaborate. And I can't ask her about it. The crone would never confide in me. Oh, it's hopeless. Even if Chun does have information that we could use, she'd never reveal it."

"Perhaps she already has," Bojing said, a wry smile on his face.

Wen crossed her arms. "What do you know?" she asked.

"Only what every good eunuch knows, my lady," he said. "That every person has a price."

"But the dowager-empress could never be bought," Wen said.

"Not the dowager-empress," Bojing said. "But Donghai, her eunuch. He has served the empress since before Hongdi was born. She trusts him implicitly."

"But can he be bought?" Wen asked.

"Not with coins," Bojing said. "But with something far more precious."

TWENTY-ONE

"*W*hat could a eunuch like Donghai value more than money?" Empress Wen asked. "He is the most powerful man in the Forbidden City, save the emperor and Wangzhu."

"He values what all eunuchs do," Bojing said. "The one thing we do not have that makes real men."

The empress raised an eyebrow and looked down the front of Bojing, then back to his face. "You mean...his manhood?" she asked. Bojing gave a single nod. "I don't understand."

"I will explain," Bojing said. "You are about to learn what few people outside of the eunuch community care to know. When we are castrated, our manhood is kept in a special jar. A *bao* jar."

"A precious jar?" Wen asked. "Why is it called that?"

"Because nothing is more precious to us," Bojing explained. "The jar is sealed with wax and tagged with our names. The jar is then kept here, in the Forbidden City, in the administration hall for imperial eunuchs.

"In order to advance in our career, we must take various

exams. Each time we appear for an exam, we must present our *bao* jar. If we do not have it, we cannot improve our lives."

The empress shrugged. "Well, what good is that? Donghai cannot advance any higher than he already has."

"That is not all," Bojing said. "When we die, we all long to be buried with our *bao* jar. We must be complete for burial so that we can be restored in the afterlife. Without it, Jun Wang, the king of the underworld, will reincarnate us as female donkeys."

"You really believe this?" Wen asked, her eyes wide. She was surprised to hear such a fantastical tale from her usually logical servant.

"I have to," Bojing said. "A son is most filial when he has a son to carry on his family's lineage. In this life, I have already failed since I can never have children."

"But it was for a noble purpose," Wen said. "Your family was so poor, they would have starved without your salary from becoming a palace eunuch."

Bojing nodded. "It was for my family, yes. But only for a short-term gain. Very materialistic. What good is food when the family line will end in a generation anyway?"

Wen could not respond to that. She could not see the logic in it. But then, she had never had to make such a terrible choice. She had never been poor. Never been hungry a day in her life. She had endless coins to donate to monks and nuns to pray her soul to Heaven after death.

"When I am dead, I have no hope to be reincarnated into a better life," Bojing continued. "For failing in my family duty, I am destined to come back as a lesser creature. But at least I can be something better than a wretched female. Then, someday, perhaps I will be blessed to have children of my own and earn the approval of the Celestial Beings."

Wen shook her head as she considered this. What a sad life, where your only hope was to die and come back as something more than a donkey. She knew eunuchs were paid well, and many of them volunteered for the operation that would provide them with such a stable salary for the whole of their lives. She didn't realize how pitiful they truly were.

"So," Wen finally said when she could speak again, "you are saying that Donghai would still have reason to value his *bao* jar."

"Precisely," Bojing said. "We cannot blackmail him into telling us anything about the emperor or his family. He has served the imperial family longer than almost anyone else. He has made mistakes, yes. Mistakes that would cost other eunuchs their life. But he is too powerful. He has too many allies, including the dowager-empress."

"And we could not torture him for the same reason," Wen said. "If he were to go missing for even a moment, the empress would be frantic searching for him. So, we need some other way to convince him to talk. This *bao* jar. But still, I don't see how this helps us."

"I propose that we steal Donghai's *bao* jar," Bojing said. "As soon as he knows you have it, he will be subject to your every whim."

"Are you certain?" Wen asked. "If I threaten him and fail, he could turn against me. Turn the dowager against me. She already despises me. But if she finds out that I hurt her precious Donghai, she would not stop harassing me until I am the one the emperor sends to the executioner's scaffold."

"I am certain, Your Majesty," Bojing said. "I know it must seem shocking to you, but Donghai will do nothing to risk his *bao* jar. None of us would. No matter how satisfying his life is now, he will not risk being reincarnated as a donkey —a *female* donkey at that!"

Wen paced, still not sure she could believe that Donghai would betray a woman he had served for almost forty years because of an old chunk of flesh in a terracotta jar.

"You realize that if you are wrong, both of us will be given white kerchiefs?" Wen said.

"I know," Bojing said with a nod of his head. "But there is no other way to convince Donghai to cooperate with you. If you want your father to be able to overthrow your husband, we must procure Donghai's *bao* jar."

Wen sank onto a chair, Bojing's words like a physical weight on her shoulders. "I don't know if I can. Has it truly come this far? Could I betray my husband? My emperor? Heaven itself?" She shook her head. "No, I do not think I can. I loved him once...I love him still. I cannot do this."

"If you have any doubt," Bojing said, "then I agree, we should not do this. While I am confident that procuring the *bao* jar will work in getting Donghai to spill his secrets, I cannot promise that the plan will not backfire somehow. It will be risking your life."

The empress stood. "Then there will be no more talk of this. Leave me."

Bojing bowed his way out of the room. As soon as he was gone, Wen slumped down onto her chair again, her hand to her mouth. She felt ill. How could she even consider such actions? She was being foolish. Risking everything. Yes, Hongdi had made some bad choices, but what emperor didn't? He had been under enormous stress with the move to Peking and the building of the Forbidden City, the accusations against Ruolan, and neighboring empires pressing in on all borders. This was not a time to try and ruin her husband, but a time to help him.

Wen called for her maid and ordered her to take a message to Wangzhu for the emperor. She would beg for his forgiveness. Tell him how much she missed him. How she longed for him. She wrote the note quickly, then held it to her heart, saying a prayer over it, hoping Hongdi would feel her love for him radiate from the page.

She waited in anxious expectation for his response.

❦

*I*n the twilight of the day, Empress-Dowager Chun rode in her sedan chair to the Hall of Rectitude, the main temple of the Forbidden City. When Chun arrived at the temple, Donghai assisted his lady in walking inside. But once she was through the main door, he stood guard to prevent anyone else from entering. Usually, the temple would be filled with ladies praying, reading, and receiving blessings from the monks. But ever since the emperor had confined the concubines and consorts to their palaces, the temple was nearly empty. There were some maids milling about who had been tasked with praying for their mistresses, but they were quickly dismissed by the monks when they saw the dowager-empress enter.

"My lady," a very old monk in a long robe said as he shambled toward the dowager, his hands extended.

"Lama Samten," the empress said as she took his hands in hers, her eyes welling with tears that she fought to hold back. "It has been too long."

The lama nodded. "Indeed. The temple took longer to complete than we had originally been told. Then the trek here was quite jarring for these old bones."

The dowager grimaced in commiseration. "Terribly long journey. But, in truth, I think my husband would be glad to know that his dream for a northern temple was finally fulfilled."

Lama Samten nodded. "The palace is remarkable. And this temple—" He waved his hand around the room. "—is far more than I could have ever dreamed of."

But it was not the tapestries, the statue of the Buddha that stood taller than five men in the middle of the room, or the sacred scrolls the empress had come to see.

"Were you able to bring it?" the dowager asked.

The lama's eyes sparkled. "Of course, my lady." The dowager sighed in relief. The lama placed his arm around her shoulder and led her through an archway in the back of the room to a locked door. The lama removed a single key from a gold chain around his neck and unlocked the door. He then escorted the dowager into the room, securing the door closed behind them.

The room was dark, with no windows, but there was a fire in a low brazier, along with several candles burning, making the room stiflingly warm. The room was filled with smoke from the flames and from countless incense sticks. At one end of the room was an altar adorned with candles, incense, oranges, bowls of water and food, a flower vase with fresh flowers, and jade carvings of buffalo and elephants. At the back of the altar was a statue of Guanyin, her gentle face watching over an item in the center of the altar that was covered by a red silk cloth.

The dowager kneeled on a pillow in front of the altar and folded her hands in front of her. Lama Samten then lifted the cloth, revealing an ancestor tablet with the name Dewei carved into it, along with the names of the person's ancestors.

The dowager sucked in a breath when she saw the tablet. It had been so long since she had last seen it because it had to be moved in secret. The tears she had been holding back finally fell from her eyes, then she began to recite a prayer as she repeatedly bowed to the tablet, making sure her forehead touched the ground each time.

Lama Samten stood aside silently so as not to interrupt the dowager. After she had bowed the traditional nine times, she then performed her prostrations again to atone for the prayers she had been unable to perform while the tablet was still in the south.

Finally, the empress completed her prayers and nodded for the lama to cover the tablet once again. He then helped the elderly woman to her feet and led her out of the room, locking the door behind them and hiding the key within his robe.

"Did you have any trouble moving it?" the dowager asked as she and the lama took a slow turn around the main temple room.

"Not at all, my lady," the lama said. "I had many other tablets to transport as well, so it hardly seemed out of place."

"But you are sure no one saw it?" she asked. She knew that asking the lama to make the tablet in the first place had been dangerous, but her guilt and sorrow over the loss of her baby, Dewei, Hongdi's twin, had become too much for her to bear. She couldn't accept that her son might be lost in the afterlife, or trapped in the bodily realm as a hungry ghost. She struck up a close friendship with the lama and finally asked him to create and then guard the tablet for her. The loyal monk had kept his lady's secret for over thirty years.

"I am certain," the lama said, taking the dowager's hand

in his and patting it reassuringly. "The other temple servants respect my authority and would never question me. No one else knows what is in that room. I told them it is simply your private prayer room and not to be disturbed."

The dowager nodded, but her heart was still unsettled. She knew that the tablet was dangerous. Proof of the secret she had kept buried for so many years. She knew the danger it posed for her son, the emperor, and for the empire. She did not love the boy, but she had lived through the last war and had no desire to see her country fall into mayhem once again—at least not while she was still alive. She knew that if Hongdi never had a son, war would be inevitable. But that was a trial for another generation.

"I need you to promise me something," the dowager said as she and the lama walked past a long wall of tiny statues, each one representing a different god or goddess.

"Anything, my lady," Lama Samten said.

"When I die, you must burn that tablet," she said.

"Are you certain?" the lama asked, slowing to a stop. "I can care for it even after you are gone. I can say your prayers and burn incense every day for the rest of my life if I must."

The dowager shook her head. "It is not enough. It must be destroyed. It is too dangerous to remain in this world."

Even though they had been talking in low voices, the lama now whispered, "But without a tablet, how will the spirit find its way to the afterlife?"

"I will be there to guide him," the dowager said, squeezing her friend's hand. "It is something I have looked forward to for the majority of my life. Only when I lead Dewei through the afterlife myself will I truly know that he is safe."

Lama Samten nodded. "I will obey your every wish, my lady."

The two finished their tour of the room in silence, not speaking again until they arrived back at the door and rejoined Donghai.

"The new temple is beautiful," the dowager said. "Thank you for showing it to me."

"I hope you will return to us soon, Your Majesty," the lama said with a respectful bow.

The dowager placed some coins into the lama's hand, and then Donghai escorted her back to her sedan chair, which carried her home through the dark and chill night.

TWENTY-TWO

*E*mpress Wen's heart was beating rapidly in her chest as she was carried in her sedan chair to the emperor's palace. He had received her missive and requested her presence. This was an excellent sign. They had not spoken in weeks, not since that dreadful night where he tried to take her by force and she had threatened to kill him if he did so. She had feared that their marriage had been rent beyond repair. But that Hongdi had accepted her request for an audience gave her hope that they could come to some sort of accord.

She had taken extra care with her preparation for seeing the emperor. She had used her best oils and lotions so her entire body was sweet-smelling. Her gown was a deep purple of the softest silk. Her ladies had brushed her hair one thousand times so it was straight and smooth, just how Hongdi had always liked it. She wore very little face paint save for some crushed rose petals on her cheeks and a tincture on her lips that made them appear plump and red. She used eye drops of belladonna to make her pupils large like a deep, dark sea. She could not remember the last time she had taken such effort with her appearance for a night with the emperor. Usually, they fell into each other's arms swiftly and easily without such pomp and circumstance. There was no need to play the game of seduction when each of them was always so anxious to feel the touch of the other.

Wen felt a fluttering in her stomach as her sedan chair halted that she had not felt in some time. She could not believe that she was anxious about seeing and, hopefully, sleeping with the man she had already been having relations with for nearly fifteen years. But necessity required change. Things had altered—degraded—drastically between the empress and her emperor. If they hoped to find their way back to each other, perhaps they needed to start again. Go back to the days of their courtship, the dance of seduction, remember their love for one another.

Wen entered the emperor's bedchamber and was disappointed to find he was not there.

"Please, have some wine," Wenzhou instructed her. "The emperor is still attending to urgent matters and will be with you shortly."

Wen nodded her thanks and once the eunuch was gone, she did indeed pour herself a large goblet of wine to calm her nerves. She finished the drink quickly and was soon feeling warm and more relaxed. She shed her outer robe and draped it over the foot of the bed. Wearing only a thin shift, she climbed into the emperor's bed to await his arrival.

❦

Several hours—and many shed tears—later, the emperor finally threw opened the door to his bedchamber.

"What is it you want?" the emperor asked abruptly.

Wen sat up, holding the sheet to her chest. "Your Majesty," she sputtered, flustered at his sudden arrival after having given up that he would come to her at all.

"Why are you in my bed?" Hongdi asked her.

"I...I thought..." Why did he think she was here, dressed as she was, so late at night?

"Well, you thought wrong," the emperor said when she was unable to finish her reply. He stepped to the end of the bed and grabbed her robe, balling it up, and then tossed it at her. "Get dressed."

Wen climbed out of bed and wrapped the robe around herself, pulling the sash taught. "Your Majesty, my love," she said, finding her voice. "I've missed you. Please, can we not make amends?"

"Amends?" Hongdi spat as though she had insulted him. "You mean nothing to me now. You are empress in name only. Were it not for your family, I would replace you in an instant." He snapped his fingers and Wen winced as though he had slapped her. Her mouth fell agape as she was once again unsure of how to respond. She was angry, yes. Hurt even more. But she knew that if she let her feelings show, any chance of reconciliation would be lost. She sank to her knees.

"I beg of your forgiveness, my love," she said, casting her eyes low, not quite to the floor, but to Hongdi's feet. "I overstepped my boundaries. Made your life more difficult. I am sorry for that and vow to never undermine you again. Please, take pity on me for my heart is broken."

The emperor hmphed. "I never imagined you would humble yourself to me in such a way. You must certainly be worried for your position to be for my favor."

"I am only worried for you," Wen said, suddenly wondering if she *did* need to worry about her position. "For us. Our marriage was never one of only practicality or duty —but love. Passion. Devotion. That I have threatened our union has ruined me. I will do whatever it takes to mend the rift between us."

Hongdi was quiet for a long moment, and Wen was desperate to see the expression on his face, but she dared not raise her eyes from his feet. She longed to know if her words were having any effect. To see if his face still blazed with anger or had softened. But instead of finding out for herself, she waited.

Hongdi took a long stride toward Wen, and she felt her body tremble for fear that he would strike her, but he did not.

"Anything?" he asked her, his voice even.

At this, Wen did raise her eyes, slowly, to meet his. "Anything," she said, her voice nearly breathless with desire and anticipation. If only he would take her in his arms, hold her, caress her. She could verily feel the crush of his body atop her.

Hongdi took a partial step toward her, his left foot nearly touching her knee.

"Kiss my boot," he said, and Wen gasped.

"What?" she asked.

"No," he corrected. "Lick it. Every inch."

She glanced down at his foot, the one she had been staring at for so long and now saw as the disgusting thing it was. It was not dirty, of course. The emperor spent his days walking around a pristine palace where servants swept and polished constantly. But in principle, it was filthy. In homes that were not the Forbidden City, men and servants removed their shoes when entering a room. Only women with bound feet did not remove their shoes since their shoes were works of art that protected their precious lotus feet. For the emperor to ask her to kiss—no, lick his boot was an insult far greater than she could bear.

Wen did not speak. She did not defy him openly. But she could not lower herself to such an act. She sat on her knees, her back rigid, her mouth tight, her nostrils flaring with each breath. She would not do it. She would not submit to such an insult—even at the cost of her marriage.

"That is what I thought," Hongdi said, walking away from her and sitting on the bed. "You could never truly submit yourself to me. You think far too highly of yourself."

A single tear slid down Wen's face, and she was grateful the emperor was behind her and could not see it.

"Leave," Hongdi said. "And do not presume to message me again. If I ever have any desire to speak to you again, which is unlikely, *I* will send for *you*."

Wen stood, her knees weak from being bent for so long, but she willed herself to stand tall and straight.

"Yes, Your Majesty," she said, then she walked toward the door. When the door opened, she was shocked to see Song Fan standing there.

Fan's eyes went large, and she dropped to her knees. "Your Majesty," she said to the empress. The empress said nothing, but merely gave a slight nod of her head as she passed through the door and climbed into her sedan chair. Fan wondered if the empress and emperor had reconciled. Though, the empress certainly had not looked happy for the half-second Fan had seen her face. She recalled that when the emperor had attacked her, it was after he had had some sort of row with the empress. Her body trembled in fear that the same thing was about to happen again.

"Fan," the emperor said, and Fan flinched at the sound of his voice. "Come here."

Fan stood and stepped into the room, but she kept her

head down, afraid of making eye contact with a man she considered to be little more than a dangerous animal. When she heard the door close behind her, she nearly burst into tears knowing there was no escape.

"Come to me, Fan," the emperor said, patting the bed beside him.

Fan took small, shuffling steps toward him, her hips forced to sway side to side as she gently balanced on her bound feet. When she reached the bed, she sat uneasily on the very edge. She winced when she felt the emperor's warm touch on her cheek.

"It pains me to think that you are afraid of me," the emperor said, his voice gentle as he pulled his hand away. "I was—*am* so fond of you, Fan. I'll never forget how you tripped over yourself the first time I saw you." He chuckled at the memory. Fan only wanted to cry as she recalled the same incident. She had thought that he was so handsome. So charming. He had reminded her of a childhood friend. And she felt so fortunate that he chose her to pass to the next stage of the examination. She had never dreamed that she would be selected as an emperor's concubine. But at that moment, as he took her hand and pulled her to her feet, she wanted nothing more in the world.

But it had all been a dream. A dream that had turned into a nightmare. Her best friend was dead and she was confined to her quarters, alone. She feared that Ruolan's ghost would haunt the palace, wronged as she was and buried without honors. She could hardly sleep. When she closed her eyes, she saw either Ruolan's headless body or the snarling face of the emperor as he violated her body. She only slept when she grew so tired that she passed out. And even then, she did not sleep long.

"Look at me," the emperor ordered, and Fan forced her

eyes to rise and meet his. "You do not need to fear me. I... regret that our first night together was..."

He sighed, unable to find the words. An emperor was never wrong and never made mistakes, which made apologizing a most challenging task. He finally shook his head. "I wish to start over. Put all that has happened behind us and start again."

The emperor was being so kind, his voice so gentle, Fan was beginning to feel guilty for being afraid of him. But no matter how she tried, she could not will her stomach to soothe.

"I would like that too," Fan said, her voice barely above a whisper.

The emperor sighed in relief and smiled so broadly, his teeth shone. Once again, Fan had a brief memory of the boy she used to play with from across the river. She was not sure why the emperor reminded her so much of Shihong. Was it his smile? His nose? Something in his eyes? She wasn't sure, but she knew she was being ridiculous. What could an emperor possibly have in common with a poor village boy?

The emperor took Fan's jaw in his hand and he pulled her toward him, placing his lips on hers. It was not an unpleasant sensation, but it sent ripples through her body, ending in the deepest part of her stomach that caused her bile to boil. She ended the kiss, licking her lips and casting her eyes down.

"I'm sorry," she mumbled.

"Don't be," the emperor said.

"I...I just need to go slowly..." she tried to explain, but her voice died away.

The emperor laughed. "I do not think I could go much more slowly than that."

Fan nodded her head, afraid to look up lest the tears start to fall and she be unable to stop them.

"Fan," the emperor said breathily. "How I have wanted you..." He took her face in both of his hands and kissed her again. She did not pull away, but she closed her mouth tightly and held her back rigid. The emperor prodded her mouth with his tongue, forcing her lips to part, but he could not move her teeth. He moved one of his hands to her hair, lightly tugging, exposing her neck to him. He sucked on her lips, then kissed her chin, her jaw, then down her throat.

Fan's breathing came out in short bursts, which the emperor seemed to interpret as delight. Fan feared she was going to faint.

The emperor pushed Fan back onto the bed and untied her sash, running his hand inside her robe along her shift-covered body. She could feel the heat from his touch, and it nearly burned her like fire. She gasped in pain and moaned in fear, which seemed to only urge the emperor on as he kissed her chest and fondled her breasts.

When he reached for her legs, pulling them apart so he could enter her, she could take no more and screamed for him to stop.

"No! Please!" she cried as she placed her hand on his chest and pulled her knees together.

"No?" the emperor asked, looking confused. "Are...are you crying?"

Fan reached up and touched her cheeks. She had not realized she was crying before now.

"I...I'm sorry," she said.

"You should be," the emperor said, getting to his feet. "What more can I do? I left you alone for weeks. I let you stay in a huge palace all by yourself. I was slow and gentle."

The longer he spoke, the louder his voice became, and the more Fan shrank into herself.

"I'm sorry," was all she could say.

"You should be!" the emperor said as he grabbed Fei by the arm and dragged her across the room. "I have done everything I can to please you, and it is still not enough."

The emperor opened the door and tossed Fei out into the night, her elbows and knees scraping on the stone walkway.

Yuying ran to Fei's side, helping her to sit up.

"Ungrateful!" the emperor railed. "Any other husband and you would not be allowed to wallow in your sadness. You would be expected to perform your duty as a wife!"

Fei kneeled in spite of the pain, and Yuying kowtowed beside her.

"You are right," she said. "I am sorry. I am a worthless woman. Please forgive me."

"I am tired of women begging for my forgiveness after they have wronged me," he said. "Begone from my sight."

The emperor slammed the door, and Yuying helped Fei to her feet and into her sedan chair.

Back at her palace, Lina tended to Fei's wounds.

"I couldn't do it," Fei said, not even feeling the pain that normally accompanied healing tinctures on open wounds. "I tried, Lina. I tried. But when he touched me, I was so afraid."

"I don't blame you, my lady," Lina said, shaking her head as she worked. "He didn't even touch me and I fear the brute."

"What am I to do?" Fei asked. "He will surely retire me now, as he did the other girls."

"Maybe that would be a blessing," Lina said as she closed the tincture and then began applying small bandages to Fei's knees. "Then he'd never bother you again."

"I'd be alone forever," Fei said. "I would never be a wife and never have a child."

"You'd be no worse off than you are now," Lina said. "Perhaps better since you wouldn't have to live in fear of him calling you to his bed."

Fei shook her head and rubbed her brow. "I am not sure which life is worse. And those are my only two options."

Lina took Fei into her arms, but Fei's tears were spent.

That night, Fei finally slept of her own accord. Being awake was simply too difficult.

TWENTY-THREE

*a*s Bojing prepared to open the curtains to Empress Wen's sedan chair, he expected to find her saddened by the emperor's rejection. The empress did her best to hide her feelings in public, but in private, he knew her to be a sensitive and feeling woman. He would have to treat her gently after such a cruel dismissal by the emperor, whom Bojing knew the empress loved very much.

But when he opened the curtains, he was surprised to see that her face was hard, her eyes cold, her jaw set tight. She needed no assistance to exit the sedan chair, and even though she had to take small steps on her bound feet, she walked with quick determination as she entered her palace and headed directly for her study.

"Close the door," she ordered Bojing as he followed behind her. He did as she commanded. She sat at her writing table, and he kneeled nearby. "Tell me more about this *bao* jar. Where can we find it? How can we procure it?"

Bojing cleared his throat. "You are certain this is the path you wish to take?"

"I am the daughter of General Kang," she said. "My

father had just as much right to be emperor as Hongwu did. Father only stepped aside because he would rather be defending the country. Riding his horse. Tending his lands. He couldn't stand the idea of being cooped up inside, sitting for hours at endless audiences. Drinking and eating himself into an early grave. Which is exactly what happened. Hongwu and my father were the same age. Yet one is dead while the other is still in the peak of health."

"But if your father had been emperor," Bojing said cautiously, "you would not be empress. The title would eventually have passed to one of your brothers."

"True," Wen said. "I might not have been empress of China, but I certainly would have been married to a king or emperor of another nation to strengthen an alliance. In that case, my value would never have been taken for granted or trampled upon as my dear husband has done this night."

"The emperor does seem to have forgotten how much you helped him in the days of his youth," Bojing said.

The empress nodded and her eyes glistened as she remembered the years she spent helping him study, improving his calligraphy, holding him in her arms and comforting him when his mother would not. She shook her head, refusing to give way to sentiment. The man she once loved was gone. The man she married would never have struck her. Would never have taken a woman to his bed so brutally as he did the concubines. Would not put his own selfish desires ahead of the needs of his empire.

Hongdi needed an heir. He never should have killed Ruolan. While the empress supposed she could never have definitively proved that Ruolan's child was the emperor's, the need for an heir was so great she would have accepted the child wholeheartedly—as Hongdi should have. Wen never imagined Hongdi would sabotage perhaps his only chance to have a child and avoid a civil war upon his death —or possibly sooner. Once his health began to wane, enemies would amass at China's gates.

The emperor's actions were worrying on almost every front. The cost of building the Forbidden City was taxing the people to the breaking point. He was not only dealing cruelly with his women, but with his advisors as well. If Hongdi ever dared speak to her father the way he had with the Minister of Finance, General Kang would probably remove the emperor's head from his shoulders without a second thought. But then Kang would not be able to claim the dragon throne for himself or his sons. He would be caught and executed, as would the rest of the family— including the empress herself. Then the country would descend into war.

The emperor was ruining the country. Taxing it to the breaking point and alienating himself from his allies. He needed to be stopped, but in a way that would allow the empress and her family to step into his place. Which was why Empress Wen needed leverage. Information. She had to know if there was anything in Hongdi's family background that could be used to remove him from the throne.

"Enough," Empress Wen said to Bojing. This was not a time to reflect on the past, but a time to act in a way that would secure their future. "Tell me what must be done."

"The *bao* jars are stored in the Hall of Precious Treasures, the administrative building for the eunuchs," Bojing explained.

"I always wondered why the eunuch administration hall was called that," the empress said, doing her best to keep from laughing. "It is named for the...precious things that were removed from each of you."

"Yes, my lady," Bojing said, his face reddening.

"So, how do we find Donghai's *bao* jar?" the empress asked. "Can the guard be bribed?"

"I do not believe so," Bojing said. "As I said, we must have our *bao* jars in order to move up in rank and when we are buried. However, some eunuchs, if they fall on hard times, might be foolish enough to sell their jar. Therefore, when he has need of it, he, in turn, will need to buy another one. There is a significant problem with eunuchs buying and selling *bao* jars."

"There is a market for *bao* jars?" the empress asked. "This is most surprising."

Bojing nodded. "As such, the guardian of the *bao* jars is a man above reproach, one who cannot be bribed. If he were easily corruptible, he could be tempted to sell the countless *bao* jars in his care."

The empress nodded slowly. "I see. So what can we do?"

"The only option would be to steal it," Bojing said. "But it would be difficult. There is always a guard present. The room with the jars is locked. And there are thousands of eunuchs in the Forbidden City; thus, thousands of jars are in the storage room. The guardian keeps a record of all the jars and their locations. I would need to find the location of Donghai's jar in his record book."

The empress stood and paced her office. It would be complicated, and if they were caught, their plan would be ruined. Bojing at least would be punished, if not the empress herself.

"Then we must surprise the guardian in some way," the empress said. "That way, he will not be able to summon one of his assistants to take his place."

"I suppose we could cause him injury in some way," Bojing said. "Though, I know the guardian, Huzhou, well.

Killing him, an innocent man performing his duty, I could not do it."

"We could poison him," the empress said.

Bojing raised an eyebrow.

"The drops I use to make my pupils large," she said, "if ingested, it is poisonous. But you would have to take a large amount to die. In a smaller amount, it will make the person seem crazy. They will see things that aren't there."

Bojing nodded. "So, we could give him enough to make him ill. His assistants will take him to the infirmary. I could take his place. As the trusted servant of the empress, no one would suspect I might steal a *bao* jar. But that is exactly what I will do."

"When the guardian returns," the empress said, "will he notice the jar is gone?"

"Only if he looks for it," Bojing said. "But since Donghai cannot apply for any promotions, the guardian would not have a reason to do so until Donghai's death."

The empress squeezed and relaxed her hands several times as she thought the plan over. She did not see why it would fail, but the risks could be great. And it could all be for nothing. If Donghai did not know anything useful, or if he would rather die than betray the dowager, they would have stolen the *bao* jar for nothing.

Empress Wen felt a warm hand on her shoulder. She turned to see Bojing smiling broadly at her.

"It will work," he said with a confidence the empress did not feel.

"I believe you are right," the empress said. "But once we do this, there is no going back. Once we have betrayed the emperor, we must see the plan through. If we were ever caught, we would be executed without delay."

"Then we must act quickly," Bojing said. "We cannot

allow anyone else to catch wind of our plan lest the emperor hears of it."

"Very well," the empress said. She left her study and went to her dressing table. The empress took a jar of expensive tea and prepared two teacups. Then, into one of the cups, she dropped a copious amount of eye drops.

"Will he be able to taste it?" Bojing asked.

"It is a little bitter, but it should blend with the taste of the pu'er tea," Wen said. She then placed the teacups onto a tray, along with several sweet and savory cakes. "Let us just hope he is thirsty."

Bojing nodded and took the tray from the empress. He carefully crossed the palace grounds to the Hall of Precious Treasures.

"Something to help the guardian through the long night," Bojing said to a eunuch who was leaving the building as he arrived. The eunuch bowed to Bojing and held the door open for him. When Bojing stepped into the room, the guardian, Huzhou, smiled at seeing his friend.

"Bojing!" Huzhou called as Bojing placed the tray on a low table. "My friend. How pleasant and surprising to see you this evening."

Bojing gave Huzhou the fist-in-palm salute and a quick bow in greeting. "I thought you could use some warm tea to see you through the cold night. I was unable to sleep and made myself a calming brew. I thought we could share it and speak of our many troubles together."

"Sounds like a most pleasant way to pass the time," Huzhou said with a chuckle. He motioned toward a chair by the table. "Please, sit."

"This is for you," Bojing said, offering Huzhou the poisoned cup. "From the empress's personal tea store."

"Mmm," Huzhou said as he accepted the teacup,

holding it to his nose and breathing in the fragrance. "The empress likes a strong tea, I see."

Bojing nodded as he took his own cup and a sweet cake. "She used to. She was much busier when she was in the emperor's favor and needed it to help her stay awake to complete her work. But now, she has little more to do than sleep much of the time."

Huzhou sipped his tea and then sighed. "Excellent quality! But, yes, we are all aware of the strife between the emperor and the empress. All of us pray for a speedy reconciliation and for a son to be born. Nothing would heal the troubles of the country more quickly than a dragon heir."

Bojing nodded and drank more of his tea, which prompted Huzhou to drink more as well.

"It must be quite lonely here," Bojing observed.

"It can be," Huzhou said. "People only come here for one thing, and promotions do not come along very often. My assistants are sleeping now, but they will arrive at first light. Then I will be able to write letters to my family during a short break. My eldest sister is expecting another child. Perhaps you could bring me some of the empress's tea she is not using to send as a gift."

Bojing nodded, wondering how long it would be before the eyedrops took effect. "Yes, of course. I am sure she would appreciate that very much."

"My sister is fortunate to have married well. She has very expensive taste," Huzhou said with a laugh, slapping his knee. Bojing laughed as well, but was also growing increasingly nervous. It would soon be dawn and Huzhou's assistants would arrive, making it impossible to steal the *bao* jar.

"Would you like a cake?" Bojing asked, offering Huzhou

the plate of treats. But Huzhou shook his head and waved the plate away.

"I regret to say that I am not feeling very well," he said as he grimaced and rubbed his stomach.

"Perhaps you should lie down," Bojing said. "You are probably just exhausted."

"No, I—" He stopped and his eyes grew big. "Bojing! Behind you!"

Bojing looked, but there was nothing there. But when he looked back to Huzhou, the man jumped up and began swinging his fists in the air.

"Get back, beast!"

While Bojing knew the drug would make Huzhou hallucinate, he wasn't prepared to see the effects in person.

"Calm yourself, friend," Bojing said. "Nothing is there."

"What?" Huzhou asked, but when he looked at Bojing, he screamed. "Vile devil! How dare you try to trick me!"

"What?" Bojing asked, but Huzhou lunged at him, knocking him to the ground. Huzhou punched Bojing in the face, then grabbed his shoulders and banged his head into the ground.

"Stop! Stop!" Bojing cried, but Huzhou was in a frenzy. Bojing realized he would have to fight back. He kicked Huzhou in the stomach as hard as he could and then pushed him away.

Huzhou rolled across the floor but jumped to his feet quickly. He assumed a fighting stance.

"I have no wish to fight you, friend," Bojing said.

"You are no friend!" Huzhou said. "I see your black face and horns. Devil from hell! Begone from this place!"

Bojing expected Huzhou to come at him again, but instead, Huzhou ducked behind a counter and reappeared with a long knife. It was then that Huzhou lunged at him.

"No! Stop!" Bojing yelled, but he knew there was no reasoning with the man. He had no idea how long the hallucination would last, but he feared Huzhou would kill him long before he knew what he was doing.

Huzhou thrust the knife toward Bojing, and Bojing grabbed his wrist, holding the weapon as far away as possible. Huzhou pulled back, out of Bojing's grasp, then thrust again. This time, Bojing grabbed Huzhou's arm and then used his knee to try and knock the knife loose, but Huzhou had an iron grip.

Huzhou was behind Bojing, so he used his other hand to grab Bojing around the throat. Bojing flinched as he felt Huzhou's nails dig into his flesh. He cried out in pain, but Huzhou had no sympathy for his friend. Bojing was unable to take a breath. He stepped on Huzhou's foot, causing Huzhou to loosen his grip. As Bojing tried to escape from Huzhou's grasp, Huzhou jabbed toward Bojing's belly.

But he missed.

Huzhou cried out in pain as Bojing slipped away from him, and Bojing watched in horror as Huzhou crumpled to the ground. Bojing ran to Huzhou's side, turning him over.

Blood was pooling around Huzhou, and Bojing's first instinct was to seek help. But then he remembered why he was there in the first place. He ran to the counter where Huzhou had retrieved the knife from and found the book of records for the *bao* jars. He found Donghai's name and the location of his jar. He put the book back and tried to open the door to the jar room, but it was locked.

Bojing slapped the door and uttered a curse. He then thought that Huzhou probably kept the key on his person. Bojing went back to Huzhou and felt around in his robes for a key. The robes were quickly becoming sodden with blood.

"Hold on for a moment longer," Bojing said. "Once I find the jar, I will send for help."

Huzhou coughed, spattering blood on Bojing's face. Huzhou groaned in pain.

"Kill me now, devil," Huzhou muttered. "Do not leave me here to suffer."

Bojing knew his only saving grace was that Huzhou still did not know who he was. He finally found the key in one of Huzhou's pockets and ran back to the door.

When Bojing looked into the room, he was astonished to see so many *bao* jars. There were half a dozen shelves that extended the length of the storage room, farther than he could see. He knew the room housed thousands of jars, but he had not been able to imagine just how many jars that was. He shook himself out of his stupor, knowing that the sooner he found the *bao* jar, the sooner he could get help for Huzhou. He looked at the nearest shelf to try to understand the organizational system, and soon, he was able to figure out the general area where Donghai's *bao* jar would be. When he found the right place, there were still dozens of jars he needed to examine to find the right one. By the time he found the right jar and stuffed it into an inside pocket of his robe, he had no idea how much time had passed. He had to assume that the assistants would be arriving soon. He flew from the room and locked the door behind him. He then went back to Huzhou to replace the key.

But it was too late.

Huzhou was no longer breathing, his life's blood covering the floor.

Bojing sat back on his heels and began to weep. This was the last thing he had wanted to happen. But he knew he had to continue. He had to get the jar to the empress in order for the plan to go forward.

"I am sorry, my friend," Bojing said as he closed Huzhou's eyes. He then noticed that his own hands, and his robe and shoes, were covered in blood. He cursed again, unsure of what to do. He would surely be caught if he tried to go back to the empress's palace covered in blood. He also did not want to leave the *bao* jars unprotected. Anyone could walk in, find the guardian dead, and steal the jars instead of alerting the guards.

Bojing stood and bowed to his friend. "I will honor you for the rest of my days," he said. Then he walked out of the Hall of Precious Treasures and began screaming, "Help me! The guardian attacked me! Help!"

TWENTY-FOUR

*D*onghai scoffed to himself when he received the summons from the empress. She technically outranked his lady, the dowager-empress, but in actuality, no one could command the dowager or those under her purview. He had as little to do with the empress as possible and did not know her eunuch, Bojing, very well. The empress was not a threat to him, nor did she have any benefits to offer. Even though the dowager-empress would not live forever, she was still healthy for her age. And her gifts to him had made him so wealthy that when she did pass, he would retire in luxury. He would buy a house and land as far away from the Forbidden City as possible. He would buy a wife and concubines and adopt several sons. He would live out his graying years as any other man.

Still, he was intrigued. The empress had never summoned him to appear before her before. What could she possibly have to say to him? The summons requested his discretion—a thinly disguised code for him to not tell the dowager about the meeting. Fine, he would do as she asked—for now. If he deemed it prudent after the fact, he would tell the dowager of the exchange later. He tossed the summons into a brazier, where it was quickly incinerated, and then he walked to the empress's palace.

He was greeted with the proper respect when he arrived. The doors were opened for him by lesser eunuchs. The maids offered him tea and bowed politely. He refused tea and held his head aloft. He didn't imagine that the empress would poison him in her own home, but after the death of the Hall of Precious Treasures guardian at the hand of Bojing, he wasn't sure what to expect. The death had been ruled a tragic accident. Self-defense by Bojing. But it had still been a strange occurrence, and all the eunuchs were waiting anxiously to see if there were consequences to come for the man's death.

Finally, Bojing appeared and he bowed to Donghai as his senior.

"The empress will see you now," he said as he motioned toward the empress's sitting room. Donghai was suspicious as to why she would see him there and not in her audience chamber, but he entered the room anyway, his curiosity growing by the second.

When he entered the sitting room, the empress was waiting for him, but her chair was not elevated since it was not her audience room. It was strange she would meet with him in a room that set her at eye-level, but not nearly as strange as the fact that there were no other maids or eunuchs present except for Bojing, who shut the door behind them. Donghai surveyed the room, expecting an assassin to leap out from behind a painted screen at any moment. He finally cleared his throat and crossed the room, kowtowing before the empress and keeping his eyes downcast.

"May the empress live ten thousand years," he said.

"You may rise," the empress said, which only meant that he could lift his chin, not actually rise to his feet. "I appreciate your expediency."

"One does not dally when the empress calls."

"As I am sure you have puzzled out," the empress said, "what I have to speak to you about is of the most sensitive nature."

Donghai did not speak. There was no need to state the obvious.

"We are all concerned about the emperor," the empress said. "His actions of late have been...erratic."

Donghai did not speak. It could be a trap. Only a fool would speak ill of the emperor, and only a man with a death wish would do so in front of the empress.

The empress gave a small smile. "I know what you are thinking. That I wish to catch you out. Have you sentenced to death. Don't worry, you are worth far more to me alive."

Donghai felt the tiny hairs on the back of his neck prickle in warning. What could she possibly want from him?

"As the dowager's confidant," the empress went on, "I know you are privy to all sorts of private information. After all, you have served her since before I was born. You have seen so much happen over the years. You were there when the Ming Dynasty was established! Oh, the things you could tell me."

Donghai no longer smiled. The empress wanted him to betray the confidence of his lady. And that he could never do. His life would be forfeit if he did. But the empress knew this. All eunuchs were a listening ear for their ladies. If a eunuch could not be trusted, he was worthless. So why was the empress even bothering with asking if she knew he would never talk?

Donghai gasped when he felt a quick slap across the back of his head. He looked up and saw that Bojing had struck him.

"How dare you?" Donghai growled. "I'll have you banished for that!"

"You will do no such thing," the empress said as she stood and approached him. He then cried out as she stepped on his hand with her tiny foot. "You'll tell no one of this either."

"What do you want from me?" he asked as he grabbed his hand to his chest when the empress removed her foot and went back to her chair.

"Information, of course," she said. "The dowager knows something about the emperor. Something about a curse."

"You can torture me all you like," Donghai said, "but I'll never tell you anything. I would die before betraying the dowager-empress!"

"I know," the empress said, but then she opened a small lacquer box that had been sitting on a table next to her that he hadn't given any thought to. He assumed it had held tea or something. But it was not tea she removed from the box. Donghai's eyes went wide when she pulled out a sealed *bao* jar. "But if you did die, would you want to be buried without this?"

"That...t-t-that cannot..." His voice crumbled in his throat. The death of the guardian. He knew there had been more to it than simply an accident. His eyes flew to Bojing. "You murdered the guardian of the Hall of Precious Treasures!"

"I didn't!" Bojing said. "It was an accident."

"But one he took full advantage of," the empress said, swinging the jar back and forth by two little fingers. Donghai felt sick at the prospect of her dropping it.

"How do I know that is really my jar?" he asked.

The empress held the jar over a nearby candle, melting the wax seal. Once it was soft enough, she removed the label and handed it to Bojing, who took it to Donghai.

"I assume you recognize your own signature," she said as Donghai held the strip of silk in his shaking hands.

"Yes," he grumbled. Bojing snatched the label away before Donghai could stop him. Bojing then gave the label back to the empress.

"Good," she said. "Now that we have that settled, perhaps we can get back to my question. What do you know about a curse?"

Donghai smirked. "You are truly a ruthless woman. No wonder the emperor finds your bed too cold to visit anymore."

The empress was not fazed by Donghai's attempt to change the subject. She held the *bao* jar over the candle flame again, this time completely melting the wax seal.

"I wonder what a forty-year-old desiccated penis looks like," she said, and Donghai began to sweat profusely. The empress removed the lid of the terracotta jar and sniffed. She grimaced. "Ugh! Smells terrible."

"Your Majesty," Donghai said, nearly getting to his feet, but Bojing placed his hand on Donghai's shoulder, holding him in place. "Please, I beg of you, do not desecrate my body."

"Then tell me what I want to know," the empress said, looking at him with cold eyes, her mouth set firmly.

"I...I cannot," Donghai said. "You know I cannot."

The empress looked away from him and upturned the jar onto the table. She laughed when she saw the member and testicles.

"That's it?" she asked, and then she laughed cruelly. The

bao had dehydrated over the years, leaving the main member looking like a dried mushroom and the testicles like two prunes.

Donghai felt a pain in his chest at the humiliation. "Your Majesty," Donghai said, his voice growing gruff with anger. "Stop this. Such spitefulness does not become you."

She stopped laughing and stared at him. "Do not presume to know anything about my character." She picked up the main member and held it toward the candle flame.

"No!" Donghai yelled, and Bojing dug his fingers painfully into Donghai's shoulder. "Stop! I beg of you!"

"Then tell me what I want to know," the empress said. "Or you can look forward to your next life as a female mule!"

Donghai shot a glare at Bojing. "Have you no sense of honor? Is there anything about the brotherhood you did not tell her?"

"I have done nothing you would not have done were you in my situation," Bojing said.

Donghai spat on Bojing's foot. "I would never betray my fellow eunuchs as you have this day!"

"Tell me what I want to know!" the empress said, directing Donghai's attention back to her. Donghai saw that the member was smoking, it was so close to the flame.

"Stop!" he said, falling to his face and folding his hands in front of him. "What is it you want? What...what curse?"

"Tell me about the emperor," the empress demanded. "Or about his mother, or father. Give me something I can use against him to get him to stop this madness!"

"You wish to betray your husband?" Donghai asked in disbelief, looking up at her.

"No," the empress said, pulling the member away from the flame. "I wish to save him. I need him to stop this foolishness. He cannot drive us to poverty. Murder innocent concubines. I need information I can present to him to get him to change his ways."

Donghai shook his head. "This is folly, madam. You risk all our lives if you continue on this path."

Empress Wen held the member back to the flame. "I don't have any other choice."

Donghai sighed and shook his head. He knew that she would destroy his *bao* to get what she wanted. She had lost the emperor's favor and was desperate to get it back—even if it meant destroying the Ming Dynasty.

"I will tell you," he said, and the empress's eyes sparkled as she placed the *bao* back on the table. "But know that if you use this information, you will doom us all."

"Tell me," she said, leaning forward like an anxious child.

"The night your husband was born, I had to make a terrible choice," Donghai said. "One that nearly destroyed the dowager. But I did it to save the empire. I had lived through years of war. Had seen so much death and destruction. I could not let that happen again."

The empress nodded for him to continue.

"There was another baby."

TWENTY-FIVE

"*W*hat?" Empress Wen said. "What do you mean there was another baby?"

"A twin," Donghai said. "When Hongdi was born, the emperor was so happy, he immediately swept the boy away to show to his vassals and ministers. Your father was there. Everyone celebrated the arrival of the dragon heir."

"Yes, Father has told me how ecstatic Hongwu was that his first child was a son," Wen said. "That it was proof Heaven was smiling on the Ming Dynasty."

"He took the child, leaving the young empress alone with myself and the midwife," Donghai continued. "And it was then that her birthing pains began again. Within moments, another child was born. Another son."

Empress Wen's hand flew to her mouth. A second son. A twin. Donghai and the empress had carried this secret for nearly thirty years. Many people viewed twins as bad luck. A portent of danger and ruin. And when it came to inheritance and lines of succession, it made things very complicated. Some people believed that the second child in a twin set had actually been conceived first. That was why it was further back in the womb. So, the second twin could claim to be the rightful heir. Of course, others believed that the child that emerged into the world first should be the rightful heir. Twin births almost always caused strife within a family for these reasons. It was not uncommon for people of all classes to drown both children upon birth. The poor did so because they could ill afford bad luck. One failed crop could result in death for an entire family. In rich families, they would destroy the children to prevent a feud later. More children could always be born.

But Wen had never heard of a case of an emperor being born a twin. To drown a son of Heaven would be unthinkable! And yet, what could they have done? Donghai was right that the appearance of a second child would plunge the country into civil war. There would always be people who supported the first son as emperor and other people who supported the second child. Then there would be others who saw the birth of twins as a sign that the Ming did not have the Mandate of Heaven. That the dynasty was cursed. People would raise arms against the Ming to establish a new rulership.

"What did you do?" Wen asked Donghai. "Did you kill the child?"

"I told the empress that I did," he said, his eyes watering. "She was barely more than a girl herself. She was lucky to even survive such a difficult pregnancy and birth. She wanted to keep the second child, foolish girl that she was. I...I had to take the child from her arms. She begged me not to, screamed and cried. But I had to do what she lacked the courage to do.

"I wrapped the baby tightly so it would not cry in the night. I snuck down to the canal that ran through the palace and planned to throw the baby into the water. But...I couldn't. I don't know why. It would have been so easy just to let go. But the water, it was so black, like ink. And freezing cold. It was winter. Even a grown man would seize up in an instant in such water.

"The whole time I pondered the child's fate, he was quiet. Calm. I looked at his face, and he grabbed my finger. He...trusted me."

Empress Wen felt warm tears falling down her own cheeks at hearing the story. How she had longed to hold a babe to her chest. The thought of having a child ripped from her arms and drowned was horrifying.

"What...what happened?" she implored the eunuch.

"The midwife," Donghai said. "I saw her leaving the palace, her work done. She saw me at the water's edge and approached me. She took the boy from me. I thought she was going to do the work I failed to do. But instead, she wrapped the child in her robe."

"'I've never had a child of my own,' she confessed. I nodded to her in understanding. I gave her a bag of coins and told her that she could not stay in the city. She had to leave. She had to raise the child far away.

"She agreed. She turned and walked away. I never expected to see her again. I told the empress that I did what was necessary to protect the empire. She thought I had killed her son. I let her think it. I have let her think it for thirty years."

"So, you are saying that there is another man out there," Wen said. "One who could have a claim on the throne."

"He could be anywhere," Bojing said.

"No," Donghai said. "Not anywhere. I know exactly where he is."

"Where is he?" the empress asked.

Donghai hesitated. He had already said too much. The

empress picked up a letter opener and stabbed one of the prune-looking *bao*.

"Tell me where he is!" she yelled.

"He's here," Donghai said, knowing that he needed to tell her everything if he hoped to get his *bao* jar back—with his *bao* intact. "He is here in the Forbidden City."

Bojing slapped Donghai in the back of the head again. "Such foolish lies! If he were here, we would know!"

"No," Donghai said. "I took precautions to make sure that no one would know. His face is hidden."

"What do you mean?" Wen asked. "How?"

"Behind an iron mask," Donghai said. "A mask shaped like a dragon."

"How?" the empress asked. "Why?"

"The dowager-empress was eaten up with guilt over the loss of her son," Donghai said. "She wept constantly. Refused to eat. She could not hold or nurse Hongdi, insisting we bring a wet nurse for him."

"That was why she was always so cold to him," Wen said. "She could never love him knowing that his life came at the cost of his brother's."

Donghai nodded. "And why she had concubines brought in as soon as possible for Emperor Hongwu. She couldn't bear the thought of having more children. She would lay with the emperor when he insisted, but she would drink a bitter tea afterward to prevent conception."

The empress shook her head. "I wish I could pity her. The loss of a child would be heartbreaking, no matter what. But for the twin to have been killed...I understand her grief. A grief she must carry to this day. But she has been so cruel to Hongdi. She should have loved the child she still had."

"In the early years," Donghai explained, "I encouraged her to love Hongdi. To hold him and nurture him. But she could not. Eventually, I stopped trying. My loyalty was to my lady, after all, not to the boy."

"So, what happened to the twin?" Wen asked.

"I sought out the midwife later," Donghai said. "I had not given her much money, only what I had on me at the time. I could not bear the idea of the child growing up in poverty. I was able to track her down even though they had moved hundreds of *li* away. I was only planning on seeing to the child's welfare and giving the family the funds to hire a tutor for him. If he could still live a happy and prosperous life, maybe one day, I could tell the dowager the truth. Perhaps in the future, when it no longer mattered.

"But when I saw the boy...I was terrified. He looked exactly like Hongdi! I couldn't believe it. I grew afraid. If someone else who knew the emperor ever saw the boy, it would be impossible to deny the resemblance."

"You said they were hundreds of *li* away," the empress said. "Surely the chance that someone else would ever see both boys was too remote to be a threat."

"Perhaps I panicked," Donghai said. "But I could not take the chance. That night, I returned to the house. I killed the midwife and her husband and set the house on fire. I stole the boy and returned to the palace with him. I took him to the dungeon and hid his face behind a mask made of iron so that no one would ever know who he was."

"You clapped his face in an iron mask?" Wen asked. "How...how long ago."

"That was fourteen years ago," Donghai said, and then he crumpled to the ground in tears.

The empress sat back in her chair, at a loss for words. She couldn't imagine the pain and horror the boy had suffered in those years. Such a punishment must be torture.

"How could you?" she finally asked. "How could you do

that to an innocent boy? To his adoptive parents? To the dowager? It would have been better if you had dropped him into the river. So much pain could have been avoided."

"I have told myself that so many times over the years," Donghai said. "I thought at the time that by sending the child away, and then later locking him in the prison, that I was being merciful. That I was protecting him. But I know I was being a fool. It was wrong, all of it. But now, my conscience is so heavy, I do not know how to heal it."

"You locked him in the dungeon fourteen years ago," Bojing said. "Did you leave him in the old palace in Nanking? Did you leave him behind to rot?"

"No," Donghai said. "All of the prisoners were moved, even him."

"He's here?" Wen said. "He is here in the Forbidden City? In the dungeon right now?"

"Yes," Donghai said. "He is."

"But no one knows who he is?" she asked, flabbergasted. "No one wonders why a man is in the dungeon with a mask? What do they think his crime is?"

"The guards do not ask such questions," Donghai said. "They only follow orders."

The empress looked to Bojing and started to say something else, but Bojing shook his head. Bojing then shook Donghai viciously.

"You are a dog who should be ashamed!" Bojing said. "You are fortunate my lady is merciful."

Donghai bent forward, putting his head to the floor again. "I am a dog," he cried. "I am worthless. I know that I can have no hope of a happy outcome in the next life. The gods are surely disgusted with me."

"If I let you leave here," Empress Wen said, "you must not tell a soul what you have told me. Do you understand?"

"Yes, Your Majesty," he said. "But what of the *bao* jar?"

The empress picked up the bao pieces and put them into the jar. She then heated up the wax again and replaced the lid so it would reseal.

"Your *bao* jar is safe," the empress said. "But it will remain here with me to ensure your silence. If you betray me, I will pitch it into the fire without a moment's hesitation. Do you understand?"

Donghai bowed once again, doing his best to hide the fury on his face. "Yes, Your Majesty."

"Good," she said. "Now, get out of my sight."

Donghai stood and backed away from the empress and then slipped out the door.

Once he was gone, Bojing approached the empress. "What do you think?"

"I'm not sure," she said. "It's a strange tale to be sure. But will it benefit us? I don't know."

"It could certainly undermine his claim to the throne," Bojing said. "Or cause people to doubt that the Ming ever had the Mandate of Heaven."

"True," she said, and then she sighed. "I didn't think it would work. I knew there had to be a reason why the dowager despised her son. But I never would have imagined she'd had another child. Never would have thought that Donghai would really give me the power to overthrow Hongdi."

"We must tread carefully," Bojing said. "If this information falls into the wrong hands, it could be used against you as well as the emperor's wife."

The empress nodded and looked at the *bao* jar that she still held in her hands. She almost laughed at the absurdity of it. That the fate of an empire relied on a eunuch's severed penis.

TWENTY-SIX

*B*efore the last star went out the next morning, Bojing left the Forbidden City, his head obscured by the hood of a cape. He mounted a horse and rode outside the city to the newly built estate where General Kang and his eldest son lived with their families.

As soon as he approached, a groom rushed over to take the reins of the horse. A servant then showed Bojing into the house as he was well-known to the Kang family.

Bojing knew that the Kang family was immensely wealthy. He had visited their home in the south many times delivering messages from the empress. But that home had been in the Kang family for over three hundred years. Many generations of Kangs had built upon it, adding to its opulence and grandeur with every promotion, every imperial gift, every decisive battle win. But even he was amazed at the size and beauty of the new home General Kang had built here in the north.

The entire compound was rectangular in form, with a massive outer wall to protect the family within. As Bojing entered the compound through a small door within the large main gate, he felt as though he had walked into a beautiful city. It was a palace equal to the Forbidden City in its stateliness, but on a smaller scale. He could easily see a dozen buildings, and suspected there were many more he could not yet see. Most were at least two stories high, many with latticed balconies where enchanting ladies sat fanning themselves, playing with their children, and chatting the morning away. The walkways were more narrow than in the Forbidden City, but that allowed large patches of green grass to grow, along with trees and bushes. The entire compound looked like a well-manicured park.

Bojing was first led to a spacious sitting room, where he was greeted by Lady Kang herself. The empress's mother, Lianyu, was still a beautiful woman for her age, and she gracefully floated to welcome Bojing to her home as he dropped to his knee.

"It is a pleasure to see you again," Lianyu said.

"You are too kind to welcome such a worthless eunuch as myself into your beautiful home," Bojing replied.

"Please, take tea with me," Lianyu said as she led Bojing to a low table with chairs around it. She did not even need to call for tea, two maids walked into the room with trays of tea things already prepared. "Have you eaten?"

"I couldn't eat a bite," Bojing politely said as he allowed one of the maids to prepare a teacup for him. He had not eaten that morning, and the ride had been long, but he did not want to impose on her ladyship's courtesy, nor did he want to delay his meeting with General Kang.

"Your home is exquisite," he said as he sipped the tea. "I do hope you are settling into your new life here in the north."

Lianyu made a laugh that was nearly a scoff. "Have any of us truly settled in? I am dreading the coming winter. The mornings are already quite chilled. If the distance were not so great, I would spend the winter with my son at our southern estate."

Bojing nodded. "We have already begun stockpiling coal and firewood, but I fear it will not be enough to last the whole winter."

"I will be sure to send my daughter extra furs for herself and her servants to make more clothes with," Lianyu said.

Finally, the door to the room opened and General Kang entered, his eldest son, Jun, right behind him. Bojing stood and then kneeled before the emperor.

"Thank you for taking the time to see me, my lord," Bojing said.

"Rise," the general said, which, since he was only a general and not an emperor, meant that Bojing could stand at his full height and even look directly into the general's face. So Bojing stood, but he respectfully kept his eyes downcast.

"I will leave you to your business," Lianyu said, standing and heading toward the door, her maids following behind. But as she passed the general, he gently gripped her elbow and pulled her to him. He kissed her cheek that was shocking in its tenderness. The woman then continued out of the room, the general's eyes on her until the door was closed again. The general then turned back to Bojing, his tough exterior reclaimed.

"What is it, Bojing?" the general asked as he took a seat at the table and poured himself a cup of tea. Jun stood aside, his arms crossed, and Bojing resumed his seat at the table.

"You requested that the empress send you information that you could use," Bojing said with a low voice.

"And?" the general pushed. "Was she successful?"

Bojing smiled. "You will not believe the story when I tell you, but yes."

"Out with it, eunuch," Jun said. His father shot him a look, but he did not admonish him. Bojing was generally accorded respect within the Kang household, but some only did so begrudgingly.

"The emperor has a brother," Bojing said.

"The emperor has many brothers, fool," Jun said, shaking his head. "Why are you wasting our time?"

"Quiet," the general said. "Bojing would not have come all this way to tell us something we already know. What do you mean he has a brother."

"A twin," Bojing said, ignoring Jun. "Born only minutes after Hongdi."

The general was silent for a moment, then he looked away, as though he was remembering something. Then he sat back in his seat. "You are certain? I was there that night. There was no mention of another child."

"While Hongwu was celebrating the birth of Hongdi, the empress gave birth to another child," Bojing explained. "Her eunuch, Donghai, spirited it away in the night. He told the young empress that the child had to be put to death. But instead, he gave it to the midwife to raise."

"How did you learn this?" General Kang asked.

"From Donghai himself," Bojing said. "Your daughter was...quite persuasive."

"We cannot trust Donghai," Jun said to his father. "He would never tell Wen anything that could help her. The dowager has always hated Wen, and her servant likewise."

"I agree," the general said, then he turned back to Bojing. "Why do you believe him?"

"I do not think he lied," Bojing said. "But you are right,

we will still need to verify the story. We have to find the emperor's brother."

"If the midwife took him, he could be anywhere," Jun said.

"Not according to Donghai," Bojing said. He then went into the story of how the little prince became the man in the prison in the dragon mask. When he was done, General Kang and Jun were both stupefied in silence. Finally, the two broke out into raucous laughter.

"What a ridiculous tale," the general said, pounding his fist on the table while Jun wiped tears from his eyes. Bojing waited for them to stop.

"Did my sister make this up as some hilarious joke?" Jun asked.

"No," Bojing said, remaining stoic. "These words are from Donghai's own mouth. He wept as he told the tale. I believe his actions have haunted him his whole life."

"This can't be!" Jun said to his father. "It is ridiculous! If there really was a second baby, Donghai should have just been a man and killed him."

The general was watching Bojing's face, rubbing his chin. "You are telling the truth, aren't you?" he finally said. Bojing gave a slow nod. "Or, at least, you believe the story that Donghai told you."

"I do," Bojing reaffirmed.

The general sighed. "Still, what are we supposed to do? Let us say this boy does exist in the dungeon under the Forbidden City. How will this help us stop Hongdi from running roughshod over everyone?"

"I'm not sure yet," Bojing said. "And neither is the empress. She was only tasked with gathering the information. I believe she wanted you to decide what to do with it."

"Hmm." The general fingered the teacup as he thought.

"Well, until we know the story is true, there is nothing else we can do."

"The only way to prove it would be to find this man in the dragon mask," Jun said.

"Exactly," General Kang said. "Somehow, we are going to have to steal the boy out of the prison."

Bojing nearly shuddered at the thought. "That would be terribly difficult. It is very well guarded, extremely fortified. It had to be that way. The emperor could not have dangerous criminals escaping from the prison and running loose in the Forbidden City."

"Of course it is well-fortified," General Kang said. "I helped design it."

Bojing blinked. "You did? I don't remember hearing anything about that."

"It was a secret," General Kang said. "So that no one could try and force the designer to reveal its details."

"So, you know its weaknesses?" Bojing said. "You could easily break in."

"Weaknesses?" General Kang barked. "You think I do shoddy work, boy?"

"Of course not!" Bojing said, cowing his head. "I...I only meant..."

General Kang laughed uproariously again. "Take it easy, Bojing." Bojing looked up and gave an uneasy smile, but he still couldn't bring himself to laugh in the general's presence. "The dungeon has no weaknesses. But since I know it's *strengths*, I do have some ideas on how I could get in and out unnoticed."

"The problem would be getting into the Forbidden City," Jun spoke up. "We can request an audience with the emperor at any time. But we can't simply walk around unescorted for no reason. And with the empress under house arrest, we will not be able to use visiting her as an excuse."

General Kang nodded. "True, that will prove difficult."

"I am sure the empress and I could come up with a plan for that," Bojing said. "We know the Forbidden City rather well, and I have many friends inside."

"Very good," General Kang said. "Let us each have time to plan. We can meet at my Peking house in two days' time. Bring two or three of your most trusted allies. I will bring some of my best men and we will formulate a plan."

Bojing stood and then gave General Kang a low bow. "Thank you, sir! I look forward to seeing you again."

"Don't be so quick to thank me, son," General Kang said, patting Bojing on the back. "We'll be lucky if we don't all end up on the executioner's scaffold."

TWENTY-SEVEN

At the appointed time, Bojing, along with three of his most trusted assistants, arrived at General Kang's Peking residence. Even though General Kang's home was not too far from the city, if he had business within Peking to attend to, it was often advantageous to stay near the palace. The general, his son, Jun, and two additional soldiers were already at the residence awaiting Bojing.

"You are sure you trust these...*men*?" Jun asked as he looked down his nose at Bojing's companions.

"I trained them myself from their first days in service," Bojing said. "They are like sons to me. I trust them implicitly."

"Even with information of this magnitude?" the general asked.

"They know we need to...*extricate* someone from the prison, but not who or why," Bojing said. "They know better than to ask questions."

The general nodded his approval. "Very prudent. Now, what is the plan?"

"There is no need to sneak into the palace," Bojing said.

"You will first request an audience with the emperor. You can decide the topic. At the end of the meeting, you will ask to visit the empress."

"She will not be at the audience?" the general asked.

"No, my lord," Bojing said. "The empress has not been invited to court by the emperor for months. Other than her morning audience with the ladies of the Inner Court, the empress does not leave her palace."

The general grunted his disapproval but motioned for Bojing to continue.

"You will then only go to the empress's palace for appearances," Bojing said. "When you leave, you and I will walk toward the entrance of the dungeon as though we are discussing important matters. When we are near the dungeon, two of my assistants will create a distraction. The guards will chase after them. At that point, you and your son will be able to enter the dungeon. My other assistant and I will stand watch at the gate, but it will be up to you to find and rescue the prisoner."

"Do you know where the prisoner is located?" General Kang asked. "And how many guards are inside the dungeon?"

"The man is being held down the second aisle to the left at the bottom of the stairs," Bojing said. "There will be at least four guards total inside the dungeon. They patrol the cells and eat and rest in shifts, so at least two people should be alert at all times."

The general nodded and pulled out a rolled-up sheet of paper, which he unfurled onto a table. He pointed to a row of cells. "Here is where the man must be, which is excellent."

"Why?" Jun asked, looking at the plans for the prison. "It is a dead end."

"It looks like a dead end," the general said with a smile, "but there is a grate here." He pointed to the edge of what appeared to be an outside wall. "The prison had to have at least some ports for fresh air, but they are not attached to any cells to prevent escapes."

"So, wouldn't that prevent us from getting our man out?" Jun asked. The general stared at his son for a moment and then slapped the back of his head.

"Are you even paying attention?" the general asked. "Once we get the man out of his cell, we will be able to remove him from the prison through the grate."

"How?" Jun asked.

The general nodded to one of his friends. "That is what Hanhan is for. He is an excellent locksmith. You and he will hide in the prison until you receive my signal. Then you will escape along with the prisoner."

"What signal?" Jun asked.

The general rolled the prison plans back up. "You'll know it when you hear it," he said. "Now, let's go."

❧

"*I* appreciate your concern, General," the emperor said to his father-in-law from upon his dragon throne, the giant pearl in the dragon's mouth dangling overhead. "But the Manchu and Mongol have shown no signs of aggression in recent months. The Mongol were soundly beaten by you and my father, and the Manchu know they cannot begin to match our strength. I believe the threat from the north is tamed."

"For now," the general said. "But times of peace are when one should prepare for war. Should the outsiders attack while we are unprepared, it could prove disastrous for us. When the capital was moved to the north, I was assured that some of the funds would be allocated to reinforcing the wall. So far, I have not seen this promise fulfilled."

"The wall will be our top priority once the Forbidden City is complete," the emperor said.

General Kang raised an eyebrow. "Recent estimates say that it will still take years, as long as a decade, for the palace to be complete. The Mongol and Manchu could easily raise an army or even join forces in a fraction of that time."

The emperor's nostrils flared and he gripped the arms of his throne tightly. "Those estimates were proven incorrect," he said through gritted teeth. "But that is not your concern, General. I have given you my answer. Once the palace is complete, fortifications will begin on the Great Wall. Is that all?"

The general bowed. "Yes, Your Majesty."

"Good," the emperor said, but as he began to motion to dismiss the general, the general spoke again.

"I would like to speak to the empress before I leave," he said. "I see she is not present. We have not heard from her in some time and her mother is concerned."

"The empress is well," the emperor said. "But her opinion is no longer required at audiences. Government is the realm of men."

"As you say," the general said. "Still, I would speak to her myself so I can soothe her mother's concerns."

The emperor sighed and rolled his eyes. Was there no end to the irritating ways of women? "Fine, do as you will."

The general and his son bowed their way out of the audience hall and met with Bojing and the other men at the door.

"That went about as well as expected," Bojing muttered to the general as he led him to the empress's palace.

"The boy is a fool," the general replied. "That was no pretense. I did need to speak to him about threats from the north. If we are not careful, he will kill us all by placing us to close to danger."

"That is distressing to hear," Bojing said. "Hopefully, after our plan today, you will find some way to convince the emperor to take the threats more seriously."

"We shall see," the general said.

The general did not stay long at the empress's palace since he had no real reason to see her other than as an excuse to prolong his stay in the Forbidden City. After an appropriate amount of time had passed, the men left the empress's palace and walked across the Forbidden City toward the gate of the underground prison.

"You and your man will not need to stand guard," the general told Bojing. "Jun and Hanhan simply need to get inside. After that, you are free to go about your business."

"What of the prisoner?" Bojing asked.

"We will remove him from the prison tonight, under cover of darkness. If he truly has his head secured within an iron mask, we will not be able to move him in the day time. Tomorrow, send your men at dawn to repair some damage along the west wall."

"What damage?" Bojing asked.

"The damage we plan to leave behind," the general said. "Get it patched up before anyone realizes how large the hole is. Then return to my country estate so we can figure out what to do with our charge."

Bojing nodded. His stomach was tied in knots that prevented him from speaking. Even though the plan seemed sound, he could not be more nervous. What if the information Donghai had given him was false? Or wrong? If the plan went sour for any reason, it could cost all of them their lives. But it was too late to back out.

Bojing looked up when he heard a yell and a crash. Two eunuchs—his assistants—had been trying to open one of the windows to the structure that led down to the dungeon. The guards at the prison gate saw them, so the boys took off at a run. The guards shrugged, planning to ignore them since they could not leave their post. But the general spoke up.

"Well?" he barked. "What are you waiting for? Arrest them!"

They both saluted the general. "Yes, sir!" And then they took off after the eunuchs.

The general then nodded to Hanhan, who pulled out a set of tools and quickly unlocked the prison door. Hanhan and Jun slipped into the prison, and then the general shut and locked the door behind them, standing guard until the regular guards returned.

"You should go," the general said to Bojing. "It wouldn't do for you to linger around here long."

Bojing nodded but hesitated. It all seemed so easy. But this was no ordinary burglar he was working with, but General Kang, the best strategist in China. Bojing finally turned and walked away, leaving the general to his work.

When the guards returned, the scared eunuchs in tow, they were grateful that the general had kept watch at the door for them. In return, the general took the eunuchs from them and dragged them away by their collars to be punished.

"Trying to sneak into the dungeon, were you?" the general sneered.

"We were just trying to get some food and water to a fellow eunuch who was imprisoned, sir," they said.

"Shut up!" the general said, "before you two join him!" But after they rounded a corner, the general set the boys free. "Get out of here. And make sure those guards don't see you for a good long while."

"Yes, sir!" the boys said as they quickly scurried away. The general then sauntered out of the Forbidden City and visited a nearby tavern for a few drinks while he waited for the darkest part of the night.

Back inside the dungeon, Jun pulled some bottles of strong spirits out of his pockets and approached the inner guards, all four of whom were sitting around a table, eating or sleeping.

"Who's up for a little game of chance?" Jun called out gaily.

The men jumped to their feet. "Who are you? What are you doing here?"

"Kang Jun," he said. "The general's son. Father is talking to the emperor and other important men, so I thought I'd just slip away for a bit of drink and a game of dice. Are you up for it?"

The men looked at each other and then laughed, welcoming Jun and clapping him on the back. Anyone with good spirits was a welcome diversion from their otherwise dreary jobs.

It didn't take long for the guards to pass out, slumped over on the table or back on the floor. Jun's bottle had only water in it, while the bottles of spirits also contained a little something extra to increase the drowsing effects.

"They'll be out for hours," Jun said to Hanhan. "Let's find this man in the dragon mask."

The dungeon was dark and dank, with dripping water

and fetid smells. The cries of the innocent and the insane echoed off the walls. Jun shivered at the idea of spending even a night down here, much less fourteen years.

When they reached the aisle the man should be down, they heard a banging sound, like metal on stone. Jun looked at Hanhan and noticed the man looked as nervous as Jun felt.

"Come on, we will be out of here soon," Jun whispered. Still, they crept down the aisle slowly and carefully. When they reached the only cell in that portion of the prison, Jun put his hand to his mouth in shock at what he saw.

"By the gods," he mumbled. Before him was the thin, filthy, hairy body of a man, but his head looked like that of a great beast. A snarling dragon. The man had rags tied around his feet for shoes and a thin shift around his waist. Other than that, the poor wretch was naked. There was a hole in the mask for his mouth and eyes, but Jun still could not imagine how difficult it must be to live inside such a contraption.

"Who...who are you?" Jun asked the man. The man stood for a second, staring at Jun, his neck bent forward as though the mask was weighing him down, which it probably was. Then the creature lunged forward, the mask smacking into the metal bars of the cage with a great *clang*, and his arms reaching toward Jun like scrawny claws.

Jun and Hanhan jumped back out of the man's reach as the man moaned and groaned.

"What do we do, my lord?" Hanhan asked. "The man must have lost his mind. He can't possibly be any good to the general."

"I'm inclined to agree with you," Jun said. "But we must complete the task my father has set us to." He looked at the man in the dragon mask and reached out, his fingers meeting those of the prisoner. When they touched, the prisoner jumped back, as though Jun had shocked him, pulling his arms back through the cage and holding his hand to his chest.

"There, there," Jun said, taking a step toward the bars. "I'm here to help you. Do you understand?"

The man stood still for a moment, his eyes darting between Jun and Hanhan, then he gave a small nod.

"Good," Jun said, giving a reassuring smile. "Now, my friend is going to open the door, okay? I need you to stand back and wait. Understand?"

The man moved to the back of the cell, all the way against the wall. Jun then nodded to Hanhan, who worked quickly. Jun went back to the end of the hall and looked down at the guards to make sure they were still unconscious. Satisfied that they were, Jun went back to the cell just as Hanhan was opening the door.

"Child's play," Hanhan quipped.

"Good work," Jun said, clapping the man on the back. He then motioned for the prisoner to come forward. "Come here." The man shook his head. "Come now. We aren't going to hurt you. We are going to try and get the mask off."

At that, the man put his hands to the mask and began screaming.

"Shh!" Jun and Hanhan both said, trying to calm the man down, but he was suddenly hysterical.

"He's going to get us killed!" Hanhan said.

The man continued to scream and shake, banging his head against the wall, making the terrible banging sound they had heard earlier. Jun finally ripped off his outer robe, initially planning to shove it into the mouth hole of the mask, but he was afraid the man would bite his finger off. Instead, he wrapped the robe around the man.

After only a moment, the man began to calm. He fingered the delicate silk of the robe. He held it up to his mask as though to sniff it, but Jun was not sure he could smell anything with his nose covered by the mask. Finally, the man pulled the robe tightly around himself and sighed. Jun thought that the man had probably not had a proper covering for his body for years.

Jun and Hanhan exhaled in relief.

"Stay here," Jun said. "I'm going to see if Father is ready." Hanhan nodded and moved closer to the door of the cell while Jun went to find the grating that wasn't on the plans his father had shown them. Thankfully, it was at the end of the row, right where it was supposed to be. It was quite small. Even without the bars, no man could fit through it. But Jun was grateful he could feel a fresh breeze on his face.

A few minutes later, he saw a leather strap poking through the grating. He grabbed it, and then sent it back through, where someone on the other side pulled it back. He ran to check on the guards, who appeared to still be sleeping. Then he went into the cell with Hanhan and the man in the dragon mask.

There was a large explosion and the ground shook. Jun felt sick. Certainly other people within the palace had heard the noise or felt the shake. They would be caught! They couldn't linger.

"Let's go!" Hanhan said, running out of the cell. But the man in the dragon mask hung back, holding Jun's robe tightly.

"Come on," Jun said, beckoning the man out. "We have to go. You are going to be safe. Free."

"Free?" the man asked, his voice sounding rough and hollow from inside the mask.

"Yes," Jun said. "You are free. But you have to come with me right now."

The man hesitated, but then he followed Jun out of the cell. Hanhan and Jun worked together to lift the man in the dragon mask out of the hole his father had made by using his strongest horses to rip the grating from the brick wall.

"By the gods," the general said when he saw the man in the dragon mask and helped him into the wagon the horses were pulling. "It was all true."

"Let's marvel over that later!" Jun said as he and Hanhan jumped into the wagon. Jun helped the man in the mask to lay down and tossed a rough blanket over him.

Hours later, the man in the dragon mask was far away from the Forbidden City, seeing the sunrise for the first time in fourteen years.

TWENTY-EIGHT

The sun was so bright, Shihong thought for sure he would soon go blind if he did not stop watching the sunrise. But he could not look away. It had been so long since he had seen the sun, years he presumed, he did not want to miss a moment. Even when he had been moved from one dungeon to another, he did not see the sun. He had been moved at night, and he thought he had been drugged for he slept for most of the journey.

He was free for the moment. The men who had taken him from the prison did not bind him in any way. When the cart had come to a stop, he had climbed out of it under his own power and looked at the sun. The sky was painted with blue and yellow and orange. He could not remember the last time he saw something so beautiful. As long as he had been in the dungeon, his life had only been the mottled gray of the walls and bars.

His neck ached as he raised his head to follow the sun. The weight of the mask caused his head to droop forward a bit, and he could feel a hump forming where his neck met his spine. But he would endure any pain to prolong this moment. He feared that the thin, bald man in the red robe would return and drag him back underground, back to the dungeon. He felt tears fall from his eyes and trickle down his cheeks, but he could not wipe them away as long as he was still wearing the mask.

He heard footsteps behind him and turned to see the older man who had driven the horse cart, the father of the man who had saved him, standing there.

"Come," the man said. "Let's get that mask off of you."

Shihong flinched and stepped away from the man, shaking his head.

"You do want it off, don't you?" the man asked.

"He...he will come back," Shihong said, his voice scratchy and weak, he so rarely spoke to anyone. "He will put it on me again."

The man nodded, then he stepped forward and put a hand on Shihong's shoulder, a hand that was surprisingly gentle for as large as the man was. "I won't let that happen."

"Who...who are you?" Shihong asked.

The man suppressed a smile. "The more important question is, who are you? Come, let's get that mask off and find out."

The horse cart had pulled to a stop outside of a large housing complex, but the man did not lead Shihong to the main house. Instead, they went to a shed nearby. Shihong saw a large forge and realized it was a blacksmith's workshop.

"Sit down," the man ordered, motioning toward a rickety chair. Shihong did as he was ordered. He was good at being told what to do.

"Can you open it, Hanhan?" the man asked. The one called Hanhan stepped behind Shihong, and he could hear and feel Hanhan fidgeting with the lock on the back of the mask.

"I've never seen a lock like it," Hanhan finally said as he stepped around Shihong to examine the whole mask.

"We will have to break it, then," the young man who had rescued him said.

The older man grunted his agreement, and the young man and Hanhan got to work on breaking the lock. They made Shihong lie down on an anvil, then they used several tools to destroy the lock. Every swing of the hammer was torture to Shihong. The impact shook his whole head and caused a ringing in his ears. Several times, he told the men to stop. He would rather stay in the mask than endure such pain. But they ignored him, some other men holding his arms and legs down to keep him from trying to escape.

Finally, Shihong heard the lock fall to the ground. The older man then pulled the mask from his face. The pain was even worse, as though the skin was being ripped from his flesh. But, finally, the mask was removed and Shihong took a deep breath of fresh air that did not taste like cold iron. He reached up and touched his face, feeling the supple flesh. He winced, as the skin was quite tender, but he could not stop. He was free. Tears fell from his eyes, and when he touched them, he examined the wetness on his fingertips.

The older man helped him to sit up and he nearly toppled forward, he was so used to the weight of the mask. He was dizzy and started to feel nauseous, so he gripped the man's arm and closed his eyes as he waited for his stomach to settle. After a moment, the world stopped spinning and he was able to open his eyes again.

"I want to see it," he said. The man looked confused, then he reached down and picked up the mask, handing it to Shihong. Shihong shuddered as the face of the dragon stared back at him. The mouth was snarling, revealing sharp fangs, and the eyes were angry. In all the years he had worn the mask, he had never seen what it looked like. He had no mirror or even clear water with which to see his reflection. He wondered what would possess the man in the red robes to encase him in something so horrible. He held the mask to his chest, not ready to let it go.

"Look up," the man said. "Let's see you, boy."

"What?" Shihong said, raising his head, his long hair falling away from his face.

"By the gods," the man said. "It's true."

"He looks just like him," the son said.

"Who is he?" Hanhan asked.

"Never you mind," the older man said. "But excellent work." He handed Hanhan a bag of jingling coins. Hanhan bowed to them all and then left the shed.

"So, what do we do now?" the son asked his father.

"Get him inside," the man said. "Get him cleaned up and fed. He's a skeleton compared to Hongdi."

"Hongdi?" Shihong asked. "Who is that?"

"We will explain everything in time," the man said, then he took Shihong by the arm and helped him to stand. Just like when he sat up, Shihong felt dizzy again, and this time unsure on his feet. But the men each took an arm and helped him to walk.

"You'll have to get used to life without that extra weight on your head," the older man said.

"You are sure I won't have to put the mask back on?" Shihong asked. He noticed they were leading him to a side entrance of the housing compound, not the main gate, and he hesitated. Had he been stolen from one prison just to be taken to another?

"What's wrong?" the man asked.

"I...I don't know you," Shihong said. "Who are you? Why are you doing this?"

The man gave him a smile and clapped him on the back. "I'm doing this to save all of China."

"I don't understand," Shihong said.

"You will," the man said. "In time."

A short time later, Shihong was sitting in a small room inside the complex. He had been brought into the complex secretly, save for two guards at the entrance. He saw no one else. The younger man brought him a bowl of congee and a spoon.

"Eat," the man said.

Shihong picked up the spoon and filled it with the rice porridge. He tilted his head and tried to pour the congee into his mouth, but most of it missed his mouth and fell onto the table.

"What the hell are you doing?" the older man asked, and Shihong's face burned in shame. He put the spoon down. He was too nauseous to eat anyway.

"I suppose it was rather difficult to eat wearing that thing," the young said sympathetically, and Shihong only nodded as he cradled the mask in his arms. "Well, let's get you cleaned up, at any rate."

The older man left for a moment and then came back with a beautiful woman. She was tall and graceful, her hair swept up in a perfect chignon, decorated with a peacock feather.

The woman shrieked and put her hand to her mouth when she saw him, and he turned his face away.

"Oh, oh my word," the woman said. "For a moment, I thought you had kidnapped Hongdi." She chuckled.

"You truly think he looks that much like him?" the older man asked her.

"Well, of course," she said. "Can you not see the similarities?"

"I can," the man said. "But I did not know if I was the only one."

"Who...who is Hongdi?" Shihong asked again.

"Why, the emperor, of course," the woman said, and the man sighed in annoyance.

"The...emperor?" Shihong asked.

"I'm sorry," the woman said. "Did I do something wrong?"

"No," the man said. "I should have prepared you. Still, I think we need to bring Wen here. She knows Hongdi better than anyone. She will have the final say as to whether or not the boy could pass as Hongdi."

"Pass?" Shihong asked.

"Never you mind," the man said. "Go with Lady Kang. Let her clean you up and get you fed."

Shihong nodded and did as he was told. Lady Kang was gentle with him as she took care of him. It brought more tears to his eyes. He had not known such tenderness since he last saw his mother, the night he was taken away.

"My mother," he said as he sat aside while Lady Kang ordered her maids to fill a large metal tub with water. Lady Kang looked at him. "Do you know what happened to my mother?"

Lady Kang shook her head sadly. "I'm sorry. I don't even know who you are. I am sure my husband thinks it best to stay quiet about you for now. But I hope all questions will be answered in time."

She then helped Shihong to undress. He was reluctant to let go of the mask he still held in his arms.

"Here," she said, "I'll just place the mask on this bench where you can see it. How is that?"

Shihong nodded and let her take the mask from his grip. She then removed the rest of his clothes and helped him into the bath. The water was so hot, it nearly scalded him, but he did not resist. He couldn't remember the last time he had bathed, or even properly washed. When he had been a child, his family had been rather poor, so he usually bathed in the river. He remembered rowing a small boat across the water to visit the family on the other side to play. He especially enjoyed the company of a girl named Fei. She had the largest eyes, like two shining moons. He wondered what had happened to her.

Lady Kang took a cloth and washed Shihong's body and hair, brushing it out of his face and running scented soaps through it until it was silky. She then washed his face, and he flinched when she touched him.

"I'm sorry," she said. "Your skin seems to be very tender from wearing that horrible mask for so long." She did her best to clean him without causing more pain, then she put some sort of ointment onto his cheeks, chin, and forehead, and the pain subsided.

Once he was clean, he stepped from the tub, leaving the water behind nearly black with grime. Lady Kang wrapped him in a soft silk robe and then oiled and brushed his hair.

"There," she said. "See how handsome you are?" She motioned toward a mirror across the room.

Shihong stood and approached it hesitatingly. His family had not owned a mirror, but he had seen his reflection in the river, so he knew what he looked like before he had been taken. He was not sure what to expect after spending so many years in prison, locked behind the dragon mask.

When he saw the man staring back at him in the glass, he gasped and his heart began to race.

"How...how old am I?" he asked Lady Kang. "How long was I in the mask?"

"I don't exactly know, my dear," she said. "But I assume you are near of age with Hongdi, so that would make you nearly thirty years old."

"Thirty!" Shihong shouted. He couldn't believe it. He had been a boy, a child, when he was taken. Only thirteen... fourteen years old. He wasn't sure anymore. He'd been in prison for fifteen years? More than half his life? He didn't know. He couldn't see the moon or the sun from his prison cell. Every day was exactly like the one before and the one after. He knew he had been locked away for a long time. But he thought it had been a couple of years at the most. He never would have imagined that fifteen years had passed in that cell.

He felt anger bubble up in him. What had he ever done to deserve such a punishment? He had been a child! The man in the red robe had stolen him away in the night, clapped the iron mask onto his head, and then threw him into the prison cell. He was never told why.

He balled his hands into fists and banged on the mirror until it shattered. He heard Lady Kang scream and call for help, but he didn't care. He couldn't look at himself anymore. He couldn't look at the man he had become.

TWENTY-NINE

"*W*hat?" Donghai roared at the quivering eunuch before him.

"Just what I said, sir," the eunuch said. "The man in the dragon mask is gone."

Very few people knew of the man in the dragon mask's existence. The prison guards knew, as did two of Donghai's most trusted assistants. But they did not know who the man was or why he was there. Everyone was paid enough to not ask questions or even speak of the mysterious prisoner. But when the guards had awoken from their drunken stupor and found the man gone, they knew they had to alert Donghai as soon as possible.

"How?" Donghai asked.

"The guards are not sure, sir," the eunuch said. "The prison was not broken into or out of. The men heard nothing."

"How could they not hear the man escape?" Donghai asked. "He couldn't simply walk through the walls like a spirit. What aren't the guards telling you?"

"They claimed that they were alert all night and heard

nothing, but..." The eunuch hesitated. He did not want to say things that might not be true and cost someone his job —or his life.

"But what?" Donghai insisted.

"I could smell wine," the eunuch said. "Strong wine. And I saw shards from a broken bottle."

"So, you think the men were drunk?" Donghai asked.

"It would explain why they did not hear or see anything," the eunuch said. "But they are right about no evidence of a break-in. I checked all the locks and they were sound."

"Still, someone could have picked them," Donghai said. "Is that what happened? Someone picked the locks and the prisoner just waltzed out of the Forbidden City with a dragon's head attached to his neck?"

"I don't know, sir," the eunuch said. "I cannot explain it."

"I suppose it doesn't matter," Donghai said as he stood and began to pace. "All that matters is that the man is gone and we must get him back. Who took him?"

"Again, the men did not say," the eunuch said. "But I assume someone brought them the wine to get them drunk so they could steal the man away."

"Hmm," Donghai said, and he had a sneaking suspicion he knew exactly who had taken the man in the dragon mask. He had told the empress about the man in the dragon mask only a few days before. And yesterday, her father had paid a call at the emperor's audiences.

"The empress is behind this," Donghai grumbled.

"The empress?" the eunuch asked. "Are you sure?"

"Positive," Donghai said. "Change into peasant clothes and go to the Kang estate outside of the city. Keep an eye on it, on everyone coming and going. Report back to me if you see anything suspicious."

"Yes, sir," the eunuch said with a bow, then he quickly scurried away.

Donghai paced as he considered his options. He was certain that General Kang had stolen the boy away. But what would he do then? The boy was thin and weak. Foolish. He'd had no education and was fed poorly. Donghai felt guilty for that. He wished he could have set the boy up in a fine home. Given him everything a son of the dragon deserved. But he could not. He couldn't risk anyone recognizing him.

He should have killed the boy when he was an infant. It would have been so much easier. But he had been weak. Merciful. His heart had been soft for the empress and he could not bear the thought of causing her pain. And yet, he had done exactly that. All these years, she thought her son was dead, and she never recovered from that. She did not grow into the great empress he thought she would be. She had only grown cold. Cruel. Jealous. Every time another concubine of her husband became pregnant, he feared for the life of the concubine and her child. While some women miscarried, some died in childbirth, and some children died while they were young, he never had any evidence that the empress had done them harm. Still, he wondered. And then with the fiasco around Ruolan, he hated to think that the empress had Ruolan put to death if she really had been carrying the emperor's child, but he would never know for sure.

He realized that he could do nothing for the moment without risking the dowager finding out what he had done. She would surely despise him if she knew. She might even put him to death. He had hoped that one day he could reunite the dowager with her lost son. That perhaps she could visit him outside the palace occasionally. That maybe he could even be turned into a eunuch and enter service. But he had not expected the boys to look so similar as they aged. It became impossible to bring the boy into the empress's life. But he couldn't kill him as he did the midwife and her husband. The boy was a son of Heaven. He would never be able to live enough lives to work off the karmic debt for such a crime.

But now everything was such a mess, he could not see a way out of it. Surely the empress's father had taken Shihong for a purpose. But what that purpose was, Donghai shuddered to imagine. For now, all he could do was wait. He would have to find out where the boy was first, and then he could act.

❀

"*M*y mother is gravely ill, Your Majesty," Empress Wen said as she kneeled before the emperor on his dragon throne. "I beg you to allow me leave to visit her."

The emperor sighed. "After the way you have behaved, you dare ask for such a gift from me?"

Wen nodded. "I know that I do not deserve such kindness. But I do not ask for myself, but for my mother. She always held you in such high regard, loved you as her own son. It is she who has called me to her side. I would never have asked such a thing for myself."

Empress Wen handed the summons from her mother to Wangzhu, who handed it to the emperor. He glanced at it and then tossed it down the stairs back to Wen.

"Fine," the emperor said. "I have no wish to see your face anyway. You may visit your mother. Let your father feed you for a few days."

Wen knocked her head to the floor. "Thank you, Your Majesty," she said. "May you live ten thousand years!"

"Go," the emperor said with annoyance in his voice.

Wen stood and backed away out of the audience room. As she left, she met eyes with Donghai, and she did her best to suppress a smirk. He had surely heard that the man in the dragon mask was missing and would suspect she was behind it. But there was nothing he could do. If he reported to anyone that the man was missing, he would have to admit there was a man in a dragon mask in the first place, and then he would have to admit who the man was. It was dangerous to taunt Donghai the way she was, but he was completely powerless. She still had his *bao* jar, after all.

Later that day, Empress Wen arrived at her family estate outside of Peking. Her mother was, of course, in the peak of health, but a gravely ill mother or father was the only way an imperial lady could ever leave the palace walls.

"How is he?" Empress Wen asked as soon as she saw her father.

"You will have to see for yourself," he said, his face grim. She steeled herself for what she was about to see.

She was taken to a room that had to be unlocked for her to enter. "Is that really necessary?" she asked.

"Yes," her father said. "He had a fit of anger earlier that scared your mother. He has fits of crying, of laughing, of melancholy. He keeps asking for his parents. He is unstable. We have to assume he could be dangerous."

"Can you blame him after all he has been through?" Wen asked.

The general shrugged. "Perhaps not, but you have to ask yourself if he could possibly be any use to us in such a state."

"I am sure we can make that decision in time," Wen said. "But I will see him."

Her father nodded and opened the door. The man was standing with his back to her, looking out a window. Wen and her father entered the room, and the general shut and locked the door behind them.

"You have a visitor," General Kang said.

The man turned and faced Wen, and her hand when to her mouth. "By the gods."

The man smirked. "That seems to be everyone's reaction when they see me. But no one has told me why."

Wen shot a look to her father.

"We were waiting on you," he said. "You know Hongdi better than anyone. If you think this man truly looks like him, then maybe there is hope."

"Hope for what?" the man asked, his temper rising. Wen looked at her father and saw that he was tense as well. This was a volatile situation.

"Father," she said, "perhaps you should step outside."

"He's too dangerous," he said.

Wen turned to the former prisoner and held out her hand, motioning toward the chairs at the table in the middle of the room.

"You aren't going to hurt me, are you?" she asked with a smile.

The man shook his head and she saw the anger flee from him, leaving only sadness in his eyes. "I don't even know who you are."

Wen nodded and took a seat, inviting the man to sit in the chair near her.

"We will be fine, Baba," Wen said, trying to melt her father's defenses.

"Five minutes," he said as he walked over to the door

and exited. But she noticed that he did not lock the door behind him. He must have been expecting to have to burst back in at any moment.

"Thank you for speaking with me," Wen said, turning back to the man. "What is your name?"

"My parents called me Shihong," he said. "But now I am wondering if I am not who I thought I was."

Empress Wen nodded. "You are quite astute. You may call me Wen...for now."

"For now?" Shihong asked. "Is that not your real name either?"

"It is," she said. "But I am sure things between us will change in time."

Shihong sighed and shook his head. He didn't understand anything that was going on around him. But he still had not gotten an answer to his most pressing question.

"What happened to my parents?" he asked her. "The people who raised me."

Wen hesitated for a moment, then she spoke plainly. "They are dead. They were killed the night you were taken."

Shihong's eyes watered, but he brushed the tears away harshly. "I knew they were, but I didn't want to believe it. When they never came for me...I knew."

"What do you remember about your life before the mask?" Wen asked.

Shihong shrugged. "I was a child. Thirteen or fourteen, I think. We lived in a little village on a river. My father was a fisherman and my mother was a midwife and healer. We didn't have a lot of money, but I never wanted for anything. We had food and were well-liked by the other villagers. I was friends with the family across the water. I would paddle a small boat over the river when the weather was fine and we would all swim together."

Wen nodded. Such a simple life. But he looked back on those years fondly. She was glad he'd at least had those warm memories to keep him company over the years.

"Tell me truly," Shihong said. "How long was I in prison?"

"Fourteen years," Wen said. Shihong's head drooped, and she noticed his neck was humped slightly. He was terribly thin. His skin pale from years of no sunlight. But it was his eyes that worried her the most. His eyes were large, like a frightened cat, and sad. Pleading. When Hongdi looked at a person, you could feel his strength. His authority. You did what he demanded without complaint. Could this scared rabbit of a boy ever command anyone?

"Half my life," Shihong finally said. "All of my manhood. For what? What did I do? I was never told why I was imprisoned. Please." He gripped Wen's hand and she jumped in surprise, but then she felt the warmth and saw the need in his face. He had to know the truth.

"You are Emperor Hongdi's twin brother," she said. "You are my brother-in-law."

"Emperor..." he said, and his face tightened as he tried to understand. "You are the empress?" She nodded. "My brother is the emperor? But I still don't understand. Why did that mean I had to be locked up?"

"Because of ancient superstitions," she said. "Your mother was a midwife. Did she never tell you what happened to children born twins?"

He sat back in his chair. "No," he said. "What happens to them?"

"Well, you were just a boy," she said. "I suppose she didn't want to tell you the harsh truth of the world. Many people consider twins to be unlucky or a bad omen. The second twin, or in some cases both twins, are often drowned at birth. But since your father was Emperor Hongwu, the empress, your mother, could not let your brother die."

"So, she locked me away instead?" he asked. "Is she such a monster?"

"No," Wen said strongly, surprised at her instinct to protect the dowager from Shihong thinking poorly of her. "She wanted to keep you. But she was a soft touch. Her eunuch, Donghai, he knew that you had to be sent away. He told your mother that he had drowned you, but in truth, he gave you to your adoptive parents. The woman you knew as your mother was the midwife who helped deliver you to the empress."

"So, what happened?" Shihong asked. "Why was I put into the mask later?"

"Donghai went to see you, to give your family money for your schooling," Wen explained. "When he saw how much you looked like the young prince, your brother, he panicked. He was afraid that someone else would realize that you were the prince's brother and threaten the empire somehow. So he killed your parents, stole you away, and hid your face behind the mask."

"But...I would never—" Shihong said, jumping to his feet. "Threaten the empire? That's insane! I was a child. I just wanted to live my life. Even now, I just want to go home."

General Kang threw the door open and stepped into the room. Empress Wen motioned for her father to remain calm as she stood between the men.

"I'm afraid that is not possible," she said to Shihong. "We may need your help."

"My help?" he asked. "What can I do?"

"That remains to be seen," Empress Wen said. "I need to

consult with my advisors. In the meantime, eat, and eat well. Rest. Know that whatever happens, you are safe here."

Shihong shook his head in disbelief as he watched Wen leave the room. *Empress* Wen. He never would have believed in his life that he would speak to an empress. That he would turn out to be a prince.

A feeling of dread settled over him. She didn't speak of simply returning him to his birth family. Of restoring his birthright as a prince, the second son of an emperor. She still wanted...something from him. And he was suddenly very afraid of what that something could be.

*a*s Wen left the room with her father, she saw him lock the door behind her.

"Must we treat him like a prisoner?" Wen asked. "Hasn't he been through enough?"

"He is a prisoner," her father said. "He is here to help us with your little husband problem. If he's of no use to us, he might as well be back in the mask where we found him."

"Shh!" Wen hissed, then she walked ahead of her father to a nearby sitting room where her brother, Jun, and Bojing were waiting.

"So, what do you think?" Jun asked as Wen sat down.

"He looks like Hongdi, certainly," she said. "But you have eyes, you knew that."

"But what does that mean?" Jun pressed. "Is that useful to us?"

"It could be," General Kang said as he also took a seat. "We could use him to have Hongdi removed as emperor. If it was revealed that Hongdi had a twin, it could put his claim to the throne in question."

"I really don't think that will work," Wen said. "People

will just say it's a strange coincidence that they look so similar. The empress would never admit that she had two children. As cruel as she is to Hongdi, I can't believe she would speak out and threaten his rule."

"She killed that girl," Jun said. "The one who was pregnant. I think she certainly is a threat to Hongdi. If he were smart, he'd send her into a convent on the other side of the country where she couldn't cause any more trouble."

"He'd never do that," Wen said. "He's loyal to his parents to a fault. Unless she did something truly unforgivable, he would never banish her."

"And keeping a twin brother secret wouldn't be considered unforgivable?" General Kang asked.

"Only if she admitted to it," Wen said. "And I don't think she would. I, at least, wouldn't want to risk our only advantage on her word. If we brought Shihong forward and the dowager denied him, then where would we be?"

"Shihong?" Jun asked.

"The man in the dragon mask," Wen said. "Didn't you bother asking him his name?" Jun shrugged and poured himself a cup of wine. He offered a drink to his sister, but she refused.

"Unfortunately, Wen might be right about that," General Kang begrudgingly admitted. "We can't trust the dowager to do or say anything to our advantage. We have to find a way to use the boy in a way that can't then be used against us."

"Using the boy at all is a risk," Wen said. "He himself could turn on us in an instant."

"You seemed to be building a rapport with him," the general said. "Do you think he would betray you?"

"I don't know him at all," Wen said, bristling. "We only just met. And he has the mind of a child—the child he was the day he was stolen away. He's had no education, no life experience since he was fourteen years old. He's angry, frightened, heartbroken. That's probably why he lashed out. He doesn't know any other way to act. He's just a boy. Building trust will take time."

"Who knows how much time we have," the general grumbled as he took the bottle of wine from Jun and poured himself a cup. "That so-called man who currently sits on the throne is just as volatile. He could send us into war at any moment. Even if he doesn't, we'll be lucky to survive the winter without money to buy rice from the south."

"You don't have enough stores for the winter?" Wen asked her father.

"I have enough for my household," he said. "But you are not a member of my household anymore."

Wen pressed her lips into a thin line. She knew her father would never let her starve, but he certainly loved reminding her that he could.

"Surely when we heard that the emperor had a *twin* brother we all had the same thought," Jun finally said. "Are we really not going to talk about replacing the emperor with Shihong?"

"It would never work," Wen said. "In his current state, he doesn't even look that much like Hongdi. He's so thin! He's a skeleton of a man."

"We can fatten him up," Jun said.

"But it's more than that," Wen said. "It's not just having the same face. It's a bearing, his mannerisms. His eyes are... pleading. Hongdi would never plead for anything. He would never even ask for something. He would demand it. This boy..." She shook her head. "He doesn't have the strength of an emperor."

"He could be taught," Bojing said, speaking up for the first time.

"No," Wen said, but Bojing disagreed.

"The emperor we have today is not the man you grew up with," Bojing reminded her. "Don't you remember how kind Hongdi was as a child. How gentle he was with the kittens that were born each spring. How he fawned over his sisters when they were small. How tender he was with you until very recently."

Wen's cheeks warmed at the memories.

"Hongdi learned to be cruel," Bojing said. "Shihong could learn, too."

"But what about his history?" Wen asked. "Hongdi's relationships with everyone? The one person just as close to Hongdi as me is Wangzhu. You cannot tell me that Wangzhu won't know instantly if Hongdi is not himself."

Bojing had to admit that Wangzhu would be a problem.

"Perhaps Wangzhu could be persuaded to our side," General Kang said. "He must know that Hongdi is a danger to himself and everyone in China."

"We could never even ask," Wen said. "Wangzhu would never betray Hongdi."

"Then we could kill him," Jun said. "One less eunuch would be a boon for the world anyway."

"Jun!" Wen said. "Hold your drunken tongue."

"I've not begun to drink, sister," Jun said. "I'm just tired of your whining and complaining. You want change, but you aren't willing to do what is necessary."

Wen crossed her arms and turned away from her brother. His words stung. The dowager had said as much to her over the years, about her not really knowing what it meant to be empress. About her not having the strength to do what was necessary for her country. She believed they were wrong. She wasn't afraid of replacing the emperor with Shihong, she was just practical. It would never work.

"And what would happen to Hongdi in this scenario?" she asked. "If Shihong was to play the part of emperor, where would the real emperor go? Into the mask in the dungeon."

"That's not a bad idea," Jun said.

"No," General Kang said. "Too risky. He would rant and rave, proclaiming his innocence. We can't risk someone listening to him. Believing him."

"Then what?" Wen asked.

"We'd have to kill him," General Kang said.

"No!" Wen said emphatically. "No. I won't allow it. Stop suggesting that killing is the answer to every problem."

"Come on, Wen," Jun said. "Be reasonable."

"I think I am the only one being reasonable."

"You're being sentimental," Jun said. "Just as the dowager and Donghai were all those years ago. If they'd killed the damn baby when they had the chance, he wouldn't be here threating Hongdi's reign in the first place.

"If you don't have the courage to kill Hongdi now, then it is only a matter of time before he comes back and exacts his revenge and reclaims his throne."

Wen sighed, refusing to agree with her brother—even if he was partially right. Donghai should have killed the baby, that much was certain. But killing a baby was much different from killing a full-grown man. Babies were expendable. Babies died all the time. It was one reason why families had so many children, so they would always have more if some of them died.

But Shihong was not a baby. He was a man. A man with a valid claim, not just to his title as a prince, but to the throne itself, even if he did not know it.

"You cannot kill a son of Heaven," Wen said, glaring at her brother. "It would be the ultimate sin against Heaven and China. The gods would never allow you to go unpunished. You know that."

"Wen has a point," General Kang hated to admit. "A sin against Heaven such as that would surely provoke the gods to not just punish the person who killed the emperor, but China as a whole. No one would be worthy of the Mandate of Heaven if we allowed the murder of an emperor on our watch."

"Then what?" Jun asked, exasperated. "What are you going to do? You've dismissed all of our ideas out of hand, empress. What is your very clever idea?"

"I don't know," Wen said. "I needed to see him first. But now that I have, I can form a plan."

Wen stood up to leave, but her father stood up as well and blocked her path.

"Do not waste this opportunity, empress," he said. "If you do not come up with a better idea soon, I will make the decision myself and you will have to follow along."

Wen lowered her gaze and gave her father a small curtsey. "Yes, my lord," she said. General Kang moved out of her way and she walked past him, out of the room and down the hall. When she passed the door of the room where Shihong was, she thought she heard movement just on the other side. Had he been listening? She supposed he was. He had a right to be concerned about his future and his safety in the hands of her father. He was a general, after all. A keen warrior who knew how to take risks and make hard choices. She thought about the story she had often heard as a child growing up, of how it had been her father who had secured the throne for Emperor Hongwu by hunting down the last children of the Yuan emperor and slaughtering them, including a girl no more than six years old. It was a story that used to bring her pride, knowing that her father would do whatever it took to keep her secure on the throne. But now, she was learning a new lesson—that no one on the throne was safe if General Kang saw the ruler as a threat to his own comfort and security.

Wen rushed from the housing compound, back to her wagon without even seeing her mother. She knew her mother was well. The tale of her being ill had only been a rouse so she could see Shihong for herself. She needed to get back to the palace and decide what to do with Shihong. A man who looked so much like the emperor was valuable only if she knew how to use him. She understood why it was tempting to replace the emperor with him, but her father and brother could never comprehend why such a foolish plan would never work.

Yet, if Wen did not come up with a better plan soon, that was likely the scenario that her father would attempt. It would fail and cost all of them their lives. Wen had to come up with something better, something more sure. But what?

THIRTY-ONE

The emperor looked down from his dragon throne at his gathered advisors. Even General Kang had deigned to appear when summoned, though he did not look pleased, with his arms crossed and his face a perpetual scowl. Hongdi gripped the arms of his throne tightly, but did his best to keep his tone even.

"I have called you all here to address the growing unrest in the north," Hongdi said. "Our scouts have reported that the Manchu are indeed amassing an army. There have been several skirmishes along the wall. Several border villages ransacked. Hundreds dead. To say nothing of the Mongol, who are causing problems of their own. There are still some within China who think life under the Yuan was a better time. How could the people be such fools?"

"There will always be people who long for the past," one of the advisors, an elderly gentleman, said. "Very few people living would remember the world under the last Mongol emperor, but the country was its largest under Genghis Khan. Some people equate size to greatness."

"The Khans were barbarians!" the emperor yelled.

"They conquered through rape and slaughter, and held power the same way. I will not allow the greatest civilization in the world to fall to such madness. We will defeat our enemies on their own land and preserve the magnificence we have built here."

The emperor raised his eyes to take in the beauty of just the ceiling of his audience hall. Painted gold and embellished with thousands of blue birds, the greatest care had been taken with every detail in building his Forbidden City. He was a builder, a visionary. He did not show his power by trampling over those who were small and weak. He would earn their respect and awe by displaying his might and power with his palaces and his immense wealth...as soon as he was able to rebuild his wealth when the Forbidden City was completed.

Most of those gathered clapped or nodded their approval with the emperor's words. But General Kang still did not look convinced.

"What say you, General?" Hongdi asked directly.

"The Manchu are not something we should ignore," he said. "As you said, they are already killing hundreds of your own people, but what has been our response? Nothing. The northern landowners who have their own feudal armies have been holding the Manchu back, but that is not their responsibility. And if they continue building their own armies to protect China, how long do you think it will be before they turn those armies on Peking?"

The gathered audience began to mumble and tisked their tongues. They knew that the general spoke the truth, but to speak so plainly to the emperor was to invite his wrath.

"My own lords will not turn their armies on me," Hongdi growled. "Those lords only have lands and armies because I allow it. I could confiscate their lands in a moment if I wished it. As I could yours, *General*."

The room went so silent, the men were afraid to breathe. The general said nothing in response, his own silence a direct challenge to the emperor.

"So," the emperor finally said, breaking the tension and turning his attention to the rest of his gathered ministers, "what would you, my esteemed advisors, recommend we do? I am not against showing the Manchu, and the Mongol if necessary, a show of force, if that is what is needed to push them back."

"Sending a contingent of our own soldiers to assist the northern lords would be a great show of support," one of the ministers said.

"And we should send grain to the villages that were attacked," another said. "Many lost their winter stores."

"We will send troops," the emperor said. "But no grain. We do not have any we can spare if we wish to survive the winter ourselves."

"That is correct," the Minister of Agriculture said. "We still need to purchase more grain as well. The winter will be upon us within weeks. If we do not have our stores filled by then, it might be impossible to do so should the roads freeze."

The emperor turned to Minister Fu, the man who had replaced the previous finance minister. "Minister Fu, have you made arrangements to purchase grain from the south?"

"I have made some progress," Minister Fu said, his head low. "General Kang has retained his southern farmlands and has agreed to have food sent up to us on credit so we can survive the first winter."

"With sizable interest, I presume," the emperor grumbled.

Minister Fu shrugged. "That is the way of things, Your Majesty." He started to slink back into the crowd, but the emperor pressed on.

"But how many years will it take to pay off what we will owe this year?" the emperor asked. "Will we be able to afford grain next year? Or the one after that?"

The minister tentatively stepped forward again. "I cannot say precisely," the minister said. "There is much to consider. We don't exactly know how much grain we will need to survive. If the winter is mild, we may have plenty of grain and we can sell some to the villages and pay off the debt. But if the winter is exceptionally harsh, we may need to request more food toward winter's end."

"That is unacceptable!" the emperor said. "You should be able to account for any outcome."

"Yes, Your Majesty," the minister said, his voice starting to shake. "I am hoping to work with the court astrologers to predict how long the winter will last."

"Then get on with it," the emperor commanded, and the minister disappeared into the crowd.

The emperor rubbed his forehead. "Since we are not spending money on grain this year, thanks to General Kang's *generosity*, we can afford to send more troops to aid northern defense and to reinforce the wall. Send ten thousand men. Would that be enough, General?"

"It would be a start," the general said. "But we do not have a defense budget that large to pay that many men."

Hongdi groaned and banged his fist on the arm of his throne. "Is there no end to the discussion of money? We are the largest kingdom in the east! How can we have no money for food or troops?"

The advisors said nothing as they looked around the opulent audience hall. The emperor banged his fist again.

"The cost of the Forbidden City should be irrelevant! We had a budget before the building work even began. Why are we in such dire straits now?"

"You ordered the work on the palace to be done more quickly, Your Majesty," Wangzhu said, speaking on behalf of the chief builder since he was not invited to the audience as a mere workman. "So the budget had to be spent more quickly, and at a higher rate."

"That is ridiculous!" the emperor said. "It should not cost more to get the job done in less time."

All present could see that the emperor was not thinking clearly, but no one would dare volunteer to try to explain the situation to him more plainly. The emperor was well-educated and should understand the basics of finance, but his love for the Forbidden City was clouding his judgment.

"What shall we do, then?" the emperor asked. "Where shall we get the money for the troops?"

"If I could make a suggestion, Your Majesty," General Kang said, and he heard many sighs of relief from the other attendees. "It might be best if the imperial family was to winter in the south, back at the palace in Nanking."

"What?" the emperor nearly roared, but General Kang was nonplussed.

"It would save money if the grain did not have to travel so far. And the winter would be much shorter, so you would not need as much."

The emperor pressed his lips and breathed hotly through his nose. He knew the ministers, weak-willed as they were, would like this plan. They had wanted nothing more than to return to the south before they had even journeyed out of Nanking's gate on the sojourn north so many months ago.

"Also, if you were further south, it would make any

northern invasion much more likely to fail," the general went on. "Peking is so very close to the border. Should the Manchu break through our defenses, it would not take long for them to reach Peking, and possibly sack it.

"But if you were in the south, the loss of Peking would not threaten the empire. In fact, if the Manchu knew you were not here but were thousands of miles south, they would probably abandon their invasion plans altogether since an attack on Nanking would be impossible."

"We are not leaving the Forbidden City," the emperor said slowly through gritted teeth.

"Your Majesty—" the general started, but the emperor cut him off.

"Do not even suggest such a thing again, do you understand me?" the emperor commanded.

The general let out a heavy sigh and gave a small bow. "Yes, Your Majesty."

"Your answer to this problem since our arrival has been to return to Nanking," the emperor said. "I never thought you were a man who would want to turn tail and run like a scared bitch."

The room took in a collective gasp. Everyone knew that General Kang had been the reason why Hongwu had been made emperor in the first place, and why Hongdi had been able to retain his throne without any threats after the last Yuan emperor's heirs were all put to the sword. General Kang was highly respected for his martial abilities, and even foreign kingdoms knew of his great reputation. No one would ever presume him to be a scared dog, much less say such a thing to his face.

The emperor and General Kang stared at one another in the tense silence. But the general knew that Hongdi was baiting him. He was the only man who could stand in defiance of the emperor if he so chose. But he had always used his power to support the new Ming Dynasty that he helped build. Hongwu had been as a brother to him. It was why he gave his daughter to Hongwu's son as a wife, to cement their families.

But Hongdi, as his own man, did not appreciate all that General Kang had done for him. Hongdi was becoming paranoid, finding threats where they did not exist. In foolish concubines. In sniveling finance ministers. In his own general.

But he knew nothing of the very real threat that General Kang had hidden in his home right now.

Shihong. The missing twin. The man in the dragon mask. Jun had taken a liking to Shihong and had been doing an excellent job teaching him about the world and making sure he had plenty to eat. It was a slow process, but the general was seeing more and more of Hongdi in the face of Shihong every day. It was still a dangerous longshot. It was certainly treason. But if anyone could take the place of the emperor and sit on the throne—the throne with a dragon overhead holding a massive pearl in its mouth that was tasked with crushing any usurper—it was Shihong.

General Kang began to chuckle. He could not hold it back. His shoulders shook as the laugh grew until finally, it was an uproar. His eyes wept and he could hardly breathe.

The advisors and ministers around the room were shocked, looking at each other with their hands covering their mouths. But the humor was contagious. They did not know why, but soon they were all laughing as well.

Hongdi scowled down at the crowd. Why were they laughing? He had just called the greatest general in China's history a bitch. Why was General Kang not angry? Why had he not drawn his sword? If he had, he could have ordered the general's death right here and now. No longer would he be able to counter the emperor's orders. The emperor could depose the empress. He could finally and completely rule all of China alone.

But the general had laughed. The general had no fear of Hongdi. He did not see the insult as a blow to his power. He laughed. He thought it was a joke. As if the emperor could ever truly strip such a man of his rank or dignity. No wonder the general refused the throne in favor of Hongwu. To the general, the rank of emperor was a step down.

Hongdi forced a smile and chuckle to his face as well. He knew that if he showed his anger or punished General Kang, he would only lose more prestige in the eyes of his ministers.

"I am glad that we can still find levity in such trying times, old friend," Hongdi finally said.

The general stopped laughing and cleared his throat. "Indeed, Your Majesty."

"I have made my decision," the emperor went on. "Round up the ten thousand men we need to defend the north and press them into service."

"You mean...without pay?" General Kang asked.

"Yes," the emperor said. "It is about time the peasants did something for their country."

"This will anger the people greatly," the general warned.

"And there will still be a cost," Wangzhu reminded the emperor since the finance minister could not be found. "The men will have to be clothed, fed, and armed. And with winter coming, the costs will be higher than usual."

"Then increase the taxes on the northern landowners," the emperor said. "Since they are the ones who need help, let them carry the cost."

"Yes, Your Majesty," Wangzhu said.

General Kang only grimaced as he bowed. He knew this was a stupid, dangerous plan. The last thing the country needed was for the northern lords to join forces with the Manchu against a greedy tyrant. Yet, he could say nothing. The emperor had not asked for advice; he had given an order. And General Kang's only option was to obey.

"I look forward to your next report, General," the emperor said, a satisfied smug on his face.

"As do I," General Kang said as he backed out of the room. As far as he was concerned, the next time he delivered a report to the "emperor," it would be to Shihong—and Hongdi would be in prison.

THIRTY-TWO

"*H*ongdi really said that to my father?" Empress Wen asked Bojing in shock.

"Yes!" Bojing replied, nearly laughing as he relayed the story of that morning's audience to the empress.

Wen shook her head. "What did Father do? He couldn't have been pleased."

"He laughed!" Bojing said, and Wen's heart dropped into her stomach.

"He laughed?" she repeated. "He...he didn't. He didn't really laugh at the emperor, did he? Please tell me you are joking."

"No," Bojing said. "He laughed so hard tears were falling down his face. And then, everyone else was so startled, they started laughing too!"

Wen stood up and began to pace the room. "Hongdi must be furious. How could he stand the shame of it? Father is lucky to still be alive."

Bojing finally stopped laughing and took a moment to appreciate the seriousness of the situation. "The emperor can do nothing to the general. He is too powerful. Too rich.

If we don't starve this winter, it will be because of your father."

"So I've heard," Wen said, shaking her head. "Father is using Hongdi to shore up even more power for himself. But why? He never wanted to be emperor. He only ever wanted to play war. He should be gladly going to the north to defend the border and staying as far from Peking as possible."

"If Hongwu were still alive, I am sure that is what your father would gladly be doing," Bojing said. "But if Hongwu were still alive, we wouldn't be in Peking."

"Wouldn't we?" Wen asked. "It was Hongwu who started this palace in the first place. Hongdi is only completing what Hongwu started."

"Hongwu never would have bankrupted the country to build this palace," Bojing said. "He would have listened to his advisors. Hongdi...He will listen to no one."

"So you think my father had turned on Hongdi for the good of the country?" she asked.

"I would not presume to know the general's plans," Bojing said. "He is a far more clever man than I. But Hongdi is not turning out to be the emperor any of us had hoped for. And now with Shihong in the general's custody..."

"My father holds every advantage," Wen said. She sat on a chair and rubbed her forehead. "Oh, Bojing. What am I to do about Shihong? I still think that using him to replace Hongdi is folly! That poor, pitiful boy could never be an emperor. He wasn't raised for it."

"I agree with you," Bojing said. "But he could still be useful to you."

"How?"

Bojing crouched near the empress and said in a low voice, "What if he could get you with child?"

Wen's eyes went large. "What? How dare you say such a thing!"

"Hear me out, my lady," Bojing said. "Shihong is also a son of the dragon. He has a claim to the throne. A son by him would be a legitimate heir for Hongdi."

Wen's eyes watered as she shook her head. "I could never be unfaithful to Hongdi. Remember what happened with Ruolan? He would kill me if he ever found out."

"But he won't find out," Bojing said. "He can't kill you as long your father remains in power. And when the child is born, it will look like Hongdi. The emperor would never know the truth."

"But I would know!" Wen said. "And it would destroy me. Eat me up like a plague from the inside. My husband... He is still dear to me, damn him!"

Wen began to cry, and Bojing sat beside her and rubbed her shoulders.

How had they fallen so far apart, Wen and Hongdi? They had vowed to love each other forever. She had only ever wanted him to be successful. To outshine his illustrious father. But he had treated her so cruelly. She never imagined that she would entertain the idea of betraying him. Of lying with his own brother to beget a son.

"It would never work," Wen said, shrugging Bojing away from her. "I have not had relations with the emperor in months. Not since...that night. If I were to fall pregnant without finding my way back into Hongdi's bed, not even my father could save me."

Bojing nodded. "That is a problem. The only solution is for you to find a way back to your marital bed."

"But how?" Wen asked. "I have tried humbling myself before him. It seems to only make him even more angry with me."

"Stop thinking like an empress and think like a woman," Bojing said. "A woman who wants a man."

Wen's cheeks blushed, but she knew he was right. When was the last time she and Hongdi had lain together for enjoyment, for pleasure, without the pressure of trying to conceive a child?

"Perhaps you are right," Wen said as she went to a trunk near her bed and opened it, pulling out a nearly sheer silk shift.

"I will make sure your sedan chair is ready this evening," Bojing said as he left the room, closing the door behind him.

That night, after a long bath and an even longer amount of time having her body and hair prepared, Wen was once again waiting for Hongdi in his bedchamber. She was nervous, remembering how he had treated her last time, but this was her last chance. She even thought that if he did consent to lie with her, she would find a way to get rid of Shihong. Send him back to his village or to another country where he could no pose a threat to the emperor. Part of her still hoped that she and Hongdi could find their way back to each other.

When Hongdi entered the room, Wen was on his bed, her body exposed except for her bound feet, which were still housed in tiny slippers.

The emperor walked to the bed and parted the curtains, looking down at her. Her heart beat rapidly in her chest. He didn't look angry. Perhaps this would work.

"What are you doing here?" he asked her, his tone unreadable.

"I've missed my husband," Wen said, and she crooked her finger, beckoning him to her.

"You think you can just call me and I will come running?" he asked.

She smiled coyly, doing her best not to lose her nerve. "It has always worked before, my love," she said breathily to conceal her quivering nerves.

The emperor took a step closer and sat on the edge of the bed. He took her hand and put her finger in his mouth. He sucked on it, and Wen whimpered.

"I have not forgotten all we once meant to each other," he said. "But I am not that foolish boy in love anymore."

Wen felt her face fall. "What do you mean?"

"I now realize that marriage to you was a trick. A trap meant to keep me and my line in subservience to your father."

"I...I cannot speak to the motives of our fathers when they agreed to our marriage," Wen said. "But from the moment I met you, I loved you. I have wanted nothing more than to be your wife. Your lover. The mother of your children. Please, come back to me."

"No," Hongdi said, standing up and walking beyond the curtains of the bed. "I would still dismiss you as empress if I could."

"What?" Wen said, climbing from the bed and doing her best to hide her nakedness in the thin robe. "Why? Even if you have no desire for me anymore, I have been a good empress."

The emperor barked a laugh. "You have been the empress you wanted to be. A woman with control over her husband. Someone who sits at his right hand and rules by his side. That does not make you a good empress. It makes you a conniving woman."

Wen felt the fury build up in her at his words.

"At least when I was by your side people respected you," she spat, all nervousness gone from her voice. "Men never laughed at you when I was a proper empress."

Wen never saw Hongdi's hand fly before it struck her across the face. She stumbled to the side and stared at him in shock. But then her anger returned.

"The men laugh in front of you and behind your back!" she screamed. "A man who cannot make an heir. Who cannot build a palace. Who cannot keep his people safe."

Hongdi lunged for her, grabbing her around the neck and shaking her. She fought back, hitting his arms and kicking at his legs even though it hurt her feet to do so.

"Killing me won't help you save face," she choked out. "The whole country will despise you."

Hongdi yelled to drown out her voice and squeezed harder. She collapsed to her knees as she tried to draw breath, but there was only pain, and the room started to go dark.

She gasped in a deep breath when the emperor released her. When her vision cleared, she saw that Bojing and Wangzhu were there, each holding the emperor back.

"Arrest her!" Hongdi screamed. "Lock her up! I want her put to death!"

Wangzhu and Bojing both looked at each other, fear on their faces. Wangzhu then motioned for Bojing to take the empress away. Bojing grabbed Wen's arm, putting it around his shoulder as he lifted her to her feet and helped escort her from the room.

"I mean it!" Hongdi yelled as Wangzhu pushed him toward the bed. "I want her dead! Don't you dare take her back to her palace!"

Wangzhu poured the emperor a glass of the strongest

liquor he could find and forced the glass into Hongdi's hand.

"Drink," he said, pushing the glass toward the emperor's mouth. Hongdi didn't fight, but drank the fiery liquid down in one gulp.

"I should have them all put to death!" Hongdi went on. "Everyone who laughed at me today should be on the scaffold tomorrow."

Wangzhu pushed the emperor back onto the bed, trying to get him to lie down. "They only laughed because they were afraid. What other man would have the gall to speak to General Kang like that? You were very brave."

Hongdi relaxed at that. "They were afraid?"

"Of course!" Wangzhu said. "If Kang had argued with you or challenged you, he could have been arrested or banished. You could have confiscated his lands. What else could he do but laugh? He was afraid of you, Your Majesty."

"Good," Hongdi said. "I'm tired of having to bow and scrape to him and his family. Did you hear what Wen said?"

"It doesn't matter," Wangzhu said, trying to keep the emperor from growing angry again at the thought of her. "She is only bitter and lonely. She is nothing."

"Yes," Hongdi said. "She's miserable. Ha! Good. She is old anyway. I should replace her with someone younger. Someone more beautiful, refined."

He jumped back to his feet and strode from the room toward the Inner Court of the ladies. He went straight to Fan's palace and knocked on her door. When her eunuch opened it, he dropped to his knees.

"Your Majesty!" he said loudly, and Hongdi heard several gasps from inside. He stepped into the palace and saw Fan heading through one of the doors to another room.

"Stop!" Hongdi said, and Fan froze, dropping to her

knees. Hongdi went to her and pulled her up to him by her shoulders. He could feel her shake in his arms. He placed his lips on hers and held her tight. He felt that she was still rigid in his embrace, so he held her away from him, trying to look into her face.

"Look at me," he said, but she kept her eyes down. "Please," he finally added.

Fan's shaking subsided and she slowly lifted her eyes to his. Hongdi smiled and tapped her on the nose.

"There is that silly girl I remember from her selection ceremony," he said. She started to smile, but it quickly fell away and she dropped her gaze again. Hongdi sighed and pulled her into his arms in a warm embrace.

"Oh, my darling Fei," he said. "No other woman has warmed my heart the way you have. How I wish I had been more tender our first night together."

"A...as do I," Fei said, her voice cracking. But as Hongdi looked down at her, she looked up at him without being ordered to.

"I loved you once," Fei said.

"It will be my mission to help you love me again," Hongdi said. Then he turned and opened the door to her bedchamber and led her inside.

THIRTY-THREE

*T*he next morning, the emperor left after the sun came up. He kissed Fei gently on the cheek and walked out with a smile on his face and light feeling in his heart that he had not felt in months.

As soon as he was gone, Lina entered the room with a tea tray. "Good morning," she chirped as she placed the tray on a table near the bed. But Fei only pulled her blankets around herself and kept her eyes closed.

"My lady?" Lina said, going around the bed. "Did...did he hurt you again? He seemed to be...enjoying himself, I thought."

"He was," Fei said, her voice raspy.

"But you...weren't?" Lina asked. Fei opened her eyes and looked at Lina with a pained expression.

"How could I?" she asked. "He barged in here, kissed me, and took me to bed. He took me so quickly, there was only pain."

"Oh!" Lina said as she fell onto the bed, taking Fei in her arms. "I'm so sorry, my lady! I thought...Well, I thought he was being more gentle....I didn't...didn't realize..."

Fei pushed Lina away and wiped her face. "No, he was. He was trying to be kind, anyway. But I...I just couldn't stop thinking about last time. I couldn't...couldn't enjoy it. I was so tense. How could he think I was happy?"

"I'm sorry," Lina said again. "Some men are like that. They only think about their own pleasure and nothing for their lady."

"At least I will never fall pregnant," Fei said. "Eventually, he will tire of me and I will be able to retire in peace."

"Oh, don't say that, my lady," Lina said. "A child would be a great blessing! For you and the empire. There is still a chance. Ruolan got with child, didn't she? It could happen to you."

Fei sighed. "I have no idea what happened with Ruolan. But look at what happened to her. Getting pregnant didn't protect her. It cost her her life. I couldn't do it, Lina. I couldn't let him lock me up and then kill me. And I could never love a child by that man even if he let me live. It would be a cruel fate. I'd rather die."

"Please, my lady," Lina said gently, "don't speak in such a way. I still have to believe that you were chosen for a reason. You are still here while the others were retired. There is a great purpose to your suffering, as the priests say. But you have to be strong. Now, sit up and have your tea."

Fei nodded as she sat up, knowing that even Lina, who had been her dear friend for so long and not just a maid, could never understand the pain in her heart. The pain her body. The fear that shrouded her always. She would sit up and drink her tea and do as she was told.

Like a good girl should.

*T*he empress left before dawn for her family estate. She used the excuse of her ill mother, but by then everyone had heard of what the emperor had done to her, so no one tried to stop her from leaving. That the emperor would try to kill his own empress with his bare hands was...barbaric. The servants, the guards, the ministers, the advisors, as each of them heard of the assault on the empress, they feared for the emperor's sanity and what kind of revenge General Kang would exact. Would he withhold food from the city? Troops? Would he simply walk into the palace and murder the emperor in his bed? Of course, any of those actions would lead to war, but still, no one could blame the general if he retaliated in some way.

But no one could have guessed what kind of treachery was truly being plotted.

When Wen stepped into Shihong's room, she was shocked by his transformation. His hair was combed and partially tied up into a topknot. He wore a fine new robe. He had put on weight. But his eyes were still wide and gentle. She realized that Shihong did look like Hongdi, but a much younger version. He looked like the Hongdi who was still optimistic about the future and gazed at her with kindness.

"What happened?" Shihong asked as Wen sat across from him at the table in his room.

"The emperor tried to kill me last night," she said, her hand lightly touching her throat. "But I deserved it. I taunted him. I should never have—"

"No," Shihong said. "You are the empress. No one should ever lay a hand on you."

Wen gave a sort of half-smile at the boy's naivety. "I am a wife like any other. My husband has the right to punish me as he sees fit."

"My father," Shihong said. "I mean, my fisherman father, he never raised a hand to my mother or me. I know some men do that. I often saw women or other children with bruises. But my mother worked hard as a midwife and healer for the village and in our home, providing us with food and clothes. Father said that even if she did step out of line, she deserved respect. I suppose you have a lot of responsibilities as empress. You deserve at least as much respect as a village midwife."

Wen felt her eyes water at his words. Not for the first time, she was sorry that Donghai tore Shihong's family from him.

"Well, the emperor is never wrong," Wen said as she regained her composure.

"Then why do you wish to replace him with me?" Shihong asked.

"What do you know about it?" Wen asked since she had told her father and brother that it would be impossible.

"Jun spoke to me about it," Shihong said. "He said the emperor was losing his mind. Was no longer fit to rule and that I should take his place."

"And what do you think?" Wen asked. "Can a boy who lived half his life on a farm and the other half in prison ever be an emperor?"

Shihong shook his head. "I didn't think so. I told Jun I could never act like such a cruel man. He told me about how Hongdi was savage to the concubines. The execution of the pregnant girl. I could never be him. Or so I thought."

"You've changed your mind?" Wen asked.

Shihong reached out and touched Wen's collarbone. "When I saw what he did to you, I realized that he cannot stay in power. He will kill you if he does."

The warmth from his touch was soothing on Wen's

neck, but she shrugged him away. "I am nothing. The emperor is what matters. An heir is what matters."

"I suppose that is true," Shihong said. "If I cannot have a son either, then the empire will still crumble."

"Do you think you can?" Wen asked. "Have a son, I mean?"

"I...I've never been with a woman," Shihong said. "I never saw a woman again after I was locked away. I have no idea. But if we are twins, I fear that I might suffer the same problem."

"There would be only one way to know for sure," Wen said.

Shihong thought about her words for a moment, and then realization dawned on him. "Oh, my lady! No. I could never violate you in such a way."

Wen waved his concerns away. "No, not me. The emperor has not taken me to his bed in months, and he has vowed never to do so again. If I were to fall pregnant, I would be put to death immediately for my disloyalty."

"Disloyalty," Shihong scoffed. "Is he not disloyal by refusing to do his duty by you?"

Wen could not reply to that. "But there is someone else. A girl. A young concubine. I am told he took her to bed last night."

"You want me to bed this girl?" Shihong asked.

"I think it would be best," Wen said. "Not only would we be able to find out if you are...potent, but it would be a way to test if you could truly pass as the emperor. If you can fool this girl into believing you are the emperor, maybe you could fool the rest of the court as well."

"I would not feel right bedding her and her not knowing who I am," Shihong said. "Could we not tell her the truth?"

Wen shook her head. "Too many people know already.

If anyone with an agenda against my family were to find out, they could ruin all of us. If you were to tell the girl the truth, then her maid would know, and her eunuch, and then it would spread throughout the palace."

Shihong went quiet for a while. He did not expect this to be part of the deception. To bed a girl who thought he was another man? It made him almost sick to think about. But if she was the only woman the emperor was willing to lie with, he wasn't sure he had another choice.

"The girl," Shihong said, "is she a fool? Would she be easily deceived?"

"I do not believe so," Wen said. "I do not know her well, but she is brave. Clever. She was friends with the concubine who was executed. She went so far as to find a way for the emperor to pardon the girl, but it would mean admitting guilt, which the pregnant girl refused to do."

"She sounds very industrious," Shihong said. "What is her name?"

"Song Fan," Wen said.

Shihong's mouth went dry for a moment. "Song Fan? Are you sure? Where is she from?"

"I don't know," Wen said. "Some village out of the city. Why?"

"I knew a girl named Fan once," he said. "She lived across the river from my family."

"Fan is a common name," Wen said. "Was this girl your sweetheart?"

Shihong blushed. "She was younger than me. And her family was much better off. I am sure I never would have been good enough for her. But, yes, I had hoped to at least ask for her as a wife one day."

"Hold on to that memory," Wen said, reaching across

the table and taking Shihong's hand. "Remember her as you do what you must."

"Yes, Your Majesty," Shihong said. "If you are certain that this is the only way, I will do what you ask of me."

"Good," Wen said as she stood. She opened the door and invited her father and brother in. "Shihong and I have agreed that he will try to impersonate the emperor."

"Are you sure?" the general asked. "As you said, it's quite complicated."

"We are going to start small," Wen said. "With the concubine Song Fan. She is the only girl the emperor has had relations with. Shihong is going to go to her in the guise of Hongdi. If he is able to fool her, and if he gets her with child, then we will see about him replacing Hongdi for the rest of the court."

"And what of Hongdi himself?" Jun asked. "Shall we..." He made a cutting motion across his neck.

"No!" Wen and Shihong said together. Wen nodded at Shihong, glad they were in agreement.

"He is still a son of Heaven," Wen said. "The gods would never forgive us."

"He is my brother," Hongdi added. "To kill him would be like killing myself."

"Fine," the general said. "We will lock him up here, in this room. Once Shihong is settled into his role and we are confident it will work, we will send Hongdi south, to our estate there to live out his days."

Everyone agreed. They would start the plan that very night.

THIRTY-FOUR

*S*hihong nearly laughed as Jun came into his room dressed in peasant clothes.

"What?" Jun asked as though offended. "Do I not look the part of a farmer?"

"Not really," Shihong said. "You're too clean. And your hands are too soft."

Jun hmphed, sticking a long reed in his mouth to chew on. "I might not be a farmer, but I'm no pampered prince. I am a captain in my father's army."

"Perhaps," Shihong said. "You are still too clean, and your back is not humped as though you have slaved over a plow all your life."

Jun moved to a tall mirror. "You may be right about that." He ran his hands over the floor and then put his hands on his face to muddy it, then he slouched. "How's that? Do I look like a poor farmer now?"

"You are getting there," Shihong said. "But I don't know how I could ever pass for an emperor."

Jun looked him over, slapping him on the back. "Yes, we should do something about your neck. It is hunched a bit."

Shihong reached up and rubbed his neck. "The mask was quite heavy, especially when I was younger."

"Maybe a bonesetter could help. I'll send for one when we get back," Jun said as he tossed Shihong a long dark cape. "Make sure your face is covered."

Jun and Shihong climbed into a cart pulled by two mules and set off for Peking early that evening. By the time they arrived, it was quite late. They left the cart at an inn a few blocks from the Forbidden City, then they walked to one of the lesser-used gates. They were only there for a moment when Bojing stepped out and waved Shihong over.

"Good luck," Jun said to Shihong, then he went back to the inn to wait.

Bojing had bribed the guard well to take a quick walk, so no one was there to see Shihong enter the Forbidden City. They then quickly went to the empress's palace, entering the servants' entrance around back.

"You made it," Wen said as she approached Shihong with one of the emperor's robes.

"Did you think we wouldn't?" Shihong asked, slightly alarmed. If she didn't think the plan would work, should they be going through with it?

"I have learned that we should never take anything for granted," Wen said as she helped him dress. "The world can change at any moment. Now, turn around."

Wen was biting her lower lip as she looked him over.

"What do you think?" Shihong asked.

"I don't know," she said. "You look like him and look nothing like him at the same time."

"What do you mean?" Shihong asked, running his hands down the front of the robe.

"Stand up," she said, and he did so. "No, not just straight, hold your chin up. Your chest. Your right arm should be behind you." She guided him as best she could. He never imagined that just standing up would be so difficult.

"It is not just his physical form that gives the emperor away," Wen tried to explain. "It is his entire bearing. He is confident. Sure."

Shihong did his best, but he knew he was failing.

"And your eyes," Wen said, turning his face to a mirror. "Your eyes ask people to believe you. They should command. When you look at someone, they should be terrified to ever doubt your words."

"How can I do that with my eyes?" Shihong asked, making faces in the mirror.

Wen sighed. "Look at me." As Shihong did so, he noticed that she was bent forward with a small smile, like a coquettish girl begging for attention. But then the empress blinked and stood up straight. She clasped her hands in front of her and looked down her nose at him even though he was much taller. She was suddenly a great lady and he felt the urge to fall at her feet.

"I...I don't think I could ever do that," Shihong said, his confidence shaken.

"Yes, you can," Wen said as she reached out and straightened Shihong's robe and dusted off his shoulders. "If you believe you can, then you will. Understand?"

Shihong nodded even though he did not believe he could do as she asked. This was going to be a disaster. As soon as the girl Fan saw him, she was sure to raise the alarm.

"Good," Wen said. "Well, either we go through with this or we quit now. All of our lives are riding on you."

Shihong felt his hands go clammy and his heart race. He knew he should walk away. This was stupid. He could never impersonate his brother. He had never even seen the man! Fan had been intimate with him. She would certainly know he was not her lover.

But as he looked at the empress and saw the dark bruises around her neck, he knew he had to try. Not just try, he had to succeed. If he failed, all of them would be put to death. He had lost half of his life to the iron mask, and all of his life to a lie on his birth night. This was his chance to reclaim some of what he had lost.

"I can do this," Shihong told Wen.

"Very well then," Wen said, and she nodded to Bojing. Bojing then led Shihong out of the empress's palace and across the grounds to Fan's palace, sticking to the shaded areas so they would not be seen. They stood in some bushes for a moment, making sure the coast was clear.

"Just knock, and then take Lady Song to her bedroom, dismissing her servants," Bojing whispered. "You don't want to try convincing three people tonight that you are the emperor."

Shihong nodded, and then Bojing motioned for him to proceed. Shihong stepped out of the shrubs and into the light of Fan's palace.

"Stand up straight!" Bojing whispered harshly from his hiding place.

Shihong started to sweat. One second into his deception and he was already forgetting everything he had been told. He took a tentative step toward the palace, and then another and another. Finally, he was standing at the door. He raised a hand to knock, but the knock was so soft even he did not hear it. He cleared his throat and took a deep breath, this time knocking hard enough for the whole house to hear.

A young eunuch opened the door and then instantly

dropped to his knees. "Your Majesty," he said. That gave Shihong a small boost of confidence, so he stepped through the doorway. He looked around the room, but he did not see Song Fan. A maid shuffled over with her head down.

"Your Majesty," she said. "My lady has already retired to her bedchamber."

"Then—" His voice was much too soft, so he cleared his throat a tried again. "Then, I will see her there." He swept past the maid to one of the doors and he hoped it was the right one. When the maid didn't try to stop him, he thought it must be. He opened the door and stepped into the room, quickly closing the door behind him.

When he looked around, he saw a young woman kneeling on the floor in front of him.

"Song Fan?" he said.

"Yes, Your Majesty?" she said, rising but keeping her head down.

Shihong was amazed he had even gotten this far. He stepped toward her and took one of her hands. "I am glad to see you."

"And I you," she said, but he could tell she didn't mean it.

"Is everything all right, my lady?" he asked. She raised her head and looked into his eyes and he froze.

It was Song Fan. His Song Fan. The girl who lived across the river from him when they were children.

"Fan," he gasped.

"Yes?" she asked.

He smiled and started to laugh, then he took her into his arms and hugged her tightly. But her body was as rigid as a tree.

"I'm sorry," he said, releasing her. "I...I..." He wanted to know if she recognized him, but there was something cold in her gaze. Something he recognized. Hurt and anger. But why? Had he done something to her? Then he realized that she was not seeing him, Shihong, but his brother, Hongdi. Hongdi had done something to this girl to make her hate him, even if she did not dare say so with her words. And now he was torn. He wanted so much to talk to her as himself, to tell her that he was alive. But he couldn't. He had to play the part of the emperor.

"I...I just...It is though I have just now seen you for the first time," he said. "You suddenly reminded me of someone I knew when I was young. A dear friend."

Her face softened a bit, and she looked at him quizzically.

"I thought the same thing the first time I saw you," she said. "That is why I could not speak. I thought you were a boy from my village."

She did remember him! And she thought the emperor was Shihong! Oh, how the gods were tricky, that they should bring them back together after so many years but they be unable to speak freely. He knew that one day, he would tell her the truth. Every part of it. Once he was the emperor, he would lay his soul bare to her.

"Funny how our minds play tricks on us, isn't it?" Shihong said as he reached up and lightly touched the side of her face. She flinched at first, but then she closed her eyes and sighed. How long had it been since the girl had known a gentle touch?

Fan had grown from a lovely child into a beautiful woman. He ran his hand over the silkiness of her hair, the roundness of her shoulder. Oh, how he wished he could tell her who he was. He felt his desire for her rise and he took a step closer. He had never been with a woman before, but Jun said that his body would know what to do, and it seemed his friend had been right. He took her jaw in his hands as he placed his lips on hers. He thought he felt her pull away, but he had to remind himself that she was pulling away from Hongdi, not him. She turned her face away and he kissed her jaw and her neck. He urged her closer to the bed, and she followed his movements. He was grateful that she had some experience as a concubine because he was eager to be with her—far more eager than he had anticipated—but she moved slowly, reluctantly, and he was forced to slow down as well. But his body reacted to hers naturally, easily, and almost before he knew it, he reached a height of pleasure he never dreamed was possible.

When they were finished, he pulled her into his arms and held her. She let him, but he still sensed hesitation in her movements.

"Fei," he said as took in the scent of her hair. "Why do you pull away from me? I long for you so."

She slowly turned to face him and there were tears in her eyes. "Do you truly not know?" He looked at her dumbfounded. He could not answer her. "Do you not know how you hurt me so badly? How afraid I was? Even when I begged you to stop!" She rolled away and sobbed into her hands. Shihong held her and rocked her as a small child.

"Fei, my precious Fei," he said. "I am sorry! Truly, I would never want to cause you harm."

She sniffed and wiped the tears from her face. "You...are sorry?"

Shihong sat up and turned away from her, burying his face in his hands. What was it Wen had said? Something about how the emperor is never wrong. An emperor would never admit to making a mistake or apologize. As the Son of Heaven, it was an impossibility for him to make an error in judgment. And yet, he could not ignore Fei's suffering at Hongdi's hands. He would find a way to make up for his brother's cruelty.

He turned back to Fei and took her hand in his. "Fei, I must go now. But I will return to you. And one day, all of this will make sense. I…I have not been myself lately…" He shook his head, torn between wanting to comfort her and being afraid of saying too much. "Please, you must trust me. Things will get better, I swear it to you."

With that, he stood up, dressed, and fled her palace. Bojing was still waiting for him in the bushes nearby and handed him his cape to cover his fine garments and face. They did not return to the empress's palace, but went back out the gate they entered. Shihong left Bojing and walked to the inn, where Jun was killing time by gambling and drinking. Shihong made sure to keep his cape pulled down so no one would recognize him. Once he got Jun's attention, Jun ended the game and they went back to the mule cart and left the city.

"So, are you a man now?" Jun asked jokingly as soon as they were out of the city.

"The ruse worked," Shihong said. "She thought I was the emperor."

"Then why the long face?" Jun asked. "Was it not as good as you had hoped?"

"It was incredible," Shihong said. "*She* was incredible. I love her, Jun."

Jun let out a hearty laugh. "I can say I have lost my heart many times to sweet maidens. Yet I still had to marry the woman of my father's choosing. The life of a noble is not as glorious as many people imagine."

"She is afraid of me, though," Shihong said. "Of Hongdi.

He was cruel to her. I will do whatever it takes to save her from him."

"Let's not get ahead of ourselves just yet," Jun said. "Once you get Fei with child, then everything will change, my friend."

Shihong nodded his understanding and prayed that the gods would show him this one blessing in a long life of misery, that Fei would become pregnant with his son.

THIRTY-FIVE

*F*ei stood just inside her doorway as she watched the first snowflakes of the season drift down, covering the ground and grass and bushes with a thick white layer. Several of the concubines left their palaces for the first time in weeks in order to catch the delicate flakes on their noses and tongues. Some of the children of the palace—the sons and daughters of Hongdi's half-sisters— ran down the paths, gathering up handfuls of fluff and trying to throw them at each other, but the snow was too dry to stick.

The sky was a bright blue, streaked with wispy white clouds, and for the first time in longer than she could remember, Fei appreciated the beauty of it. While the despair and loneliness in her heart and stomach were still ever-present, they seemed farther away than usual. As if there was light at the end of the tunnel, even if she couldn't see it quite yet.

"Tea, my lady?" Lina asked, handing Fei a steaming cup.

"Yes, thank you," Fei said as she accepted the teacup, letting the heat seep into her fingers as she breathed in the cold winter air around her. She blew on the tea and then sipped, letting the hot water slip slowly down her throat into her stomach.

"Perhaps you should come inside, my lady," Lina said. "Your nose is already quite red."

Fei sighed and went to her sitting room while Lina closed the door. Fei's chair was situated near a brazier that was burning split logs at a roaring pace. She sat in the chair and pulled a heavy blanket over her legs as she picked up an embroidery hoop to continue working on a red decorative scarf she would send to the dowager when it was completed. Fei assumed the old woman wouldn't even notice it and would simply chuck it aside or have it sold. But it was expected of all the consorts and concubines to send gifts to their mother-in-law regularly, so Fei did so without complaint.

But she couldn't seem to focus as she held the hoop with a half-finished chrysanthemum in one hand and a threaded needle in the other. Her mind continually drifted to last night and the emperor.

"Lina," Fei finally said. "Did the emperor seem... different to you last night?"

"I hardly see him at all," Lina said. "So I'm not sure I'd know. He did seem a bit rushed. And I was surprised when he left so early instead of staying the night."

Fei nodded. "Yes, that was odd."

"What was odd?" Yuying asked as he entered the room carrying more firewood.

"The emperor," Lina said. "Fei was just saying he seemed to be a little different last night."

"Hmm," Yuying said, then he returned to his work stacking the wood.

"What?" Fei said, getting a distinct feeling that Yuying had noticed something as well. "What did you see?"

"Nothing, my lady," Yuying said. "I opened the door and he went straight to your room...but..."

"Go on," Fei said.

"I don't know," Yuying said. "When I saw him, I had to look twice to make sure...This must sound stupid, but to make sure it was him."

"You didn't recognize him?" Fei asked, something niggling at the back of her mind.

"It felt like my mind was playing tricks on me," Yuying said. "I knew it was him, but at the same time...it wasn't."

"I know what you mean," Fei said, leaning back in her chair and tossing her embroidery aside. "I felt something similar. He looked the same, but something felt...off. He was different, somehow."

"He didn't hurt you again, did he, my lady?" Lina asked, concerned.

"No," Fei said. "Just the opposite, in fact. He was so kind. Gentle. He even apologized for hurting me."

"Lina nearly fell over from the shock. "He apologized? That doesn't sound like the emperor at all!"

"I know," Fei said with a small chuckle. "He also said that he hadn't been himself and that one day, everything would be clear to me."

"Do you think he was drunk?" Lina asked, her voice a whisper as if someone might hear her.

"I didn't smell any alcohol," Fei said. "Perhaps opium?"

Yuying nodded. "Perhaps. The emperor does imbibe once in a while, though I have never heard of him taking so much he loses his senses."

"Well, he has been under a lot of pressure lately," Lina said. "There's a first time for everything."

"Yes," Fei said, turning her head to the window and watching the falling snow.

*T*hat evening, the emperor came to Fei's chambers again. She was surprised to see him so soon, but she kneeled and did not even consider turning him away.

"Fei," the emperor said, taking her hand and pulling her up to stand. "You are looking as beautiful as ever."

Fei looked at his face, into his eyes, felt the touch of his hand. She did not have any of the apprehension or doubt from the night before. He was the same as always. She thought that he must have been taking opium the day before and that is why he had seemed different.

"What is it?" he asked her.

"Nothing," she said. "I just wanted to tell you how much your words meant to me the last time you were here."

"I am glad to hear it," he said with a smile. "I meant every word."

"Your apology meant more to me than I can ever say," Fei said.

"What?" the emperor asked. "What apology?"

Fei stepped back, afraid she had angered him. "When you apologized for hurting me. Don't you remember?"

"If I hurt you," the emperor said, "that was not my intention. But I would never apologize for only taking what is my husbandly right."

"Of course," Fei said, kneeling again. "I'm sorry. I must have misinterpreted your words."

"Quite so," the emperor said. Then he reached out and tugged her robe open. Fei put her hands down to try and stall him.

"Wait," she said. "Can we not go more slowly? Take our time?"

The emperor smiled, but not one of playfulness. He looked more like a hungry wolf over an injured rabbit. He pulled the sash from her robe in one yank.

"Playing coy, now?" he said into her ear as he gripped her arms tightly. He bit her lobe, and she winced. Then he kissed her cheek as he pulled open her robe and fondled her breasts.

"Please...please," she begged, hoping he would slow down. She was becoming tense at his aggression.

"Oh, yes, Fei," he said, a huskiness to his voice as he completely disrobed her and pushed her to the bed. "Beg me, girl. Beg."

Fei whimpered as the emperor ravaged her once again.

❦

The next morning, when the emperor was gone, Fei continued to lie in bed, watching even more snowflakes fall outside her window. They were so beautiful. She dreamed of being a snowflake, floating on the breeze as far from this place as possible, and then melting at the first sign of spring. It would be a short life, true, but oh, so much more blissful than this one.

She had been mistaken in thinking that the emperor had changed. In hoping that he was sorry for hurting her and would do his best to do right by her in the future. He must have been drugged the other night, for last night he was as cold and unfeeling as ever. If anything, he had been worse than before. He seemed to enjoy dominating her, hurting her. The more she begged him to stop, the more aroused he became. She vowed that the next time he came to her, she would remain silent in the hopes that it would end more quickly.

But the next time he appeared, he was once again gentle and kind. She wept at the softness of his touch, and he kissed away her tears. She wondered if he had again been smoking an opium pipe, but she could not smell it on him and he showed no other signs of being drugged.

When the emperor made love to her that night, she felt some twinge of pleasure for the first time. She held him close, wishing that he would remain this man for all of time.

But it was not to be. For the next several weeks, whenever the emperor came to her, she never knew what mood he would be in. Gentle or rough. Kind or cruel. And he never seemed to remember their conversations from one night to the next. She soon realized that there was no point in trying to talk to a man who was often drugged when he came to her, for that was the only explanation. He was not the same person each night, and the drugs addled his brain.

Each time the emperor came to her, she grew more quiet, more reserved. When he took her, she withdrew into herself, dreaming of being a snowflake on the breeze. The emperor would finish, and she would have almost no recollection of the event after, which calmed her mind.

When the emperor came to her in his drugged state, she knew that he wanted her to be more responsive. She sensed that he cared for her. But she knew it wasn't the real emperor she was talking to. The more he pressed her to open her heart and mind to him, the deeper into herself she crawled until there was only Fei and the snow.

"*A*re you feeling all right, my lady?" Lina called to Fei. "Yes, just a moment," Fei replied. But everything was not all right. It was all wrong. All terrible.

Her moon phase was late.

She paced the room, tears in her eyes, her stomach sick. She didn't want anyone to know. Not even Lina. If her maid knew, it would be her duty to inform the Ministry of Household Affairs. They would then send a doctor to confirm her condition. Then the doctor would inform the emperor.

Would the emperor then kill her as he had Ruolan?

The mere thought of Ruolan was enough to send her into a panic. As miserable as she was, she didn't want to die. She didn't want to be sent down into that filthy, stinking prison with the wild animals and that beast with the dragon head.

But she didn't know what else to do. How could she hide it? Lina would know that she was due for her moon phase, and if she didn't bleed, it would be her duty to report. Fei couldn't ask Lina not to fulfill her duty. If it were discovered that Lina knew Fei was pregnant and kept the information quiet, Lina would be punished.

Lina knocked again. "Should I send for a doctor, my lady?"

"No!" Fei said. "I'll be right out. Just a...a bit of... cramps!" Oh, why did she say that? She was certainly going to be in trouble now.

"I see," Fei said through the door. "I'll prepare a hot poultice for you."

Fei then heard Lina walk away. She had bought herself a couple of minutes, but not any more than that. As Fei tried to think, her eyes fell on a knife sitting with her supper tray from last night. She picked it up, wiping the sauce from the blade. It wasn't very sharp, but it would have to do. She held the knife to her palm, but then she realized that Lina would know something was wrong if she saw a cut on her hand. Instead, she pulled up her robe and made a small cut on the inside of her thigh. She bit her lower lip to keep from crying out. It would have been easier if she'd had a sharper blade. But as she started to bleed, she picked up an undergarment and pressed it to the wound. By the time she stopped bleeding, she was surprised to see that the cloth looked similar to her cloths when she did have a moon phase. She sighed in relief. Then, she heard Lina knock on the door again. Fei went over and undid the lock.

"Sorry," Fei said.

"Not to worry, my lady," Lina said, ushering Fei back to the bed. "You just rest and put this on your tummy." She helped Fei get comfortable and then placed the poultice on her. Lina then went around the room and collected the laundry. She didn't even look twice at the stained undergarment.

"I had hoped that since the emperor had visited you so many times, there might be a different outcome this month," Lina said with a sigh. "I suppose it's just not meant to be."

Fei said nothing as she laid back in the bed and stared up at the ceiling. She knew about pregnancy and childbirth since she had younger siblings. She knew that unless she did something about it, the baby would come.

She just didn't know if she had the courage to do what was necessary.

THIRTY-SIX

$\mathcal{A}$s Shihong left Fei's palace, he felt frustrated, confused. She had barely spoken a word to him, didn't look at him, didn't respond as he tried to make love to her. It was as if she was a hollow shell of herself. And the kinder he was to her, the more withdrawn she became. He wished he could talk to her, ask her what was wrong. He suspected it had something to do with Hongdi, but he couldn't find out without revealing that he wasn't really the emperor. He wished she would fall pregnant. As soon as she did, Empress Wen and General Kang would believe in him enough to let him take Hongdi's place. Then he could tell Fei everything.

He turned down a path along her palace toward the gate. He no longer met Bojing outside the palace but went straight to the inn to keep from lingering.

"Your Majesty?"

Shihong had been so deep in thought, he had not heard the eunuch approach him. But as he turned to face him, he felt his heart freeze in his chest.

"I thought I just left you in your chambers..." the man said as he looked at Shihong curiously.

"I...I...Yes..." Shihong tried to talk, but the words died away in his mouth. For some reason, he never imagined he would see the eunuch who had imprisoned him again. He didn't even ask about him. When he found out how long he had been in the mask, for some reason, he assumed that the old eunuch must have died by now. But he hadn't. He was right here in front of him. He was even older now, his skin hanging off his even thinner body, but he had the same dark eyes and thin lips.

"Your Majesty?" the eunuch asked again.

Shihong couldn't speak. His breathing was rapid and he was sweating. He shook his head and took a step back. He had to get away. But the man grabbed his wrist, his grip cold as ice and Shihong screamed.

"No! I won't let you!" Shihong said.

"It's you!" the eunuch said. "Dewei! The twin. What are you doing?"

"Let me go!" Shihong yelled, but the old man was surprisingly strong.

"Guards!" the eunuch shouted, then he turned back to Shihong. "Whatever you are up to, it stops right now!"

Shihong knew he had to do something. He couldn't let the monster put him back in the mask. He stopped pulling and lunged forward instead. The eunuch was caught off-guard and Shihong was easily able to wrestle him to the ground.

"Help!" the eunuch cried.

"Shut up!" Shihong said, wrapping his hands around the eunuch's throat. He squeezed, and the eunuch clawed to escape. "I won't let you put me back in the mask!" He slammed the eunuch's head down on the stone walkway.

Once. Twice. After the third time, the man stopped calling for the guards. Another slam to the ground and his hands fell to his sides. Shihong was still squeezing when he felt hands on his shoulder.

"What have you done?"

Shihong looked up and saw Bojing there.

"He...he was going to put me back in the mask..." Shihong tried to explain.

"We must go. Now!" Bojing said, pulling Shihong to his feet and rushing him toward the gate. He pushed Shihong outside. "Go to the wagon. Talk to no one. Look at no one!"

Bojing watched as Shihong shuffled away, his head bowed as though he was carrying a great weight.

Bojing went back inside and called for the guards. There was no way to hide that Donghai had been murdered. He just had to hope that the search for the killer would yield no results.

❦

Fei stumbled back away from the window to her bed. She had rushed over when she heard screaming outside, but she never imagined she would see something so terrible. The emperor had killed Donghai! But why? At first, the emperor had looked terrified of Donghai, but then they started shouting at each other and the emperor dragged Donghai to the ground and killed him.

Fei felt sick as she heard the shouts of the guards who had arrived. She ran back and locked and covered the window to her room. She didn't want anyone to know what she had seen. If the emperor knew she had witnessed his crime...

She sat in a chair and pulled her legs up to her chin and

held herself tightly. Was it even a crime? She didn't know. She knew that the emperor—and the empress—had the right to punish, or even execute, any member of the court for wrongdoing. But what she just saw was not an example of imperial justice. It had been murder.

She knew the emperor was cruel. He had ordered Ruolan put to death. He had taken her body against her will more times than she could count. He had beaten the empress. And yet she still never imagined he could kill a man with his own two hands.

Her hands went to her still-flat stomach. She already feared that the emperor might kill her once he knew she was pregnant. But now, she knew that he would. He would kill her with his own two hands just as he had Donghai. He would never believe that he was capable of siring a child after what happened with Ruolan. He would kill her and she would be disgraced. He would demand the bridal gifts back from her family and punish them for raising a whore for a daughter. They would be ruined. She couldn't let that happen.

She had to get rid of the child. She knew it was possible. She had heard such things whispered about when she still lived at home. But she didn't know how it was done. She needed help. She would have to find a way to ask Lina what she needed to do.

❀

The cries of the dowager-empress reverberated over all of the Forbidden City.

"No! Why?" she screamed as she kneeled by his body in the emperor's audience hall. The guards had brought Donghai there as soon as they had found him. The back of his head still oozed dark blood onto the bright red carpeting. The emperor sat on his throne and glared out at those gathered. This late at night, very few had responded to his summons, but more would come. The word would spread that there had been a murder in the Forbidden City.

The empress stood over the dowager, patting her shoulders and crying along with her. She cared nothing for the dowager or Donghai, but as the empress, it was her duty to mourn alongside her mother-in-law.

"My oldest, most loyal friend," the dowager said through her tears as she stroked Donghai's leathery face. "How could this happen? No one was more loyal to the throne than you."

Empress Wen knew that to be true. Who else would have done such horrible things to Shihong as Donghai had?

"You must find out who did this!" the empress screamed at Hongdi. "This cannot go unpunished!"

The emperor raised his hand to calm his mother. "Of course," he said. In truth, he hated Donghai. The man was sneaky. Calculating. A crony of his mother. One good thing about his mother one day dying meant that he would be rid of Donghai as well. Instead, the old man had finally gone too far in his machinations and had gotten himself killed. Hongdi would have been satisfied in calling it a terrible accident and letting the murderer go free. But if he wanted to live in peace with his mother, he knew he could not do that.

"I want the killer found immediately," the emperor said. "We cannot allow someone so dangerous to run about the Forbidden City. Bojing."

The empress's eunuch shuffled forward, keeping his head down. "Yes, Your Majesty."

"The guards say that you found Donghai's body," the emperor said. "What happened?"

"Yes, Your Majesty," Bojing said. "I was only doing a nightly check around the empress's palace before turning off the lanterns when I heard yelling."

"Could you hear what was being said?" the emperor asked.

"Sadly, no," Bojing said. "I was too far away, so the voices were muffled. But I ran toward them nonetheless. But by the time I got there, I only saw Donghai on the ground. The killer had fled."

The emperor nodded, then he turned to the Minister of Palace Security. "Secure the palace. No one comes in or goes out. I want every room in the Forbidden City searched. If you find anything, or anyone, out of sorts, report to me immediately."

"Yes, Your Majesty," the minister said as he backed away. He snapped his fingers and a group of guards followed him out of the audience hall.

The dowager continued her weeping, but her voice was much lower now. Only the empress could hear her words. "My friend. My dearest friend. This is all my fault. This is a punishment for my great sin."

The empress did her best not to smirk. She was right about that. Bojing had told the empress what happened when he was sent to bring her to the audience hall. Shihong had killed Donghai. She suspected that the man had seen Donghai and panicked. She didn't blame him. Donghai had kidnapped him, imprisoned him, locked his head in iron, and murdered his family. If anything, Donghai's death had been too quick. The wicked man should have suffered. Still, she supposed there was some cosmic justice at play. And he would certainly never be caught. He would be safely back at her father's estate by now.

She just hoped that no one else would be accused of Donghai's death in his absence.

THIRTY-SEVEN

"*B*y all the gods, what happened?" Empress Wen asked Bojing when they were back in her palace.

Bojing sighed and shook his head. "Donghai saw Shihong as he was leaving Fei's palace. He threatened to expose Shihong. Shihong did the only thing he thought he could in the moment."

Wen shook her head and clenched her fists. "The dowager will badger Hongdi endlessly to find the killer. This could ruin everything! Did anyone see or hear them fighting? It looked brutal."

"I didn't see anyone," Bojing said, but there was a twinge of doubt in his voice.

"But...?" Wen pushed.

"I was in such a rush to get Shihong out the gate," Bojing said. "I-I-I glanced around, but I didn't look carefully."

"And?" Wen asked. "Do you have reason to believe someone saw something?"

"They were not far from Lady Song's palace," Bojing said. "And Fei was certainly still awake. The lanterns around her palace were still lit. It was how Donghai saw Shihong in the first place. It would be hard to believe that Fei or her servants didn't hear *something*."

Wen rubbed her forehead. "We must be cautious," she said. "If anyone suspects we are involved, even without Shihong, the dowager will ruin us.

"Bring Fei and her servants to me. I will speak to the girl privately."

❧

*F*ei was shaking as she sat at a low tea table in the empress's palace. She clenched and unclenched her hands together several times to stop them from trembling, but she was sick to her stomach. Somehow, the empress must have found out what she had seen. Would she find a way to punish Fei in order to keep her quiet about Donghai's murder? Even though Fei had not done anything wrong, the empress could always invent a crime and pin it on her. As the head of the Inner Court, it would be the empress's responsibility to punish any errant concubine, and no one else would be able to say anything about it. Even the emperor rarely contradicted the empress's rulings when it came to the women of the court.

Or did the empress know about the baby? Fei still hadn't told anyone, but she had been so tired lately and too nauseous to eat. She knew that Lina suspected something was wrong with her, but she hadn't asked. She had the bloody undergarments as proof that Fei wasn't pregnant. But maybe she had still told the empress of her suspicions.

Fei was near to tears when the empress glided into the room and sat on the other side of the tea table. Fei quickly stood and kneeled, nearly crumbling all the way into a kowtow, her knees were so weak with dread.

"Please, sit," the empress said as she lit a candle under a teapot to warm the water. "I only invited you here for a little chat."

Fei nodded and tried to smile, but her face was frozen. She sat on the stool but kept her eyes down on the table.

"So, which do you like?" the empress asked, motioning to several pots of tea. "A flower tea? Jasmine? Chrysanthemum? Or maybe something a little bitter? This pu'er is especially heady."

"Whichever you like," Fei said, her voice so quiet even she barely heard it.

The empress smiled as she poured the hot water over the cups and spoons and other tea items to warm them. She then refilled the teapot with fresh water from a pitcher and placed the teapot over the flame again.

"You seem a little nervous," the empress said as she added some dried flowers to each of their cups. "I know we have not spoken very much, but I mean to change that. The emperor has taken such a likeness to you, it is my duty to make sure that you are doing all you can to please him."

"I am doing my best, Your Majesty," Fei said. "But I honestly do not know why he keeps coming back to me. He always seems...irritated. His moods are quite changeable. I never know what to expect."

The empress chuckled. "I do not think changeable moods are limited to the emperor. I believe all men can be rather...temperamental."

Fei shook her head. "I wouldn't know, Your Majesty."

The empress took the teapot and poured the hot water into her own teacup. "Something seems to be bothering you, dear. Mind telling me what it is?"

Fei's heart sped up and her mouth went dry. She shook her head again. "No, Your Majesty. Nothing."

The empress smiled, but it was not one of friendship. Fei thought she could see the tips of her teeth past her lips like a viper.

"Come now," the empress said, and she moved to pour tea into Fei's cup, but she spilled some of the hot water on Fei's hand. Fei cried out and pulled her hand away to blow on it.

"Oh!" the empress said. "Clumsy me! Are you all right?"

Fei's hand was burning and her eyes teared up, but she nodded anyway. "Yes, Your Majesty. I'll be fine."

The empress filled the rest of Fei's teacup. "Are you sure there is nothing you need to tell me?"

Fei looked up and the empress was not smiling. She was looking directly into her eyes.

"Tell me," the empress said coldly, all pretense of kindness gone.

"I...I saw him," Fei said. "I s-s-saw..."

"Saw what?" the empress asked.

"Saw the emperor kill Donghai," Fei said, and the tears fell from her eyes. She covered her face with her hands, scared of what would happen next.

The empress put the teapot down and nodded, putting a finger to her mouth to think. So, Fei had seen Shihong kill the eunuch. This was not good. If Fei told anyone that she saw the emperor in the garden, Hongdi would know something was wrong because he wasn't in the garden, hadn't been to Fei's palace, and certainly didn't kill Donghai. But what could she do? She couldn't arrest Fei. Or cut out her tongue. She was Hongdi's favorite, for some inexplicable reason. He would never allow the empress to exert her proper right over Fei as a member of the Inner Court.

"You understand how serious this is," the empress said. Fei lowered her hands to her lap and nodded with a sniff. "If anyone, even the emperor, knew what you saw, your life would be in great danger."

"The emperor...doesn't know I saw?" Fei asked.

The empress reached out and took Fei's hand. Fei flinched, but the empress held fast. "Not yet. And he need never know as long as you, and your servants, keep your mouths shut."

"They don't know anything!" Fei said with a sudden strength she didn't know she had. But she couldn't let her servants suffer on her behalf. "I was alone in my room when I saw what happened. They were not with me. I am sure they saw nothing, and I didn't say a word! I swear."

The empress nodded and released Fei's hand. "I believe you. But we will have to question them just the same."

"I understand," Fei said. "But please don't hurt them. They are innocent."

"We will see," the empress said. "You never know what secrets a servant may be hiding. They might not have seen the emperor kill Donghai, but if they are keeping *anything* from me, I will discover it."

The empress sat back and sipped at her tea, looking so sure of herself. How long would she torture Lina and Yuying, trying to get something out of them? And what if Lina told of her suspicions about Fei being pregnant? Would Lina be punished for not saying anything sooner? How long would it be before the empress told the emperor? And how long would it then be before she was arrested and tossed into the dungeon to await her execution? She dropped her head and dissolved into a fit of crying again, unable to stop herself.

The empress was confused by Fei's response. What was she afraid of the servants revealing.

"If there is something else you need to tell me, Fei," the empress said, "I suggest you do so now. It will go better for you if you confess."

"No," Fei said. "If I confess, I will be signing my own death warrant."

That certainly piqued the empress's interest. "Dear, you better tell me. Especially if you want to save your servants from certain torture."

Fei wailed. "I'm pregnant!" she practically screamed.

"What?" the empress asked, jumping to her feet. "How long?"

"A month perhaps," Fei said. "A little longer? I'm not sure. The emperor has been coming so often. But I've only missed one moon phase, so I can't be very far along."

"You missed a moon phase?" the empress asked, slumping back down onto her stool. "Why wasn't I informed?"

"I hid it from my maid," Fei said. "I cut myself. Bled on my undergarments so she wouldn't know."

"But-but-but why?" the empress asked. "This is wonderful news. Why would you hide it?"

"Wonderful?" Fei asked. "How long will it be before the emperor sends me to the scaffold as he did Ruolan?"

The empress nodded. She understood the girl's concerns. The death of her friend was probably enough to scare her away from having children for life. But she could not stop nature. Well, she supposed the girl could if she knew how. But now that the empress knew, the girl could not cause herself to miscarry without grave consequences.

"Now, now," the empress said. "There is no need to fear.

The emperor had...reasons to suspect Ruolan. You know how flighty the girl was."

"Ruolan was innocent!" Fei insisted. "His Majesty killed his own son!"

The empress pressed her lips into a thin frown. "If you want to live, you will *never* utter such words again."

"My life is forfeit either way," Fei said. "I should at least die with dignity, as Ruolan did."

"Stop this nonsense," the empress said as she stood and called for Bojing. "You are not a martyr. You are going to be the mother of the next emperor!"

Fei began to weep again, and the empress rolled her eyes.

"Bojing!" she called, and the eunuch quickly appeared. "Take Fei back to her palace. We have something incredible to celebrate. Fei is pregnant."

Bojing nodded and a smile crossed his face. "Praise the gods."

"What of my servants?" Fei asked. "Yuying can walk me back."

"Not just yet," the empress said. "I am quite curious now just what they have been keeping from me. Bojing will escort you back. Your servants shall be returned to you soon."

Fei stood and let Bojing lead her out of the empress's sitting room. At the door, she stopped and turned back to the empress.

"You aren't going to tell His Majesty right away, are you?" she asked.

"Of course I am," the empress said. "If anything will take his mind off this dreadful little problem with Donghai, it will be knowing that he is finally going to have an heir."

Fei's stomach clenched and she gave a small bow as she

left the room. She barely heard or saw anything as Bojing led her home. She entered her palace and closed the door behind herself, locking it tightly.

She was alone. Ever since she had first arrived in the Forbidden City, she had never been alone. She always had a servant with her. Even as she slept, Lina was on the floor nearby. If she was going to do anything to stop this baby from coming, she had to do it now. But what could she do? She didn't have the medicines to stop it. And if she tried to cut it out...Well, she had no idea if that would even work, and she would probably bleed to death.

Besides, if she did anything to cause a miscarriage, the empress would suspect she had done it on purpose. She would certainly be put to death then. Was there a greater sin than killing a future emperor?

Fei fell to her knees and wept. She did not know what to do. She had no one to ask for help. She couldn't leave the palace. All roads seemed to lead to the same end—her death.

She touched her stomach. She couldn't even feel the little life growing within her. Was it even real? Would it feel pain? Would the gods see fit to reincarnate it in the next life? She had to hope they would.

Fei went to her bedchamber, shutting the door behind her. She picked up the red scarf that she had been embroidering for her mother-in-law. It wasn't white, but it would have to do. She climbed up onto her bed, grabbing the railing around the top that held the mosquito netting in place to make sure it was solid enough to hold her weight. It seemed to be.

She wrapped the delicate silk around the railing, tying it into a strong knot. She then tied the other end around her neck. She stood on the edge of the bed, tears streaming down her face. This was not the life, or the death, she imagined she would have the day she first came to the Forbidden City. Why did the emperor have to save her from being sent home? If he had allowed her to be dismissed, she never would have known such pain, such fear, have shed so many tears as she had since she became an imperial concubine.

The gift of being chosen by the emperor had been nothing but a curse. It was a sin for her to take her own life. The life of her unborn child. She would most likely not be reincarnated. She would not be honored by her family. She would wander the earth as a hungry ghost, tormented by the demons of the underworld. And yet, that life was preferable to dying under the executioner's axe.

Fei placed her hand on her belly. "I'm sorry."

She stepped forward.

THIRTY-EIGHT

"*I*t worked, then," Bojing said when he returned to the empress's palace. "Shihong is capable of fathering a child!"

"It would seem so," the empress said. "And it couldn't have come at a better time. Fei saw Shihong kill Donghai. It is only a matter of time before the weak-willed girl spills her guts to someone. Her servants, if not the emperor himself."

"She did seem greatly distraught as I walked her to her palace," Bojing said.

"She thinks the emperor is going to put her to death as he did Ruolan," Wen said. "But I can't imagine the dowager being able to plant such seeds of doubt again. The girl never leaves her palace."

"I wouldn't put anything past the dowager," Bojing said. "Her heart is rotten. And after losing Donghai, she might have the girl put to death just to feel some sense of revenge."

"Then we must not tarry a moment," Wen said. "Go to my family. To Shihong. We will replace Hongdi tonight."

"Tonight?" Bojing asked. "Are you sure? Is Shihong ready?"

"He was able to fool Fei for weeks," Wen said. "He must be doing something right."

"What about Wangzhu?" Bojing asked. "He knows the emperor better than anyone. He will certainly know that something isn't right."

"But what will he be able to do about it?" she asked. "He doesn't know about the twin. If he says anything about Shihong not being Hongdi, everyone will think he is crazy. In fact, maybe that should be Shihong's first act as emperor, have Wangzhu locked away."

"How will we do it, then?" Bojing asked. "It will not be an easy thing to switch them out. We will have to somehow remove Hongdi from the palace."

"I have already thought of that," the empress said. She went to her tea table and picked up a small tincture bottle. "My mother was able to procure this. She says that it will be able to render even the strongest man unconscious for at least a day. I will summon Hongdi here and tell him about Fei's pregnancy and offer him a drink to celebrate. Once he is asleep, you can bring in Shihong as you always do. But instead of then ferrying Shihong out, you will take Hongdi. Then, Shihong will be able to take Hongdi's place and no one will be the wiser."

Bojing nodded. "I think it will work. I will leave now. We will return after dark."

"Good," Wen said. "I will tell the emperor after dinner. Once he is full of food and drink, it will not seem strange that he has fallen asleep."

Bojing nodded. "And what of Fei's servants? They have revealed nothing of interest so far. Should we keep questioning them?"

"Oh, I had forgotten about them," Wen said. "Release them. They are of no use to me."

"Yes, Your Majesty," Bojing said, and he bowed his way out of the room.

For the first time in months, the empress's heart felt light and hopeful. Hongdi would be gone. Fei would deliver a child. And Shihong would restore her to her rightful place at the emperor's side.

❦

*I*t was twilight when the first scream rent the air of the Forbidden City. The empress raised her head, as the sound was quite close. Then she heard yelling and more screams.

"Bojing?" she called, but then she remembered that he had gone to fetch Shihong. She called for another servant. "What is going on? she asked when he entered her room.

"I do not know, Your Majesty," he said. "But it seemed to be coming from Lady Fei's palace."

"Why would—" The empress's voice died in her throat as she jumped to her feet and shuffled as quickly as she could on her bound feet toward the door. It was freezing outside and there had been another snow the night before, blanketing the Forbidden City in white, but Wen did not stop to grab a fur wrap. She held tightly to the hands of two maids as she walked through the snow toward Fei's palace. Fei's servants were outside on their knees, keening and wailing as though they were in the greatest pain.

"What has happened?" Wen demanded.

"She's dead!" the woman screamed. "She's dead! My mistress! My mistress!"

The young man bent forward and pounded his fits on the ground as he cried.

Wen's heart froze in her chest as she took a step back. She was going to be sick. How could this happen? What would it mean for their plan?

No. She couldn't believe it. Fei was pregnant with the heir! She wouldn't have...But she remembered how distraught the girl had seemed over the pregnancy. How she was sure the emperor was going to put her to death. She hadn't...she hadn't really believed that so strongly she would kill herself, had she?

Wen stepped through the snow and past the crying servants into Fei's palace. She turned toward Fei's room and saw that it was true. Even from her place by the door, she could see the body swaying at the foot of the bed.

Wen gulped and staggered toward the room. "Stupid... stupid..." she muttered. She entered the room and felt sick when she saw Fei's eyes, open, staring at her. Accusing her. She never...she never should have threatened the girl. She had scared her. Made things worse. She hadn't realized just how delicate the girl's constitution was. She didn't know... she didn't know...

She turned to the side and was sick on the floor. Then she let out a wail of pain of her own. She had failed. For the first time, the dowager was right. She had failed. Fei had been her charge and she had not protected her. Now Fei was dead. The child was dead. Their plan...Oh! Shihong! Her father! Bojing! They would be coming to the Forbidden City tonight! She had to stop them.

But as Wen turned to leave Fei's room, Emperor Hongdi and his mother were entering. Hongdi fell to his knees and tugged as his robe, tearing the precious silk.

"No! No! Why?" he yelled. "Who did this?"

"She did it to herself," the empress said, kneeling by his side and wrapping her arms around him.

"No!" Hongdi said. "I don't believe it. She was my favored lady. She wouldn't have. Who convinced her to do this."

"Your Majesty," Wen pleaded. "You are distraught! This is terrible for you. But there was nothing that could be done."

"How do you know?" the emperor demanded, turning to her, his breaths coming out hard. "What did she say to you?"

Empress Wen shook her head. "Nothing. She was..." She didn't know what to say to remove the blame from herself. Whether Fei had been pregnant or not, her distress had been apparent for months, ever since the death of Ruolan. Wen should have been taking better care of her, but she did not. She hated that the emperor had been giving Fei his attentions, and she had neglected Fei because of it. Worse, she had used Fei. She had sent Shihong to her under false pretenses. When Fei had said that the emperor was changeable, she was talking about Shihong and Hongdi, each using her for their own pleasure night after night, and Fei never knowing who would be coming to her bed. No wonder she was afraid and heartbroken. No wonder she had thought that the only way to attain some peace had been to hang herself.

"I was told that you had tea with the girl earlier today," the dowager said. Wen looked up at her. The woman did not look upset at Fei's death at all. In fact, she looked almost pleased. Not pleased that the girl had died, but pleased that she finally found her chance to ruin Wen for good.

"I...I did," Wen said. She couldn't lie about it. "I was trying to get to know her better. I know I had not been giving her the attention she needed and I was attempting to make amends."

The emperor ripped her arms from around him and he pushed her to the ground. He pointed to Fei. "You call this making amends?" he demanded.

Wen shook her head. "No. I had no idea. She didn't tell me she was this sad."

"Because she wasn't," Hongdi said. "She lived in the greatest palace in the world! I showered her with attention and gifts. No, she wouldn't have done to this me. Not to me!"

"Donghai was killed just outside of Fei's palace," the dowager said. "Did you have something to do with his death, empress?"

"Of course not!" Wen said. "I have barely spoken two words to the man in my life."

"Yet the day after he is killed, you have tea with a woman you despise who also ends up dead," the dowager said. "Are you sure you didn't order Fei to kill herself? To keep her from talking about something she may have seen? To keep her from telling the emperor that you killed Donghai?"

"No!" Wen said, pulling herself up to her full height and looking down her nose at the dowager. "I had nothing to do with Donghai's death. Or Fei's. This is all just a terrible tragedy."

"Son," the dowager said, lightly touching Hongdi's robe, "you know how Wen has tried over and over again to entice you back to her bed. She must have seen Fei as a rival for your attention. Whether she killed Donghai or not, she must have certainly entreated Fei to take her life in order to get her out of the way."

Hongdi turned to Wen with a snarl on his face. "You bitch."

"No!" Wen said, falling to her knees and clasping her hands in supplication before her. "Please, please, you must believe me! I would never hurt Fei. She was a kind, quiet girl. And I would never do anything to ruin your happiness. Remember how many times I told you to take a concubine to bed to spread your seed? I have never been a jealous woman."

"I can hardly even remember those days," the emperor said. "I have changed in that time. As have you. You were once a loving wife and a magnanimous empress. But now, you are nothing but a scheming shrew."

"No. No!" Wen said, shaking her head, tears falling. Everything she had built was falling down around her. "I would never. Never!"

"Take her away!" the emperor shouted to the guards that had gathered nearby. "Take her to her palace and lock her away! She is *never* to be let out, do you hear me? I want guards around her palace at all times. She is not to see or speak to anyone ever again."

"Yes, Your Majesty," the guards said as they grabbed the empress's arms and dragged her from Fei's palace.

"No!" the empress yelled. "Hongdi! My love! Please! Stop this!"

"Shut up before I have your tongue sliced from your lying mouth!" Hongdi yelled at her. He then turned his gaze back to Fei, her lifeless body still swinging in the breeze from the cold air that was filling the palace from the open door.

"Cut her down!" Hongdi demanded, then he left Fei's palace. He needed to be alone.

THIRTY-NINE

$\mathcal{L}$ate that evening, after most of the Forbidden City should have been asleep, Bojing paid the guard at the gate a substantial bribe to leave his post for an extended period of time. The guard seemed hesitant, but the lure of the money was too great. Once he was gone, Bojing opened the gate for Shihong, General Kang, and Kang Jun. They slipped into the palace silently, staying in the shadows as they wended their way toward the empress's palace.

It was dark at the empress's palace, with all the outdoor lanterns extinguished. But there was a small light still on inside. Bojing did his best to survey the area to make sure no one would see them, but it was nearly impossible in the dark.

"Are we too early?" Jun whispered.

"Or too late?" the general replied. He sniffed the air, but he could not sense anything amiss.

"The emperor should be asleep now," Bojing said. "But we must be quick. Come." He waved for the men to follow him. But no sooner had they stepped onto the main path to reach the empress's front door than four guards rushed forward, their weapons drawn.

"It's an ambush!" the general hissed as he drew his sword.

"No! Stop!" Bojing cried out, holding his arms up. One of the guards reached out and grabbed Bojing by the collar, hitting him across the face with the hilt of his sword. Bojing collapsed as his nose and mouth began to gush blood.

The door to the empress's palace opened, and all of the lights inside were quickly lit, illuminating the scene just outside. The empress stepped forward and saw Bojing on the ground.

"What is happening?" she screamed.

"E-E-Emperor?" one of the guards said when the light lit on Shihong. The guards fell to their knees.

"Run," the empress said to her father and brother. But as the general turned to do so, Wangzhu ran up.

"What is going on here?" he asked. Then he caught sight of Shihong. "Your...Majesty? But I only just left you..." He turned to General Kang, who still had his sword drawn. "What is the meaning of this? You are attacking the emperor's own guards? Who is this...person?"

General Kang sighed and returned his sword to its sheath. "It's over," he said to no one in particular, but Shihong knew that all their lives were in great peril.

"Arrest them all," Wangzhu ordered the guards, but they hesitated to do so in the presence of Shihong. "What are you waiting for, you fools. Do as I say. That man is not the emperor."

The guards stood and took the general, Jun, and Shihong by the arms.

"What about the empress?" one of the guards asked.

"Double your numbers on guard," Wangzhu ordered. "But she may remain here for now."

The empress helped bring Bojing to his feet and took him inside as the guards who remained closed the door behind her.

"Who are you?" Wangzhu asked Shihong as they walked.

Shihong only shook his head. He was not sure what to say. He looked to General Kang for help.

"We will answer only to the emperor," the general said.

Wangzhu scoffed. "You broke into the palace at night and are armed. That right there is enough to have all three of you executed without delay."

"But you aren't going to do that," Jun said.

"Why not?" Wangzhu asked, his arms crossed.

Jun motioned to Shihong. "The emperor would never forgive you if you failed to inform him about this."

Wangzhu hmphed, but he turned and led the small group to the emperor's palace. His own curiosity was strong enough that he wouldn't dare do anything to the men without getting answers.

"Your Majesty," Wangzhu said as he entered the emperor's sitting room, where the emperor had been reading over some papers for the next day's audiences. "I must speak to you urgently."

Hongdi raised his eyes and his blood ran cold when he saw Shihong. He stood up slowly, dropping his papers aside.

"What is this?" he asked.

"They were caught trying to sneak into the empress's palace," Wangzhu said.

Hongdi was unable to look away from the man who looked exactly like him. Nor could he speak. He stepped closer, wondering if perhaps the man was wearing a mask, but he was not.

"Who...who are you?" Hongdi asked.

Shihong felt his eyes water. Suddenly, he was glad they had been caught. This was his brother! His twin. He could never do something to hurt him.

"I am your brother," Shihong said, tears leaking from his eyes.

"I have several brothers," Hongdi said, some of his senses coming back to him. "But none of them look so similar to me. Why have we not met before?"

"I am your twin brother," Shihong said. "We have the same mother. Were born on the same night."

Wangzhu and the guards gasped and Hongdi's eyes went wide.

"What? No," Hongdi said. "That is impossible."

"It's true!" Shihong said. "Our mother's eunuch sent me away to protect you. Then he later imprisoned me within a dragon mask. The general saved me."

Hongdi looked at General Kang for the first time. "General? What is the meaning of this? You were at the empress's palace? Why? What were you going to do?"

General Kang did not answer, but stood stoically.

"Find the dowager," Hongdi said.

"It is quite late—" Wangzhu started to say.

"Now!" Hongdi yelled. Wangzhu bowed and scurried away. Hongdi then turned back to Shihong, looking him over. "You are thinner than I am. Your shoulders rounded. We don't look so much alike upon further inspection."

"It is like looking in a mirror," Shihong said as he looked at his brother. "For fifteen years I wondered why I had been locked away, my face hidden. But now I know. The old eunuch was right to worry that people would think I was you."

"Mother's eunuch?" Hongdi asked. "You mean Donghai. Did you kill him? Have you been in the palace before tonight?"

Shihong drooped his head. "I did kill him. I was so afraid. He said he would report me. I would be locked back in the mask." His breath shuddered. "I could not let that happen. I was so scared..."

The door to the room opened and the dowager rushed in. "What is happening? I was told to come—" Her voice died away when she saw Shihong and Hongdi standing next to each other. Her hands went to her mouth and she fell to her knees.

"Mother!" Shihong said as he went to her, kneeling to help her stand. She reached out and touched his face.

"Are you really here?" she asked. "Not some demon sent to torment me?"

"It's me, Mother," Shihong said. "I am alive."

The dowager wailed and clutched her heart. "Donghai! Donghai, what have you done?"

"He did what he had to do," Shihong graciously said, not wanting to cause his mother more grief. "He sent me away with the midwife. She raised me as her own."

"I...I always wondered what happened to her," the dowager said. She wiped the tears from her eyes and let Shihong help her stand. "This is a glorious day! My son has returned."

"No, Mother," Hongdi said. "This man is a traitor. He broke into the palace. I think he meant to kill me."

"What?" the dowager said, clutching Shihong's arms tight. "No. That's not possible."

"No," Shihong said. "I would never allow anyone to hurt you. We are brothers, both sons of the dragon."

"Then what was your plan?" Hongdi asked. "You would not have come with General Kang if you had peaceful intentions."

Shihong looked away, shamefaced.

"That is what I thought," Hongdi said.

"No," the dowager said. "It can't be true. Tell me it's not true!"

"I'm sorry, Mother," Shihong said. "I was planning to take Hongdi's place. We were going to send Hongdi to live in the countryside in peace so I could rule as emperor."

"How dare you!" Hongdi said as he lunged at Shihong, pummeling him as best he could. Shihong shrank back, putting his arms over his face. The guards rushed forward to separate the men, pulling the emperor off of Shihong.

"Don't touch me!" Hongdi screamed. "I am the emperor! No one is to touch me!" He then turned to General Kang. "Are you a coward, to sit there so silently? How could you betray me? Your emperor! The son of your dearest friend."

"You are not the man Hongwu raised," General Kang said. "You are cruel. Spiteful. Foolish. You have wasted money on this monstrosity of a palace. Violated your own concubines. Dishonored your empress."

"You know nothing of being emperor!" Hongdi yelled. "I have always acted within my right."

"Perhaps," General Kang said. "But you are also impotent."

Hongdi's eyes went wide and he stepped back in shock.

"You are incapable of producing an heir," the general went on. "By refusing to accept one of your nephews as heir, you doomed your country to civil war after your death. To protect the country I built with your father, yes, I was going to replace you with Shihong."

"But perhaps this...man," the emperor said disdainfully at his brother, "is unable to produce a child as well, if we are supposed to be twins."

"We know he is able," General Kang said. "He is the father of Lady Song's child."

The emperor shot a look at Shihong. "What?"

"Shihong has spent several nights with Fei," the general said. "She is with child. We believe it is Shihong's. Not yours."

Hongdi felt great pain at the mention of Fei, but that was quickly followed by rage.

"You...you did this," he said, turning to his brother. "This is all your fault! You killed Fei!"

"What?" Shihong asked. "What do you mean?"

"Fei is dead!" the emperor said. "She hung herself in her palace this afternoon."

"No!" Shihong cried as he fell to his knees. "No, no, no! Not Fei. It can't be true! Not my Fei!"

Hongdi grabbed Shihong by the collar and pulled him back up. "She was never your Fei! She was mine!"

"I knew her as a girl," Shihong said. "We were from the same village. I hated deceiving her, but I was going to tell her the truth once you were gone. She...she can't be dead."

The emperor pointed his finger at Shihong, General Kang, and Kang Jun. "You are all traitors. You were going to kidnap me. Kill me. Take my place. Take my throne! You are all under arrest for treason. And you will all die for treason!"

"No!" the dowager screamed. "No, please, Hongdi, I beg you. Please don't take my son from me again."

"*I* am your son!" Hongdi yelled. "What about me?"

"I'm sorry. I'm sorry," was all the empress could say as she sobbed into her hands.

Hongdi turned back to the men. "What about Wen? Was she involved? You were captured outside her palace."

"No," Shihong said. If he could save at least one person from dying on his behalf, he would do whatever it took. "She knew nothing. We were going to tell her tonight. Ask for her help."

"What is this about a mask?" Hongdi asked. "This dragon mask? You said Donghai hid your face behind it. Where is it?"

No one answered him.

"Fine," the emperor growled. "Wangzhu, send guards to search the general's estate. And bring back any other evidence of his vile plot."

"Yes, Your Majesty," Wangzhu said.

"All of your lands are forfeit," Hongdi said to the general. "Your family will be evicted post haste. All your goods and coin will revert to me."

General Kang said nothing, which only stoked Hongdi's anger.

"Perhaps your whole family should be put to death," Hongdi said. "I would not want my country to be tainted by your traitorous blood."

"No!" Shihong said. "Don't blame the general's family. I am the one who should be punished. I was the one who planned to take your place."

"Silence!" Hongdi said. "You will get your punishment soon enough, *brother*. Take them away."

The guards led the three men away to the prison, and the dowager continued to cry.

Hongdi slumped into a chair. A brother. A twin. How was such a thing possible? How could he never know?

"You lied to me my whole life," Hongdi said to the dowager.

The dowager crawled over on her knees to her son. "No. I thought he was dead. All this time, Donghai told me the boy was dead. I didn't see a reason to tell you."

"Even if you thought he was dead, I should have known," Hongdi said. "Don't you see? This is why my reign has been riddled with strife. Why I have not been able to produce an heir. We were cursed, Mother. You know that twins are a bad omen. You or Father must have done something to cause the gods to punish you so. This isn't my fault. It's yours."

"I have wept every day for your brother," the dowager said. "But if I had told your father the truth, he might have killed you. I had to let Donghai take your brother away to protect you. To protect the kingdom."

Hongdi shook his head. "You were a terrible mother. You never showed me an ounce of affection. Even now, you do not cry tears for me. You cry them for him."

"He was an innocent babe," the dowager said. "I thought he was dead. You were alive. I had no need to mourn for you."

"Well, continue your mourning," Hongdi said. "Because once I find that dragon mask, I will clap his head in it once again. And then he will wear it to the scaffold."

"No!" the empress cried, falling on her face. "Please spare your brother! I beg you."

"This is the only outcome there can be, Mother," Hongdi said. "He betrayed me. Tried to usurp me. It doesn't matter that he is my brother. The only just punishment for treason is death."

The dowager continued to cry, but she knew that there was no way to change his mind.

"Get out," Hongdi said. "I expect you to be present for the execution."

The dowager struggled to her feet and then staggered from the room, crying all the way. The pain in her heart was greater now than it had ever been. Her greatest wish had always been to have her son back. But no sooner did she have him back than he was about to be ripped from her arms again. She could not let him die. If he did, her heart would not be able to take it. She would die with him.

She did not return to her rooms but went to the hidden shrine dedicated to her lost son to pray for guidance and strength.

FORTY

*W*angzhu returned from General Kang's estate several hours later. He handed the dragon mask and several papers to the emperor.

"What are these?" Hongdi asked.

"Letters between the empress and her father," Wangzhu said. "She was part of the scheme."

Hongdi motioned to one of the guards. "Arrest the empress and have her imprisoned with her family."

"Yes, Your Majesty," the guard said.

Wangzhu then handed the dragon mask to the emperor. Hongdi took it with a shaking hand. He turned it over and saw what looked to be skin and blood on the inside.

"How could Donghai have done such a thing?" Hongdi asked. "And why a dragon?"

"From what I have gleaned from the letters," Wangzhu said, "Donghai feared that people would see Shihong and that rumors of you having a twin would spread. He was afraid that such rumors would turn people against you. So, he put Shihong into a dragon mask as a mere boy, around fourteen, to keep that from happening."

"Why a dragon?" Hongdi asked as he ran a finger over the snarling mouth of the mask.

"Perhaps to, in his own way, honor the boy's lineage?" Wangzhu suggested. "It is a shame Donghai is not here to ask."

Hongdi nodded and handed the mask to Wangzhu. "Take this to the guards and have it put back on Shihong."

"Are you sure?" Wangzhu asked. "It is quite cruel."

"Do not question my orders again, Wangzhu, or you will join him on the scaffold."

Wangzhu nodded and bowed, backing his way out of the room.

❦

"I am sorry," Shihong said to General Kang through the bars that divided their cells. "I failed you."

"The plan was doomed from the start," the general said. "It was too ambitious. I never should have agreed to it. Some great general I am."

"You are a great general," Jun said. "And people will remember that for generations to come."

"Not my generations," the general replied. "I am sure the family will curse me when they are living on the street. They will not mourn me after I am gone. I'll wander the earth as a hungry ghost for the rest of time."

"You cannot tell me that you are giving up," Jun said. "Not you. Not General Kang."

"I am old, my son," the general said. "I should be resting. Enjoying the fruits of my labor in my retirement. Yet I will die as a traitor to the country I helped build. I am only sad that I will not see my friend Hongwu once I am gone."

Jun started to say something else, but Wen's high-pitched screams interrupted him.

"Let me go!" she yelled as two guards brought her around the corner and to a cell across from General Kang, Jun, and Shihong. She kicked her tiny feet and tried to pull her arms free, but it was useless.

The guards opened the door to the cell and unceremoniously tossed her inside. She landed face down, her hands and dress covered with brown muck. The guards laughed as they locked the door behind her. Wen stood up and grabbed the bars of her cell, shaking them.

"Let me out of here!" she yelled. "You'll pay for this!"

"Cease the infernal screeching!" Jun said, covering his ears.

"Shut up!" Wen said to her brother. "You might have given up, but I won't. I will not die like this."

"What are you going to do about it?" Jun asked. "At least die with dignity."

"I'll not die!" Wen said, but some of the fight had gone out of her as she realized just how perilous her situation was. There was nothing she could do. They had all been caught, and they had her letters as proof. She was going to die.

She was about to say something smart to her brother again, but she stopped when she heard guards returning. These were carrying the dragon mask. The guards opened the door of Shihong's cell and grabbed him, forcing him to the ground. As he saw the firelight from the torches gleam on the iron mask, he screamed and fought, but he could not escape.

"Don't put me back in the mask!" Shihong cried. "Please!"

But the guards just laughed as they did exactly that.

They left Shihong on the floor as they left and locked the cell.

Shihong sat up slowly, the weight feeling much more heavy than he remembered it. He could hardly sit up, it was so heavy. He put his hands to his face, but when he touched only cold metal instead of warm flesh, he began to weep.

Empress Wen turned away and sank to the floor, wrapping her arms around herself. Shihong's cries were sheer torment, but no matter how tightly she placed her hands over her ears, she could not drown them out.

❖

"Your Majesty?" Lama Samten said as he entered the small sanctuary. "It is the middle of the night. What are you doing here?"

"I have committed a great wrong," the dowager said, not looking up. She was kneeling before the altar, her hands folded into her lap. "And I see no way out that does not end in my own death."

The lama kneeled beside her. "Do not say such a thing. The gods always provide a way forward."

"Not for me," she said, shaking her head. "All this time, I have been praying for the soul of my son, but he was alive all along. Living a life of torture within an iron mask."

"What do you mean?" the lama asked her.

The dowager shook her head. She was afraid to say too much lest even more people become implicated in her sin. She reached out, and the lama took her hand to help her stand. She picked up one of the candles from the altar and dropped it onto the kneeling pillow, setting it alight.

"Your Majesty!" the lama said as he went to put the fire out, but the dowager kept her hand tight on his arm.

"Leave it," she said. "The altar is meaningless." She led the lama out of the room and closed the door behind them. She leaned against it, listening to the pop and crackle of the fire as it consumed the altar.

"Please, my lady," the lama said. "What is wrong? Let me help you."

She shook her head. "There is nothing you can do for me. Even when I am gone, I cannot allow you to mourn for me. The gods will punish or reward me as they see fit. But I thank you for your loyalty, old friend."

With that, she left the temple and climbed into a sedan chair, ordering the chair bearers to take her to the prison. When she opened the prison door, the wailing of her son ripped into her very heart. She kept a hand on the cold and damp wall as she made her way underground. At the bottom of the stairs, the guards leaped to their feet at her appearance.

"Your Majesty!" they all said.

"Stay here," she ordered them as she walked past, deeper into the prison, toward the pitiful cries of her son.

"Your Majesty!" General Kang said, surprised when he saw her round the corner toward his cell. But she ignored him, walking to the cell with Shihong. She felt a knife to her chest when she saw that he was once again wearing the dragon mask.

"Mother!" Shihong said. "You came! Can you help me?"

The dowager nodded her head. "For the first time in my life, I can do something for you." She reached up into her hair and pulled out a long hairpin so sharp, it could have been mistaken for a dagger. She slipped the sharp end of the pin into the lock and worked it until the lock fell free. She then did the same thing to Shihong's mask. Shihong sighed with relief as the mask clattered to the ground. He then embraced his mother.

"Thank you!" he said. "Thank you!"

She held him tightly. "Whatever happens next," she said, "I hope you will think kindly of me."

"Of course, Mother," Shihong said. "I could never think ill of you. You thought I was dead. You never would have allowed me to be imprisoned in such a way if you had known I was alive."

The dowager nodded and kissed her son on the cheek. "I must retire now. Do what you must."

Shihong nodded and watched as his mother slowly left the prison. He looked down and realized that she had placed the hairpin into his hand.

When the dowager reached her palace, she went to her bedroom and closed the door behind her. She went to a trunk that was full of embroidered gifts from Hongdi's many concubines. She pulled out a long white scarf and wrapped it around her neck before climbing onto the bed.

FORTY-ONE

Shihong used the dowager's hairpin to open the door to General Kang and Jun's cell, then he freed the empress.

"We should flee," Shihong said. "Leave while we have the chance."

"And go where?" General Kang asked.

"Anywhere!" Shihong said.

"But we have no money," Jun said. "No weapons. No food."

The general nodded. "Right now, the emperor's men are raiding my home, taking everything I have worked so hard to accumulate for themselves. If we don't stop them, there will be nothing left."

"So, you think we should ride out and fight the emperor's men?" Shihong asked.

"No," Empress Wen said. "We need to complete our mission."

"What?" Shihong said. "You can't be serious. We were caught! If we don't leave, we are certain to be put to death."

"Not if the emperor pardons us," the empress said.

"Why would the emperor..." Shihong then realized what the empress meant. If he took Hongdi's place, he could pardon the general and his family and restore his lands and treasure.

"We were already caught once, though," Shihong said. "What will keep us from being caught again?"

"We are supposed to be in prison," General Kang said. "It is still dark out. The emperor will not expect us to try our plan again."

"So, what do we do?" Hongdi asked.

"Wait a moment," General Kang said, and he nodded for Jun to follow him.

"I'll stay here," Empress Wen said, stepping back into her cell and pulling the door closed behind her but not locking it. "As soon as Wangzhu comes to dress you in the morning, give the order that I, my father, and my brother are to be released."

"What about Hongdi?" Shihong asked.

"Let my father take care of him," she said. At that, they heard yelling and screaming from down the hall. When Shihong went to see what was wrong, he found that the general and Jun had managed to overpower and kill the guards even though they didn't have weapons while the guards did.

"You are both very brave," Shihong said.

"Come on," the general said. "We need to get to the emperor's room before dawn."

❦

*H*ongdi could not sleep. He paced his room, pouring himself a third cup of wine.

A brother. A twin. All this time, he had wondered why

he had struggled to rule his kingdom. Why he had never been blessed with an heir. He had been doomed to failure from birth. His mother should have done the right thing and put both of them to death. Perhaps the gods demanded a blood sacrifice in order to bless the new Ming Dynasty. She could have given birth to another son later. One born without a curse.

But he hoped the curse would soon be lifted. Once the man in the dragon mask was put to death, there would be no more twin. No more bad omen. He could rule China knowing that the way forward was clear.

He was disappointed that Fei had taken her own life. But he never could have loved her again or accepted her child knowing that his brother had taken her as his own woman. But with Fei gone and the empress out of the way, he would choose a new empress, and together, they would finally have the child he needed and deserved.

As he walked, he felt a cool breeze waft past his shoulder. He turned, but saw nothing.

"Hello?" he called out. "Wangzhu?" But there was no response. He thought that he must be getting tired. He removed his outer robe and sat on the bed, draining the last of the wine from his cup. He let out a long sigh as he stretched out on the bed. He closed his eyes, hoping to get just a little bit of sleep. It would be dawn soon, and he would make sure the executions were carried out as soon as possible.

He laid there, with his head on his pillow for some minutes, but he couldn't settle down enough to sleep, in spite of the wine. He opened his eyes and tried to yell, but a hand fell over his mouth. Shihong, General Kang, and Jun were all standing over him.

"Hello, Emperor," General Kang said. Hongdi tried to fight back, but Jun and the general held him tight.

"What are you doing?" Hongdi asked as they dragged him from the bed and tied his hands behind his back. "How did you escape?"

"We didn't escape," General Kang said. "We were set free."

"By whom?" the emperor demanded.

"Your own mother," Jun replied.

"That wicked old crone!" Hongdi said. "I should have dispensed with her a long time ago."

"You would kill our mother?" Shihong asked, worry scrunched in his brow.

"She's not a mother," Hongdi said. "She's a cruel, manipulative, vindictive woman. Never trust her."

"I am sure our mother and I will form our own relationship," Shihong said.

"Come on," General Kang said, then he looked at Shihong. "Do you know what to do?"

Shihong nodded. "In the morning, I will pardon all of you."

"No," the general said. "Not all of us. Not the man in the dragon mask."

"What?" Shihong and Hongdi both said at once.

"You want me to let my brother die?" Shihong said. "No. I could never!"

"It is what he was going to do to you," the general said.

"I am the son of the dragon!" Hongdi said. "If you kill me, the gods will curse you all! Any usurper so sits on my throne will be crushed by the dragon's pearl!"

Shihong shrank back. This was not the plan he had agreed to. He couldn't imagine killing his brother. It was wrong.

"You won't be sentencing him to death," Jun said. "He will just be taking your place on the scaffold. Remember, your own brother would have let you die this day."

Shihong shook his head and rubbed his face. He knew that Hongdi was a bad man, that Hongdi had sentenced him to death. Had put him back in the dragon mask.

"But I am not Hongdi," Shihong said. "I will never be as cruel as he is."

"But if you don't let him die," General Kang said, "Hongdi will never let you rest. Look at him. He will never stop fighting you to regain his throne."

"That is quite true," Hongdi said even though he knew he was digging his own grave. He had a feeling that, no matter what Shihong decided, General Kang would kill him anyway. "I will never take your name. Your place. You are nothing but a peasant. A filthy, stupid boy in a cage. I'll kill you. One day, I promise I will kill you."

Shihong took a step back and nodded his head at General Kang. Hongdi laughed as the general and Jun bound and gagged him and dragged him toward the prison. But once he saw the dead bodies of the guards, the laughter died away. He was taken to a cell, where the dragon mask laid on the floor. When he saw it, he dug his feet into the ground.

"No, no, no!" he tried to say, but his words were muffled. The general left him gagged as the dragon mask was placed around his head and locked shut. Hongdi was then tossed to the ground as the door to the cell was shut. He leaped to his feet and shook the bars, but it was no use. The general, Jun, and Empress Wen all laughed at him from their own unlocked cells.

"You'll never get away with this!" the emperor mumbled. He reached up, but there was no way to remove the gag from around his head. The hole in the front of the mask was too small, and the gag was tied in the back, where he could not feel anything but cold iron. He looked out the small grate in the wall and could see the first light of day.

❀

*S*hihong did not sleep, but paced his room, waiting for dawn. When the door to his room opened, he slipped behind the bed so that the eunuch, Wangzhu, could not see him clearly. Wangzhu was carrying a tea tray, which he placed on a table in the middle of the room.

"Did you get any sleep, Your Majesty?" Wangzhu asked.

"Not at all," Shihong said. "I...I thought long and hard all through the night. I wish to pardon the empress and her family."

Wangzhu turned to the emperor, an eyebrow raised. "Are you sure? They are traitors, Your Majesty. No one would blame you for sending them to their deaths."

"I know," Shihong said. "But I still wish to show them mercy. They are...family."

"Very well," Wangzhu said. "I will alert the guards of your wishes. What of the man in the dragon mask?"

Shihong went quiet for a moment. "Let the execution proceed as planned."

"But...he is family, Your Majesty," Wangzhu said, stepping closer to the bed to get a better look at the emperor.

"Not anymore," Shihong said.

Wangzhu peered at the man standing across from him. There was something different about him today. Perhaps learning that his own brother had tried to overthrow him was enough to bring about a change in his demeanor.

"Very well, Your Majesty," Wangzhu said, and he bowed his way out of the room, closing the door behind him.

❀

*E*mpress Wen, General Kang, and Kang Jun were all released, but they did not leave the prison. They wanted to be there to see the man in the dragon mask taken away.

The guards opened the door to Hongdi's cell, and each took one of his arms as he was led out.

"No," he tried saying. "Wen! Wen, please, don't let them do this. You loved me once. We loved each other once." But no one could understand him. And if they did, they didn't respond. Even though her hair had fallen down and she was covered in prison muck, there was a small smile on Empress Wen's face.

"Maybe now I will finally have a son," she whispered as he was dragged past her.

Hongdi felt sick to his stomach at the idea of another man taking her to bed. He suddenly regretted the cruel way he had treated her over the last few months. She had always stood by him, always supported him, and he had beaten her and locked her away. She had been right all along about everything. They never should have moved north.

But now it was too late. The guards dragged him up the stairs and into the cold light of morning. It had not snowed the night before, but the ground was icy cold under his bare feet.

He was taken through the small door in the main gate, where a scaffolding had been hastily assembled during the night. A crowd had already gathered to watch the execution, and the people gasped when they saw the man in the dragon mask brought forward.

"He must be hideous!" a woman cried.

"Cursed by the gods," a man said.

"Traitor!"

"Murderer!"

Hongdi realized that the people had no idea what his supposed crime was, they just wanted blood.

"No!" he tried saying. "I'm the emperor!" But no one could understand him.

He was ushered up the stairs, where the executioner was waiting with his sword.

"Please, I'm innocent," he tried to tell the man, but he was pushed down onto his knees, facing the crowd.

The people laughed and pointed at the man in the dragon mask.

And as the executioner drew his sword, the cheers were deafening.

EPILOGUE

Shihong shuddered as he heard the cheering from the crowd outside reach a crescendo and then fall away. His brother was dead. The emperor was dead. And he had let it happen. He thought he would cry. Feel sick. But instead, all he felt was an immense peace. A feeling he had not had since he was a child playing on the river with Fei and her siblings.

Shihong cleared his throat. "I wish to pay my respects to Fei, Lady Song," he said when Wangzhu returned.

"As you wish, Your Majesty," Wangzhu said. He approached Shihong with a wet cloth to wash his face and body. When the two men were face to face, Wangzhu hesitated, and he glanced away for a moment.

"Is there a problem, Wangzhu?" Shihong asked.

Wangzhu bowed his head. "No, Your Majesty." Then, he continued with the emperor's morning routine as usual. Shihong knew that Wangzhu was aware that he was not really Hongdi, but there was nothing that Wangzhu could do about it now. Shihong had just allowed his own brother to be executed. Wangzhu had no reason to think that

Shihong would show him mercy if he spoke up about Shihong's true identity.

Once Shihong was dressed, he went to Fei's palace. There were several ladies outside who had dared to leave their palaces and mourn for Lady Song. Shihong blessed them for their piety as he passed them and entered the building.

Fei had been washed and dressed by her maid and eunuch and was lying in repose upon her bed. With her hair combed straight and her cheeks rosy, she looked as though she was sleeping.

Fei's servants were kneeling by the bed, weeping, and they did not rise to greet the emperor. Shihong did not blame them. They most likely blamed the emperor for their lady's death.

Shihong kneeled beside Fei's bed across from them. He kissed Fei's head tenderly, then he placed a hand on her stomach.

"I wish for Lady Song to be buried with honors befitting an empress," Shihong said.

"Yes, Your Majesty," Wangzhu said, his voice soft.

"When my time comes," Shihong went on, "I wish to be buried by her side."

"Of course," Wangzhu said. "But that will certainly not be more many years."

"We should take nothing for granted," Shihong said. Then he stood and left the palace. The sun was shining brightly, and Shihong realized that his future was secure.

Empress Wen and her father and brother approached him and bowed.

"It is good to see you, my friends," Shihong said.

"Everything seems to have gone according to plan," Wen said.

"I suppose it has," Shihong said as he took in a deep breath of the cool, clean air. "I can never thank you all for what you did for me. Because of you, I now have a life to live."

"And an empire to rule," General Kang said, clapping Shihong on the back.

"I have no idea how to even begin," Shihong said, feeling a bit unsure of himself again.

"First," Wen said, "you must attend to morning audiences. You are already late."

"But...what will happen?" Shihong ask. "What should I do?"

"Don't worry," Wen said, a smile on the side of her lips. "We will all be there to help you."

Shihong exhaled and nodded. "We should go then." He held out his arm for Wen and she placed her hand daintily upon it as they walked to the audience hall together.

When they arrived at the audience hall, Wangzhu announced the emperor's presence. Everyone in the room, from servant to high-ranking minister, kneeled to the floor in a kowtow before Shihong, a man who had been sentenced to death only the day before.

As he walked toward the throne, he lifted his eyes up to the great golden statue of a dragon that hung above it, a pearl gripped in its mighty jaw. Shihong stopped at the foot of the dais, a lump in his throat.

"The emper—Hong—Umm, my brother," he whispered to Wen. "He said something about anyone sitting on the throne who was not worthy would be crushed by the pearl. Is that true?"

"Only one way to find out," Wen said.

Shihong gulped and slowly, carefully climbed the stairs to the throne. He then turned and looked out at the people gathered before him. He exhaled and sat on the throne, but just on the very edge. He waited expectantly for something to happen, but nothing did. He relaxed slightly and sat further back in the throne. He cleared his throat.

"The audiences may proceed," he said, his voice carrying through the hall so that all could hear him.

"May the emperor live ten thousand years!" Wen declared.

"May the emperor live ten thousand years!" everyone in the room replied in unison.

THREADS OF SILK

http://amandarobertswrites.com/threads-of-silk/

When I was a child, I thought my destiny was to live and die on the banks of the Xiangjiang River as my family had done for generations. I never imagined that my life would lead me to the Forbidden City and the court of China's last Empress.

Born in the middle of nowhere, Yaqian, a little embroidery girl from Hunan Province, finds her way to the imperial court, a place of intrigue, desire, and treachery. From the bed of an Emperor, the heart of a Prince, and the right side of an Empress, Yaqian weaves her way through the most turbulent decades of China's history and witnesses the fall of the Qing Dynasty.

Fans of Amy Tan, Lisa See, Anchee Min, and Pearl S. Buck are sure to love this debut novel by Amanda Roberts. This richly descriptive and painstakingly researched novel brings the opulence of the Qing Court to life as Yaqian and Empress Cixi's lives intertwine over six decades.

MURDER IN THE FORBIDDEN CITY

http://amandarobertswrites.com/qing-dynasty-mysteries/

When one of the Empress's ladies-in-waiting is killed in the Forbidden City, she orders Inspector Gong to find the killer. Unfortunately, as a man, he is forbidden from entering the Inner Court. How is he supposed to solve a murder when he cannot visit the scene of the crime or talk to the women in the victim's life? He won't be able to solve this crime alone.

The widowed Lady Li is devastated when she finds out about the murder of her sister-in-law, who was serving as the Empress's lady-in-waiting. She is determined to discover who killed her, even if it means assisting the rude and obnoxious Inspector Gong and going undercover in the Forbidden City.

Together, will Lady Li and Inspector Gong be able to find the murderer before he – or she – strikes again?

Readers who enjoy historical mysteries by authors such as Victoria Thompson, Deanna Raybourn, and Anne Perry are sure to love this exciting start to a new series by Amanda Roberts.

THE EMPEROR'S SEAL

http://amandarobertswrites.com/touching-time/

The Emperor's Seal – the divine symbol of the Emperor on earth – is missing. The Empress will do whatever it takes to get it back.

Jiayi has a gift – she can travel through time just by touching historical artifacts. More than anything, she wants to escape the clutches of the Empress and run away to a foreign land. Finding the Emperor's Seal could be her only chance at freedom, but is she willing to risk the wrath of the Empress?

Historian and wannabe archaeologist Zhihao has no love for the Empress or the Qing Dynasty, but when the Empress orders him to find the Emperor's Seal in exchange for funding China's first history museum, he cannot refuse. It is only after he accepts the assignment that he realizes the key to finding the seal lies in the hands of a palace slave.

Civil unrest and encroaching foreign powers threaten Jiayi and Zhihao's mission and lives as they hunt for The Emperor's Seal.

ABOUT THE AUTHOR

 Amanda Roberts is a USA Today best-selling author who has been living in China since 2010. She has an MA in English from the University of Central Missouri and has been published in magazines, newspapers, and anthologies around the world. Amanda can be found all over the Internet, but her home is AmandaRobertsWrites.com.

Website: http://amandarobertswrites.com/
Newsletter: http://amandarobertswrites.com/subscribe-threads-of-silk/
Facebook: https://www.facebook.com/AmandaRobertsWrites/
Instagram: https://www.instagram.com/amandarobertswrites/
Goodreads: https://www.goodreads.com/Amanda_Roberts
BookBub: https://www.bookbub.com/authors/amanda-roberts-2bfe99dd-ea16-4614-a696-84116326dcd1
Email: Amanda@AmandaRobertsWrites.com

ABOUT THE PUBLISHER

RED EMPRESS PUBLISHING

Visit Our Website To See All Of Our Diverse Books
http://www.redempresspublishing.com

*Quality trade paperbacks, downloads, audio books, and books
in foreign languages in genres such as historical, romance,
mystery, and fantasy.*

CPSIA information can be obtained
at www.ICGtesting.com
Printed in the USA
FSHW010516080520
70057FS